is the counterfactual novel to beat all counterfactual novels . . .
Sesshu Foster and Arturo Romo float high above the the landlub-
bing bulk of American fiction."

—Mark Doten, author of *Trump Sky Alpha*

"Forget the zombie apocalypse, forget priapic gun-crazy Hollywood
dystopias—all these troubled times require is an economy ticket
on the East LA Dirigible Air Transport Lines. Enter the isotherm
with Foster and Romo and cruise high over the trashed and blasted
landscapes of imperial decay. *ELADATL* is more than a novel—it's
the secret history of the secret history, the map they always kept
hidden, a dream inside a dream of a dream. Hilarious and prophetic
and profound, truer than truth, and realer than all realities currently
available for purchase, *ELADATL* is strong medicine against the
erasures of history, a mega-vitamin for struggles yet to come. This
book combats despair."

—Ben Ehrenreich, author of *Desert Notebooks:
A Road Map for the End of Time*

"Sesshu Foster's second novel *ELADATL: A History of the East Los
Angeles Dirigible Air Transport Lines* is not some preciously honed theoretical tale scripted as an abstracted warriors' syllabus, but instead, it
gives a powerful account of a curious quotidian revolt that accompa-
nied the East LA Balloon Club and the Bessie Coleman Aero Club rife
with the contradiction that singed their arcane thriving. This novel
not only explores the actual quest for physical elevation, but, more
significantly, with the complication of inner elevation, attempting to
rise above a circumstance studded with racism and looming financial
debacle. Mr. Foster's novel magically inscribes the trenchant character of an opaque and transitional zeitgeist."

—Will Alexander, author of *Kaleidoscope Omniscience*

"*ELADATL: A History of the East Los Angeles Dirigible Air Transport Lines*
is one of the wildest, most creative and deeply-cutting novels I've read
in years, a genuine piece of newness in both content and form. Sesshu
Foster and Arturo Romo have managed, from the mind-bending perch
of alternate time and space, to construct a perfect lookout from which
to view the deranged spectacle of late-capitalism America. To wade
through this surreal narrative archeology—composed of everything
from oral histories to inspirational posters to lunch menus—is to
experience, in the finest sense, literature as fever dream."

—Omar El Akkad, author of *American War: A Novel*

"Sesshu Foster and Arturo Ernesto Romo co-pilot the *ELADATL* phantasmagoric journey across historic/imagined skies with magnificent views of a post-industrial East Los Angeles wasteland that is dotted with cinematic/cultural phantoms: Raquel Welch, Oscar Zeta Acosta, Anthony Quinn, and Brown Berets who invoke the mantra, 'Don't believe the fake dreams of the secret police.' Human skin, dirigible skin, chorizo skins, are simultaneously celebrated as art while being attacked by Zeppelin gunships. *ELADATL* lifts the reader into a free intellectual airspace where airships of new thinking reign."

—Harry Gamboa Jr., author of *Urban Exile: Collected Writings of Harry Gamboa Jr.*

"'The strange future of war over Los Angeles, zeppelins versus dirigibles . . .' Sesshu Foster and Arturo Ernesto Romo capture the uncapturable. 'Experience levitation and death,' 'attune your cellular vibrations to the frequency of Star Beings,' 'the merciless winds of the human heart,' 'the Atmospheric Trash Vortex.' Who is the I here? 'The welcoming hosts at the front door, you want to look inside?' The nightmare does not erase the comedy. 'The CIA behind the million faces, hair and fingernails still growing.' 'Sign your sorrow over . . . they're taking everything; let's give it to them, the sober whisky of Love.' Unforgettable read. 'Isn't someone in charge?'"

—Sharon Doubiago, author of *My Beard: Memoir Stories*

"A fierce, bittersweet, and hilarious antidote to our increasingly deracinated personhoods and neighborhoods, *ELADATL: A History of the East Los Angeles Dirigible Air Transport Lines* inspires us to hold our ground in a here and now that includes futures and pasts we both know and can barely imagine. Set against the absence of Hollywood—that perfect hierarchical structure that occludes most of the actual labor that goes into making the finished product—Sesshu Foster and Arturo Romo take us through the hood and under the hood while celebrating and mourning the intimacy of social life in all its vicissitudes. Along the way, our fearless guides introduce us to the living politics of a particular place whose accumulated experience reverberates throughout the cosmos."

—Ammiel Alcalay, Founder and General Editor of Lost & Found: The CUNY Poetics Document Initiative

ELADATL

A History of the
East Los Angeles Dirigible
Air Transport Lines

SESSHU FOSTER &
ARTURO ERNESTO ROMO

Cover Design: Jeff Clark
Book Design: Isa Knafo / mosastudio.work

Library of Congress Cataloging-in-Publication Data

Names: Foster, Sesshu, author. |
Romo, Arturo Ernesto, 1980- author.

Title: ELADATL : a short history of the East Los Angeles
dirigible air transport lines / by Sesshu Foster & Arturo
Ernesto Romo.

Description: San Francisco, CA : City Lights Books, 2020.

Identifiers: LCCN 2019058872 | ISBN 9780872867703
(trade paperback)

Subjects: LCSH: Imaginary organizations—Fiction.
| Airships—Fiction | Air travel—Fiction

Classification: LCC PS3556.O7719 E53 2020
| DDC 813/.54--dc23

LC record available at https://lccn.loc.gov/2019058872

City Lights Books are published at the City Lights
Bookstore, 261 Columbus Avenue, San Francisco, CA 94133.

WWW.CITYLIGHTS.COM

ELADATL

TABLE OF CONTENTS

SKY CITY

In order to advance the proletarian interests of the community, and to counteract the military-industrial propaganda of the oppressor government — which goes so far as to categorically deny the existence of the High Low Radiance Corridor, disregarding cars that disappeared many years ago reappearing nowadays, falling out of the sky to wreak havoc on community members, community gardens, and street traffic—this is pirate radio Ehekatl 99.9 on your dial, broadcasting from various hilltops in Northeast Los Angeles (during our irregular broadcast hours of 2 a.m. to 6 a.m.). Tonight we examine the Mysteries of East L.A., confirm the existence of one of the biggest and most mysterious of them all: the long-rumored but never-before-sighted Sky City. We bring you a live eyewitness investigation by one of our undercover reporters, from her night job as a pilot-trainee at the allegedly phony and/or "clandestine"

East Los Angeles Dirigible Air Transport Lines. Pirate radio
Ehekatl 99.9 is ready to provide first-hand evidence that Sky
City is real. Our reporter, with her unsuspecting master pilot
watching over her shoulder, has assumed the flight controls
of a 700-foot-long state-of-the-art postmodern dirigible and
has ascended to 11,000 feet in altitude (the signal's fading in
and out due to air-pressure fluctuations, not to mention the
engine noise, but we can't help that). We go live directly to our
report in progress:

"Which is it gonna be?"

"Which is what gonna be?"

"Which is it gonna be?"

"What? The heading's off the compass bearing, altimeter
right there in front of you, pitch and yaw, wind direction.
Remember there's two gauges fore and aft, that's important
in a ship this long, both hands on the wheel—"

"Which? Is it gonna be a story or what?"

"You want a story? 'The ELADATL Agnes Smedley drifts across the misty night above the devastated West,' too boring for you?"

"You know, your usual, whatever it is, surrealism bullshit. People get tired. That's not really considered a story, is it?"

"It's not—"

"Is it?"

"It's not—"

"Come on!"

"It's not surrealism!"

"What? That's not what they call it?"

"No."

"It's kind of psychedelic or something, isn't it? Doesn't that qualify—"

"Surrealism goes back to World War I. It was French. It's supposed to be a reaction to the First World War."

"Thank you, doctor. Doctor Barnswallow."

"No—thank you! I always like a little European history and iced tea on night flights over the greater L.A. basin."

"I'd like a little iced tea with my iced tea."

"Now you can get virtual iced tea with—or in place of—your actual iced tea."

"Doctor Barnswallow!"

"Mister Doctor Barnswallow to you."

"So what's the best love story you know? I mean one that you actually know about. Not—"

"You mean not like *Romeo and Juliet* or *Wuthering Heights* or—"

"Exactly. Something that happened to you—"

"*Brokeback Mountain*, eh? What about, like, *The Fly*? That's kind of a love story. There's a love story in there. The scientist's wife has to kill him by crushing his fly head to put her husband out of his suffering. I feel like something like that happened to me. Or it could!"

"You know what I'm sayin'. Best thing you can come up with."

"Something I heard about?"

"All right. Something you heard about. Someone you actually know, though."

"Personally, eh? Somebody we know personal. Personal-like."

"Who you know. Yeah."

"The love of a middle-aged Arizona couple for their Chihuahua? The love of a whole people for their land? The love of an old retired dude for a patch of lawn and his lawn chair?"

"For a woman!"

"I thought—"

"Make me spell it out!"

"Thought so. A woman always wants a story about a woman. How about someone you know, someone you and I both know?"

"Let's see if you know any. You ever know any? Let's see if you were paying attention."

"I see. It's a test. Everything these days is like a test."

"Let's go back to the facts, then. You're a flagrant anarchist, an individualist subject to no party discipline, who can't even get his partners to show up for work—Jose Lopez-Feliu, Swirling Wheelnuts—so you have to yank me, an innocent communist newspaper girl, off the streets, teach me to drive this thing toward the dawning of a New Something Era—"

"Complaints and whining, that's the thanks I get for teaching you a saleable skill? You'd rather still be selling that useless cult propaganda sheet?"

"Cult! You anarchists can't even—"

"All right, all right! The whole yawning proletariat shall one day bust a move in a Bollywood dance number, waving a sea of red flags—"

"You think they won't? Just like everything else in

America, media for the people is winking out in the darkness. My organization happens to be developing real alternative community news outlets! For all you realize, my captain, I could be broadcasting this across the greater Northeast Los Angeles heights and the San Gabriel Valley on a pirate radio station, to arm our communities with the knowledge that you won't—"

"Pirate radio!"

"You laugh, my captain! But the workers are the ones who deserve collective ownership of the skies. If your fleet of solar-powered dirigibles proves to be—"

"If! If? You mean *when*!"

"That is exactly what these flights may prove, Captain, sir! But come on, tell us—say—for the sake of our listener-ship (even if you don't believe our listenership exists, like the authorities don't believe this dirigible exists, like they deny the existence of Sky City), tell me the story behind it all, a personal story, give 'em a sense of your personal motivation for heisting abandoned materials, welding titanium-frame airships in collapsible folding sections, creating solar technology capable of eluding the forces of the downpressor government (I know, you said you can't afford the insurance, but you can afford our listeners the true story)!"

"Comandante Che said the real revolutionary was guided by feelings of love. At the risk of appearing ridiculous."

"Let us not go gently down the slippery slope of sarcasm, Captain. How's that square with the one about that girl you used and abused, she was so young and sweet, what was she? Just a baby—eighteen, nineteen, baby sister of your best friend, she looked up to you both, threw herself at you like only a kid could, but there was something sinister going on between you and your compa so you took it out on her, kept her on the line, strung her along until you were in such a state you couldn't recognize her as something fully human—in the end, what?

Left her all in a mess? Gave her a dread disease? Wrecked her car? What were you planning next, kill yourself? Double-suicide, Japanese-style? Is that where love gets you?"

"Sounds like you heard that one before. The whole story in a nutshell, eh? I'm not sure that has anything to do with me."

"So they say. In the twentieth century, you know, they thought the world was going to end with an apocalypse—death and destruction raining down on all nations through nuclear war, viral agents, genetic engineering, ecological disaster. There wasn't even going to be enough left of us to make fossils out of—that's what they were having nightmares about. They had no idea, not the vaguest, about what would happen via global warming, the obliteration of the auto industry, the end of aerospace, the bankruptcies and complete economic collapse, death of the oceans, the landscape erased and replaced by a scene of utter devastation, the past not even the vaguest dimness, not even nostalgic, not even a memory evoked by *I Love Lucy* reruns—"

"But what?"

"What?"

"So what about it?"

"I was just going to say that I agreed to train for this position because besides needing a real job (I'm tired of selling revolutionary newspapers up and down Figueroa Boulevard) and liking you personally, as a person I mean, and respecting your loco plan to build clandestine (because uninsured) dirigibles in abandoned warehouses and foreclosed office parks, to be launched at the perfect moment—"

"There is no perfect moment."

"You said it, Captain. But this is my idea, hear me out. They have denied the existence of Sky City, the downpressor government, till their political credibility (such as it is, strained even among their most vocal supporters, probably about ready to combust like the so-called evangelical vote) depends on this lame fabric of lies. We prove the existence of Sky City, Captain, and it will bring the downpressor government to its knees."

"Then the people will rise up, eh? I think that's a fantasy. Legend from the mists of time."

"I don't make these things up. That's too much of a whole lot of extra work."

"John Brown said the slaves would rise up across the South when he took Harper's Ferry. Che went down saying he only needed fifty more men in Yuro ravine."

"Sure. But what they didn't have was a radio audience of potential millions; you got the perfect broadcasting platform up here floating over the entire city. They'd be on the edge of their seats, I bet. Even if all they could hear was the droning of propellers (three on each side driven by electric engines powered by the dirigible's self-charging titanium frame) and the occasional weird John Cage–like structural noises that the great airship makes while nosing its way through the wild empty darkness. It's kind of spooky up here, just me and you. You marked our location?"

"Just northeast of the Burbank airport, acres and acres of lots, old abandoned hangars and warehouses and service facilities that used to—"

"Boys' hangout. Playground for youth—"

"Yeah, well, when they planned for the expansion of the airport they didn't plan on the airlines going out of business. All these empires coming to an end, leaving junk landscapes in their wake—socialism imploded, Sea of Azov dried up, capitalism exploded, toxic waste everywhere, dead forests like old ideologies on fire, public entitlement programs gutted, billboards for shit that people can't recognize let alone hanker after, malt liquor and "Gentlemen's Clubs," cell phones and household cleaners, ads peeling off to reveal the coruscating undersurface, a face somebody might've seen on TV decades ago, dimly recognizable except that now nobody cares. What's left that's worth risking your life for?"

"Isn't that Mount Washington or Glassell Park over there? San Fernando Road doglegging away from the river?"

"Our hometown."

"Scene of the crime."

"It's all conspiracy and no crime, Cadet—just trying to survive, fanning insignificant dreams and desires like a tiny campfire on the stormy side of some immense mountain, maybe squatting in some empty building, making unpermitted renovations . . . calling it the headquarters of East Los Angeles Dirigible Air Transport Lines! Taking calls at all hours. Attempting to broker deals for the production of great new fleets of revolutionary airships. Where other people looked at the huge old empty hangar and saw a derelict building with smashed-out windows and orange fiberglass insulation furling in the breeze, we saw opportunity. Vast opportunity, I might add."

"Wow, can I work in telemarketing? Hello, Mister Investor, this is the East L.A. Dirigible Company. We are headquartered in Burbank. Yes. That's right, for a loose ten thousand pesetas you got hanging in that sack there—"

"Scoff and mock! Scoff and mock at will. Professionals have made careers of it. But where are those professional mockers and scoffers when you truly need 'em? Where are the Marx Brothers now? In Hollywood Resurrection Cemetery where all the smart-asses end up, watching the movies from the solid side of the wall, listening to punk bands on Día de los Muertos."

"Sorry, sir. Sarcasm isn't maybe my best side. I apologize. But why the big secret? Why operate clandestinely?"

"Why do you broadcast on pirate radio? Why don't you publish your own newspaper, resurrect the *L.A. Times* and call it the *Post-Everything Herald*? Next you'll be asking me why do we bother to resist in the first place, commie girl. What, do you expect the same government that was behind Wounded Knee and AIG and every war that bankrupted the whole world system to show up in our driveway with a suitcase of cash and papers to sign? You think they'd overlook our lack of friends in government, no investors, no credit, no permits, insurance, licensing? Don't you even read your own newspaper?"

"Okay, okay—"

"No, no, follow me on this now. When it made it here, Western Civilization brought the equivalent of the Black Death to the Tongva. But from this angle, we're watching the whole show in decline. Industry came to Los Angeles like Steve McQueen heading to the Tijuana cancer clinic, like Janice Joplin in room 105, fixing in the Landmark Hotel, like Sam Cooke shot with his pants down at the Hacienda Motel, like JFK in the Ambassador Hotel—"

"RFK. Ambassador Hotel Wilshire Boulevard was Robert Kennedy—"

"You know what I'm getting at. Look down, two o'clock, south by southeast."

"At the cops? That looks like one of those, what do they call it? Pursuits where they go slow?"

"But look at the streets—what I'm saying is that they got streets and buildings named after those 'people,' but it's all just like black-and-white shadows, soundless flickering in the collective memory of some windy abandoned hangar—"

"Did your ears pop just now, too? Mine just did."

"Tupac and Biggie Smalls, heroes of the crack wars, where are they now? Che T-shirts, brown berets, and the grape boycott, where are they now? Purple Hearts, field jackets, the Doors at the Troubadour on Sunset, all those rock stars living in Laurel Canyon, Topanga and Malibu, where are they now? Sam Yorty calling Tom Bradley a communist? Freeway Ricky Ross's conduit for CIA crack cocaine, the prison post-industrial system! The San Fernando Valley porn industry boom and bust? All those unemployed porn stars trying to find work as strippers? The Desert Acres real estate bubble? L.A. riots of '65 and '92 and 2021, etc? Crystal meth, Earth Day, public education, rap music, U.S. Steel, the Merchant Marine? What happened to all of it? It didn't just blow away on a Santa Ana . . . "

"That was then."

"This is now! Hey, you can see water in the arroyo! It's gone now, but I swear I saw it shining."

"So what if there's no aerospace industry? Fifty thousand gangbangers and 100,000 cops, they're still there. Maybe if you sift out suicidal Christian cults, the movie business, the real estate shuck-and-jive, $1.37-per-gallon gasoline, 'physical culture' and food fads—that was what was real, finally . . . "

"Cops?"

"Or gangbangers. Did you see? The cops had 'em lined up on the sidewalk back there. In the spotlight."

"Well, we aim to love it anyhow, as is. So what if the twentieth century was a wash? We aim to love it by floating our boat. We aim to change the whole look of this landscape. This solar-powered dirigible will rise from the El Sereno hills, ferried across the San Andreas Fault at night, in the early hours before dawn, to some secret mooring location. An underground movement to develop pollution-free air transport, to revolutionize and revitalize the Southern California grid. Job creation for the masses, turning around the bankrupt culture of despair, the Cults of Eating Shit and Liking It. We will use the current state of total neglect, disrepair, and the entropy of urban centers to launch an inversion. An electro-titanium dirigible on the scale of the Graf Zeppelin will appear like the rising sun over the San Gabriel Valley, and, when the people see what can be done, they will rise up, across the nation, in every dead city and wasteland suburb, the will to live and the desire to prevail, the prevailing of desire—"

"What do I get if I invest my life savings in this imaginary scheme? A pound of queso fresco, a clay statue Colima dog?"

"Such a deal! Where else can you find an offer like that?"

"So why wait? What better time for them to rise up than right now?"

"What, why—If it weren't for the lack of a handful of investors—"

"What, you're gonna pretend cash is all that's holding you back?"

"We can't operate forever out of abandoned buildings, always moving storage and assembly sites one step ahead of the bulldozers. We don't have outlay for lithium batteries, critical materiel; everything is borrowed against up to our eyeballs. Every time I need a new part, I find Vice President of Sales Swirling Wheelnuts out back sitting on a woodpile in the weeds drinking up the profits, clinking beers with passersby—"

"I think you're holding back the real reason."

"I assure you, it's all a house of cards improvised on the head of a pin, balancing on tiptoe, walking through fire—"

"You got the look of motion sickness on you. But I don't think it's from vertigo, from any fear of actual heights."

"You think it's not daunting, piloting pirate dirigibles across the night skies of Southern California, conversing in code on the radio so as to fool air traffic controllers into thinking that you're either some aircraft heading away from them on a standard corridor at lawful altitude, or an emergency craft making an unscheduled rescue? To give at least a radio appearance of being legit while avoiding all visual recognition, collisions, and charted air corridors?"

"I know you can spin it for the customers—huge, hovering airships droning across the south-facing slopes of the San Gabriels in the dark, hiding behind black clouds, pretending to be the slowest helicopter that never was, maneuvering through air pockets, isotherms, and cold fronts, carrying forth into the

New Era forgotten alternative technologies, salvaged through derring-do. But a while ago you had something like this same green look on your face when you told me you were waiting in your car in the alley outside The Smell to pick someone up—"

"No, Isaura had to drop off something for the band—"

"Whatever—you saw her come out of the club, smashed. The guy she was with had to carry her out. They fall against the side of your car (I see you sitting stone cold in the dark and not even twitching at this point) and slide off the hood (very slowly off the wheel well, as you described it) and stumble down the alley."

"Yeah, I told you about that. That was the guy she married."

"Her enabler, I know."

"You said that."

"Not true?"

"I wouldn't begin to know."

"No?"

"I don't pretend—"

"No? Come on—she was calling you. I know you were taking her calls."

"Once or twice a year. Yeah, I might get a call."

"Maybe more than that. She's drunk or wasted and always starts crying. She's gone from L.A. to El Paso, Austin to San Jose, San Jose to Chicago, Albuquerque to San Diego, burning her bridges everywhere. The constellation of mutual friends is winking out one by one. Even you stopped lending her money when she told you it was for her mom, and then you found out it wasn't. Her mom has one in jail, one out on parole at home, and this one—"

"I knew her when she was better than that. Everybody just sees the latest mess. She used to be somebody else. Some other person entirely."

"You got that color in your face again."

"I heard she broke up with that guy, anyway."

"Of course! Within six months of the wedding she and the guy are fighting all the time. Eventually she calls the cops, apparently there's visible bruising and redness, so they arrest the dude. She changes the locks and gets a court order barring the guy from getting back inside his own house for three months! When he does, he finds she backed up a moving van to the place and cleaned him out. She was off to Texas or Chicago or wherever when the guy walks in and finds it clean as a whistle— "

"Sniggling and giggling. Here, let me assume the controls. Go use the restroom, even if only to check it out—upstairs, down the hall to the left. Check out the workmanship—wall-to-wall tile, full-length mirrors, brass fittings—better than anything Boeing or McDonnell-Douglas ever produced. No second-class Third World train with a hole in the floor where you can see the ground going by. Go. I'll play music for you on the PA."

[Musical interlude: "Little Train of the Caipira," by Heitor Villa-Lobos, Toccata, Bachianas Brasileiras No. 2 for Orchestra]

"You were right! This thing does have great bathrooms! What a blast of gleaming brass—no wonder you don't have money to pay your bookkeeper. Give me those controls back, would you? I'm feeling much better now, more relaxed. You know, this ship is mighty spacious. It's like we're in the belly of the whale, but once you get the hang of it, with your hands on the wheel—"

"It's not a hummingbird. It's not a helicopter."

"It's not an eighteen-wheeler. It's not an oil tanker or ship of state."

"You do seem to be getting a feel for it."

"I think I am! Does this mean I have a job?"

"Looks like it."

"Outstanding! Congratulations to me, new girl pilot! No cop choppers or—"

"No surveillance or hostile interference visible at this time. All screens are clear. Steady as she goes."

"Good! Look at all those people sleeping down there. America's dreamless sleepers. Tired out, tossing and turning—I can see them all in their beds. Dreaming of a blank future! I wonder what they'd think if they could see this ship in the clouds?"

"You got a real imagination on you."

"I can see them. I can see everyone."

"I can't see anything down there but streetlights, houses, big shadows of trees on the avenues. It's a dark landscape, dark fields of the republic rolling on under the night. I can't see any people at all."

"I can see everything from up here—their individual lives flickering like candles. What a feeling."

"It's all just a blobby blackness sprinkled with a few random lights to me."

"Wow, what happened to you?"

"I don't know. I think I got burned out working on all these secret plans, underground utopias, machines to transport our future. I think they were killing too many people while I was working hard on something else. Time went by, stuff happens."

"Really? You look down there across the whole city at night, you don't see those souls burning and scattered like stars against the dark?"

"I don't even see the stars any more. I think you might be talking about the streetlamps."

"No, I am definitely not talking about the streetlamps. I am talking about the people."

"Yeah."

"You're embarrassed about that, I see."

"It is a little embarrassing."

"Is it?"

"Sometimes I feel like my feelings for people went out with the last century. I'm looking down on the eviscerated cities of America day and night from my floating vantage like a squinty-eyed Captain Nemo, and I feel like I lost most of my soul somewhere along the way. Or maybe it just dried out completely and stuck on me like a scabbed-over herpes sore on the corner of my mouth."

"Yeah, that could be kind of embarrassing. What're you gonna do about that?"

"Thanks for the sympathy. I appreciate that."

"Welcome."

"Really."

"Hee hee."

"I have bared my scars and here you are snickering."

"Sorry. Habit."

"See those yellow gauges off to your left. That means that bank of batteries are reduced; switch over to Bank Three. Bank Two off, Bank Three on."

"Roger that."

"That's the professional air transport lingo I like to hear."

"I feel like I'm really flying this thing."

"We're flying!"

"We're flying?"

"We're zooming."

"So gimme the rest of the story. And not just some cheap allegory either, like we're the all-seeing Eye of Surmise, of the Flying Id above the dreaming mind of America, asleep in its bed of ideological rubble, its subconsciousness submerged in the ruins of everything it has consumed and discarded like the Indian nations and the Civil War dead and the slaves and the Chinese who built the railroads and the Mexicans in the fields. Dead-dreaming America except for cops and gangsters running around shooting at each other. That's not a story."

"I didn't say it was."

"So just say it. You're taking me to Sky City aren't you? If not now, then. . . . But wait a minute. This all has something to do with her, doesn't it?"

"I didn't tell you I saw Isaura last month."

"Really?"

"We had lunch. She wanted to talk."

"Uh-oh!"

"She looked good. Looked great, as a matter of fact."

"I've seen pictures."

"Better than the pictures."

"Pictures may lie. What did she want to talk about?"

"She's turned her life around. She's taking care of herself now."

"That's what she told you? Did you laugh? Did she ask you to lend her a down payment?"

"She looked like she's got a handle on it. She might have been coloring her hair, but she looked like she put down some demons. Maybe they went down hard, but they went down."

"Her? After what everyone's told you, in the face of your own experience, you're going for that? After everything she's done? No wonder she keeps calling."

"She didn't mention money once, except to say she could pay me back."

"Really. I don't know whether to believe you. Is there any actual verifiable fact associated with her at all?"

"I'm relating it exactly as I have been told. I heard she's been working in South Central, gang intervention for at-risk kids, getting them off the street, into school, changing some lives. I did some checking up."

"News to me! Secondhand, too. I can't say as I am believing it yet."

"I relate it just as I was told. She said she got into it after the riots of 2021. She had to drive through an intersection where the TV choppers were circling. She was on her way to work that morning, and she saw cars mobbed, people dragged from their vehicles and beaten. One car on fire. They smashed out the windows and—"

"Yeah, I saw it on TV."

"For Isaura it wasn't on TV. She'd almost made it through—people were on the ground—when a guy smashed out her window and hit her in the head with a piece of concrete. He grabbed the steering wheel and was jerking it away. She said she hit the gas and dragged him along till he fell off. Blood pouring down her head, glass all over."

"She didn't, like, pause at that point, light a cigarette and look at you from the corner of her eye and ask for a favor?"

"She wasn't sure how badly she was hurt. She felt wet, she knew she was hurt but not how bad, and she wanted to live. The guy was trying to grab the wheel from her and push his way into her car, and she was thinking, 'I am not going to die like this! I am not going to die today!' She had decided, then and there, when she hit the gas pedal and got herself through the intersection, dodging groups of people and other cars, the whole neighborhood in chaos, that she was determined to live. She was out of the intersection but not anywhere she could get out and make sure she was okay. So she leaned over and drove as far as she could—her windshield was smashed and she couldn't really see through it— without looking where she was going, peeking around every once in a while. Then she got dizzy and had to pull over to the side of the street and stop. But a woman had seen her. The woman told her to move over and stay down, and drove her out of there. She looked ten years younger when I saw her. She'd lost weight. She was taking care of herself. She looked like the sister of the Isaura I knew. That was the promise she'd made to herself the day it looked like—"

"You believed her?"

"Whatever she said to herself when she got through that

intersection, it carried down through the years. She changed her life."

"Hard to believe."

"Some of this shit is real. Exact words. Verbatim."

"Was she happy?"

"She seemed very happy, yeah."

"There's hope for us all?"

"There is, yes."

"If she can do it, we can do it?"

"We can do it."

"Maybe I can do it. Not sure. What about you?"

"Maybe, eh?"

"Is that a dead reservoir there, by those white buildings?"

"Hahamongna. Most of the big shore places are closed now, there's hardly any lights . . . And as the moon rises, over there that's JPL, Jet Propulsion Laboratories. You may not believe this, but at one time they had hundreds or thousands of people working on a Mars mission. There's plywood on the windows now. Check your altimeter, we're catching a rising draft off the San Gabriels. Time we start the climb."

"Where is she now? Why aren't you hooked up with her? Is that all over? She burned even you one too many times? End of story?"

"You know, I looked for her."

"She disappeared again? Where to now? Maybe she's over in Ethiopia somewhere."

"I always knew where she was, before. I could always call somebody who knew."

"What now? Now what?"

"I checked my people. New York, no, eastern seaboard, nada, I even checked Miami. Texas was out, Chicago was a blank. St. Louis, somebody there pointed back to L.A., San Diego pointed back to L.A. The same thing with the Bay Area."

"Montana?"

"Overseas! London, Lisbon, Brazil, nothing. Capetown, nothing, Melbourne, the same. Ho Chi Minh City, Shanghai, some of it by Internet, but still. Not even a whisper, no trace at all, and, anyhow, it all pointed back to L.A. as last residence. L.A. is like the black hole you can't escape from."

"Except apparently she escaped. Maybe you missed something."

"Could have, but we found her last apartment, talked to the landlord. Her family boxed up her stuff and cleaned out the place after she'd been gone for a couple months. I talked to her sister. Her sister was worried about her for the first time ever. I promised I'd keep looking. But she was the one who realized where Isaura must be."

"Where?"

"That's where we're going."

"El Monte?"

"We're underway already."

"Coachella Valley? Victorville? I thought we were on a run to rescue illegals from dehydration or transport sneaky drugs expressed from cochineal beetles or something. Or to conduct mysterious scientific research over a crater in the desert."

"I admit I mentioned some of those possibilities."

"That was a cover story."

"I had to say something halfway plausible. It's not like we don't find ourselves engaged in practical pursuits to pay the bills. We can't all be like you—spend our days selling revolutionary newspapers on street corners along Figueroa Boulevard and then spending all night in The Echo or The Airliner or dives like that."

"Oh, low blow!"

"Deny it."

"I stopped going to The Echo last year. But, wait—where to now, then?"

"Exactly about the time Isaura disappeared, the National

Oceanic and Atmospherics Administration published its data on atmospheric anomalies caused by global warming. Hurricanes along the Gulf Coast and eastern seaboard chronically engorged, Florida swept under the sea surge, gone like Bangladesh. Tornadoes hopping from Oklahoma to Colorado, touching down in Pittsburgh. Africa turning into a hellish baking continent of Saharas to the north and Namib deserts to the south. Australia and southern Europe burning off, desertifying. Vast areas of the earth depopulating, turning into heat-blasted wastes."

"Didn't Al Gore win the Academy Award for that?"

"The earth is turning into Venus. We're churning out thick stratospheres of smoke, debris, waste gases that have a measurable cooling effect. Making a dark planet of blasted ideologies, bloated sick passions, corrupted by viral pandemic apathies—"

"Tell me something I don't know. That's why the working class has to subscribe to the *Daily Red Revolutionist*. Then the revolution—"

"We're going up to check out that ring of litter, particulates, and trash that rains down on the globe now. That's why you brought the radio transmitter aboard in your cute Guatemalan bag, right?"

"You knew about that? I didn't mean—"

"My police scanner picks up all frequencies. For this airship to remain invisible, I've got to monitor all currents. These multicolored gauges and flashing lights aren't Christmas decorations."

"Where to, then? What's the course adjustment?"

"You're the one driving."

"We're on a heading 130 degrees, 80 knots, 60-mile-an-hour wind speed from the northwest, resulting in heading correction of about five degrees."

"Perfecto!"

"But where?"

"You just said—"

"You know what I mean. On this heading, we won't see much out this way except vast freeway interchanges, concrete flood plains and flood control channels, gravel pits, the Budweiser brewery and the Rose Hills Cemetery, Fry's electronics, massive warehouse districts, and truck distribution facilities. Chino Hills."

"See, even you—"

"When the moon comes out, they'll be able to see the dirigible's shadow sliding across all that cement. It's all parking lots and gravel down there."

"We'll be climbing."

"We're already at 13,000 feet. How much higher can we safely ascend?"

"We're going to the Sky City, rookie. That's why you're flying this ship. You aced the interviews, and I collated a whole file on your skills."

"But then you must've, I mean—you knew? You knew about my membership in the Punk Faction of the Red Underground Party, affiliated with I.T.S.C. point one?"

"I knew about all of that except for the I.T.S.C. point one part—I don't give a damn about that! I've seen you around the neighborhood since you were carried around in diapers by your mom when she was looking for your MIA dad. Basically, I see that you got heart; who else would sell those damned newspapers on the street corner and even get me to subscribe to that fishwrap?"

"It's true, then? It's really there?"

"Sky City? I want you to adjust the ailerons for maximum climb (maximum torque) and drop the last of our water ballast, because we're entering the isotherm. My studies on Sky City's origins and existence have provided me with reasonable information that Isaura and her yellow Volkswagen bug were likely swept up in the most recent series of tornadoes and other atmospheric disturbances that maintain the conglomeration of debris in the stratospheric rings—agglutinated by force—careening through the upper atmosphere, encircling the planet. If my information is correct (and I've every reason to believe it is, since we've gotten this far based on my calculations), Isaura's only one of hundreds—perhaps thousands—of people trapped in their vehicles and other bubbles of shelter within that swarm of packing sheds and pipelines, condo construction materials, cars and planes, entire trains, and a couple small towns torn out of East Texas and Oklahoma—ripped off the face of the earth by windspouts, all slammed together in the blood-brown rings swirling around our planet. I expect the diversity and variety of the debris to include enough plant and animal life and atmospheric water to have sustained a totally marginalized and invisible population, in spite of the occasional 1979 Pontiac El Caminos, delivery vans, old tires and broken water heaters that fall out of the sky at approximately 145 miles an hour terminal velocity, landing in school yards and shopping mall parking lots, which the government blames on Muslims and maintains is yet another thing soon to be fixed by tax cuts."

"14,000 feet. Fourteen thousand four hundred."

"Steady on this course."

"15,000 feet. Fifteen four hundred."

"Oh yeah, we'll be there in just a few damned minutes. Just like an entire distorted aquatic ecosystem and weird society has developed around floating villages on stilts in the midst of the Great Pacific Trash Vortex, I expect we'll find the marginalized poor are the inhabitants, forgotten and stranded in Sky City, fending for themselves. They've reconstructed a semblance of lives and livelihoods in the wind, dust, and trash storms of the sky—"

"If we get there—"

"When we get there. You're going to come about, so the gale-force currents don't crush the lateral bulkheads against the swirling edges and jagged parts of the debris rings. In fact, it's almost time you turn about and reverse course, transfer the remaining ballast into the nose—"

"But—"

"If you don't do it quickly the winds will crush the power-generating titanium frame against the trash in the vortex. Before we get to the edge, the rift in the stratospheric isotherms, I'll leave the ship strapped into a paraglider, and I expect I'll instantly get sucked up into the vortex, straight into Sky City. The hard part won't be getting in—the hard part will be not ending up ripped to pieces by a tangled mess of radio antennae and radar dishes strung up in high tension power lines, flatcars and water tanks, oil tankers, and remains of Amazonian rain forests. But if I can drop anchor on a stable structure of some kind, I should be able to pull myself in on the ropes or rappel into shelter."

"What about getting back on the ground? What about getting home?"

"I'll be in radio contact if I make it. First I want you to drop down a thousand feet and circle clockwise at fifty knots against the south-by-southwest wind. If I find survivors, I'll bring them out via paraglider. One at a time, as many as I can."

"The first eyewitnesses! Everything will change when they start telling what they've been through. Ambassadors of the New Era! You, Captain, will be a hero! Our Party has always maintained the existence of this phenomenon and some others, recognition of which by the masses would provide us with the credibility that would be the first step to power. I'd almost believe I was shaking and trembling if I didn't know it's the steering wheel vibrating like crazy. How can the ailerons take it? Won't there be structural damage?"

"Titanium. Steady as she goes. You realize, don't you, that these people might not tell a story that serves the interests of your Party? From the Plan de Ayalá to the Plan de Aztlán, from the Soviet Five-Year Plans to Let a Hundred Flowers Bloom, none of these ideas ever look the same in the daylight. On the ground. Oh now—are you crying? Don't cry, kid!"

"Sorry!"

"Come on, I'm relying on you. I'm gonna release my paraglider into the slipstream, and it's gonna be hell getting back against those gale-force winds. Meanwhile it's all on you, whether any of us lives or not."

"I know. Sorry! It's just a little . . . I struggle my whole life in the streets with the blown-out industries of civilization collapsing all around us, and survive to be here, to be able to see this day—"

"I'll take the wheel a second. Dry your eyes; you've gotta see clearly to make the maneuver, turn about, and descend into a calmer air column."

"I'm all right. Just . . . I know everything might not go the way they say. I don't really think it will. Nothing ever goes like anyone plans. I'm grateful we even get the ghost of a chance. Even if I find out later it was all some fairy tale, sci-fi fantasy daydream, I won't even care at that point. Because we took the chance. That's all I've wanted. I'm so grateful, at this moment, that's all. Whatever happens."

"I am too! I thank you for your heedless skill and reckless youth, new pilot! Let me shake your hand. A comradely embrace. Take the wheel. You've given me a chance at the happiness of a lifetime, and for the masses it's a glimmer of a new day. Here on, it's up to you."

"Thank you, sir. I'll turn about and make the descent; I'll get the berths ready for our first survivors while I stand by. Karl Marx and Friedrich Engels, would you look at that?!! That looks like some terrible thunderhead—you can see the debris sticking out of it like torn-out tree roots, stuff swirling inside of it like flocks of birds—"

"That's just the leading edge of the tumorous fulminating debris cloud. According to my charts, the densest interrelated conglomeration is a few miles south of us—"

"Augusto César Sandino, what is that? What just hit us?"

"That's the lead edge of the wind I was telling you about. I estimate that thousands or millions of plastic bags, whipped by a hurricane-force gale, are layering like warm slush on the fins, rudder, and engines—"

"Already? Sounds like the ocean smashing against us."

"Just the beginning!"

"Very hairy and scary, señor!"

"Just the beginning!"

"Oh!"

"Yeah, it's going to test the tensile strength of the titanium frame for all it's worth! To think that for years I disguised the frame as the outer housing of the Zep Diner on Main Street, people stepping inside as if it were an ordinary restaurant. I'd hate to lose the income from that business. I built my whole life on carnitas and pozole. Are we almost about?"

"110 degrees. 135."

"I'd better go suit up."

"Good luck, sir! 160. Two more minutes!"

"How do the engines feel? How's the ballast?"

"Ballast set, 125 degrees, nose tending to drop 5-10. I can barely hold it up."

"But it's holding?"

"Holding. Holding for now. Feels like four to five minutes at the most. The position is already degrading."

"I'm going, then. Remember, you drop a thousand on my signal."

"Terrible wind shear—"

"Yeah. Good luck, kid! Radio headset channel on—I'll be talking to you."

"Roger that. Let me know if—"

"What?"

"Good luck!"

"You won't be able to see the paraglider. I'll communicate over the headset."

"I'll be listening for you."

{"I'm out! [continuous hiss of static, sometimes rising to a sound like tropical rain on a sheet-metal roof, electro-static slapping and snarling] . . . Paraglider wings whipping like a banana peel . . . I will buy a subscription [percussive clanging resounding through titanium struts, weird twanging like a Nels Cline guitar solo] . . . It's really blasting . . . no control of glider . . . visibility lim . . . [hissing of static slashed by sudden silence] . . . in range . . . outskirts of Sky City above me, looming towers of wrecked cranes festooned with jagged sheet metal, trailing cables, plastic sheeting . . . Just a few . . . to hook the ropes . . . [loud popping, percussive clanging] Yes! Now if I can secure the glider! [grating metallic shrieks] Cables . . . swirling like octopus tentacles in the cloud—}

"ELADATL Agnes Smedley descending to three miles. Waiting for your call."

{[electric crackling, popping] [insistent hiss of static, then silence]}

[Cue: "El Pueblo Unido Jamás Será Vencido" by Quilapayun]

"This is Ehekatl 99.9 on your dial. Stay tuned."

CHICKEN MAN

Afternoon light etches a brittle hardness into the corrugated San Gabriel Mountains. They were always there to the north and east, green shoulders hunched protectively over the city, ignored mostly, like we ignored the elders who watched over us because we thought we were in some kind of rush, thought we'd already known everything about them for a long, long time. The San Gabriels are still there, of course, but the city as we knew it is gone. And with it, ourselves. We have become others to ourselves, or ghosts, those selves we thought of as our permanent, private property turned out to be transient as secondhand clothes. Late afternoon orange light cutting across the folds of the mountains, shadows seeping out of the canyons into the lavender dusk like snowmelt stored deep in the heart of cracked granite. Once in a lifetime, the yucca throws up its tall crisp stalk and blooms, creamy white blossoms. Later, the whole plant dies, the stalk drying golden in wind and sun. Later, the seedpods rattling black in the wind.

✿

Ben recommends the Dino's Chicken and Burgers in Pico Union, but I was closer to the Lincoln Heights location. An order of their famous chicken dripping radioactive orange marinade, french fries drenching a paper basket, trying to eat in the car—you get impatient to eat while driving (can be a disaster), hard to cuss yourself out now because why bother, did you really think you could steer with one hand, stuffing a fistful of greasy bird breast into your face with the skin sliding off your fingers with a fire engine and paramedics coming at you? Sirens, and glare so you can't hardly see to get over to let the emergency vehicles pass, plus you could once in awhile clean your windshield so it won't look like a cross between an Oklahoma dust storm and a starry night in the Sierras projected onto the brilliance of mid-afternoon? It's hard to see anything, while the roofline of a mini-mall in the middle distance polarizes into its own silhouette every time you look directly at it, leaving you seeing spots, groaning because some secret reservoir of orange grease inside the chicken breast is splattering your T-shirt, your pants, and the passenger seat as you thrust it aside.

Traffic moves somehow, people in vehicles crammed together stare at other drivers grimacing, cars bottlenecked behind an 18-wheeler changing gears in the intersection. Too late for this T-shirt now, toss the chicken back into the basket, wipe your hand on your shirt so as not to slime the steering wheel even worse, accelerate past vehicles crowded at the on-ramp, veer into the right lane ahead of the truck, dashing into the shadows of the Golden State Freeway overpass, heading toward the L.A. River.

I punch the radio button, and Warren Olney is reporting on a mass murder in some outlying California town, somebody killed a whole crew of Mexican workers on a chicken ranch. Six, all told, maybe one survivor, Warren Olney said, men who had ventured far from their homes in Michoacán and Jalisco, only to meet terrible deaths—shot, stabbed, and in one case run over repeatedly by a pickup truck—at the hands of an apparently crazed individual. "Is it racism or a sign of deepening economic stress when individuals commit these terrible crimes? As in last week's murderous attack on a Mexican family in southern Arizona, these crimes seem to be on the rise in the United States. Does it mark a fearful new chapter in the xenophobic history of the American West, as in the days of anti-Chinese pogroms, lynch law and vigilante 'justice'?" Warren Olney said he was going to devote his program to these issues.

I hadn't tuned in in time to get the full details. Where was it? Who did it? Was this somehow connected to Mexican cartels and gang wars? Was the chicken ranch actually a secret meth lab? Were the killings a cover-up? What was the poultry-meth connection? I sucked chicken out from behind my incisor and probed the area with my tongue, straining to hear the facts as I drove. I gathered that the violence had taken place in some rural area. I pictured in my mind a chicken ranch I'd seen once as a child outside of Lancaster.

It had impressed me a lot at the time—sterile industrial lines, a facility of sheet-metal hangars sitting under desert heat in utter silence. I had spent the day riding out in a van to see "the ranch," a piece of real estate the father of one of my friends had purchased as an investment. My friend Raúl said his mom was angry that his dad had spent their savings on this piece of rocky desert. Raúl's dad told his family it was going to be their getaway from Los Angeles, their "ranchito." Raúl, his little brother Beto, and I were all curious to see the ranchito. We drove out on branching dirt roads across sun-stricken desolation. The landscape reflected an almost malevolent heat. When the van stopped in a barren patch of bulldozed ground ringed by piles of old construction debris, odd bits of trash and discarded car parts, we saw that the ranch consisted of chalky, alkaline soil, tumbleweeds and creosote brush, and dark volcanic rocks.

The sole structure on the property was a battered mobile home, hot and airless when Raúl's father opened it up and we pressed in behind him, rank with some bitter plastic stench, reeking like a wet dog. Raúl's mother stood outside with her arms crossed over her chest in the leaning shade of the trailer, with such a sorrowful expression on her round face that we couldn't look at her. We thought she was about to burst into tears, and perhaps there'd be a typical big nasty fight and we'd have to ride back to the city in a choking atmosphere, full of recriminations and the chance that we might get slapped across the face if we said anything. So Raúl said, "What's that over there?" and we three ran off into the bushes to get away as fast as we could.

Instinctively, we made for the highest point on the property, a very low rise—not even a hill—some distance away. We didn't want to be anywhere near if the adults were going to start screaming at each other. The low rise didn't look very far, but Raúl and I had to cajole little Alberto to keep up with us, because it must've taken us at least half an hour or so of struggling through brush, down into and back out of gullies, struggling up sandy embankments that collapsed and covered us in chalky dust, ducking under dusty branches that coated us in sticky resin. Beto was whining about going back, rubbing his eyes red with some cactus fuzz or something in his hair and eyes, and about to cry, so Raúl and I kept telling him that the low rise was "ruins!", but he didn't know what ruins were so we said that there was a treasure there. Alberto really had no idea what treasure was either and kept insisting that we'd better go back, so we told him that people had buried big piles of money and toys and stuff in a secret cave on the hill. We actually found two crushed, decaying beer cans on top of the low rise when we finally got there, and Raúl and I both told

Alberto that pirates drank beer here before they buried their treasure. Beto was such a baby, we didn't have to bother to explain how pirates bury their treasure in the desert. In fact, there were shallow depressions and holes where it looked like someone once dug into the rocky ground. Raúl jumped into one and started kicking at the ground with his foot, telling Alberto that he bet he'd be the first one to find something. I was a little leery of what he might find and didn't move to help, because it reminded me of old backyard graves of family dogs. I noticed there were white buildings maybe a mile or so in the distance, pale against the volcanic ground. Dozens of windowless, featureless sheet metal buildings arrayed in long broken parallel lines. Who lived in the metal buildings, like barracks, without windows, out here in the broiling desert? There was no sign of movement, no vehicles, nor people, nor anything. There seemed to be no fence around the buildings, so I figured that they were not a prison, like the county jail compounds—Sybil Brand for women and Peter Pitchess for men—located behind high fences near my house, in the neighborhood where Raúl and I lived.

Who builds these long buildings out here in the desert, who works here? It reminded me of the movies, where scientists are working on top-secret projects. Blankly metallic in the afternoon sunshine, I knew they were too far away to ever get Beto there and back. I wondered if there was a way Raúl and I could tie little Beto to a bush, or just tell him not to move while we ran as fast as we could to go investigate those strange buildings. We might find some real treasure! But Raúl said Beto would cry, and his mom was already pissed off and didn't need a reason to whip the crap out of him. When we got back to the van and asked Raúl's father about the windowless buildings as long as city blocks, he told us that it was a chicken farm. I said, "I thought scientists were working on something there." He shook his head, "Chickens come from there."

✧

The United States was at war when we were growing up, as we came of age, during our young adulthood, throughout our lifetimes, and after we died. The wars could never stop, it was too late for that now. People didn't mention it. It wasn't worth thinking about. United States equals WAR. So? They got Mexicans to fight in the wars and deported them afterward. Some wars, if you blinked you missed them. Grenada, Panama. Of course, the industrial-military complex conducted full-blown wars in Iraq and Syria and Afghanistan—and those soldiers, privatized mercenaries and civilian contractors, didn't want to work in KFC and Popeye's frying chickens like Mexicanos, though they did eat mountains of chicken.

Myself, I like to take two chickens, fryers five or six pounds each, slice them from the neck through the breast cartilage down to the bottom, spread the ribcage apart and place them backside up on a cutting board and press down till the ribs crack and the chickens flatten about as flat as they can be. Rub both chickens with achiote paste that you can cut with lemon juice and mashed garlic in liquified butter, maybe with chipotle powder and/or red pepper flakes if you want to increase the necessary heat. On the barbecue over semi-low coals, it takes about an hour and you have two red juicy fiery chickens to serve to your guests with the side dishes. My friend Rick has a killer curry chicken recipe he cooks in a wok and serves over rice, so hot it burns your mouth, but these days I prefer my barbecue chickens, which when flattened cook all the way through without having to be turned, over a bed of Mexican mesquite charcoal. They brown nice and crisp on top like that.

After listening to a *Recent Rupture Radio Hour* (Ehekatl KXPO 99.9 FM), which features guests like Chicano Moratorium organizer Chalio Muñoz, I was especially intrigued by urban agriculturalist and chicken farmer, Liki Renteria. What he said about raising poultry for personal needs in an urban setting was eye-opening and enlightening. On his rough estate on a slope in Happy Valley, adjacent to Eugene Debs County Park (where it would seem his chickens have the run of many acres of urban green space, however fraught with raccoons and coyotes), Liki Renteria farms hundreds of heirloom variety pullets and cocks: Cuckoo Marans, Salmon Faverolles, Speckled Sussex Triplets, and Dark Cornish Plymouth Barred Rocks. Renteria, a favorite guest on the radio show for several reasons, answered many questions from the audience about raising your own organic food in an urban setting. I've been lucky to catch him on the radio lately on a couple of episodes, where he answered questions from the audience with alacrity and generosity. Audience members (seemingly a wide spectrum of Eastside residents of all ages and genders) could not get enough, asking him about food pyramids, urban ethics, sustainable agriculture, legal issues, and even questions about the effect of select foods on personal relationships. I was deeply impressed with all the information and began to believe that it might be good to purchase some big fat Rhode Islands for myself.

✿

Recently Tina and I were at some "industry" (show biz) lawyer's house in Laurel Canyon, a benefit for arts programs for children with AIDS. Tina told me I should go when somebody asked me to read some poems there, and, even if I didn't want to, she was curious and it was for a good cause, etc., even if it was going to take us an hour or more to get across town in traffic, if there were no accidents. The usual bottleneck on the 110 through downtown to the 101, bottleneck there too, breaking up a bit by Alvarado to Highland, south to Hollywood and due west on whatever it is, people driving so rude, night falling, lights of the city coming on in the glittering chill, winking and twinkling as we drove up into the hills. Tina reread Google-map directions as I drove rushed and gloomy.

"I don't care if I'm late," I sulked, but I drove fast (anyway I tend to drive fast). Tina soothed me, nonchalantly, "We'll get there." I had to park a couple blocks away on a narrow winding street hemmed in between tall walls, tall hedges, tall structures obscured by trees. I gave my name to a couple at the door who checked it against a list. The hostess, a TV actress, met us as we were walking in—she looked at me with wide eyes as if tentatively recognizing me based on somebody else's verbal description and thanked me for coming, telling me I was to follow the musician ("That's your cue, just let us know if you need anything. The program this evening is bursting, so please keep it under three minutes. Will that be satisfactory?" "Sure," I said, "I won't go longer than even one minute."). I'd been staring at the actress, her face round and shining like the moon, thinking that I had seen that face before on TV and in movies where it appeared normal-sized. She turned to other arrivals. We moved forward through a crowd. What's her name? I asked Tina. Tina said she thought her name was Something Something, but then corrected herself, saying, "but I'm probably wrong." I forgot the name a minute later. The party was all white people except for a few black people who apparently also worked in television or film. I recognized another actress who used to be Jackson Brown's girlfriend and who we used to see, sometimes with him, in downtown protest marches and demonstrations. She was in some terrific famous science fiction movie that academics loved to reference when discussing the future of Los Angeles. People were dressed in clothes they might wear on TV and also regular clothes, jeans, T-shirts or whatever. Nobody was talking to us just yet so we ambled through the living room where people milled with plates of food, drinks in hand. "Man," I whined, "when is the musician going to play? They haven't even started the program yet. Maybe the musician will be on first and then me and we can get out of here. What does this guy do, anyway? To earn enough to buy this big house overlooking Hollywood." Tina told me that he was a former communist in the 1960s, lawyer for the Black Panthers and other radical groups, lately he mostly did "entertainment law," made lots of money and tried to give some of it back. I scanned the spines of books on the nearest bookshelves. Social issue or political titles, nonfiction trade hardcover books (*Uneasy Rivals: Men and Women in Today's Workplace*, *Long Walk to Freedom: The Autobiography of Nelson Mandela*). Easy reading, not very interesting. Outside there was a deck where caterers grilled imitation Thai chicken satay on skewers, which we stood in a short line for and set on a bed of rice with Chinese chicken salad (made from the same frozen cuts of white meat, it seemed). I handed Tina a plastic cup of sparkling cider as we pushed through knots of people glancing at us so coldly their looks were almost openly hostile, out onto the hillside, laid out in a grassy open garden under oak trees. "This is very nice, very nice indeed," Tina said. "I can't wait till I get the fuck out of here," I said. "You gotta do your one good deed today," Tina said. I tried to tear the satay off the bamboo skewer with my teeth without stabbing myself with the skewer's charred point. The meat sort of crumbled like charcoal in my mouth. "This chicken is dry," I said. "My favorite," Tina said. "Yeah, right," I said.

Tina said the gardens alone were worth the trip. I couldn't see it, but I said the gardens were nice, to show that I could appreciate horticulture where she was involved. It was a nice warm evening above the city. When she was finished with her food I took her plate and we sauntered the path that wound down the hillside.

✿

One time I went to Liki Renteria's farms in the hills of Happy Valley, following Jose's detailed directions, without which I probably would have ended up lost somewhere, driving into some unfortunate alternate reality of sci-fi Los Angeles, never having the opportunity to join the UFO Club of Greater East Los Angeles, to miss out on ever finding my destiny. I went to the farm to kill chickens. Or roosters, rather, because the hens serve the purpose of laying eggs and therefore don't need to be killed, but the roosters just fuss and fight all the time, and harass and rape the hens, and need to be killed. Because I am a chicken eater, and I eat chicken every week, I felt it was my duty to help Jose and Liki cull their chickens. By the time I got there, up on the hillside by the shed, they had the big pot heated to exactly 140 degrees, or whatever the exact scientific temperature is for immersing the dead chickens in extremely hot water so that their feathers slough off as easily as feathers fall out of a torn pillow, and Jose and Liki were already at work, cutting the roosters' heads off, letting them bleed out in buckets, throwing the bodies into a big pot, which was (it was immediately apparent upon entering the area) releasing a stench of chicken death, of scorched dusty feathers, of bird blood, bird fear, punctuated now and then by the snapping off of yellow chicken feet, also tossed into a bucket, to be later thrown away, because no one—except Olga—wanted to cook or eat chicken feet. Liki handed me an apron and a knife. "There's gloves if you want them," he said.

Liki's Chicken-Killing Machine consisted of a piece of plywood onto which he had screwed a plastic orange traffic cone, upside down. At this point, there was a wash of blood streaming down the plywood into the bucket where the heads ended up. The cone made cutting the rooster's head off easy. You stuffed the rooster head first into the cone, so the head protruded out of the bottom. The roosters blinked, mouth open, wondering what the hell. They were so trusting. They'd lived their lives on this hillside, fighting with each other and raping the hens, endless free food, safe in the wire pens (once in awhile menaced by raccoons or coyotes who dug underneath or climbed overhead), and now they were hung upside down, with their head sticking out of a traffic cone? What was that awful smell? Why is there blood on this board? They don't try to peck at you. This is uncomfortable, you pulling my head like this. You pull their neck out, stretch it for the knife and cut off the head. The body flaps and kicks. Blood spurts out and drips toward the bucket. Toss the head. After the body stops moving, pass it to Jose and Liki who are scorching the feathers and removing them. That's the dirty job. After the dark feathers are yanked out, the outer feathers and long wing feathers and underfeathers, with that stench of filth and death, pale goose-pimpled naked chicken skin revealed itself, and I had never seen it before, but after the feathers came out—out of the same pores the feathers came out—long filaments of pale mucous extruded in spaghetti-like secretions.

No wonder we like our chicken fried crispy.

✿

Many years later, decades later, after Swirling Alhambra disappeared and the others were killed, after Sergio died, I was walking across the parking lot of a mini-mall. I had gone jogging in the hills in El Sereno, and my knees were killing me, and I was thinking that I was going to have to give up jogging, that I was getting older and closer to death—all those gloomy thoughts that I was always torturing myself with in a self-centered way, especially when I was working out. Except, of course, I felt pretty damned good afterward, cooling down, walking through the last light of the afternoon, twilight falling, car headlights streaming by on Huntington Drive. I passed giant piles of used tires towering over the fence of the bright yellow tire shop that I admired for its large plastic sign, which had been painted over and re-lettered so many times that when it was lit up, it was a perfect gibberish. The mini-mall parking lot was half-empty in the dusk. The jiujitsu students were taking a break in the parking lot. The tall dark woman in her late twenties who was apparently the lead black belt of the group glanced at me. I'd spoken to her once or twice somewhere, probably at a meeting at the Eastside Cafe. She was giving her group a break out in the hot summer dusk, and they were chatting while she stood looking stern. They were mostly young people—nobody as old as me. One storefront was empty, between a pharmacy and a "health food store" (window filled with supplements) and some curandera's office. I ducked in the doorway of the empty storefront for a look; the door was flung open as if the store had been looted or abandoned. The fluorescent lights were on, and debris was scattered in corners of the place. Was the economy in such disarray that landlords could no longer even police their properties? It wouldn't be surprising as a sign of the further downturn in the ever downward spiraling of dust-empire America. "You want a future? Go to China and see if you can make it there!" said some former storefront psychic-turned-politician on the front page of the *L.A. Times*. I walked through the empty storefront and out the rear door, which I'd expected to lead to a parking lot behind the buildings, but I found myself in a hallway full of medical equipment: gurneys, examination tables and computers, boxes and boxes of stuff, paperwork, stools, cabinets large and small, all stacked the length of one wall. I found a suite of rooms in the rear of the building, an abandoned medical clinic that was occupied by the group I'd only heard rumors about, Bugs Not Bombs (at least that's who I'm pretty sure it was, that's who I supposed it was based on what they were doing). With their little logo of an electrified cockroach. Anyway, somebody must have recognized me from somewhere, from those community meetings or whatever, somebody nodded at me (they didn't kick me out, as I walked through they ignored me—it was like I was some ghost, vestige of old days, neither a threat nor of any relevance), I walked through, heading purposely toward the rear exit, as if looking for the rear exit, which indeed I was. This group, Bugs Not Bombs, was a bunch of hacktivists targeting war machine NSA spy computers and police state war computers and Rand laboratory defense contractors, etc. They were going about it casually, as if marinating carne asada for a barbecue. They conferred quietly, talking in low tones, glancing at me now and then as if waiting for me to make my exit—which, just as casually, I did. I had the feeling they were doing their usual thing, using computers abandoned by a failed medical clinic, sending off a viral malware or spyware and waiting for signs it was working its way through systems, firewalls, servers and clouds. "I think it's working," someone said. They were quiet, waiting. I opened the door to exit, and paused. They seemed tense, awaiting a signal. (Maybe the signal was going to be cop cars roaring into the parking lot just outside this door, or an alteration of numbered patterns on the screens?) I exited, closing the door behind me.

THEY SAID SOMEONE
WILL COME

Sergio pumped the camping stove, a backpacking stove with
a cylinder of kerosene that had a pressure pump arm that he
had to pump to prime the vaporizer, the nozzle, to emit kerosene vapor could be lit with Strike Anywhere matches. That
was how he understood it to work, even though it was always
trial and error in the beam of a flashlight, dust motes wafting
through its pale light inside the vast dark of the hangar, random
punctuations of the interminable night.

One valve had to be open, or both—he always forgot the
details of the correct sequence to follow, it always took a long
time to start the stove (he was never certain it would start)—

The match got too low, and he flinched and flung it into
the darkness, shaking his hand.

He could hear his breathing.

After the (he stopped to listen, but he could only hear
his own breathing, couldn't see anything beyond the beam
of the flashlight aimed at the stove perched on the corner of
the rusty steel desk)—after the stove was lit he would pour
water in the pot for tea.

But first he had to get it lit.

It was always like this getting the stove started. He had never decided finally and absolutely once and for all that he should get a new stove. The trouble was that this one always worked. He'd told Jose and Swirling more than once that he needed a stove if he was going to be sent out on solo reconnaissance missions. They always agreed to anything he asked for, since he was dependable (that in itself somehow seemed a miracle) and took care of everything on his own. Then they'd given him a couple old relics, propane or butane stoves, that were too heavy or were missing parts or had no gas canisters. Swirling just shrugged. "You have to drink tea?" he asked.

Sergio was tired of working with jokers or pissing alcoholics.

Whatever those guys were.

Because he was a recovering alcoholic, and he just wanted to drink a fucking cup of tea.

He distracted himself by griping in his mind about the losers he had to work with in the East Los Angeles Dirigible Air Transport Lines. Swirling only heard what he wanted to hear, Jose didn't know how to tie his shoes, and then the big boss, Enrique Pico, always away on BIZNESS. After a while, Sergio got the pump to work, the nozzle to gassify, and he lit a flame that rushed from fluttering yellow to focused blue. It emitted a small roar.

The water would only take a couple minutes to boil.

The desiccated leather chair with alkali scum of evaporation on its cracked seat looked like it would collapse if he sat on it, so he pushed it aside. It rolled with a hollow gritty noise that resounded within the office, with its wide, empty window-frames yawning out into the abyss. He'd make do temporarily with a file cabinet he laid on its side (bits of debris skittered internally, fragrance of rat shit).

Sergio relished a moment of decision, selecting a bag from his stash of matcha green tea, Ceylon breakfast tea, Pike Place Market cinnamon tea, African rooibos and Chinese restaurant oolong.

As the tea steeped, enameled cup hot in his hand, Sergio picked up the flashlight and went off looking for a chair, with the expectation that instead he might find treasure. "At the very least I will find a chair." Part of his mind was focused on the thought that finally, now, with a cup of tea (some corner grazed his thigh, some steel angle—he immediately stopped.)

He pointed his flashlight and his headlamp down and saved himself, saved his own life (One more step and he might have fallen through the hole. Into blackness of space. Something huge and heavy falling from above had apparently torn away the steel railing and bent the walkway down into the blackness, so that one more step and he might've slid off into nothingness of space till he landed some second or two later with a hard slap on the concrete and debris several floors below, he saw now, with his heart thudding in his ears.) barely a tremor in his hand as he lifted the cup to his lips.

What had fallen? One of the huge, almost car-sized units formerly attached eight, ten stories or whatever it was above the plant floor? Or something brought down by teen vandals? He'd better keep his wits—or his one wit that he had left— about him. Sergio told himself that he had not had his cup of tea yet, that was his problem. That was why his thinking was muddled. That was why.

Matcha green tea would restore his thinking, he would be thinking right again. His head would be good again. He stepped back from the brink, back from the slippery slope of Death. Switched off the flashlight, then the headlamp, dropping the curtain of sudden pitch black. He sipped from the cup, allowing his sight to recover some glinting details of ambient light from the immensity of the abandoned aircraft plant they'd sent him to reconnoiter. He could hardly be irritated that they had assigned him no partner, no backup (crucial if you fell in utter darkness and broke your legs or your spine, a partner could get you some help before the death agony), since he had assiduously promoted his own reputation for utter independence, total reliability and unassailable, overwhelming competence. Dismissive as he was of others, having established urban reconnaissance skills at a far superior level in his own eyes and then in theirs, sometimes (he listened for any sound, but heard only the creak of his weight shifting on the grating, his own breathing and the sound of his slowing heartbeat, fear remaining localized like a chill in his thighs and stomach) yeah, sometimes it was stupid to go out without a partner. You could die out here. Just one wrong step, some mistake.

He switched his lights back on and checked the stability of the walkway overall, deciding it was only the outer edge that had been compromised. This by stomping on the steel grating and listening to the quality of the reverberations at a couple points. Which sounded all right, basically, so far, but in his report he would advise that work teams should exercise extraordinary caution when traversing the higher levels of the plant. And he'd need to try to think right if he wanted to survive to make that report. Why all the lame thoughts, poor thinking on his part?

Just the way it goes. Try to snap out of it. (sip of green tea) About him swirled an impenetrable darkness, falling out of the universe of night, pouring through the shattered roof eight stories above the cavernous hall. Torn, crumpled railings and bent walkway threatened death in various directions, leading him toward instant emptiness, though he had his head-lamp switched on. Little swirly flecks or motes floating across murky currents of dank air reeking of rust, mold, dust heaps of history.

Sergio had no use for the emptiness pouring out of

dark night and space. He furiously swept out his "office"—masonite debris, broken glass, former telephone books that were now wavy, porous blocks of cellulose, empty cans of something, strange dirt (from where?), went flying off the gangway into space. Though it was just a glorified glass booth (with some shattered panes, and a large Plexiglass window, discolored and aged with intricate fractal webs of cracks), it had a file cabinet (bottom drawer did not open), massive steel desk with cracking, charred Formica top, miscellaneous chairs (all damaged but quasi-functional), and, importantly, an old beige rotary telephone, which he plugged into a line that could not have been operative for decades. Immediately he began receiving calls.

Sergio took call after call. "East Los Angeles Dirigible Air Transport Lines, how may I direct your call?"

"No, sorry, he's not here."

Sergio sniffed, trying not to sneeze. These recycled offices always attacked his allergies with the infinitesimally ground-up particles of blasted lifetimes, stymied Chernobyl/Fukushimas of collapsed economies.

"No, those guys are never around. They might be out back. Can I take a message? They might get back to you."

Sergio took a number of calls, and after 45 minutes he unplugged the phone. He set it on the corner of the desk at a jaunty angle, indicating its readiness to receive more calls when he plugged it back in. He set the pad (with the "ELADATL Con Safos" logo in one corner) and pencil beside it, topmost notes visible.

Then he zipped up his favorite nifty jumpsuit (with the Amoco patch over his heart that said "Ray"), hefted his tool belt, his water bottle, and his broom, and made his way along the steel mesh gangway that ran the length of the building to the stairs at one end.

They said someone would come, meaning he could count

on help, but they always said that. And their volunteers were worthless even when they did show up; he had to spend more time babysitting them, keeping them from killing or maiming themselves in the hazardous environment of the abandoned facilities that were a major part of (and supplier of parts for) his job. Which was, that is, rehabbing and renovating the abandoned plants so they could be used to produce either a movie of a dirigible or the actual aircraft itself (depending on whether you spoke to Swirling or to Jose or to Ericka, or whichever ELADATL faction you might speak with, though you didn't have to worry about getting into a face-to-face argument, because the factions hardly communicated except by Internet static, flinging little insults and wannabe cutting remarks like sparks spitting off a chain dragging behind a junk truck on a 3 a.m. street). Either the movie about dirigibles that the Fictive faction insisted would be the necessary first step aimed to cure ELADATL's financial ills, or the clandestine dirigibles proposed by the Real World faction, which they insisted were necessary to restructure the entire transportation grid of California, which would transform the entire collapsing once-dominant U.S. economy (with a blockbuster summer dirigible movie just a spin-off and product-tie-in, its profit earmarked for more worthwhile, maximalist goals). Of course, the movie faction insisted that they themselves were the realists, while the other faction was a bunch of idealists, voluntarists, and adventurists, total lunatics untethered to reality. The rejoinder from the pilots flying actual clandestine dirigibles through the unlicensed air spaces of night was that they were the real realists, and the movie faction was just a bunch of armchair fantasists, artists, and hipsters dedicated to the idea (but not the practice) of actual lighter-than-air flight. When it got really nasty, each side was talking shit about who had money and who didn't, who lived where, who was from L.A. and who wasn't. The infighting was often bitter—fulminating over endless persecution by the feds, the police, the Mexican Mafia, you name it—causing drunken brawls and minor bloodshed in forgotten dives across East L.A.

Rank-and-filers like Sergio had to wonder if these natterings of brittle, fatigued leadership were signs of doom, crackbrained utopian delusion (as he had been told, and often, by losers in the street). ("Word in the street—")

He had to keep his mind on one thing at a time if he wanted to stay alive in the pitch blackness of the abandoned aircraft plant, which stood in partial ruins over a 3-mile-wide underground lake of Chromium-6-tainted water. The ruined plant (abandoned by Lockheed Martin in 1991) tried to maim and kill him via rusted railings that detached when leaned on, stairsteps that fell away into the abyss when you let down your full weight on them, random holes in the flooring where pipes and conduits or elevators or stairwells had been removed, etc. Even if he just stepped into a shallow hole and broke an ankle, like one of his short-term volunteers had done, it could mean days of misery before anyone came looking for him (that was one chirpy volunteer's first and last ELADATL experience).

They would only have a few week's use of this plant until it was razed to make way for the many bulldozed acres that were to release Chromium-6-laden soil to the winds for a couple of years until the developers figured out how to put a big-box shopping mall on the site. And when the leadership, minis and maxis both, found out about a plant's "availability," they always called in the forward team. Sergio was the forward team.

Given the shortage of members (who usually could be found reading angry spoken-word poetry in Long Beach coffeehouses, or singing sad versions of sones huastecos on the sidewalks of Koreatown, or defecting to the Food Not Bombs collective in Highland Park, or making clever online comments about the latest movies rather than actually putting in hours of labor), particularly on the graveyard shift that was his specialty, this forward team was Sergio alone.

But they said someone would come.

☼

They didn't say for sure who it was that killed Sergio on a night like this. They denied the rumors that it was an internal ELADATL security squad sent by one faction to take out a suspected member of the other faction, or an FBI Cointelpro-style provocateur playing that role. Most likely, they said, it was a psychopathic loner who read too many Conan the Barbarian comic books while listening to Classic Rock who chopped Sergio to pieces with a machete, who waited till Sergio was busy hammering, welding four hours straight, dragging scavenged steel frames into a circular pattern laid out on the ground floor in advance, concentric constellations of blue LED lights casting a distant pale glow like distant stars made of ice chips, reaching above his head to climb back up the ladder, when out of the dark he heard the faint indication of a footstep—

☼

That was one of his repeating nightmares, which Sergio replayed and discussed in his mind while measuring out great concentric circles in charcoal on dank concrete (lit at crucial intervals by solar-powered lights stolen from the front yards of helpful homeowners across the state of California— ELADATL officially thanks them here for supporting the next new era economy). He didn't know that his assassination was actually in writing somewhere—it had gone past the whisper campaign and moved through the final planning stages; he thought it was only in his imagination that he was going to be killed doing his clandestine duty for the people of California and the underclasses of the Americas (North and South), but what if his paranoia—that distant ticking or those slight sounds from odd corners of the pitch-black great hall of the generator room, deep inside the cavernous building—was a killer actually making his way stealthily toward him across the vast dark space.

Sergio did his best to remind himself that he was just paranoid, as usual; you had to keep your wits sharp to survive the usual dangers of any postindustrial wasteland. A little voice at the back of his mind suggested that perhaps the minis had tipped off some malevolent Homeland Security death squad that Sergio represented the maxis' best hopes in their effort to take over the entire ELADATL organization and replace the leadership with radicals who represented a direct attack on the capitalist 1% that ruled America with fascist force backed by NDAA legislation and endless piddly-assed laws against everything and your mother. Municipal ordinances, local laws, institutional regulations, state codes and federal legislation against terrorism and conspiracy and thinking, rules about everything from where and how you could walk the earth and chew gum at the same time, draw breath and how long, not to mention which verbal expression might be allowable when they towed your car from the 30-minute parking zone. God forbid if you showed up at the collective meeting and ever forgot Roberts Rules of Order, and—

What was that sound?

He could swear he heard a dry tick, like the steel blade of a machete accidentally scraping on cement.

Hopefully it was nothing, because he still had the front carapace of the dirigible to weld into place in the five hours left before dawn, if he was going to be ready by the time Swirling had said he was going to arrive with a carload of potential investors for the movie (if they were that kind of investors) or the dirigible fleet (if they were those other, harder-to-find investors). The aluminum conduit, thermostat and drain cocks, brass tubing, blower unit housing, cold air ducts and coolant lines that Sergio welded, bolted, drilled, hacksawed, ground, sanded, engineered, framed, scaffolded, lifted, pulleyed, swung, chained, tied, hammered, sledged, screwed, fused, wired, electrified, cantilevered, extended, raised, oxy-acetylene-torched, arc-welded, stapled, grommeted, tacked, maneuvered, moved, hurled, spun, forced, handled, sorted, joined, expoxy'd, Super Glued, powered up, connected, hot-wired, grounded, ionized, jerry-rigged, and banged together would have to look visually impressive so as to impress the hell out of motion picture producers, on the one hand; and it would need to have an actual chance of getting off the ground, in order to meet the requirements of the outlaw capitalists captivated by strange dreams of lighter-than-air solar-powered or self-charging airships on the other. In short, he had one night in which to make ELADATL happen—or not. Others put in a similar predicament might have been resentful. Sergio certainly was.

But he had work to do. He was doing it!

What was that?

Did a couple of the distant LED lights just flicker, out there beyond the perimeter of darkness?

Anyway, how could he see anything, green spots in his eyes after welding the concentric circles of the hull into place, and the gangways too, laid out and welded along port and starboard. By that time, Sergio was glistening with sweat, his skin blackened by carbon dust and fiberglass insulation dust and ancient dust. His hair bristled through the goggle straps; strands of black hair hung in his face, his forehead smeared where he'd brushed it repeatedly away. He figured he probably needed a haircut.

They said he'd never seen it coming. He was so engrossed in his work, as usual—building an entire dirigible by himself (or the representation of one, according to the movie faction)—that he hadn't even heard the figure zigzagging through the emptiness of the great hall toward him as he bent over the framing, electrode holder in a thickly gloved fist. Occasionally, he'd jump up, rush over to the portable generator and shut it off.

Sergio would grab the big 25-watt HID rechargeable spotlight and furiously swing the 20,000,000-candlepower beam in great arcs in every direction to verify that he was totally alone. As the vast shadows of building materials, framing and debris leaped wildly back and forth, he felt alone in this strange endeavor—not just in some existential sense but, more importantly, there at the base of the ladder. Darkness shuddered and wobbled in big clouds in all directions above him, but the great hall, with its various foundation struts and structures scattered across the floor resolved into shaky definition under the white spotlight. Then he switched it off, giving his eyes a moment to readjust to the darkness, reaching upward—

That is—he heard the slight—

Too late—

✿

Fuck it, he had to put that bullshit out of his mind and get his work done. This paranoid thinking—occupational hazard of certain jobs on a graveyard shift—was going to cause him to weld a hole in his hand or something stupid like that. Maybe he should take a break and have a cup of tea. The trouble was, to get back upstairs to his "office," fire up the pain-in-the-ass camp stove and boil water would take half an hour, which he didn't have. Probably—

BAM!

Lights out!

That was the way he expected to go out. Some psycho loser was going to take him out when he wasn't looking, or he was gonna fuck up and touch a hot wire and bite his tongue through, shattering his teeth, 150,000 kilowatts torching every hair off his blistering skin. Meanwhile, he positioned himself above the juncture to begin his next bead.

He should have taken a tea break. He should have fired up the stove back in his office and made a cup of organic South African rooibos.

Or, something he'd done more than once, he should've poured a cup of cold water and thrown a tea bag of anything in it and come back later to drink it. Even that would have been better than nothing.

As it was, he knelt down to lift a heavy stanchion armature onto his shoulder and drove an eight-inch-long piece of steel wire (that he had somehow miraculously avoided all night) through his leg, through the meat of his left calf and the pants leg of his favorite grease-stained jumpsuit. He gasped, a tremor of agony shaking his entire body, and leaned slightly to his left, tossing the heavy stanchion far enough that it would not rebound onto his own injured limb. He stifled the screech that rose in his throat as he lifted his leg off the wire, the length of it sliding out with a friction audible in Sergio's hissing exhalation. He growled a long string of banal cusswords and sat on the one bare patch of dusty cement floor he could vaguely make out, his attention drawn to the nastiness flaring up his leg. He wrapped his hands around the wound, which he could feel leaking warmly through the fabric, sighing. "Ow, fuck," he added.

Then he limped toward the stairs at the far corner of the vast ruin. He'd have to pour hydrogen peroxide into both sides of this wound so he didn't wind up with tetanus. He'd get the cup of tea that had been in the back of his mind for some time.

On the final night, did he even see the figure that separated itself from the shadows?

✧

Although he always kept a pair of bolt cutters handy in his truck at all times, Swirling was glad he did not have to interrupt his spiel about the dead economy, California's once-great, eighth-largest (or fifth-largest according to some estimates) world economy and its ever increasing population, 38 million at last count, the dead economy freeing up space both actual and intellectual for airships of new thinking, forward bound, filled with the helium of dreams.

Sergio had, as usual, cut through the chain and hung the lock so that it appeared locked; so Swirling could swing out of the cab, with the Germans safely tucked inside as the dawn streaked brightly across the puddled expanses of empty pavement, pull some keys from his pocket to "unlock" the lock, open the sagging chainlink gate, and drive his quiet, bemused bunch through to the still vaguely impressive facilities.

It was clearly all fallen into disrepair but the Germans had been told all that. They had been told all sorts of things, parts of it certainly true.

Like the edgiest of venture capitalists, these guys checked their cell phones as often as teenagers. With their open-collared polo shirts and paunches and eco-shoes and salt-and-pepper close-cropped bullet heads, they were not really interested in the grimmest and grimiest of dull details. They expected that to be taken care of in advance. Maybe just one or two morsels to titillate like an appetizer. They wanted the secret glory of the supposed outside risk (that was primarily yours to bear), but mainly they expected insured return (of some kind!) on their money.

That was all fine, Swirling reflected, as he drove across the railroad tracks that cut through the plant, through another gate that Sergio had (as instructed) opened in advance, even though it was worrisome that Sergio had stopped answering his calls sometime after 4 a.m.

He hoped that Sergio had not injured himself or been killed. That would certainly put a damper on the meetings with this group. ELADATL needed this capital to get to the next phase. Sergio had never failed him before, that's why Swirling was putting him in charge of all the forward teams (once they organized some forward teams).

Meanwhile, Swirling covered his worry about not hearing from Sergio for hours during this most critical period by raising the decibel levels—roaring through the expanse of the former plant with its mounds of clumpy debris and its empty rectangles of razed foundations shining damply in the dawn light, speeding through the grounds at fifty miles an hour like a low-flying twin-engine P-38 "Lightning."

Swirling tossed out all kinds of facts and random commentary while he drove, drawing his charges' attention to this or that and away from his own jittery nerves. When he arrived at the runway—which had been in use as a parking lot but was still recognizably a runway—with the B-1 building adjacent, the huge hangar doors were not open. In the mean light of dawn, they looked permanently closed, nonfunctional, battered and corroded.

"Gentlemen! Time to view our newest prototype!" Swirling said.

He leaped out, swaggered to the center of the nearest hangar door and banged loudly, repeatedly.

"What the hell," he muttered, banged again, his fist hitting the door that reverberated thunderously inside the cavernous building.

"If he's working, sometimes he can't hear," Swirling explained, glancing at the Europeans from the corner of his eyes. They commenced looking about in the morning breeze and grinned at him, unwavering steady pinpoints of gravity in their eyes.

Swirling was banging again, desperately, when the huge sheet-metal door gently lifted, softly rising into the air.

It went up about twenty feet and stopped, revealing the great hall with its sad, strange stacks and piles of sheet metal, piping and debris scattered about the huge frame of an obvious dirigible, five or more (top obscured in dimness) stories high and hundreds of feet long, what you could see of it, as rays of morning light penetrated the dimness of the interior.

As usual, Sergio had ultracapacitors hooked up to oscilloscopes and generators to produce random electrical thrumming and sizzling far down the tail end of the ship, and he'd left his welding apparatus shooting sparks and had to run over and switch it off, all for effect. This ship produced its own sound track.

The German investment group rushed forward, as if hypnotized by their own expectations. One of the investors with a cigarillo in his mouth (one of their slim brown cigarillos) caught Swirling's glance, removed the cig and pinched it away in his pocket, grinning and shaking his head.

Swirling took to nodding, as if everything was on schedule.

Sergio made it on schedule.

Sergio dropped the nylon line of the manual pulley he'd had to rig to get the huge door to slide on its broken old tracks; he limped over on his damaged leg to shake hands with the investors. Swirling was explaining some ideology about dirigibles, some shit about self-charging titanium frames and solar power to these guys who had to remove their sunglasses to see into the dimness.

Sergio was tired. He stood behind Swirling till Swirling finally noticed him and introduced him to the members of the investment group, "This is Sergio, head of our Forward Teams division." Swirling gave the bloody rag wrapped around Sergio's calf a glance and said, "How're you, boss?"

Sergio frowned, tipping his head toward the hangar door.

The two walked out toward the shining expanse of morning. The Germans talked happily.

"You all right?" Swirling asked again.

"Look, I got blood all over my favorite jumpsuit. Get me out of here," Sergio said, "I want to change my clothes and have a cup of tea. I don't want to be late. Unlike you, I got a day job."

"Absolutely! Let me give our friends the story behind this ship first, then we're on our way! What a beautiful morning, eh?"

KRAKEN ATTACKS AND DESTROYS L.A. ZEPPELINS

"I Am a Lineman for the County
and I Drive the Main Roads"

1.

It all starts on Bunker Hill. Some people say we emerged
from the 2nd Street tunnel to the stairs, ascending Angel's
Flight to the top of the hill, a bunch of us with Elote Girl with
cornsilk in her long dusty hair and her sack of corn that she
sells steaming with mayonnaise on the street corner. That's
not really true, of course, not in the literal sense (what is?),
that's pure reductionism, but that's what I am going with
because, because—anyway, yeah—we need a simple gesture
at the beginning—especially for things that seem to have no
real beginning or end.

Because it's not easy to think of the teriyaki-flavored Buddhist chain of cause-and-effect events (lingering aftertaste of ginger) that caused me to be dangling from my line, roped securely to my harness outside the 45th floor of the United California Bank Building, watching the war, the war they had going on at that time between the zeppelins and the dirigibles, the skyship versus airship war for the skies of Los Angeles, when the Kraken appeared out of the clouds and forever changed the world as we knew it.

I might be the first person in modern times to see the Kraken.

The sudden swirling vortex of a huge black thunderhead lashing out at the skyscrapers with hellish flashes of lightning, lightning bolts popping and exploding from it like the thrashing arms of a wild monster, purplish and black—so overwhelming that at first I thought I might be seeing spots and about to faint, or maybe I was having a stroke brought on by years of stress and thinking wrong thoughts; at the same time, it occurred to me that perhaps two of the dirigibles and zeppelins firing away at each other had collided, exploding directly overhead, and this descending darkness signaled they were about to crash down upon me, so I hid my face against the black glass of the high-rise, raising my arm over my skull to ward off the massive debris that I felt most likely would follow the great shadow.

Gale-force winds whipping my (fake) company jumpsuit so that my collar slashed at my neck and my hair stung my cheeks as it flicked about insanely didn't bother me in the least, even when they caused my line and anchor rig to sway back and forth across the black glass divoted surface of the building, and all it took was a couple snags or scrapes against the window edges to send me spinning dangerously, so that my line was going to wrap and perhaps shear, and I was going to smash hard into the side of the building, which whirlpooled around (and around) me, like I had become the hopeless center of a lunatic universe spiraling totally out of control.

I had not had time to spike a piton in a window-cleaner's track as a stabilizer. I knew what was about to happen, and I wasn't looking forward to it. I had the piton filched from a cargo pocket and gripped tightly in my fist when it did happen. The slack in the line combined with a drop in the wind slammed me face-first into the reflective obsidian glass of the building (I glimpsed my reflection careening forward) so hard that I blacked out.

I came out of it feeling like I was coming up for air. I felt myself floating toward a fluid surface and gulped air, trying to breathe and clear my vision.

But I wasn't swimming, I was spinning forty-five floors above Hope Street, downtown L.A. gone blurry and faint below. The piton I'd been gripping was gone; I was feeling at my smashed face with my numb fingers. They came away bloody; my nose seemed to be broken, along with one or more front teeth. I tasted blood.

But I could see, more or less, and the impact with the building had somewhat slowed the spinning, so I found another piton and executed an E, lifting my right leg and my right arm parallel to flail the building, stiffly and weakly, attempting to halt the spin. I wasn't sure, but a couple of burning airships might have landed atop the tower above me, and burning pieces and raw ejecta might fall on me at any moment, but I didn't have time to consider that, I had to knock a piton into a window-cleaner's track or spacer column. So first I clawed my grappling hook onto the next spacer that came around—it took several tries and I was worried my spin would accelerate, but I got the hook on a crease without losing it or my grip, and knocked a piton in. I clipped my harness to the piton and looked up.

We were all looking up.

When I looked up, the window was flying to pieces, and I didn't even have time to turn away before I was hit. Three masked gunmen had emerged from a black Honda firing dozens of shots, blasting the window apart and missing all the patrons but striking me in the head. As I went down beside the counter I didn't even have time to register what I felt. I'd come from China only the year before, working to bring over my daughter. I rode my bicycle to work every day.

When I looked up, turning my face from my mother's shoulder as we walked on Eastern Avenue, on our way back to the apartment with my sister and my aunt, this giant bucket thing like a big steel fucking arm swings loose on this huge truck going around the corner, crushing us all against the cinderblock wall, killing us instantly except for my little sister who suffered severe head injuries and me just a toddler never to grow old enough to talk or say the word "crane".

When I looked up I couldn't see a thing, not a light of any kind. Who knows, but maybe I wasn't even looking "up." I'd gone down in the black hole of the tank to save my co-workers, who'd failed to come out or answer my shouts. I thought I might be able save them, but I couldn't locate them—instead I blacked out. I must've took a little breath or somehow tried to breathe.

When I looked up, I was flying through the air into the street, the driver had run the red light. It had been a nice warm evening, mom was pushing me in my stroller. It was at the downtown L.A. Art Walk.

When I looked up into the Red Line tunnel, we saw or really just heard the 4 x 4 concrete blocks stabilizing the shaft in the Santa Monica Mountains above us shift and buckle. They basically exploded. I jumped aside a yard or so at the most before they landed on me.

When I looked up there was the big school bus, and it didn't stop. I was pushing my bike like my parents said to in the crosswalks, but the driver didn't see me somehow, even in broad daylight.

By the time we arrive at the job, we've lost so many of our people it's hard to even call us a "team." When I had time to glance sideways, I saw traffic whizzing by on the 10 San Bernardino Freeway through the photochemical afternoon haze of delimited expectations. I saw fuzzy remnants of black plastic tarps or whitish plastic bags partially buried in the sand, soft and wind-tattered like petrolate feathers on windswept soil under a broken fence line. One time I saw a wheel ejected explosively from a collision in opposite lanes come bounding and bouncing over the center median like a missile, as if charged with all of civilization's automotive kinetic energy. I saw skinny topless girls lolling on faraway beaches of a faded old titty calendar on the wall in the oily dank garage bay with hydraulic lifts while waiting for a mechanic beside the Coke machine. I saw neighborhood teenagers trying out skateboard tricks in parking lots under the streetlights out of sight of cops. That was when I had time to glance sideways. I glimpsed the high-tension lines marching toward the horizon of the Chocolate Mountains and the black stains of cooking grease trailing from the back door of the restaurant to the grease pit next to the dumpsters . . .

I always carried my tools close to my person: Swiss Army knife, bottle of aspirin, fake ID with social security card, pictures of actual children, scraps of paper with contact information for children and wife, work gloves, anti-entropy ideology (which starts by replacing the word "cool" with the word "folded" or "unfolding"), climbing kit: pitons, harness, belaying devices and descenders, carabiners, ropes, hooks, clips, chalk, gloves and stuff. First Aid tape and whatever little medical first aid kit I could get. In a bag with extra little baggies. You get killed so many times for carrying too much gear or too little, it helps you get your gear kit in order, over the long haul.

Five hundred years climbing cables of law-enforced genocide. They're killing us too many times.

In his ground-breaking analysis of Pacific Rim urban planning for the new millennium, "Laundromats, Liquor Stores and Storefront Psychics: Los Angeles Rules the World," UCLA social scientist George Carlin writes, "I don't like ass kissers, flag wavers or team players. I like people who buck the system. Individualists. I often warn people: "Somewhere along the way, someone is going to tell you, 'There is no "I" in team.' What you should tell them is, 'Maybe not. But there is an "I" in independence, individuality and integrity.' Avoid teams at all cost. Keep your circle small. Never join a group that has a name. If they say, "We're the So-and-Sos," take a walk. And if, somehow, you must join, if it's unavoidable, such as a union or a trade association, go ahead and join. But don't participate; it will be your death. And if they tell you you're not a team player, congratulate them on being observant." Such an expert analysis of modern industrial trends. Which is why George Carlin is considered an expert on such topics by crowds in auditoriums and lecture halls on universities and TV shows, by people who sit back and clap.

But we don't go for that.

As I said before, we emerged as a people from the earth, from the depths underneath our feet or conduits beneath the 4-10 sub-basements with their nylon earthquake shock-absorber pylons, the motion-isolator supports, flexible electrical conduit, utility service tunnels, etc. We enter the buildings from below and begin to climb. Our teams and crews are often eliminated by security or predatory gangs or the mishaps and accidents that always happen.

We never give up. That's not our official motto or anything, just the way it is. So they kill us.

When the experts are on stage saying their thanks, thanking the producers, their moms and God, nodding at standing ovations and sitting on panels with the checks in the mail or in jacket pockets over their hearts, we're in the shadows—standing in the aisles with a flashlight or at the back door staring out over the parking lots. We're cleaning up after the shows are over, locking the doors and holding the gate till the parking lot empties. We're walking the gangways high over the convention floor pulling cables and junction boxes, coiling the cables and turning off spot lamps. We're driving around the parking areas cleaning up trash or evicting a drunken couple fucking in a vehicle against the back fence and sending the neighborhood skaters on their way. We're cleaning the hall and emptying trashcans, sweeping and vacuuming carpets in aisles, hallways and lounges, from floor to floor. We took tickets and set up for Republicans and evangelicals, Democrats and Teamsters, SEIU, AWP, panels and keynote speeches, celebrity benefits, anime conferences, and porn industry galas.

Which history of famous porn stars mentions us by name? Which economic study of the industries of desire and disgust records our extensive labor?

You've seen us pointing at the exit with flashlights, nodding as you go, standing with our hands folded waiting for the show to be over, pushing the cleaning cart, sweeping corners and swabbing toilets. You didn't notice us at the time, maybe you nodded as we came out of the elevator. Our uniform blended in, we got on with the work.

We emerged from the earth to ascend, bound together, our teams networking via safe houses and contacts. We were those "so-and-sos, trade unionized"—together, we proceeded. Via portals and tunnels, harnessed and geared as we moved into the day. Roped, strapped in, tool belt, carabiners clicking. Strapped into blowers, blowing leaves, strapped into trucks, driving endless routes, jammed in traffic, staggering out of back doors at all hours carrying slopping steel pans and tubs to the grease pit—turning back again—tied to soiled aprons—frying, grilling, chopping, blasting pots, pans, and trays with spray in clouds of steam boiling out of the dishwasher when we open it and stack it higher. (Hey, didn't I see you at the Grand Canyon or Yosemite National Park, getting your lunch? Didn't you leave your magazine in the motel room—so I glanced through it before I tossed it?) Stacking cars on the parking structure, stacking pallets and dead cars in wrecking yards, stocking shelves in the big box stores all night . . . flatten cardboard boxes and aluminum cans, and fill shopping carts to push down the avenues . . . delivering parts from San Pedro docks to warehouses throughout L.A. and the Valley, crawling under fleet vehicles, changing brake pads, pulling transmissions, welding mufflers and radiators, climbing through ceilings two stories from the ground to pull wire through conduits, numb minds and fingertips, breathing dust and plastic resin, blackening our faces and exposed skin with soot and tuolene solvents, roof tar, and herbicides, staple gun in one hand, sweat-marked lifelines on the other.

You saw the grave markers. Those pegs scattered across the broken ground, little ribbons of fluorescent orange tape flying. Ground prepared for new construction. Someone gone for every orange tape flicking in the breeze across the bladed clay ground of an open field.

Maybe you saw the markers alongside the highway, white crosses and plastic flowers to commemorate lives lost on the way, or the pile of votive candles, real and fake flowers, mylar balloons ("We'll miss you!"—"Rest in Peace"—"Love"—"Smile Now, Cry Later"), handwritten cards and sometimes stuffed toys, against a fence or under the streetlamp on the corner where it happened.

✿

On one job, while climbing a steel cell tower over by Altadena, I reached the 200-foot level and spotted an expensive alloy clip still attached to a guyline, and I knew something had happened to the last steeplejack, because for what we make to risk our lives at these heights, you don't leave that kind of gear behind. (I left it clipped in place as a commemoration of whomever it was, and a reminder for the next guy.) It was like the time I was working my way alone (as member of a team or crew or collective we have to play our individual role on jobs requiring hazardous solos) through some far corner of some sub-basement level, I don't even remember where, of course, and I came across another crew's duffle bag emptied and discarded behind the pipes—(I'd found it accidently; leaning against the pipes to wipe my face in the stultifying heat, I touched a strap—and pulled out the bag). You get those messages once in a while: "Somebody like you came this way. Somebody like you was doing exactly what you are doing. Likely they were killed doing exactly what you are doing. Watch yourself." What happened? Who took out the other guy? Who stole his gear and discarded the bag? That's exactly the kind of intelligence you never get from the people contracting the job. Their line always is, "Don't worry. We're just scouting new talent. The last crew had no problems at all." At most they might say something like, "The last group was involved with drugs. They got sloppy, made mistakes. We let them go. You guys are clean, eh?" You never get the real story.

Sometimes there are the unmistakable signs that individuals are living inside the walls, merging with the infrastructure. Old retirees or women living in utility closets or under bridges or under the stairs. That's how the owners want us. My favorite writer, Rick Harsch, coming from a long line of subway tunnel families and high-climbing ironworkers, author of the trade classics *Belaying and Rappelling with Guts,* and *Sensual Builder-ing and Erotic Stegophily: I Like it on Top*, writes, "The fucking fascist-capitalist assholes both as a class and as individuals goddamn want us motherfucking dead or fucked up and frozen in catatonic postures of shit-eating horror, blind-sided by their horrible motherfucking goddamn fuck-off piss-ass delusions of grandeur, those motherfucking assholes—that's why we have to camouflage in the infrastructure." Possibly the most famous quote about why we must unobtrusively excel at the highest techniques of parkour and structuring, else we are lost. No wonder his books are passed hand to hand and studied by fading LED lamplight deep underground in dank utility tunnels with intermittent rumbling of heavy traffic or subway trains or mineshaft cave-ins.

Word came down that you didn't want to get a reputation for being too good at your job either, as employers had paid local gangs to take out crews or units that got too proficient or too prominent and asked for higher rates, driving up wages. One crew, among the best in their line, was driven to a service road in the Verdugo Hills, shot in the head at close range. One team came under fire at a gas station, four killed—including a fourteen-year-old bystander. A family was found slaughtered at home, bludgeoned, stabbed and shot—the rest of the team was never found. Of course, the media suggests that these crimes are endemic to our community, a desperate elimination of the competition, through overwork or drugs or epidemic violence or "secret histories" or "genetic modification." It was counterintuitive, but tunnel rats respected for their acuity suggested that powerful contractors with connections to the Philippines and Central America, to Citibank and Bank of America, respectively, wanted a more disorganized labor pool—that historically had been more to their liking. Legislators and attorneys general suggested that crews would be subject to indefinite confinement and torture in secret prisons if they were discovered operating without permits and licensing, in order to protect public order. Some even suggested this would "protect" the workers themselves in the aggregate by "sacrificing" a portion of individuals. Anguished unheard death agonies in the secret prisons should be considered, some in the media argued, as a small price to pay for lower taxes. Pundits or academics would say that it was just competition between aboveground and underground, between base and superstructure ("inside" and "outside") workers that had taken a violent form, maybe just random or isolated cases of crews or teams fighting among themselves because they were infected by Southland gang cultures and the dirty criminality of Lakers fans, though I personally never saw anything like that, it made no sense. It was true that "things happened," that is, whole groups disappeared, leaders were assassinated—throughout the years with the accumulation of thousands of deaths and disappearances—with no official inquiry or media attention or importance placed on any of these lives gone, so that they were erased—history was erased, as if tens of thousands, hundreds of thousands, or millions of vanished lives had in fact never existed. What was actual, instead—in fact, in actual hard fact—were the corporate logos and company names we affixed, rappelling from the roofs of high-rises and skyscrapers to place the subconscious beacons on the dusky evening skyline.

Ceaseless supply moving to demand, our teams and crews entered from underground, repurposing motion detectors, rerouting alarms, switching video-surveillance monitors over to the Saturated Fat Network or Pornographic Home Industry, as we installed marijuana gardens or organic vegetable plots behind the fence line. I didn't have anything to do with it myself, but drug gangs paid some workers to tend marijuana plots and heirloom tomatoes for supply to locals. I appreciated picking my own fresh chiles, potatoes, summer squash, Anasazi beans, kale, and chard. With hydroponic gardens installed in sub-basement levels and dry-irrigation crops sown on freeway medians and embankments behind rows of oleander, we occupy the overlooked and forgotten spaces. Politicians whip citizens into a self-righteous frenzy about imaginary sins and corruption, while we raise the city around them— we push wheelbarrows, carry hod, shoulder drywall, and solder plumbing. We electrocute outselves and fall sixty feet down dark shafts. We fix cars, tend babies, begonias, lawns, or laundry, empty bedpans and piss bottles, shift old people in bed, strip the beds and change bedding, bathe the enfeebled, disabled, and demented. From either side of the window, behind glass, everything on the other side appears normal, routine, ordinary.

Buildings and boulevards, avenues and malls, freeway exchanges, parking lots, and vehicles, the whole built cityscape was real, but we who lived inside walls, we had no visible life. The visible life was of products.

Perhaps what I would see in a single dangling wire (a disconnected TV cable line) dangling from a telephone pole or a steel power pole was something that others could not see. Anyway, what we saw everywhere could always—and in every case—be denied. By a tap on a screen.

In the baleful gaze of the woman peering out from her covers in a crawlspace under the stairs as three of us ascended I saw the history of a whole people.

If our peoples were deemed to not have existed—or if allowed some sort of existence but never really counted—if the service workers who tended the grounds, swept the walks, cleaned the offices, corridors, and hillsides, did misdemeanor community service picking up trash on the freeway medians and embankments wearing orange reflective vests, framed tract houses on building pads bladed across landscapes and kept green the greenways of executive golf courses and resorts, transforming swaths of the terrain—in fact, we who also reconstituted the world of the financial towers downtown overnight, in the dark while the rest of the world slept, so they might awaken in the morning and find "their" world as they presumed it to exist (a world possessed by all those possessed by it)—the artifice of this material world sustaining that comforting illusion people may cherish at any given moment: that all was as it had ever been—served up with pastries baked for the coffee shop from 2–4 a.m. and delivered by trucks negotiating the predawn streets in submarine hues of greenish shadow and gleam, freshly roasted coffee beans delivered to those same locations, fleets of shining taco trucks and lunch wagons sprayed down, washed, restocked, and steaming by the hundreds in dark yards before they rolled in along the avenues under the streetlights—it was as if the civilization was sleeping, dreaming of a distant Hollywood life of a ghostly Shangri-la where somehow sweaty faces and grimy necks, toil-weary backs and arms, calloused hands and dirty torn fingernails were themselves the strange dream.

In the morning, people rushing to work might notice the others at the end of their shifts, might have been awakened by a truck banging down dumpsters or caught some vague fleeting bit of conversation between the garbagemen before turning back to sleep, or while trying to beat rush hour might have paused at the light behind a work truck laden with welding equipment and oxyacetylene tanks emblazoned with yellow warning stickers looped with rubber hose and did not bother, never thought, never imagined or dreamed of marginal lives channeling the velocity of their own into the mainstream of broad daylight except to feel some impatience, perhaps, at having to pause for a truck at the light. In the spotlit gaze of unblinking storefront security cameras and mannikins, we became as shadows.

Maybe you saw cops pull people out of a vehicle. A couple of cruisers with their light bars at daybreak, starting early. No wonder traffic was slowing. Men kneeling on the sidewalk, hands behind their heads. Maybe you'd pay special attention if one was a woman. Did they pass that confinement law or whatever the new law was they were talking about? You couldn't recall.

✧

"Let's get back to the original line of questions we were going over, eh? What about the war between the zeppelins and the dirigibles in the skies over Los Angeles?"

"I heard something about it, I don't remember exactly what. I figured it didn't have anything to do with me, frankly. I have enough trouble trying not to get killed by gangs or random, crazed, heavily armed individuals, or by accidents on the job."

"Really? You don't know anything about the Volunteers of the Zeppelin Attack Dirigibles and their defense of hillside communities and crowds of protestors?"

"I probably saw something about it on the news. Yeah. Pretty sure."

"You're sort of disappointing as a narrator."

"Hey, they subcontracted me on this job. That's the way it works. They contract out, no questions asked. Our crew had to retrofit the foundation at the basement levels—jacking up one side of the building at a time, imagine—to meet new codes."

"But still, the War of Los Angeles is pretty important. It's a major social issue, and you don't seem to know much about it."

"If you let me check with my co-workers, my backup probably can—"

"No. No, no time for that here. Besides, your compas are even more injured than you are. I don't know if they regained consciousness. They're being tended to."

"Sorry, I never was asked about social issues before."

"Don't you care about your community? I mean, you live in this city too."

"I tend to keep my head down—or up, in this case—"

"It's in all the papers."

"Yes. Mainly my reading is confined to work-related questions. Did I tell you about my favorite quotes by my favorite author, Rick Harsch, author of *Belaying and Rappelling*—" "Yes, you already mentioned that.

"Did I tell you about his motivational instruction, 'The fucking fascist-capitalist assholes both as a class and as individuals goddamn want us motherfucking dead or fucked up and frozen in catatonic postures of shit-eating horror—"

"Yes, yes."

"I said that?"

"You did."

"Often, we find such concepts useful, like when you are thinking how to extract your own crushed or broken fingers from the belaying device at fifty stories or more —"

"No doubt. We are rather more interested in the first documented sighting of the Kraken."

"I never suspected for a second the existence of such things. Never in this world! Imagine?"

"This may be the first documented sighting of one, yes. That's why we're trying to get this down. We'd like to complete your testimony, for the record."

"So really, you don't really want to hear about my job situation, is that what you're saying?"

"Basically. Yes."

"Oh."

"As you were saying, you were roped outside the 45th floor of the United California Bank Building dangling above Hope Street and 6th, sent crashing into the side of the building by gale-force winds out of black thunderheads above you?"

"That's right. I thought I was dead right there. Before we go on, can I get some medical attention for my face and my hand? I'd like to get my face sewn up and my fingers splinted."

"We'll get you some primary care as soon as we finish this interview."

"It's getting hard to see. I'm worried about losing the sight in my left eye. I feel as if I might black out."

"Yes, let's proceed with answering the questions, shall we? That way, we can get finished as soon as possible and then we'll get you fixed right up. Your co-worker is a lot worse off—in critical condition—and we'd like to get him airlifted out of here as well. We just want to document the important details while we're waiting."

"Can I have a drink of water?"

"Of course. I have some M & Ms, would you like some?"

"I don't think I could hold them; these fingers are really—"

"Of course. You must be in a great deal of pain."

"About a five on a scale of ten."

"Let's get on with it, then we can get you to the doctor. You said you knocked in a piton and clipped on your line. 'I clipped my harness to the piton and looked up.'"

"I clipped my harness to the piton and looked up."

2.

"It did start on Bunker Hill (or underneath it)."

"As you know, the sky has become a striated vortex of polyethylene or polypropylene snow or dust (resin pellets), capable of sudden, dynamic weather formations that defy climatology. Who can account for strange orange clouds suddenly blowing in after the Santa Anas, raining down not the stinging desert sands and alkali chalk scoured from the floors of high deserts, instead they draw burnt sienna curtains over the atmosphere, glinting winds sifting almost invisible semitransparent flakes and sharp, reflective flecks across the terrain, threatening urban citizens (particularly young children or the elderly and infirm) with asphyxiation, or at least severe eye and lung damage resulting from breathing yellow particulate. What do people hiding from the weather in shopping malls, abandoned public buildings like libraries or schools or in a Starbucks say about the Orange Gyres? They speculate that some secret U.S. government agency like the National Oceanic and Atmospheric Administration has conspired with radical environmentalists to foment Orange Gyres over the urban centers of the planet in order to hide the wholesale theft of internal combustion automobiles and major appliances like refrigerators, microwaves, and other popular consumer goods from former First World nations. China (and sometimes Brazil) always figures in these theories. Water heaters, 1970s Oldsmobile Cutlasses, store mannikins, screen doors, and refrigerators occasionally falling to earth out of massive orange thunderheads that blot out the sun only adds to the conspiracy bullshit."

"As you know, I said fuck you (in my mind) to your generous offer to unlock the glass case in the lobby, remove the directory of suites and offices, step through into the service corridor ("watch your head, some of these pipes are hot—as you know"), skedaddle semi-sideways the length of the elevator core, ascend a series of ladders and gangways to the sixth floor (where you could feel the radiant heat of the eastern face of the building through the wall) to a nearly perfect air-conditioned cubicle ensconced inside that "inframundo" with CCTV feeds to a central flatscreen panel and digital feed from security sensors indexing energy use, infrared cameras, and movement sensors, giving the operator in his or her comfy pilot's chair total access to all spaces, interior and exterior, of the structure."

"And you with your 'fuck you.' Don't you feel childish?"

"Sorry."

"It could have been the perfect job for you. No more climbing up the outsides of the tallest structures in the city core during shitstorms and wars."

"It's not really my thing."

"Compunctions! What does this squeamishness come

from? Why? You don't want to inform on a prostitute ducking into a broom closet to change her rag and shower in a mop bucket, flush ragamuffins out of the Hope Street garage entrance planters to protect the shrubbery, not even inform us that one of our former security supervisors has returned to his old habits and unrolled his bedding beneath the generator housing in sub-basement A, when it's clearly unhealthy to do so (given the magnetic fields) and unsanitary for all involved? That we must comply with all state, federal, and municipal codes for the welfare of all concerned? You know this is a cushy position that must pay several times your current income. Even if the office is difficult to access. "

"Nah."

"Oh, not your thing. Steady work, paid vacations, health benefits, full package, inside job."

"Thanks."

"Inside job! Come on!"

"Thanks."

"'Fuck you,' eh?"

"Ah, well."

"All right, all right. Back to our original agreement. Install the jacks, lift the building ever so gently so that no one notices anything, retrofit and align the isolator columns, service the shock-absorbers, upgrade the flexible conduits, and give us the premium-quality maintenance of the elevator core your people are known for. Sixty-two stories' worth!"

"Certainly." (It was the warm handshake, the brotherly squeeze of the shoulder followed by the wink that stayed with me. The wink especially. A wink, really? A wink.)

"Come on. What's a wink?"

"That's what we wondered. Then the accidents started happening."

"Accidents? Really? Your team had quite the safety record previously. I shall have to note these 'accidents' for our insurance representative. They'll be contacting you. What happened?"

"After we'd finished up in the sub-basements, we were cleaning up to leave when Sergio went upstairs and found the exit locked. It wouldn't be the first time that management forgot about us and forgot to allow us access to leave."

"No doubt some oversight by the plant supervisor. I'll check on that."

"So we packed up and tried the alternate routes. We had to drag some of our men out by their feet, because the air ducts were full of carbon monoxide. They nearly died trying those routes."

"That's terrible! You're suggesting engine exhaust fumes from the street or some other source is finding its way into our HVAC air ducts? Not good! Something else to check on. Go on. You had other incidents."

"Yeah. We made our way to the central elevator core—"

"How? How did you get to the elevator core?"

"We made our way to the central—"

"Yes, but how? How did your people—"

[. . .]

"You'd rather not say? Really? No problem. It's not really important. A little unusual perhaps, but go on—as you were saying—the central elevator core."

"We planned to steeplejack the corporate logo as per the contract and get signed off on the job. To do so, we had to ascend to the roof. All elevators began descending as soon as we emerged into the shafts. It was as if whoever was monitoring building security was trying to physically eliminate us."

"I wonder if that could be related to a computer error we noticed that morning. Perhaps your coworkers tripped a safety device when they entered the shafts."

"We've never heard of 'safety devices' that send elevators down on workers in the shafts."

"All right. I'll check with the plant supervisor and security. What else?"

"We gained the nothwest stairwell of the building and began ascending."

"You did, yes. How did—"

"We gained the northwest stairwell and one of my men was hit by a piece of steel rebar. Stabbed through his leg above the knee, just missing an artery. He was bleeding badly when we pulled it out of his leg."

"There's no record of any work involving rebar on that day anywhere in the building. Perhaps your man somehow injured himself. Did you see this occur personally?"

"Yes."

"Please, go on."

"I left Saul behind with him, saying we'd finish the job quickly and be right back for them. After we left them, they did not answer their cell phones. We left them messages, but they didn't return our calls. We don't know what happened to them."

"Really? We don't have any records of unauthorized personnel exiting the building from that area. Perhaps they got tired of waiting and left to seek medical assistance. Did you consider checking the hospitals in the area? Perhaps they know something about your friends. Don't worry. I'll have someone check. So, yes, go on—"

"We were attacked on the roof."

"Yes?"

"Three individuals attempted to gain access to the roof while we were preparing to go over the side."

"They attacked you?"

"We assumed they were going to."

"What did they do?"

"They advanced toward us. They told us they were building security. They were armed."

"Then what happened?"

"We were complying with their request to see identification and papers when I got a funny feeling."

"A funny feeling?

"Yes. So, so we disabled them and put them back in the stairwell and locked it."

"This was when your coworker was injured?"

"No, he was fine at that time."

"Were the other men injured?"

"Yes, they were all injured. One was badly injured. He caught a spring-loaded grappling hook in the face, and the other, the claw end of a wrecking bar."

"Well, I'll have to check with security to see what they have to report. As far as I know, no reports were made of security personnel in the roof area. But I will double-check on it. Curious, indeed. So you defended yourself with your steeplejack equipment, got into your rigging, and went over the side. Then what did you see?"

3.

~~When I looked up, a pickup truck was stopped on the freeway, and someone was lying in the lane ahead of it, on the pavement shiny with blood and broken glass. Then I caught a glimpse in the side mirror of a big rig truck going too fast to stop.~~

When I looked up, out of the sudden swirling vortex of a huge black thunderhead lashing out at the nearby skyscrapers with hellish flashes of lightning, lightning bolts popping and exploding like the thrashing arms of a wild monster, purplish and black, it occurred to me that perhaps two of the dirigibles and zeppelins busy firing on each other had collided, exploding directly overhead, and this descending darkness signaled they were about to crash down upon me, so I hid my face against the black glass and sharp edge, raising my arm over my skull to ward off the massive debris that I felt most likely would follow the great shadow.

To tell the truth, with all the wars in the news, War on Drugs, War on the Poor, War on Litter, War on Terror, War on Crime, War on Time, I have not had too much time to pay attention to the War of Los Angeles, with the Dirigible Attack Zeppelins hunting down and destroying the home-made ELADATL airships. I'm sure somebody will win or lose or something, making the skies over Los Angeles safe again for human-powered flight. I suppose. I'm a long way from being able to afford a bicycle plane or one-man gyrocopter, I'm a pedestrian. I do know several people who have been injured by falling debris, but look around, there's so much trash, psychological and ideological, littering the landscape, it's hard to pinpoint any real source. Meanwhile, I got a job to do.

Impact with the building slowed the spinning somewhat, so I found another piton and executed an E, attempting to halt the spin. I wasn't sure, but a couple of burning airships could have landed atop the tower above me, and burning pieces and raw ejecta might fall on me at any moment, but I didn't have time to think about that, I had to knock a piton into a window-cleaner's track or spacer column. First I clawed my grappling hook onto the next spacer that came around—it took several tries, and I was worried my spin would accelerate, but I got the hook onto a crease without losing it or my grip, and knocked a piton in. I clipped my harness to the piton and looked up.

The attack zeppelin appeared to descend from the clouds, closing upon an ELADATL dirigible (they were close enough that I could make out the insignia and writing on the sides), which seemed to be damaged, attempting to maneuver using the Central Library tower as cover. Out of the roiling column of the black cloud came the Kraken, its purplish tentacles unfurling, writhing and flexing as they coiled about the zeppelin. Before the zeppelin exploded, I caught a blimpse of the wires or strings controlling the tentacles, which I noticed were moving stiffly, and shiny as papier-mâché. I actually think the Kraken was made out of papier-mâché. Of course, I never said anything about that.

FOLLOWING YEARS WITHOUT COMMUNICATIONS FROM DOWNTOWN, THIS WAS WHAT OUR AGENTS REPORTED

Tina or Sergio brought it to our attention: a file of old letters addressed to Enrique Pico and other officers of the company, which it seemed had probably never been answered. Given the types and number of complaints in these letters, we decided to mobilize a systems check of all transport lines and stations, from top to bottom, and the support facilities as well.

Here is one such letter from a passenger:

Dear Enrique Pico

On July 3rd, 2002, I arrived at the Fresno station of your East Los Angeles Dirigible Air Transport Lines looking for a flight to San Gabriel. To make a long story short, I had walked to Fresno from Valley Children's Hospital where I had caught a small ELADATL shuttle in front of the

supermarket in North Fork from where
I had walked away from a snuff-out,
the mountain road all hot holding my
toiletry bags, mugwort stuffed in my
pockets, in thick clarity. I was very
tired and your staff were hard to find
and not friendly at all.

Sergio printed my ticket and said
the airship would arrive one hour late
because they were having difficulties
up there. When Sergio went on break,
I talked with Joey, who told me he
would announce the arrival and that I
should go to sleep because the flight
was delayed. The chairs in the station
were plastic, like cheap plastic ones
and they were scattered all over the
station tipped over and upside down,
and I couldn't sleep at all.

The station was big and there was
a dynamic echo, however there was no
food available because the concession
stand looked like it had been burnt
inside and boarded up. Everything
seemed blank and sick. I watched TV
for five hours. The shows kept repeating. Paquita la del Barrio concert
special, ESPN SportsZone, Fresno
KFSN local news, Paquita again. It
was actually getting hard to arrange
or locate my feelings. Joey wasn't
listening to me, even though I kept
seeing dirigibles come and go, first
silver ones, then slightly orange
ones, then brilliant pinks, coral
reds, dull oranges, deep blue ones
then black iridescent ones.

Later in the night, I talked to
Sergio and he asked why I hadn't

boarded one of the orange dirigibles—
he pointed to my pink ticket. It's
already gone, he said. Next one comes
at midnight, it's running late, it
might be pale blue by the time it
gets here.

The inside of the station was all
greenish by this time. Because I
had walked through dense hot pine
forests, old logging towns, down into
the San Joaquin Valley, across Fresno
into the half-dead bank district
(Fallas Paredes, Botanica Poder Del
Mestizo) and dead governmental center
(people waiting in lines forever,
all depressed) to the green ELADATL
station, I was very tired when I was
trying to solve my problem with Joey.

And Joey was giving me the
runaround. Sir, he said, I am not
responsible for you missing your
flight, I have been professional and
diligent in my duties—every flight
that leaves I announce here on this
microphone mounted on this desk. The
sound travels effectively up the wires
from the microphone, to the speakers
and if the speakers are broken and you
can't understand what I'm saying or
if sir, the speaker isn't working at
all, I have been diligent in my duties
to you and my company in announcing
the outgoing and incoming flights and
in no way sir have I been spending
the last five hours watching TV in
the back room. And sir, I have also
not been drinking this whole time, my
eyes are just like that, I was kind
of born looking this way.

So I ended up staying up late waiting for the next dirigible to San Gabriel, which I boarded at 3:25 am. I enjoyed the carpet lining the walls of the pale blue dirigible and the ashtrays were a plus. I spent the whole time on the viewing deck. I arrived in Stockton eight hours later and the station was closed—I wasn't tired anymore, I was over being tired!

The station in Salinas was also closed, even though I called and they said they were definitely open. I waited outside in the wind the rest of the night. This was inconvenient but educational. I double checked with LA's central office over the phone and they said it was no problem, that they would alert the pilot to accept my pink ticket for the flat blue dirigible to San Gabriel. I felt relieved to know my ticket would transfer despite the 20-hour delay. There was a type of concrete bench beneath a palo verde, and so I watched its shadow sweep around me when the sun rose—it moved so slowly. 107 degrees and dusty wind, Christian radio stations, agricultural birds, white skies, I was gritting my teeth, I'm sure. The Flat Blue was late by about four hours and when a Black Opalescent came in its place, I attempted to board but the pilot would not accept my pink ticket despite assurance from L.A. He said that he had not heard anything from L.A. He said that my ticket was not a ticket for this or any other flight and that if he accepted my ticket and let me go home then he would have to let everybody else with a pink ticket board and that even though there was nobody else at the station, it wasn't really his job or his choice to let me board. I asked him to have a heart because it was late and there were no hotels open and I could redeem my ticket at the next stop in Delano. He said I'm sorry but the only way to keep this airship company running is to follow the rules and where would America be without the rule of law? There were moths on the inside of the airship, I could hear them hitting the balloon's skin.

So then I spent the night drinking coffee in a 24-hour Denny's and they said excuse me sir, we need to vacuum the carpet so you can't stay. Then I spent time walking in between the trees in an almond orchard until the next flight in the morning. I counted 180 complete rows of trees—there were some owls, so quiet, purplish.

When the sun came up, another Pale Blue arrived and I boarded using my pink ticket—the pilot said that of course I could board it was official policy to let a pink ticket board any dirigible as long as they redeemed their ticket at the next stop, in this case Monterey Park.

I'm writing this letter to you so that you can fire Joey. Please fire him because he was drinking alcohol and hanging out watching TV when he should have been working. I'm including some photographic proof of my ordeal as well as a pro/con chart of my experience. Thank you and looking forward to hearing about improvements to ELADATL.

Pro: Excellent website with many available flights

Con: Almost none of the flights listed on the website actually exist

Pro: Sergio in Fresno was polite

Con: Joey was negligent and rude

Pro: Your stations may be very hot inside but the lights are a pleasant shade of green

Con: The blinking of the lights and the heat inside gave me a headache which was disorienting

Pro: Your dirigibles are beautiful and majestic, the way the city lights look down below in the blackness, distorted through thick rounded glass, slipping like jellyfishy floating lights along the perimeter of the viewing deck was amazing. The carpeted walls make for a quiet flight

Con: The ever changing and confusing color shifts of the dirigibles throughout the day is unnecessary— how the color of the ticket and the color of the dirigible relate is *not mentioned on your website or printed literature*

Pro: TV in the Fresno waiting room and plastic chairs to sit in

Con: Salinas station closed and looked like it was burnt inside, is it ever opening?

Pro: Price of tickets is low

Con: Sodas cost seven dollars at stations

We responded immediately by organizing teams of agents to serve as inspectors, sending them out to check on all the lines, our ships, stations, and maintenance and ancillary facilities. The reports we received back were like a slap in the face by an octopus. Twice maybe. Their findings are below:

AGENT: Tere "la Radio" de la Torre.
Some girls will try to please; Tere is not one of those. In fact, when we said we needed people to go station to station, down the line, check on operations or the actual existence of some of the stations, she said she was not interested. But you work here, we said. I did—I used to work here, she said doing something with her bag, looking into her bag, not looking at us. Maybe, she said, I could test out this vintage Leica 35-millimeter camera and that sounds like the perfect so-called assignment. I'll let you know what happens.

Report: Little Tokyo Station
En route from Union Station, much of Little Tokyo (and the high-rises of downtown and destroyed Bunker Hill in the background) looked so changed that I was taking it all in, snapping pictures here and there:

✿ a leaf crimped in the perfect shape of a woman's smile, fallen to the cold gray sidewalk

✿ chalky white convolutions of limbs of a dirty ficus tree with litter in its crotch, evoking human limbs writhing in an obscurity of desire

✿ two intimidating late-middle-age women wearing fur coats (one white, one gray) as well as glittering veils over their faces that looked exactly like plastic bags but must have been breathable

✿ shop window poster of a four-foot-tall prawn or shrimp embracing or perhaps playing a violin

✿ orange/blue face of Jesus with crown of thorns, eyes seeking heavenward, the rest of the poster in tatters, all that's left clinging to a wall

✿ an old Nisei in a wheelchair at the bus stop and a unicorn

✿ spectacular colors of sky behind roof lines, wires transect fleeting, hurried clouds

✿ etc., you got the idea

Okay, then I asked a bunch of people, a whole bunch of random people on Second Avenue, and then again some more groups of people that I bumped into (I was asking everybody, I assure you) if they knew anything about the dirigible stop or ticket station and mooring mast of the East L.A. Dirigible Lines, "Hey, do you know where I could get the dirigible that goes out to Montebello?" "The Freeway Flyer?" "No. What about the one that goes to Claremont and Pomona? The dirigible." They shook their heads. Nobody knew anything about it. It's true they were all like, uh, white people. Maybe some weren't white, some were Nihonjins, but they were just typical downtown hipsters. You know? They didn't have clue one, I could tell.

If I hear anything, I'll let you know. That's good enough, isn't it? It took me like hours. I don't know. Almost all day.

Yeah? What shall I write on my invoice?

AGENT: Armando Restrepo, gay Peruano poet, architect, publisher of Red Cholo Books (they have published four books so far, two of which were his own)

Armando has an uncool genial, friendly demeanor sort of like Alberto Luz, if you know him. I was eating lunch at Zankou Chicken when he spotted me, came over to say hello, and I gestured that he should sit down.

"Mano, I have something for you. You know I work for the East L.A. Dirigible Air Transport Lines?"

"I heard something about that. Sorry, knowing you, I wasn't sure if it was bullshit, I mean, somebody's idea of a cover story, or—"

"We have a job for you, and your friends, if you know of someone who needs work."

"Sure. What's up?"

"We need some investigators to access urban areas and vertical air space to do some investigations as to where some dirigible stations and passenger airships went to. They fucking disappeared, someone or something tore them down and crushed their dreams and folded them into a dead-end vortex of lost time and we need people to help us find them."

"I don't have experience at—"

"No, certainly, we understand that. But you know people, you have some connections from the old days, even if it's just a few contacts, and you have the right instincts."

"I don't know."

"We'll pay a hundred per report, three hundred if there's real information in it. We'll go as high as five hundred and up if you give us a line on the actual whereabouts of working dirigible stations or the physical whereabouts of the airships themselves."

"Really? A hundred for starters, eh? Three for information, five and up for actual material. Hmmm. What's the catch?

Where would I have to go?"

"Take your pick. The whole city is pretty much wide open. We have agents downtown, Little Tokyo, Chinatown, we got that covered, Lincoln Heights, City Terrace—"

"Boyle Heights?"

"Boyle Heights, yeah, the Eastside is pretty good, of course, but you name it, anything else—Pico Union, K-Town, Glassell Park even—"

"Echo Park, Silver Lake?"

"Yeah. Los Feliz to South Central."

"All right."

"Really? That's great. I knew we could count on you."

"Of course, man. How long we've known each other? Are you kidding? Where do you want me to start? Culver City or some—"

"No, no! Start anywhere you like. West of Western or east of Vermont. It's up to you. Listen, write your contact information here."

"All right."

"Thanks!"

"Wow, you still got a grip on you."

"I'm glad I'll be able to tell Jose, Ray Palafox, and Tina that I saw you and you'll be working with us. They'll be really happy. They'll be really excited."

"That's great, man. I better get going. I'll talk to you soon, eh."

REPORT: This agent never filed a report.

AGENT: Tina Lerma

Tina is outstanding and invaluable, that is to say she is hard-working, dedicated, and not crushed by cynicism and burnout (not yet!), she is capable and brilliant, that is to say she is not fazed or distressed by our absurd "margin" of error (which so far largely exceeds our "margin" of success), in short, even though she was so damned indispensable in the capacity of company spokesperson, front desk, media coordinator, dirigible pilot substitute, and early shift food prep assistant, I had no other choice except to tap her on the shoulder and ask her if she might ("One time deal, guaranteed! I promise!") consider "running an errand." Errand? she looked up, doubtful—brow arched, querulous gleam in large brown eyes.

REPORT:
Swirling Alhambra has typical ideological perversions of North American males: he is obsessed with sex (I can tell by the blinking of his squirrelly eyes), he is hypnotized by visual phenomenology of the world—appearances, as they are to many human beings, the billboards of his brain—maybe that's why he's enchanted by speed and things that go fast like flying dirigibles in his mind. He has no patience for details or inner workings of actual relationships or substantive issues, he just wants immediate gratification, immediate results, and like most of this kind of Norteamericano, therefore, he will never amount to much (you have been warned), but he does have, as many do, various lesser talents, occasionally amusing or practical; for example, he can do a back flip, landing on his feet, from standing position (used to be able to, anyway). If you ever want to get to know him better, ask him sometime how he lost his driver's license.

Ha, none of that has anything really to do with my official report, but when Swirling asked me to undertake THIS assignment, ON TOP OF EVERYTHING ELSE I DO AROUND HERE, I wanted to note that for the record.

In short, me and my friend Melissa (Mel) went everywhere looking for those darn ELADATL stations. We drove out to the desert, probably the most obvious place, where we had been told of an old dirigible hangar outside Joshua Tree. In Joshua Tree we stopped in for breakfast with the locals (flashing their Lycra biking and rock climbing finery), and I fed Mel and me organic multigrain pancakes with blueberries and blue agave syrup. Mel wore yellow sunglasses with green lenses, but she was a bit too shiny in the endless sunlight, with her fair skin and all (unlike me, I just brown) so, popping back in the Toyota Prius, I opened the glovebox and pointed at the sunscreen. "Noah Purifoy's compound displays engineered prototypes of the dirigible station that was built in the nearby Mojave," I said, "so I was told."

"Not those prehistoric fossils of stone dirigibles?" Mel asked. The last time we were out this way, I jaunted out about 200 miles toward the Mojave Preserve to the relatively unknown petroglyph sites that depicted the earliest known designs of lighter-than-air airships anywhere in the world, just to show Mel how indigenous to the Late Pleistocene these ideas were, emerging like shadows in the moonlight of historic America. Mel had not been especially impressed.

"No. We're searching for their modern equivalents, say from the late 1940s, early 1950s."

"I know you explained the crucial differences, last time, between fossilized remains of ancient stone dirigibles and the random stegosaurus ridges of volcanic rocks (both of which look kind of like the backs of great dinosaur fossils, half submerged in the desert floor), but it was hard for me to tell them apart. Even when we climbed into the caves and hollows you said were the cockpits and crews' quarters. So what if the Paiutes or the Yuma or whoever had marked them with wavy lines that indicated uplift and navigational astrology? Looking out across the vast overheated expanses of those desert valleys, it looked like all those black rocks were floating above a shimmering sea of heat waves. Sky reflecting silvery radiation across blue valley distances." Using her tongue, Mel dislodged something like oatmeal from her teeth with a dismissive snick.

"This time we're looking for actual modern establishments, Mel. Contemporary architectural stylings, Art Deco actual infrastructure, probably still connected to the grid, in working order. Come on, you're not going for it?"

"I just don't see it like you do, is all."

"What're you saying?"

"Sergio."

"What about him?"

"You like the way he tells it."

"I think it sounds right to me. Everybody's gotta do what's right the way they see things."

"All right."

"Ay, Mel."

"Ay, yourself. Let's go on then. Let's go see what there is to see. See if we can find anything."

I zigzagged from the highway off some dirt lanes (east by northeast, by my reckoning—tires crunching dusty down gravel lanes past glaring melancholic bungalows, fenced-off lots, kind of junkyard residential outposts), following handwritten instructions from a friend. We parked at the entrance of the Purifoy compound.

"Here," I said.

We exited both sides of the vehicle into the white glare of desert sunshine, our eyes sort of crinkling with its intensity. I felt like a piece of tin foil, thin and shiny. Mel seemed excited, slamming the car door and scooting off across the peach-colored sand. She was saying something, cooing brightly.

I scurried around the front of the Prius after her.

"Oh my God," Mel was saying, more excited the more she saw.

There was a sprawl of derelict cabins, it looked like, scattered in the sand and creosote bushes. The cabins were about the size of sheds, really, scrabbled together out of horrendously weathered sunburned boards, discard wood with the grain blackened and coarsened by weather, splintering, nailed together with sheet metal of numerous derivations (also weather-scarred, stippled, torn or folded, rusty). The walls of some sheds were draped with various kinds of debris or cordage, maritime fashion, as if in preparation for a voyage across the Desert of Time. Likewise, twin catamaran hulls thrust jauntily upward, beside a row of brightly colored kiosks festooned with hubcaps or something like arcane signage of some unknown type. I approached them to peek inside the windows, to see what they were selling. I caught a glimpse of piles of manual typewriters and/or adding machines. On dusty desks, blind computer monitors and droopy derelict computer keyboards.

Everything signified infinity and time.

Beyond these structures and past some smaller, freestanding sculptures that stood like sentinels, like mute wordless signage, were two side-by-side greenish prefabs or mobile homes, a long work table under an awning between them still covered in Purifoy's debris and objects he worked with till he died (on this spot, I presumed, inside one of these smoke-filled prefabs), age 86.

But where did Mel go? Arrrgh! She'd run off and left me alone.

Suddenly I felt like an intruder in Purifoy's work area. Where he died. Maybe just on the other wide of these walls, this door. I glimpsed my reflection in the sliding glass door and felt someone's eyes on me, and then I was moving, I got the hell out of there.

"Hey, Mel!" I chirped.

No answer, so I blurted out, "Mel, Mel!"

I caught up with Mel running her fingers along curls and bent lengths of coolant pipe strung underneath rectangular stelae plated with sheet metal and aluminum flashing, causing it to tinkle and chime in a Mel-breeze. Mel grinned up at the musical thingamajig, thingamabob, thermomelodic whatchacallit, as the sky stroked its perky decorative antennas.

Mel grinned at me.

Noah Purifoy had been an assemblage junk sculptor, co-founder of the Watts Towers Art Center in South Central L.A. A child-sized train made of bicycle wheels, jerry-rigged freight cars made of piping and aluminum ducting, beer kegs and containers rolling on straight tracks led us from a shocking igloo (shocking because it looked so forlorn, a failed attempt at a survival structure, amalgamated from an abandoned wickiup patched with sheet metal awning and located in the brilliant merciless sun—to cast some delicate shadows across scoops of pocked sand)—toward a large white crenellated castle or windowed carousel structure atop or beyond a real or illusory earthen rise.

We were walking through a whole town (a junk town, a town of junk, like so many are), or a movie set of an imaginary city. There was a graveyard. A gallows, with viewing platform. A theater, "Adrian's Little Theater" (empty). Three crosses ready for crucifixions, with a comfortable seat provided. A row of legs without torsos, pointed in our direction. Could they watch us without eyes? Observing with the tips of their shoes?

More theaters or amphitheaters with empty stages, empty seating. Walls built of rickety plywood, casting rickety shadows, barely this side of existence.

Everything perched on sand, on the edge of nonexistence.

All these once-new products, materials, things—they have this ancient life now.

Energy generators constructed of steel, tin, and aluminum stood like the penultimate obelisks of a failed civilization. Energy collectors partially hidden behind corroded protective fencing or decorative silver-painted and chrome grillwork of automobiles plumbed the radiation. Vertical energy broadcasters stood like sentinels, technological artifacts masked as expressionless masks, masked as unlettered texts. In all directions wide blue sky, in all directions pastel-colored warm pockmarked sand.

A raft of radiator pipes and bed frames, bedsteads and iron plumbing stood over the pale sea of sand like an oil platform.

An ark, a massive heavy wooden boathouse, sank peacefully into the silent cool earth. It was cool in there, with the eerie mildew stink of rotting books and magazines. Printed matter in the form of old paperback dime novels or discarded library books were scattered about, but I didn't want to pick up any of it. Tattered fabric hung here and there, unseemly insulation. The desert felt so harsh there seemed little chance that much in the way of fauna could live inside the ark (like the theater, like the igloo, like the carousel, like the bleachers, it was all empty), but I expected tiny creatures, mice or beetles, lived in the crevices and margins of this architected debris. A scorpion perhaps. Maybe a mama scorpion and her babies. Sometimes bits of the ghost town or imaginary city displayed wispy movements in the subtle desert breeze.

All this humanity, all this evidence of human activity, and no people.

I emerged from the opposite end of the ark in a hurry. "Mel," I squawked.

"What?"

I couldn't tell where her voice was coming from.

I paused in front of a monolith constructed of gauges, gadgets, redacted equipment and elbows of machinery, little dials forever frozen. I looked at the partly erased notices, the hard-to-read or effaced numerals, and tried to take a reading. What was the monolith measuring? I understood this monolith must measure eternity. What's the measure of eternity? Everything looked broken. Eternity went off the charts; it went off the scale.

One smeared or obscured gauge made me want to cry.

One blank featureless cracked crystal suggested to me that we could sigh.

One emphatic straight up pointer implied that we'd best

laugh. These were our little indicator arrows, tickling units to register the infinite.

When I peeked inside one structure, what I took to be a bank of circuits against one wall, like gauges ripped out of a airplane cockpit, turned out to be on closer look a geometric grid of dominos, their white spots on black tiles or black spots on white bones, fastened to chrome surfaces of toasters or discarded appliances. I recalled the interior of a garage opening out on the sidewalk as I walked by (was it in South Central L.A. or Puerto Rican Bushwick in Brooklyn? The same as in Miami and Havana, Lisbon and Sao Paolo?) where the middle-aged and then years later the old men sat, fingertips pushing these tiles forward, these bones, over and over, endless permutations of games, hours, through how many days or years . . . to death? And, of course, if you walk by, some men will watch you go by, relentlessly as the spots on dominoes.

"Mel?

"Yes?"

"Where are you?"

"Here. Over here."

"I don't know. Girl, I'm not seeing you."

"There it is!"

"There's what?"

"There it is! What we've been looking for?"

"What, Mel, where?"

"It's a dirigible station, I think!"

I caught sight of Mel's white top floating off toward a semi-circular hangar of some kind, like a large shining tin can half-buried in the ground. Through the glare and the heat waves, Mel looked like she was floating toward the corrugated, galvanized structure. She was levitating, and the structure itself was wavering along its base, as if rising. "I left my damn water bottle in the car," it occurred to me.

Mel and I ran slipshod, loping over the sand to the hangar.

We reunited under a pergola of loops buried in the sand that formed a kind of open-air tunnel, leading to large double-armored doors welded with bold strips, plaques, plates, shields of stippled, rusted, folded, bolted, riveted, and dimpled metal. But the doors were chained shut and locked with a hefty padlock. "Gah," I said, huffing, if not exactly breathing hard.

"Whooooooo," Mel exhaled.

Mel leaned over and put her eye to the crack between the doors.

"What's in there?" I asked.

Mel mumbled something I didn't catch. "Something, grish-graw errr-err something space."

"What?" I asked, "What do you see?"

"Hold on, will ya?" she said.

"What's in there?"

"Looks empty." She stepped back, taking out her phone—commencing to take some pictures. The doors, the pergola, herself smiling, the terrain, me pulling on the door handles (making the chain sway and click) and leaning over to put my eye to the crack in the door. For a minute, at least, I couldn't see anything. I couldn't smell much either, though there was some sort of dusty, musty odor in the air escaping from the interior. It smelled vaguely hot and old and empty.

When my vision adjusted, I could generally make out the empty gloom of the Quonset hut interior. The place was empty, unused, far as I could tell. I saw a folding chair . . . a box against a far wall that might be a tool chest. . .

"What's this?" Mel said.

When I turned around to see what Mel was talking about, I saw her bending down to pull a magazine out from under the bottom of the door. A faded publication called *Filth Saints/Manifestos/Ballons*. Gritty dust drifted out from its yellow-stained crinkly pages. It was dated 1988. Mel and I squatted by the doors of the hangar scanning the stiff pages as she gingerly separated and turned each one. That was where we first saw the name (now famous) of the founder of the East L.A. Balloon Club, Ericka Llanera.

We took the magazine and sauntered out of there. (Mel had to swivel her neck, shooting more pictures as we were walking.) We got back in the car, drove around to some famous UFO sighting locations that I had researched online, like the big rock formations where a bunch of stoners supposedly burned some famous rock star's body (I can't recall by name, 'cause I never heard of him). One humungous boulder covered with black fire stains, the whole area blackened in charcoal debris from giant bonfires and tire tracks, cans, litter, and smashed beer bottles in all directions. We didn't find a lost dirigible station in the desert, but we brought the magazine back to town as key evidence to show Jose What's-his-name and Swirling What's-his-face.

AGENT: Melissa Arana
How can I even begin to describe Mel? Grumpy, ha ha. Usually. Some people just get scared or intimidated sometimes, she looks so serious. LOL. Gah. That's just the way she is, I know for a fact she can be just as silly or romantic or anything as anybody. She's half Mexican, light hair, small, smart, unique, she's my beautiful friend. Don't mess with her!

REPORT:
I don't really like pampas grass. You will find out, if you get it on your skin or in your clothes, you will be in for the worst time of your life. The seeds, the tall plumes of pretty dry flowers that look like feathers. I know. But if you get it on you, you can't get it off and it has tiny microscopic fibers that penetrate your skin. And, oh my God, if you get any in your eyes! We played with that stuff when I was a kid, me and my brothers. The blades of the grass slice your skin like razors.

Do you know the story of Frances Farmer? She was a movie

star; her mother had her committed to a psychiatric hospital where they gave her a lobotomy.

What about Bessie Coleman? She was the first American to get an international pilot's license (which she got in France, because they refused to teach her how to fly in America), and the first African American woman to get her pilot's license, back in 1921, but she could only make a living doing dangerous stunt flying, and it killed her. In 1926, she lost control of her plane, and it spun out and threw her at 2,000 feet above the ground, so she died. She was 34. Of course she was the inspiration for the Bessie Coleman Aero Club.

Now this is basic history of the skies of Los Angeles, so you are supposed to know this already.

The Bessie Coleman Aero Club was founded in 1929 by William Powell here in L.A., where Powell learned to fly because the Los Angeles Warren School of Aeronautics was the only place in the country where he was allowed (because he was black) to take flying lessons. Powell—who owned a chain of five gas stations—became a licensed pilot, navigator and aeronautical engineer. He started an airplane company, Bessie Coleman Aero, to lay the foundation for a new future for African Americans. In his book, *Black Wings*, Powell wrote, "There is a better job and a better future in aviation for Negroes than in any other industry, and the reason is this: aviation is just beginning its period of growth, and if we get into it now, while it is still uncrowded, we can grow as aviation grows." Powell had a major plan and this was his plan. "Negro leaders—why do you sleep? Black men and black women, arouse your imaginations. Act before it is too late. Do not let the aviation industry become completely monopolized by other races who will give you and me only the most menial jobs. Get into aviation now while we have a chance to get black airplane manufacturers, black airplane distributors, owners of black transport lines and thousands of black boys and black girls profitably employed in a great paying industry." That was Powell's plan. It would eliminate "continually begging the white people for jobs." He started a black aviation newsletter, where he offered scholarships to black students, male and females alike, who wanted to learn to fly.

Everywhere in the nation, black people were discriminated against, excluded, exploited, and oppressed. There were lynch mobs, racial covenants in real estate, John Birch hate groups, segregated schools, Jim Crow laws, Ku Klux Klan terrorist organizations, and white supremacy holding forth in the media. Powell said the aerospace industry that was just beginning would allow Negroes to "slip the surly bonds of earth," leaving all that horrible bullshit behind as black people literally flew into the future. His plan almost worked, as Bessie Coleman Aero Clubs formed in major cities across the U.S., if only the Great Depression hadn't ruined his businesses, and then Powell himself died of lung failure caused by injuries from poison gas in World War 1.

So William Powell's plan didn't work out. It's true.

The Bessie Coleman Aero clubs went bankrupt, faded away.

Powell's vision faded away too and has been forgotten for the most part.

These people and their dreams all became part of the history of the skies over Los Angeles.

But Ericka Llanera didn't want people to forget about it or think it was all just dreaming. She published articles about Powell, the Bessie Coleman Aero Club, and the Black Wings Company, the second aircraft manufacturing company William Powell founded, and the even earlier Sonora Aero Club, which Charles Dellschau documented in unpublished manuscripts located by Fred Washington, Enrique Pico, and the East Los Angeles Dirigible Air Transport Lines, which we have spent months and years researching in order to document the remains of that infrastructure, of their lines that once extended throughout Southern California, into Northern California and through the Southwest—old abandoned airfields, anchoring stations, hydrogen and helium filling depots, hangars, etc.

That's why, in 1971 (the same exact year that Fred Washington discovered Dellschau's important manuscripts, rescued from the gutter outside a burning house in Houston, TX), Ericka founded the East L.A. Balloon Tours and its support group, the East L.A. Balloon Club, with limited service using two gas-fired balloons, launching from hilltops in El Sereno and City Terrace with the help of then-boyfriend Ricky Wong (sometimes called Rinky Wing Wong and mocked in songs by 1970s East L.A. punk bands).

I don't really like the idea of floating around in a balloon high above the ground, if you want to know the truth. This is all Tina's idea. Sometimes I just go along with her ideas, because she's my best friend and so great.

I don't really like the desert. How can people stand to live out here? It's crazy, the sun is like a horrible blast furnace, and the wind never stops fucking blowing. Plus, you can tell it attracts crazies that can't get along with people. Tina had us wandering around out there, driving gravelly dirt roads to nowhere that would all of a sudden just stop or bend and head off in a random direction—raising plumes of dust that could be seen for miles.

We'd have to get out and ask directions, walk up to some damn trailer, that looked like an abandoned piece-of-trash trailer out against some far rocky outcropping of vaguely menacing boulders (like Indians would hide behind in old movies to shoot down at cowboys), and we'd honk the horn first (Tina said this was the protocol, the way they do it in these "areas"—you honk driving into someone's property as a courtesy, "or they might be alarmed"—I'm thinking GUNS when she says that)—and then we'd get out, slamming the car doors loud, with the sound echoing against the rocks sometimes. WTF, Tina acts like she's never scared, she always acts like that, just steps forward, no matter what she feels or thinks, she's there—but I am not happy about being in some deserted corner of the desert way out behind the mountains walking up to a tiny beat-up aluminum trailer not even in the shadow of the big pile of rocks it's parked in front of—it's been baking in the goddamned heat all day, so if the crazy person who decided to live way out here wasn't crazy to start with, they must be deranged by solar radiation by now (sometimes with old junk cars in the tumbleweeds and siding or indescribable trash piles of nasty clothes, ruined building supplies, discarded appliances that could never have been used for their original use out here)—all this has filled me with unease, and I'm on the verge of panic, thinking about horrors of kidnapped children buried perhaps on the property in coolers somewhere and other stories that the desert will never reveal or tell. And Tina walks up to the trailer and knocks politely on the door, going, "Hello!" (Nothing, silence, maybe wind noise.) Hi there! Hello!"

And I am looking at the little windows of the trailer for any sign of movement.

I will be screaming and running to the car in a split second.

I don't really mind driving long road trips with Tina. She said we might get paid. Who knows when they pay her for all the work she does, if ever.

She does it because she believes in it, obviously.

I gotta say, though, that vast stretches of the country seem like they are populated by people with sad, terrible lives, you could see how they would embrace a meth epidemic as the best fucking thing that's happened in their area for some generations.

Plus, I don't like the food they eat in rural areas. You might think, hey, it's a rural area, they have farms, cows and chickens, organic vegetable gardens with rows of flowers, sunflowers by the fence—they'll eat fresh at least. But you go through these little towns and they eat, like, Jack in the Box. I hate Jack in the Box, it's the worst shit industrial slaughterhouse debris crap packed in a styrofoam box. Some of those towns, it's either that or microwave food from a gas station or 7-11. Drive a thousand miles in big circles around the West, with some locals giving you the evil eye (two girls traveling together—luckily we can't begin to imagine what they might be thinking), and you are grateful to fall out at some mom-and-pop diner, where you're all, "Really? You serve breakfast all the time? You do? Oh, thank God, can I have oatmeal?"

That's right, so we drive hundreds or thousands of miles in Tina's little car, and where do we find the clue? In that little magazine we found outside of Joshua Tree, on the ground at that artist's compound.

And what does the magazine have, next to a picture of Oscar Zeta Acosta (with the caption, "Have you seen this man?") but the last known address of the main office the East L.A. Dirigible Air Transport Lines.

Of course that meant venturing downtown, thrice-blessed with total destruction of public spaces and working-class neighborhoods through 1-2-3 punches of Urban Renewal (1957–1989), Gentrification (1986–2021), and Elision (2021–present). Tina and I rode our bikes along the abandoned Gold Line route since that or the Arroyo Seco bike trail, which is more dangerous, or less? If there was something crazy going on on one of them, we'd switch over to the other. Cyclists we knew zipped by, making visual contact with a wave or a nod, so we weren't worried. This terrain we know. (But who knew it would be so torn down and messed up now, compared to when we were growing up? Well, everybody knows that by now.)

A few things I noted:

1. Huge letters supposedly memorializing 10,000 dead of "L.A." obscured by sulphuric orange haze wind

2. Rebel hotel still on fire

3. Encampment "A" at York and Figueroa cleared (again), just some cardboard and discarded clothing at the triangle in the intersection under the ficus trees

4. Encampment "B" northeast of Avenue 43 visibly larger

5. Memorial to girl recently killed at Ave. 43, just a clump of votive candles, balloons, and flowers (like a slap to our faces when we stopped to look at it) Tina wrote a poem she tied on the fence and I added a folded paper flower.

6. Coyote by Debs Park

7. Squirrels in the arroyo

8. Something shiny glistening in my expectations, can't imagine what it could be—gives me a good feeling

9. Tina and I shared lentil kale salad sandwich with Stacy and the Vanagon kids

10. Snakes of light stand up zigzagging across the middle of the street, not that I'd tell Tina about them or she'd think they're cancer-related; anyway they go away after awhile without headaches

11. Avenues looking dull or normal without dancing snakes of light

✿

In spite of a world half-destroyed, a nation sunk in ruins of once proud ideologies, surrendering its will to fashion, self-delusion, self-absorption, self-defeat, and bad writing, I'm always happiest riding my bike. Tina's rump and legs oscillating ahead in and out of view as I lean forward, hillsides of Highland Park chaparral-like greenery streaming by above the dry sycamores of the arroyo. Everything dappled and gold-tinged, the sunlight beating on everything, staining bright edges of foliage, vehicles and objects with gold leaf. We speed through a world so shining sparkly, it's like glancing at it through tears. Hair whipping once in awhile in her mouth, Tina spits it out to shout something back at me, laughing. So what if weary exhaust fumes swirl overhead, enter our lungs. We are alive, rolling toward downtown!

Palm trees float overhead—the way ladybugs must see dandelions.

Torn-down frames of rotten couches, sacks of garbage strewn beside the light-rail tracks—we keep an eye out for broken bottles.

We're rolling along, huffing and puffing. Floating overhead, skeletal dirigibles, winged seeds, pollen and spiders, smoke—contrails. But we keep an eye out for debris and sharp objects in the path rolling underneath.

L.A. rehearsed its part in this apocalypse more times than Tokyo or anywhere. In *Omega Man*, Chariot Heston drove around deserted downtown in a 1969 Pontiac Catalina, shooting shadowy vampires— a 1971 analog for Mexicans. In *Soylent Green*, Soylent Green was people—Heston ate it. In *Earthquake!*, Heston was again crushed when the Big One brought the city down. In *Blade Runner*, the city is overrun by Mexicans and Asians speaking gibberish, and do white people thank God for all-you-can-eat ceviche, sushi, pho, Szechuan, birrierias galore and Yucatecan cochinita pibil? No, for white people (who act like robots in movies like *Blade Runner*) such miscegenation is Kiss of Death to the Apartheid Imagination, plus in that movie it rains all the time. In *Kiss Me Deadly*, a radio isotope blows up a Malibu beach house, razing downtown Bunker Hill in real life. In *Zeppelin Attack Dirigibles*, people use imaginary futures to attack the desolated present, aided by a papier-mâché Kraken. This was all fictional in those movies. Mike Davis wrote a book on it.

L.A. passed unscathed through all those symbolic

apocalypses, only to be destroyed by actual waves of public policy, gentrification, real estate bubble, bundled derivatives, income redistribution, privatization, and budget cuts.

It's all good, zipping downhill fast, till we get to the river. One of the bigger earthquakes after 2019 knocked the bridge into the river—the bridge had stood since the 1930s, I imagine—now Tina and I shoulder our bikes and carry them down the trail made through the chunks of bridge material, twisted cords of bent rebar, weeds, and steeply sloping former traffic lanes now painted with graffiti messages like "N9NN!" and "SYK" and "YIYI" and "I HEART MY DOG" and "WHERE IS FLORA?" and "YOU KNOW WHERES FLORA?" and "KAKA" and "gog," etc. I suppose that the bridge now covers dangerous catacombs of underground hideouts down in the great canyon of the Los Angeles River sluiceway with its vast concrete walls, unseen water roaring and gurgling below the pieces of tilted road, gaps in the asphalt anywhere between a few inches to four feet or more, which you have to span by taking a running jump—black water down there— and on the upstream side, just at the level of the top of the span, the great green pool of water backed up behind major sections of the bridge. Huge collection of foul-smelling trash coagulated at the base of the five-story-high concrete wall. Blue sky reflecting on the calm green water and sometimes mallards paddling around, quacking.

It's cooler, with a breeze that smells green like the river.

You always have the feeling of being watched.

Tina forges ahead, pushing her bike where the roadway's still level enough to proceed by walking, and then we're jumping crevasses or climbing great blocks of concrete rubble, handing each other our bikes across a gap or holding them over our heads as we go. A mom and dad with a small kid pass us going the other way. We step to the side to stay out of their way. If we dislodge a chip of gravelly cement or a chunk of asphalt, it falls with a clatter that echoes weirdly off the far wall, eerily—I don't like it, that crackling echoey sound. I pause to listen to the force of water underneath us. On the far side, the high southwestern wall side of the bridge, luckily, collapsed in a giant stairstep jumble, and people have constructed wooden walkways, fairly sturdy with handrails on the steep parts, zigzagging up a couple gaps that would have been too big to climb without a rope, allowing for easy foot travel. We shoulder our bikes and huff up to the top, breathing hard when we get there (wind comes cool through the big nostril holes of the tunnels, tiles glistening somewhat, it smells dry—different than the river), we catch our breath— to zoom through the tunnels.

We are zipping, we are tearing through.

It's going to be a longer (uphill) ride back.

Our clothes flap like magazine pages.

We're pumping, pumped up.

We hoot and howl, yip and yowl. There's not an echo, except a kind of wobbly cone of reverberation. A kind of pinging off yellow ceramic tiles lining the tunnel.

We fly fast, Tina pedaling to keep up with me. I'm laughing.

Past the burned out car, long since rusted out.

Out of the first tunnel—then three more. Blast of sunlight, almost blinding, obscurity of gloom momentarily—we go hurtling into it—

What if some big debris was in the way, a branch? What if someone was there? Hopefully we'd see them in time. In a second, our eyes adjust.

The tunnel stretches ahead of us, swirls of dirt and leaves having drifted down the roadway over the years. Sometimes our wheels crunch sticks or twigs or leaves.

Tina is still laughing. Our lives are flashing by like this— hurtling, we're pedaling— Tina's laugh stops, but it's still in my mind. I love Tina. Years of our lives have gone, "as if in a flash," says my inner narrator. Some inner voice who often comments on things.

That thought is punctuated by the memory of Tina's laugh. So beautiful! Clean and clear. It rings inside me. The inner narrator has no answer for it, except to laugh. I laugh too.

FROM THE FILES
LABELED "ELADATL
OFFICERS,
SACRAMENTO
BUREAU FBI,
NOT FOR PUBLIC
RELEASE"

Clockwise:
PROPAGANDA,
JOSE LOPEZ-FELIU,
MARIA MEDEL
VILLALOBOS,
AUGUSTINA
SANDATE,
RAY PALAFOX,
HECTOR
"HUMBERTO"
VERDUSCO

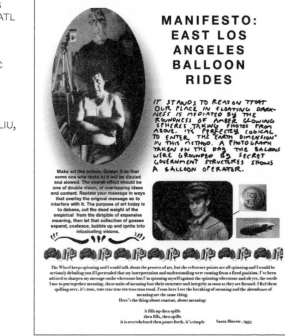

MANIFESTO: EAST LOS ANGELES BALLOON RIDES

IT STANDS TO REASON THAT OUR PLACE IN FLOATING DARKNESS IS MEDIATED BY THE ROUNDNESS OF AMBER GLOWING SPHERES. TAKING PHOTOS FROM ABOVE, ITS PERFECTLY LOGICAL TO ENTER THE EARTH DIMENSION IN THIS METHOD. A PHOTOGRAPH TAKEN ON THE DAY THE BALLOONS WERE GROUNDED BY SECRET GOVERNMENT STRUCTURES SHOWS A BALLOON OPERATOR.

Make art like poison. Design it so that some one who looks at it will be dizzied and slowed. The overall effect should be one of double vision, of overlapping ideas and content. Restate your message in ways that overlay the original message so to interfere with it. The purpose of art today is to debase, cut the dead weight of the empirical from the dirigible of expansive meaning, then let that collection of gasses expand, coalesce, bubble up and ignite into intoxicating visions.

The Wheel keeps spinning and I would talk about the process of art, but the reference points are all spinning and I would be seriously deluding you if I pretended that my interpretation and understanding were coming from a fixed position. I've been advised to sharpen my message on the whetstone but I'm spinning myself against the spinning whetstone and oh yes, the words I use to put together meaning, these units of meaning lose their structure and integrity as soon as they are formed. I feel them spilling over, it's true, true true true tru troo troo trool. From here I see the breaking of meaning and the abundance of meaning are the same thing.
Here's the thing about content, about meaning:

it fills up then spills
then fills, then spills
it is overwhelmed then pours forth, it's simple   Santa Muerte, 1935

H. VERDUSCO

FILTH SAINTS/MANIFESTOS
BALLONS

#2 1988

#2 1988

ISSUE #2
°COLLAPSE OF SPATIAL VECTORS OF WESTERN
CIVILIZATION by Dr. Eufencio J. Rojas
PLUS: FILTH SAINTS' PREDICTIONS/ DIRIGIBLE CONTENT

ERICKA LLANERA DOCUMENT RETRIEVED
AT THE NOAH PURIFOY COMPOUND

Right: RESIDENCE OF ERICKA LLANERA, EDITOR OF *FILTH SAINTS/MANIFESTOS/ BALLONS*, AND WHO ALSO ATTEMPTED AN EARLY "RESSURECTION" OF THE ORIGINAL EAST LOS ANGELES DIRIGIBLE TRANSPORT LINES. ARROW INDICATES SITE OF SUPPOSED "CODEX JOLINAUS" MURAL LOCATED IN AN APARTMENT ADJACENT TO LLANERA'S.

Left: POSSIBLE NENSHA (THOUGTOGRAPHY) PHOTOGRAPHS OF ERICKA LLANERA AS A CHILD *Images and items found in the apartment*

CHICANAS IN THE MOVEMENT

Chicanas reject feminist tokenism

Regeneración

Ericka Llanera in earlier days

CATS AINT GOT
NOTHING ON THESE CATS
CARBOLIC SMOKE BALL
CURE-ALL-ALL

calimesa the lo
hill before epic
desert of Coachell
Chiefly stated
every
thing
here that was once
living is now dead

HE ALSO REALIZES THAT
STRUCTURES SUCH AS THIS
ONE ARE BOTH NIGHT-
MARES AND THE PRODUCERS
OF NIGHTMARES

EASTSIDE WALKING
LEVITATION MANIFESTO

QUESTIONS

1. PLATELETS OF FAT STICKING PLAQUE
TO OUR BRAINS?
2. ARE YOUR THOUGHTS USUALLY ROBBED
OF OXYGEN AND TURNING DIM?
3. BLACK CLOUDS COVER YOUR MIND
BECAUSE OF CHROMIUM POISONING OF
YOUR BRAIN STEM?
4. BRAIN DAMAGE HURT YOUR FEELINGS?
5. WAS LOVE DENIED BECAUSE OF YOUR
STUPIDITY?

5

*Drawings and materials recovered
from Llanera's Lincoln Heights
residence*

"A HOLE PUNCHED THROUGH,
THOUGH ON ITS FACE IT REMAINS
SILENT, THERE'S SOMETHING
SHOUTING FROM BEHIND"
IS HOW EUFENCIO ROJAS ONCE
DESCRIBED LLANERA.

Top: THREE TOKENS FROM THE EAST LOS ANGELES DIRIGIBLE TRANSPORT LINE, INCLUDING A DAY PASS WITH FOUNDER ENRIQUE PICO'S PORTRAIT

MEMBERS OF THE BOTANICA PODER DEL MESTIZO, INCLUDING FOUNDER RICARDO DESUAREZ RENTERIA (INSET PHOTO), STRONGLY INFLUENCED EARLY DIRIGIBLE DESIGNS.

KNOW YOUR
LLANERA ENGINE

ALL PARTS MACHINED
FROM PROPRIETARY
ALLOY (SRGIO 41) AND
NICKEL PLATED

"LILY POINT" NODULE
INNOVATION MULTIPLIES
ORGONE ENERGIES LOST
IN OLDER MO-JOE CELL
DESIGNS

IMPROVED MACHINING
TECHNOLOGIES:
FLUTED TRANSFER
CHAMBERS CREATE
MORE STABLE ORGONE
SHIFT AND
METABOLIZATION
WITHIN CONFINES OF
ENGINE ITSELF

INNOVATIONS IN
FLANGE DESIGN:
REPEATED HEXAGONAL
PITTING ALONG INSIDE
EDGE OF FLANGED
TUBING EFFECTIVELY
SOLVES "VESICLE
PROBLEM" OF EARLIER
ENGINE DESIGNS

HEXAGONAL
CORRUGATION IN
JO-CELL INSULATING
SHEATHING DOUBLES
EFFICIENCY OF ORGONE
ENERGY ACCUMULATION

SECONDARY ORGONE
ACCUMULATOR
ENCOURAGES BUBBLE
TRANSFER THROUGH
SODIUM FILTER

EAST LOS ANGELES DIRIGIBLE
TRANSPORT LINES
ENGINEERING DIVISION

AT THE HEIGHT OF PICO'S ORIGINAL EAST LOS ANGELES DIRIGIBLE AIR TRANSPORT
LINES, THE COMPANY HAD A THRIVING RESEARCH AND DEVELOPMENT ARM. THE
SO-CALLED "LLANERA ENGINE" APPARENTLY RELIED HEAVILY ON WATER VORTEX
THEORIES OF VIKTOR SCHAUBERGER, DAS WESEN DES WASSERS. AT VERLAG.
ORIGINALTEXTE, HERAUSGEGEBEN UND KOMMENTIERT VON JÖRG SCHAUBERGER.

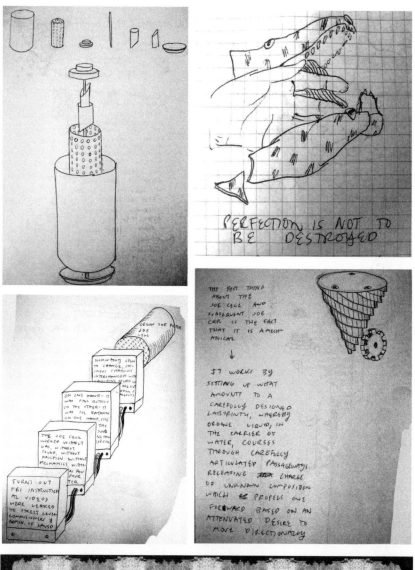

SKETCHES AND THEORETICAL DIAGRAMS OF ENERGY SYSTEMS. UNATTRIBUTED
DOCUMENTS FROM ERIKA LLANERA'S FILES

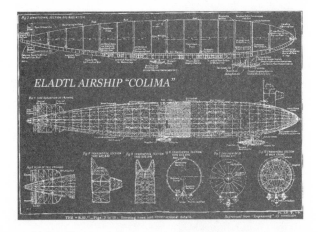

ELADTL AIRSHIP "COLIMA"

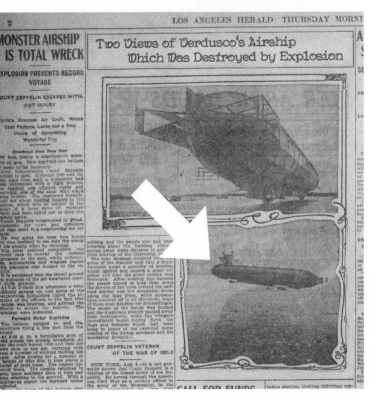

ELADATL AIRSHIP COLIMA XOLOTL

CRITICAL SEQUENCE OF EVENTS
THAT CLOSED DOWN THE
EL MONTE TO OAKLAND LINE
FOR ONE YEAR AND RESULTED
IN THE RESIGNATION OF HECTOR
"HUMBERTO" VERDUSCO

DEAR SWIRLING ALHAMBRA,

It is with great pleasure and pride that I am writing to offer you the position of Poet of the Universe, a prestigious residency at our Zoltan Monsanto Campus, located in a remote area of City Terrace adjacent to industrial flats below the El Sereno hills east of Lincoln Heights.

We are quite proud and pleased to offer you this marvelous all-expense-paid two-year award based on your superlative record of controversial publications, your reputation as spokespersona for the pirate airship community, and your extra-logical covert activities. As you will see, these accomplishments make you a supremely qualified candidate for this fellowship.

You may not be familiar with the Zoltan Monsanto Institute for Cognitive Dissension, so I shall say a few words about it before describing the prized position of Poet of the Universe, which the New York Times has called, "literally an illusory Dream job for dreamers," and the Washington Post has described as, "like a Macarthur Award for Outsiders in the Unknown."

The Zoltan Monsanto Institute for Cognitive Dissension originated in 1953, when the death of Josef Stalin allowed select scientific figures in the American Intelligence Community to return to their research endeavors in ESP-Transference and Kinetic Manipulation as related to UFO Clubs throughout history, particularly those that multiplied throughout the American Southwest during the 19th and 20th centuries, aided by funding from "anonymous" donors with apparently indefatigable sources of disposable income.

By the 1960s, the Zoltan Monsanto Institute had developed an international profile for its utterly original, even controversial proposals on Cognitive Dissension and Kinetic Folding of an Indifferent Universe; though to outsiders (or even local residents in the neighboring communities of El Sereno, Monterey Hills, the Hemon District, and Happy Valley, as well as Lincoln Heights), the Institute was virtually invisible, perhaps as an unintended or intended result of a type of "psychic cloaking" practiced by certain faculty members who were said to have been variously Soviet defectors, Nazi rocket scientists, CIA rejects, or members of the Ayn Rand Society.

Upon the untimely demise of its beloved Chancellor Emeritus, Doctor Zoltan "Z-Bird" Monsanto (1878 - 1959), the Institute created the position of Poet of the Universe as a tribute to Dr. Monsanto's vision of poets as "acute folders inside an origamaic universe," as well as a nod to his own life-long activity as a versifier and lover of poetry, especially (his own specialty) the Poetry of Dream Architecture and Horticulture.

In keeping with Dr. Monsanto's great scheme, therefore, it is my privilege to offer you the position of Poet of the Universe at the campus of our world headquarters in East Los Angeles. The details of this position are . . . Cypress . . . The moths of blackness . . . Spiky ornate leaves of eucalyptus trees . . . hills on

fire ... night travels ... midnight corrofuscations ... like the red
roof of the mouth white with mildew ... lizardy swish-swish
... Sixto at midnight driving a VW bug through the intersection
of City Terrace and Eastern ... The position of these details is
... 34.0811° N, 118.1778° W Stipend $22,000 per year ... or per
day ... or per minute ... We will decide ... we ... together, we
will sit at the metal table outside on the patio for a discreet
conversation, you and I and ... somebody else (no worries if
they are uncontrollably shaking and trembling) ... They may
be a figure clothed in obscurity or an ancient past ... They are
another figure you may notice or may not notice ... looking at
you ... They may be imperceptible, no matter ... I say Thank
You already, to you, to them ... for your indulgence ... for
your one sleepy eye ... for your shoes (look at your shoes)
... the afternoon in the trees (no one in the trees) ... Someone
vanishes around a corner (the same person from before) ...
The white wall of the entrance of the building ... I say to you
... You reply ... You know ... a movie of Studebakers, Packards
and Fords oscillates inside eggplant nausea ... glint of beer
bottle alongside railroad tracks ... the moment passes ...
I know you already know this ... phrase of a Leadbelly song
... the moment is passing.

✿

The position of Poet of the Universe does require you to reside
on campus for two years in the apartment appointed for the
poet/dream architect. The Institute provides a sumptuously
supplied second-floor apartment, outfitted with every modern
convenience, including streamlined toaster, all-electric
stove with built-in oven, kitchen wall-clock with perfectly
accurate local time (please notify us if you require a different
chronology), RCA color television and stereo entertainment
center with diamond-tipped Hi-fi record player, a complete
collection of modern jazz and pop LPs (from Jo Stafford to Nat

King Cole). This bright, airy, modern apartment is accessed via stairs external to the modest two-story building, so you must be physically able to ascend stairs to the level of a second-floor landing, as this is part of the "Monsanto tradition." We are sure you will find this all-electric, air-conditioned ultra-modern apartment to your liking during your two-year stay, especially compared to your present lodgings. We deliver Folger's coffee. You may select piped-in radio programming from stations across the continental U.S. at virtually any hour via our intercom system. Rusty tint of late-afternoon sun slanting in from the direction of the Union Pacific railroad tracks . . . Clock face on the wall striped with shadows of venetian blinds, silhouette of a potted plant, suddenly time itself has shifted . . . Darkness . . . Light . . . Dark . . . A flickering light . . . You understand.

    This

    sihT

Once you have read this letter we are certain you will agree to these terms. You'll have to agree, as have all the previous winners of this award (such as REDACTED), that it is a great honor to receive this position's $22,000.00 per annum . . . per month . . . per day . . . per minute . . . I shall now inscribe for you the details of the slight, insignificant, and easily complied-with duties of the position. As Poet of the Universe, we ask that you keep a "log" of poetic notions related to "time" and "intersectionalities" or "native plants" or "angles" or "colored moments" or "seconds." This "log" may be existent or non-existent. It may consist of actual notes in your favorite notepad or it may appear in frames of a black-and-white montage of flipping calendar pages from 1940s films. It may occur within the life cycles of indoor plants you are indifferent to, or inside the minds of people who do not understand that you love them (or did, once, when you lived—when supposedly you were alive).

If you are a Dream Architect in your guise as Poet of the Universe, we will ask that (weather permitting) you take your regular afternoon (or late morning) beer naps in the hammock supplied for this purpose on the balcony overlooking the rooftops of the industrial workshops, foundries, garages and neglected neighborhoods of El Sereno ("Hillside Village"), Hazard, and Lincoln Heights west of Soto Street, and keep your sketchbook at hand. Or, we ask that you supply a type of photographic apparatus inside a corroded black sack made of vapors and mirrors that will record your hidden thoughts via sonic impressions thrown against thin brown glycerin sheets. If you prefer the use of microscopic beads of silver oxide or aluminum oxide, these will of course be provided to you.

SQUISH LADY
BUG HERE

Now that we have your attention for one historical moment, we'd like to reiterate our thanks to you—again, again we'd like to thank you—in advance—for your work over these past decades in the area of poetry and poetics of the universe, and, moreover, your impeccable contribution to the pirate airship industry, which was crucial to the lives of several hundred people embroiled in spider webs of karmic freeways and car-crash destinies of urban spaces. Although few if any of the many projects you were a part of ever came to fruition, including the incipient "Southern California Labor Party," the aborted "1000-Foot Retinal Monument to Carlos Bulosan," and the troubled "Anthony Quinn Center for the Ericka Llanera Files," nobody could say that your work on these and other ancillary projects was for naught, since they did result in increased humidity in localized areas, new plant growth on hillsides, and heightened awareness of the effects of pollution in intertidal zones; as well as providing fodder for doctoral dissertations by dozens of lecturers, adjunct professors, and part-time faculty at numerous institutions across the Western Hemisphere; not to mention kickstarting the careers of two actors, a radio personality, and several regional writers.

We will consider it a great honor to have you join us as Poet of the Universe. Besides the requirement of the residency itself and lending a congenial aura to our usually totally deserted industrial compound/campus (hidden behind brick walls on the other side of the Southern Pacific railroad tracks in a particulate haze of twilight or murky afternoon heat waves radiating from the telephone poles running from the San Gabriel Valley toward downtown), we are asking that you instruct one workshop in the Poetics of Dream Architecture for our clerical staff and other nonessential staff members we can round up at the drop of a hat. We also ask that you give a public reading from the balcony of your residence one afternoon in the orange last light of day, for the faceless masses we will gather. Posters of this event appeared in 1991 and 1986.

If you have any questions regarding these or other clerical duties that may be requirial (requiroid) of you, we expect any uncertainties you may have to be cleared up by calling (916) 651-4022 or 202-225-6235. In order to accept these minimal duties, all you must do is return the portion below after signing your signature next to the indicated images ascertained in each photograph:

1. I RECOGNIZE THE PERSON IN THIS PHOTOGRAPH AS "TINA LERMA," WHO WILL BE FOUND SHOT TO DEATH IN HER DRIVEWAY, PRESUMABLY BY SICARIOS OF THE MEXICAN MAFIA FOR SERVING AS CONSULTANT IN A MOVIE ABOUT EAST L.A. DIRIGIBLES THAT WAS FOUND STYLISTICALLY OBJECTIONABLE.

I AVER THIS TO BE FACT, (SIGNED)

_____ DATE _____

2. I RECOGNIZE THE PERSON IN THIS PHOTOGRAPH AS "JOSE LOPEZ-FELIU," WHO WILL SUSTAIN FATAL HEAD INJURIES AFTER FALL-ING DOWN THE STAIRS TO HIS APARTMENT AFTER (CONJECTURALLY) GOING OUTSIDE TO FETCH THE NEWSPAPER, NOT REALIZING THAT HIS HOME DELIVERY SUBSCRIPTION TO THE LOS ANGELES TIMES HAD LAPSED TEN YEARS EARLIER. (ACCORDING TO ANOTHER SOURCE, THE ALTERNATE VERSION OF HIS DEATH WILL BE THAT HE STEPPED OUTSIDE ONE MORNING AND WAS WHIRLED AWAY BY A TORNADO THAT DESCENDED OUT OF NOWHERE. IT WAS THE SECOND TIME HE HAD SUFFERED SUCH INDIGNITY.)

SINCERELY, (SIGNED) _____ DATE _____

3. I RECOGNIZE THE PERSON IN THIS PHOTOGRAPH AS "SERGIO TAMAGO," WHO WILL BE MURDERED IN AN UNSOLVED MACHETE ATTACK INSIDE AN ABANDONED AIRCRAFT MANUFACTURE PLANT IN BURBANK, CA, ONE OF A SERIES OF SUCH (UNSOLVED) ATTACKS IN THE BURBANK (CA), VAN NUYS (CA), EL MONTE (CA) AND LAS VEGAS (NV) AREAS. ARE THESE ATTACKS CONNECTED TO SPASMODIC ACTIVITIES OF CARLOS CASTAÑEDA TENSEGRITY CULTS?

I AVER THIS TO BE FACT, (SIGNED)

_____ DATE _____

4. I RECOGNIZE THE PERSONAGE IN THIS PHOTO AS "ENRIQUE PICO," WHO WILL DIE FROM A SUPPOSED STROKE WHILE HOSPITALIZED IN PARIS FOR "MENTAL FATIGUE" AT THE BEHEST OF HIS PERSONAL ASSISTANT, THE FAMOUS ALCOHOLIC BUDDHIST WHO NOBODY REMEMBERS. SOMEHOW PICO'S FAMILY AND ASSOCIATES WILL NOT BE NOTIFIED UNTIL TWO WEEKS LATER. BY THEN, HIS REMAINS WILL SOMEHOW BE "LOST" AND UNACCOUNTED FOR.

I AVER THIS TO BE FACT, (SIGNED)

_____ DATE _____

5. I RECOGNIZE THE PERSON IN THIS PHOTOGRAPH AS "SWIRLING WHEELNUTS," WHO WILL BE FOUND CHOKED TO DEATH IN HIS CAR AT 5 AM ON THE OUTSKIRTS OF THE NEW WALMART PARKING LOT IN SAN BERNARDINO, CA, HAVING TRIED TO SWALLOW TWO BURGER KING BURGERS AND A 32 OZ. DIET COCA-COLA ALL AT THE SAME TIME (WRAPPERS INCLUDED).

I AVER THIS TO BE FACT, (SIGNED)

_____ DATE _____

6. I RECOGNIZE THE PERSON IN THIS PHOTOGRAPH AS "YERICA YANERA," WHO WILL BE FOUND TO HAVE COMMITTED SUICIDE BY HANGING HERSELF WITH A GAP SHOPPING BAG IN THE CITY OF COMMERCE SHERIFF SUBSTATION, FOLLOWING HER ARREST FOR "ERRATIC EYE MOVEMENT" AND "LONELY DRIVING" ON THE STREETS OF EAST LOS ANGELES.

I AVER THIS TO BE FACT, (SIGNED)

_____ DATE _____

7. I RECOGNIZE THE PERSON IN THIS PHOTOGRAPH AS "RENATO FRIAS," WHOSE BODY WILL BE RECOVERED DURING THE PERIODIC DRAINING, DREDGING AND CLEANING OF THE LAKE IN LINCOLN PARK, BY CONTRACT WORKERS FOR THE CITY OF LOS ANGELES PARKS AND RECREATION DEPT. THE BODY WILL BE TOO DECOMPOSED TO ASCERTAIN CAUSE OF DEATH, BUT INDENTIFICATION WILL STILL BE POSSIBLE DUE TO CERTAIN INIMITABLE FASHION SENSE.

I AVER THIS TO BE FACT, (SIGNED)

_____ DATE _____

8. I RECOGNIZE THE PERSON IN THIS PHOTOGRAPH AS "AUGUSTINA SANDATE," WHO WILL BE PROUNCED OFFICIALLY DECEASED BY THE UNITED STATES OF ALZHEIMER'S EVEN THOUGH HER BODY WILL NEVER BE FOUND, AS HER CAR WILL BE RECOVERED FROM THE NATIONAL PETRIFIED FOREST OF MEMORY, INTERIOR STAINED WITH FATAL AMOUNTS OF BLOOD AND BITS OF COURAGE.

I AVER THIS TO BE FACT, (SIGNED)

_____ DATE _____

9. I RECOGNIZE THE PERSON IN THIS PHOTOGRAPH AS "MELISSA ARANA," WHOSE DEATH WILL BE OFFICIALLY PRONOUNCED AS "HOMICIDE," AFTER AN "ACCIDENTAL" DRONE STRIKE BY FORMER CHINA LAKE–BASED HUNTER–KILLER DRONE OPERATORS WHO ALLEGE THEY WERE MERELY "TESTING" GENERAL ATOMICS MQ 9 REAPER ON "BORDER CROSSERS." CRITICS ALLEGE THAT THIS SCENARIO IS A DUBIOUS CIA COVER–UP, DUE TO THE FACT THAT ARANA WAS "BUG–SPLATTERED" AND "EXPLODI–YODIED" ON A DIRT ROAD OUTSIDE JOSHUA TREE, CA, OVER 110 MILES FROM THE U.S.–MEXICO BORDER. THREE OTHER PERSONS IN THE VEHICLE AT THE TIME ARE ALSO LISTED AS "ACCIDENTALS."

I AVER THIS TO BE FACT, (SIGNED)

_____ DATE _____

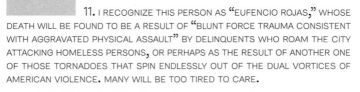

10. I RECOGNIZE THE PERSON IN THE PHOTOGRAPH AS THE 4–YEAR–OLD "JANE ARANA" (CHILD OF SERGIO TAMAGO AND MELISSA ARANA) "ACCIDENTALLY" BLOWN TO PIECES WITH HER MOTHER (ARANA) IN REPORTED "DRONE INCIDENT" DESCRIBED ABOVE.

I AVER THIS TO BE FACT, (SIGNED)

_____ DATE _____

11. I RECOGNIZE THIS PERSON AS "EUFENCIO ROJAS," WHOSE DEATH WILL BE FOUND TO BE A RESULT OF "BLUNT FORCE TRAUMA CONSISTENT WITH AGGRAVATED PHYSICAL ASSAULT" BY DELINQUENTS WHO ROAM THE CITY ATTACKING HOMELESS PERSONS, OR PERHAPS AS THE RESULT OF ANOTHER ONE OF THOSE TORNADOES THAT SPIN ENDLESSLY OUT OF THE DUAL VORTICES OF AMERICAN VIOLENCE. MANY WILL BE TOO TIRED TO CARE.

I AVER THIS TO BE FACT, (SIGNED)

_____ DATE _____

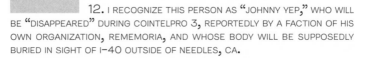

12. I RECOGNIZE THIS PERSON AS "JOHNNY YEP," WHO WILL BE "DISAPPEARED" DURING COINTELPRO 3, REPORTEDLY BY A FACTION OF HIS OWN ORGANIZATION, REMEMORIA, AND WHOSE BODY WILL BE SUPPOSEDLY BURIED IN SIGHT OF I–40 OUTSIDE OF NEEDLES, CA.

I AVER THIS TO BE FACT, (SIGNED)

_____ DATE _____

13. I RECOGNIZE THIS PERSON AS "ERIC GARNER," ... AS "EZELL FORD," ... AS "PHILANDO CASTILE," ... AS "KELLY THOMAS," ... AS "AMADOU DIALLO," ... AS "RUBEN SALAZAR," ... AS "REKIA BOYD," ... AS "SANDRA BLAND," ... AS "ALEX NIETO," ... AS "ANDY LOPEZ," ... AS "CAU THI BICH TRAN," ... AS "HECTOR MOREJON," ... AS "WESLEY EVEREST," ... AS "AIYANA JONES," ... AS "TAMIR RICE," ... AS "AMILCAR PEREZ LOPEZ," ... AS "OSCAR GRANT," ... AS "4 MILLION VIETNAMESE," ... AS "_____," ... AS ...

I AVER THIS TO BE FACT, (SIGNED)

_____ DATE _____

The Poet of the Universe will be able to stand on her or his balcony at dusk and view her or his domain as night falls.

Blue deepening east over the San Gabriel Valley, the last flash of daylight casting a red-orange sheen on the Union Pacific tracks parallel to Valley Blvd.

The Poet of the Universe will stand on her or his balcony as night falls and consider her or his options.

Please consider this offer seriously.

We look forward to hearing from you at your first convenience.

Sincerely,

Ralph Beria
DIRECTOR OF PROGRAMMING
Offices of the Poet of the Universe
DREAM ARCHITECT DEPARTMENT
ZOLTAN MONSANTO INSTITUTE

LONG LIGHT OF AFTERNOON

The world ended at Paul's Kitchen, 1950 S. Atlantic Ave.,
Monterey Park, CA 91754, (323) 724-1855, so people can be
forgiven if they failed to notice. Maybe it was because of the
horror of greed and murder and the hypocrisy of war and capitalism, maybe it was because of the rape and slaughter of poor
people in every corner in every continent, for thousands of
years, eons, then the whole species ran out of gas, out of humanity, spit and spunk and courage and sympathy, everything it takes
to survive as a human being—they had always thought it was
endless, like the fish of the sea, the birds of the sky, the buffalo
and elk and grouse on the plains, but they didn't take the warning when they had their chance. It was over.

Finished.

Or maybe it was something else, something we'd never
find out about.

Maybe something broke and couldn't be fixed somewhere
out there in the desert behind the mountains, out in Nevada or
Arizona or out on the vast Pacific. Maybe there was just some
shift in the wind, some almost inaudible puff not amounting

to an actual word in the broad empty sky, and that was it. That was all.

But why Paul's Kitchen?

Why?

There is no why.

I hated their food. Paul's Kitchen was one of those old-time Americanized chop suey joints serving "beef with broccoli . . . Sweet and sour pork . . . Egg flower soup . . . Chashu chop suey . . . Shrimp egg foo yung . . . House special chow mein . . . Yang chow fried rice . . . Sauteed bok-choy" blandly covered in cornstarch glaze, vegetables overcooked so the celery had no crunch for the old Niseis who loved the place, aunts and uncles who always wanted to meet there, relive the old days when Paul's Kitchen meant that they were enjoying a special night out on the town, "China meshi," faded nostalgia for lost post war decades when Chinese eateries had an armlock on exotic oriental cuisine like shrimp wonton, spare ribs with black bean sauce, "shrimp Cantonese." (The Chinese, massacred en masse in downtown L.A., Rock Springs WY, Hells Canyon, OR, hung from bridges or oak trees up and down California like effigies, regular target of American-style pogroms from the 19th through the early 20th century, Chinese were like exotic cousins, the French to the Brits, or maybe the Italians, they always got it worse than you did, even if it was all the same and it was your neighborhood being torched, your house shot up, your people loaded, forced, onto transport, maybe you could speak of the Chinese with casual condescension because the FOBs never stopped coming, plus you got a little fortune cookie afterward to marvel at. "Happy news is on its way to you," you could be assured.) But I wasn't tuned in to those old stations my aunts and uncles leaned toward in the radio cabinet of memories, tubes glowing green in that darkened recess. Those attitudes didn't warm my heart, burnish old sick fears with the shock that we'd survived, that we'd come this distance through the years, through generations in the sugarcane in Hawaii, in the fields and truck farms of rural California when it was rural for real, as starving as Okies, Arkies, through TB, Asian exclusion, dispossession, internment camps, "relocation," anti-miscegenation, and hatred, came through it all to sit back and relax in the red vinyl booths and believe it was all over and done with (though it was becoming apparent to me that it was, it really was all over and done with). "No," I was thinking. "Come on, not Paul's Kitchen, forever and always. This can't be how it ends."

If something was all over, good—that past had no kick for me, no more than the cold, uneaten bok choy slopped on the plate, coated in cornstarch with canned mushrooms and carrot slices.

✿

My luck, Paul's Kitchen. History evolved and reached its final incarnation in a second- or third-rate Chinese eatery "inexplicably" beloved by Japanese Americans (though I did just explain it, but, still, like a lot of overdue explications, in the end it really doesn't explain much).

Turns out, some things you think are nothing—you may have forgotten all of them already—they turn out to be the high point, the acme of civilization spiraling down through history. Paul's Kitchen, who would have thought?

You know, that time you helped your grandmother cook or cleaned out her yard, that could turn out to be the high point of your life, looking back on it. Before it all started to go.

✿

As usual, I could distract myself from these situations by attending to the needs of Leonor and the children, make sure they had what they wanted or needed. I was ever a soldier for the collective, they could rely on me. Would I lead our youngest by the hand through the crowd, find restroom door and lean outside it while waiters and busboys hustled back and forth brushing by? Would I please try to retrieve the order from our waiter and change it, so as to change the wan sullen cast to the middle girl's face? Make plain to her that we were giving her the dish she wanted, even if that in itself was not much solace for having to sit right next to her sister? Would I distract the eldest from her own resentment by praising her recent performance to her mom, describing her speed, grace, and stamina in some adroit exercise of memory, delivering precisely recalled details that effectively limned the actual stride of her spirit. So she would know that she was loved?

As usual, everyone was a little tired. I leaned across to Leonor (later, when I reconstituted this scene in memory, or maybe I dreamed it, she was no longer there—I saw myself speaking to empty air, and all these figures were phantoms, shapes of colored air, movement of lights—and I knew then that I had taken her for granted once too often) to say, "A line formed outside the restroom. Got there just in time. It's the crowd in the back room. I said hello to Marisela. She offered to order me a rum and coke at the bar in back. The ELAC Latin Jazz Band's on stage now. I wanted to see if Sara was playing flute with them. I don't know, so many people were coming out in the hall, I didn't even get a peek inside."

"Why is it so crowded tonight?" our eldest asked.

"Everybody just had to be here," I said.

"But why?"

"House special chow mein?" Luckily, at that moment the waiter arrived, demonstrating both poise and prowess, balancing three steamy oval dishes on one arm and another in hand.

"Can we all have chopsticks?" my wife asked.

"Certainly," the waiter assented.

(I recall her exact words, because I recalled them. I went there for that purpose. I went back specifically to get all the bits left that I could. I wanted all of it, our life together. It was not our favorite place—we only went there when people like our relatives invited us. On other visits to the mostly empty restaurant, crowded with phantoms of memory, I pulled Leonor's words from moist air. It was even harder to get back any of the words my children said. They say the hardest things to remember are the least dramatic, the most ordinary, the most common moments you all shared together. When I heard her voice intoning "chopsticks" amid the roar of conversation noise, I just about reached out and grabbed the exact syllables out of space above the celery noodle slime and gleaming orange chicken. The thought that this life would be lost me to one day sickened me in a sudden spasm.)

I must have gasped.

"What's the matter?" Leonor said.

"I bit my tongue."

"Don't eat so fast. You're as bad as the kids," Leonor said.

"Daddy, did you bite your tongue?"

"Chew your food carefully. Or you'll bite your tongue too," Leonor said.

"Let me see, Daddy. Let me see your tongue."

I stuck out my tongue.

"Mama, daddy stuck his tongue at me," the youngest said, not quite laughing.

Leonor glanced at me. I shook my head solemnly, intent on a clot of chicken I lifted with chopsticks.

Leonor looked at her saucy curly-headed daughter's rapt face. I stuck my tongue out, quickly, so that when Leonor glanced back at me I was masticating chicken-morsel.

Our daughter shrieked with joy. Her voice must have carried all the way out the front door, high above the overbearing noise of the crowd. Her sisters chuckled.

Leonor turned to look at her girls and I stuck out my tongue. Our girl shrieked ever louder with pure joy. "Mama! Mama, daddy stuck his tongue out again!"

Leonor glanced at people watching us from nearby booths and shooshed the agitated girl, who squirmed against the vinyl seat. Her eyes fixed on my mouth, ready for the vanished tongue. She was practically vibrating, you could see her preparing to scream again even louder. "Hush, baby, hush now," Leonor admonished her, "Your daddy needs to act his age. You girls stop encouraging him and eat your food."

The girls looked at me. I shrugged.

The littlest one looked at her mother and me, glancing one to the other, uncertain. I smiled.

✿

Johnny Yep and his compa, Eddie Jaro, watched us from the booth across the way. That gave me something to chew on. I'd heard that they'd had a falling out decades ago, that Jaro had a hand in Johnny's disappearance. The revolutionary organization Johnny led went underground, and Jaro turned up years later as some kind of consultant, broker, and community redeveloper. Who could have imagined? They were together again over sweet and sour pork and egg foo yung, giving us the eye. Johnny Yep dug behind an incisor with his fingernail and sucked at his teeth: Pinche poet, you giving us the eye?

But who was I to tell Johnny what time it was?

Eddie Jaro was all bizness, digging into his plato. He always knew what he was about. He wasn't about to give any time to any of these lightweights. Matter of fact, Johnny, watch your back. You might disappear for good on a night like this.

✿

Among all these people, at one of these tables sits the Virgin Defacer, who has spraypainted the faces off the Virgin of Guadalupe on stores all over the Eastside. What's his problem? He probably eats Chinese food with a fork. He likes sweet and sour pork—living his secret life—he's drinking a Coke.

I think there must be a way to find out who he is, in this crowd. (I'm always thinking of stuff like this.) The last time I was in a big crowd like this somewhere, at the Son Jarocho Fandango in Placita Olvera or Day of the Dead at Self-Help Graphics, I was probably trying to figure out how to find this guy. But I didn't find him (we were only going to interview him, to find out what his issues were), so I go on thinking about him. That's probably just the way he likes it.

But there must be some way, if you could think of exactly the right way to go about it, to do something, or say something, just loud enough, just the right thing, so that he'd turn and look at you. And you'd know it was him, by the look on his face. Because he'd be the only one who knew what you were talking about. Because he lives a secret life.

Sure, lots of people live secret lives, double lives, invisible to the public or to most other people. My daughters were squabbling about having to sit next to each other, and who was crossing the invisible dotted line that separates one girl's space from the other girl's space, and one of them marked the boundary with the piece of paper that the chopsticks came in, and the other girl moved it over farther, and the other girl put it back on the boundary that she had declared to be her side of the vinyl bench, and the other girl flicked the piece of paper to the floor as if to say, "we don't need no more danged borders 'round here," and the other girl almost leapt onto the table in protest, "See! See the way she is! She keeps getting on my side on purpose! She's doing it on purpose!" while the other one was countering, "Oh shut up, you don't need to be such a spoiled baby about everything! Just shut up!" and Leonor already warned the older girl, "Don't tell your sister to shut up, that's rude." "She is being rude!" the younger girl agreed, "she keeps pushing my arm on purpose! She makes me drop my food like that!" "You aren't even eating with that arm! If you drop your food that's because you don't hold your

chopsticks right! Look at the way she holds her chopsticks."
"I hold them like I want to. That's not why I dropped it on the
floor. It's because you keep jostling me! And touching me!"
The younger girl gave her sister a shove, mostly in anger at
her sister being right all the time and making her laugh at
herself besides! This caused her sister to bump her water glass,
sloshing water that quickly reached the blue formica edge of
that flat world and cascaded onto my lap, though I already
had (unconsciously, instantly) staunched most of it with a
fistful of paper napkins snatched from the tin receptacle—all
whilst scanning the crowd, repeating in my mind, "Okay, Virgin
Defacer, I know you're out there. What's the secret password?
What's your secret sign? By which gesture or what means will
you reveal yourself?"

✧

"What's up, Poeta?" Johnny Yep sneered at me with his elbow
over the back of the seat. He used to be a friend of mine in some
other life, but that's when we were kids.

"Looking for somebody," I said.

"Really?" Johnny said, leaning forward to mutter something to Eddie Jaro, who nodded. "And who might that be?"

"I doubt you know him."

Johnny said something to Eddie, who snorted. "Yeah?"
Johnny said.

"Some tagger. I don't know his real name."

"Tagger?" Johnny said. "I probably don't know him. Who
gives a shit about taggers?"

Eddie didn't pay any attention to this exchange.

Johnny turned, as if with a shrug, but I glanced at the side
of his head a couple times because Johnny left a lasting impres-
sion of watchfulness. I saw him remove his elbow a couple
times from the back of the vinyl seat, a couple times turning away. I thought his stare was still fixed on me, but every

time I glanced across, I saw the side of his head—he leaned forward—or lifted his hand to his face. I didn't want him to catch me looking at him again, so I looked elsewhere. Jaro inclined his head toward Johnny, as if leaning forward to suggest something in a brotherly way, such as, "Johnny, we got something going on out at the ranch where we need your expertise. You remember, we set it up as a training facility outside Lancaster, on the edge of the desert? We finally set up a meeting with [names redacted]. We could take a run out and be back by morning."

✿

Some of the "last words" that Jaro may have said to Johnny Yep supposedly surfaced later in trial transcripts, where defense attorneys for various members of the organiztion on trial for capital murder and weapons and conspiracy charges used the Freedom of Information Act to secure redacted surveillance records and transcripts of monitored phone calls to allege that "Minister of Defense" Armando Loya had been a government informer and provocateur who had framed various members of the organization using fraudulent FBI documents to suggest that they were government informers. Some of these were found tortured and executed in the same period when Yep disappeared, and it was asserted that Jaro, Loya, and the "military wing" of the leadership had been responsible. In turn, the organization's official line was that these assassinations were the work of government agents or criminals at war against the group's anti–drug dealing and neighborhood empowerment activities. Those of us from the neighborhood whose childhood friends grew up to become drug dealers knew that the cops cultivated informers among them (our ex-friends told us as much when they came out of the revolving door of jail and the courts, when we saw them on the street again), so that assertion was more than likely true. But there were questions after the disappearance of Johnny Yep.

"What's up, Poeta?" Johnny had sneered, before returning to his confidential conversation with the comrade most likely to betray him, if memory served.

"Hey Johnny, why are you dead?" I had wanted to ask. Instead, I devoted myself to keeping my daughters from fighting (sticking out my tongue or whatever the situation called for), and now and then peeking into the back room to check on Los Illegals or Los Perros or Tierra or whomever it was, and ask Marisela if she had any thoughts on who, among us, was actually the Virgin Defacer.

✿

The end of world dragged on and on. Over glazed plates of shrimp curled in MSG, overcooked bok choy, orange chashu pork. Christian fundamentalists argued at first that the end of the world was the fault of communism, then they said it was due to Muslims, foreigners, and terrorists, but then they said that the long, drawn-out nature of the end was also due to homosexuals and drugs. But clearly people who blamed Hillary Clinton or third party voters or contrails had not a fucking clue, since there never was and never would be a single special reason. That is, except for the last orange light of afternoon.

⬛

THE FAMOUS TV SHOW
(THE STUNTMAN'S TALE)

He wasn't killed today so he had a free day, in theory, to take his son to school and pick him up afterward, perhaps take the kids to the park, meanwhile re-plumb the leaky sink, peel off old roofing from the garage and take it to the dump in his pickup, perhaps purchase new clothes to make it easier for him to show up for work and to look for work and not have people looking at him the way they recently had been looking at him (so it seemed to him, with peremptory derision indicated by immediate insolent dismissal and pointed disregard—he was thinking if he could just get some partial acknowledgment out of the receptionist's eyes) because there didn't seem to be much demand recently for our unnamed unaccredited "man" dying, being killed a dozen ways, including thrown from a horse (which itself was tripped on a wire, tossing him as dehorsed rider face-forward into the dirt in an explosion of dust), shot, clutching himself or twitching, falling off high boulders of the canyon onto hidden air cushion behind granite boulders, riding back and forth in the dust cloud of other riders (most of them white boys in brown paint, whooping), shot to pieces, fired upon, stepped on by massive horses, getting big bruises and broken ribs, too bad—maybe he'd get lucky and some Chuck Norris or Sly Stallone wannabe would remake a Vietnam jungle wish-fulfillment battle scene where America wins this time, he could scoot practically invisible through the Malibu State Park chaparral (nameless gook) only to get blown sky high out of a prop palm tree just as he was about to fire off a fatal shot: taken out by casual offhand RPG from the hero or his cool cohort, while a digital flock of white birds fly off over patched jungle shot. "Kill me, kill me, kill me," some voice whined in his subconscious while he wondered whether it was really worth it to spend $30 on a shirt.

☼

There was a famous TV show where the narrator came on to introduce the subject matter of each evening's fantastic episode in an eerie semi-ironic monotone, cigarette smoke curling offhandedly from the unsucked cigarette in one black-and-white hand, every Ronald Reaganesque hair in place, in un-ironic black tie, white shirt, and suit jacket, he'd say something like, "Our dauntless hero, a famous dirigible pilot in his day used to extremely hazardous duty in the violent storms of the upper atmospheres at the edge of space, is about to find out that there's an even stranger zone whipped by merciless winds of the human heart, a zone where love may be the most dangerous weather of them all, in tonight's episode . . ." etc., as eerie zither and bongo music rose and the title sequence appeared against a black background punctuated or punctured by what a viewer might presume to be stars and not condensed nodes of weird leftover electronic 1960s sparkles.

☼

This is how to simulate the "Atmospheric Trash Vortex" or "Orange Gyres":

small fans placed immeditely in front of the camera, blowing on buckets of dry ice and water, to stream wispy vapors;

medium fans placed waist high into whose airstreams assistants toss handfulls of confetti and tiny bits of paper streamers or ribbons;

large fans that blow on great murky cheesecloth screens hung like banners, which ripple and billow in the background like waves and like clouds, additionally, some of this air spills over the set, causing it to creak and sway with realistic tension and gale force, against which the actors must lean in order to advance and must shout in order to be heard;

every now and then a prop person throws newspapers, boxes and pieces of cardboard, various foam or paperboard objects roughly the size and configuration of five-gallon drums, detergent bottles or food containers, etc., into the windstream—sometimes small items such as cigarette packs get sucked from the grasp of grips and swirl into the windstream (production stalled for a matter of minutes one afternoon when the lead actor nearly swallowed and choked on a cigarette butt that flew into his mouth);

behind the curtains and billowing sheets of "atmosphere," large pieces of sheet metal strung on frames are "played" with soft mallets or rubber hammers to manufacture rumbling thunder and crashing lightning and other "ambient" sounds (lead actor choking, hacking, coughing, spitting);

addition of animated flying items, large black birds flapping or flailing like crushed spiders, old model cars mostly as silhouettes flapping by, etc.;

the above all combines to produce what we believe to be the most realistic Atmospheric Trash Vortex or Orange Gyre yet presented to the viewing public!

the lighting is muted, sometimes flashing as with lightning, but otherwise we simply focus spots strategically on figures or create silhouettes, and tight facial close-ups as we see fit, because—face it—the audience has to see something! Even if our consultant, Liki Renteria, assures us that in an actual Trash Vortex or Orange Gyre, visibility will be extremely limited or lacking entirely. ("You wouldn't be able to see your hand in front of your face," says Renteria. "Objects will just fly out of nowhere!") But we can't film a TV show in the dark! We'll have to lighten the visibility to at least low fog level, called "San Francisco" in the industry.

☼

Actors may occasionally be blown off their feet and have to resort to grasping at stanchions or the hidden scaffolding that underpins the set in order to save themselves. Limited visibility enables them to wear padding under their raggedy flapping "atmosphere suits" that cushion some of their sudden falls and take the brunt of their sliding horizontally across the set, only to fetch up against the far end of superstructure, the improvised and unstable ramshackle raft-like edifices of Sky City. (Liki Renteria assures us his verbal descriptions of the improvised habitation in the cloud vortices are highly accurate, and we're lucky to have them, given the total secrecy of the govenment's investigations so far. Liki Renteria suggests they have not really penetrated the cloud vortices for lack of mimimal competence and fundamental courage. He suggests that, like the citizens of New Orleans after Hurricanes Katrina and Meredith, any citizens swept up into the trash vortices in the sky have been abandoned by the very government forces sworn by law to protect them. In fact, the security forces view these people as outsiders, outlaws, and threats to civilization, and "rogue federal units" are implicated in suspected killings, torture, or disappearances of vortex survivors reputed to have returned to earth—so says Renteria.) Some actors will be attached to guy wires and hauled off suddenly into total blackness of howling space in order (at proper points in the narrative) to indicate the fate of anyone who does not grab it fast, whatever they wish to keep they think will last, it's all over now, baby balloon.

We have numerous prototype dirigible replicas in production at all times, since they tend to suffer accidental destruction at a high rate.

The model dirigible is seen piercing the cloudy skies—generally "floating" across a cloudy sky attached to an unseen wire strung across the set and propelled by pyrotechnics of some sort—or pulled along by a hidden wire—as lightning flashes dramatically on its tumescent carapace, sometimes with water droplets streaming poignantly across its metallic skin, opalescent in pearly glow of lighting designed by union members of the Motion Picture Studio Professional Electrical Lighting Technicians Ass., and sometimes enhanced by passive reflectors held in place by grips to create a "moonlit effect."

✿

My favorite dirigible models are:

ELADATL "Colima"—papier-mâché dog head atop an airship constructed mostly of chicken wire and duct tape, the dog head replicating the iconic ceramic superstructure bridge that perched atop the legendary airship that vanished under mysterious circumstances. Unfortunately, our model (just like its namesake!) was blown up in a spectacular propane accident on set during filming, but luckily the explosion was caught on film from several angles, and the writers worked furiously to change the story line to include its destruction. "That ship is jinxed, get me out of here," someone was heard to say.

ELADATL "Ehecatl"—a sleek, courageous airship of friendly, open demeanor, much heart, supposedly has a preying mantis as its mascot.

ELADATL "Jolina"—all-black pirate airship, all-female crew, strange stoic raven-haired impulsive captain thought to be grumpy and aloof because of "lack of love" and lonesomeness.

ELADATL "Agnes Smedley"—awkwardly constructed of papier-mâché and tin cut with metal shears, spliced together with duct tape and cheesecloth, powered by Smokey Joe racial stereotype fireworks that sputter and glow and smoke as the ship is pulled across the cinematic skies of projected cloud vistas and darkening atmopheres while—

✿

In one of the show's story lines he was, of course, the evil Chinese Fu Manchu villain, black-pajama-clad gook, weakling sneak-killer. With the other killers, some regular white guys in yellow face, they swung down on ropes "seemingly out of nowhere" after the sudden appearance of the evil Fu Manchu Mother Ship, with its communistic red curvy oriental Cadillac tailfins and slanty-eyed windows maniacally glittering with freakish light as their stoic Asian faces (lit from below) peered malevolently down at the Sky City. Their job, it seemed, was to exert China's hold over the Western Hemisphere from above, starting with infiltration and takeover of America's Sky Cities—a devious plan, since the government had refused to acknowledge the existence of these outposts of disposable civilization sucked up into the trash-laden upper atmospheres. So the Chinese agents (who could be said to be controlled by a rogue agency internal to the Chinese government, for "plausible deniability") could descend upon America from above, dropping out of its own atmospheric layers. And who stood in the way of their total control, first of the skies, then all of America and the entire Western Hemisphere, but Our Hero, who was looking for the love of his life, on his way to rescue her from where she was trapped in an Orange Gyre.

Happily for the story line (so-called), he could kill all of the "invaders" (reluctantly, but he had to). He just had to, because they were so mean, devious, inarticulate, violent even beyond obvious self-interest in their own survival; they rushed at him on the various levels of the Sky City ramparts and balconies and rickety, gale-swept walkways that sometimes ripped apart in the huge winds, sometimes at opportune moments when the hero was trapped, tossing black-clad Chinamen ninjas to the roiling winds of night. The wire harness would suddenly jerk him backwards, our nameless figure of a low-budget extra (and villain), off the set and off-camera. Then he could get back to work and reenter a later scene.

So that was the "story." He was (of course) glad to get the work. He did decide to purchase the $30 new shirt. Might as well look the part, when asking for work, of a professional working man. As he fastens a safety line and leaps with his big knife drawn upon the back of the unsuspecting hero, a woman's shriek pierces the howling gale—the hero pirouettes in a spinning roundhouse kick that connects with the villain's jaw, knocking the evildoer against his own safety line, which snaps. Dragged away—elbow banging painfully into a stanchion—he's sucked up into swirling storm clouds of the upper atmospheres. The body count in this movie had to approach that of Pearl Harbor, therefore he would (re)appear to die in several more scenes. He could purchase another shirt; he decided to purchase earrings for his wife when he got a chance. He would buy the kids some healthy snacks. He would take the wife out for dinner! In one penultimate semi-climactic scene, he dangles from a high tower (upon which the red, black, and white Pacifica Radio call letters "KPFK" in weather-beaten ancient sans serif font from the 1990s can still be read through foggy wisps of shredded clouds), after being beaten to a pulp mano a mano by the Bruce Lee martial arts prowess of Our American Hero. But as our unknown extra (henchman) slides into the gaping maw of the abyss, the All-American Hero grabs his defeated opponent's wrist, showing utmost generous humanity toward the nasty, duplicitous loser. He offers mercy, showing his great American respect for life! And what does the villain do (with close-up facial grimaces spliced in during editing, provided by a son of late Syrian-born actor Michael Ansara, who looked vaguely Asian, especially with taped eyes when he played Klingon aliens) but pull out a scary Filipino escrima dagger! The Hero's sorrowful eyes widen! In a gesture meant to convey the notion that even this sneaky, cruel, inhuman Asiatic has come to understand and respect (almost worship) the moral superiority of his conqueror, the vanquished Asian creep cuts off his own hand with one mighty slash! Because he'll never be anything other than just a cruel, evil Asiatic killer and his pale vanquisher is too good! Then he nods with understanding and respect at his would-be rescuer, and he plummets upward! To certain death! (Redeemed and dead— the perfect Indian.) The scene is filmed several times, to make sure his final Nod of Respect is visible through the vapors and flying trash.

Our Hero soulfully contemplates the Asiatic's severed hand in his own for a moment, and then tosses it over the edge. It swirls around in the tornado-force winds as if waving goodbye and flies out of sight. The solemn Hero tries to get back to rescuing the Love of His Life, but little does he know, the nameless uncredited dark extra has reentered the stage from below with others of his ilk and is working his way up to attack him again! Through a trap door! Oh, will he ever know peace? To think, according to Liki Renteria, this is all "based on a true story." Twelve minutes of screen time left before the credits roll.

Our unnamed, uncredited, unknown heavy or gangster extra, Indian, killer of innocents and of luckless whites, horde member, future zombie of plague apocalypse, mob torch bearer chasing the White Hero Monster, Napoleonic battlefield corpse, pistolero, bandido machine-gunned by cynical Peckinpah outlaws, pirate falling from Disney's high mast, German casualty in trench warfare of World War 1 epic shoot, killed at Marne and Vicksburg and Monument Valley and fake-front towns of the manufactured West, not to mention blown up, riddled with M16 full-auto fire, blasted dozens of times in rice paddies and simulated East Asian jungle foliage, chanting "Oogah boogah" from the scaffolding in torchlit scenes for Francis Ford Coppola's gook shoot-'em -up Apocalypso Whatever, another shadowy figure lurking backlit behind high window, stupid thug running herky-jerky forward into the headlights right into blazing copper's blazing guns, he happily took the bus and joined the crowds on the democratic sidewalks of downtown Los Angeles. Bright day, taking his time purchasing two shirts, so he could look his best soliciting more such jobs. He was certainly on his way to success in his chosen line of work. He knew how to paint his face white, black, yellow, red. He could have long abominable shaggy yak hair, neat sneaky braids, or appear completely bald. He could grimace, yowl, growl, creep, clutch, saunter arrogantly, overbearingly overconfident right into the expert sights of the expert shots that never missed and never could, because his chest was wired to explode with erupting squibs of blood, that's how he could afford to grab fried chicken drumsticks at the downtown stand a couple blocks from Grand Central Market where his dad had taken him when he was a kid before running out of his life forever and leaving him to grow up on these streets on his own (he thought of them as his own too). With his fingers still greasy, he stepped into the crowd under the theater marquee (of the dead grand old movie theater now used as an evangelical Spanish church— "Pare de sufrir"), pushing his way through and expecting to see some mildly grotesque street performer (whatever the contemporary equivalent might be for a man and a monkey, the grimacing death's head monkey thrusting forward its little monkey cap, snatching with its little hands and their tiny black nails at any dirty coin proferred) but instead it was a thick-necked red-faced cop kneeling on some scrawny kid's back, dislocating the kid's shoulder, twisting his arm behind him, the kid howling in agony and the cop screaming curses at the kid for what reason? "Do something, do something, that's you down there, you know it too, when nobody stood up for you, nobody did anything, that was you—" one voice exhorted in his mind, while the other said louder and louder—"Piss on that, let the kid deal with it himself, he'll learn the same way I did," —already the first voice finished, "you cheap bastard, cowardly bastard, you bastard! Rub two new shirts together in a crisp paper bag and suddenly you're too afraid to step out in front of the crowd and open your—" as he found himself stepping forward, pushing past dazed bystanders, some unseen hand (like that of a child's) pushing him forward, he could hear his own voice saying, "Wait a minute! Wait a minute, he's just a kid, you're hurting him, you're breaking his arm—"

✿

The missing front tooth, a few more scars on his face, did not count against a man in his line of work, though of course the thirty-dollar shirts were long gone by the time his wife paid his bail, the clothes he'd been wearing before he was handed the orange jailhouse jumpsuit so ripped to shreds he had to have her bring him a change in a paper sack when she came to pick him up. She was outraged (not at the cop when he explained what had happened, through the aching of his broken face, with his new lisp that he was going to have to get used to, this new way of speaking with swollen rubbery mouth—no, she was thoroughly enraged at him, what was he thinking going near a cop—"all I did was grab his arm and pull him off, give the kid a chance"—she just clamped her jaw closed and drove, her last word was ever that bitter silence), and he sensed it would be so much the worse if he mentioned the little earrings he'd purchased for her were in that shopping bag, failed gesture, puny and ineffectual in the face of the season of worry tormenting her. All that anyway just a memory he might review daily, had already done almost hourly all during the previous week he'd spent in jail while she, prompted by his one phone call out, got his cousin to secure and cosign the bond. Weeks later, felony assault on a peace officer arraignment approaching, he could come home to the place emptied of her and her possessions, her purposes and aspects, "I'm not going down with you. I choose not to be one of the women who enable the self-destruction of her man. I'm not holding your hand and going down that road. You get paychecks for them killing you off in big ways and small, but you finish the job off yourself on your own time. This is my life too. I don't have to be part of that choice (you say it's no choice, due to lack of choice). I care too much about us both. We are responsible for us. You made choices that hurt us both. Take care of yourself."

So what if he should have known, could have expected it. That was in the future, anyway, the strange future of war in the skies over Los Angeles, zeppelins attacking dirigibles against a seething black-and-orange sky, where an unpredictable papier-mâché Kraken surprised onlookers, suddenly appearing (as if guided by puppet strings from above, off-screen) to destroy the huge airships, clasping them in giant suckers of writhing tentacles, turning them into fireballs, escaped gases, and deadly lightning (from the dark clouds or somewhere). So not only did entire crews of good guys and bad guys have to lurch back and forth as the cameras lurched back and forth to imply the violent forces with which the airships were destroyed, but also sometimes he and the rest of the crew had to fall out of suddenly ruptured gondolas, screeching for all they were worth as the skies exploded around them. So what if he could hardly breathe when he landed on the piles of cushions, his broken ribs unhealed as yet, his shattered zygomatic arch pounding in his cheek with the force of a continual punch, his left eye so full of broken capillaries and blood it had gone partially blind, red, and later red-and-yellow and an object of discussion. He did his best to keep his broken nose out of the game, broken finger taped to its mate. The aspirins he ate all day with coffee made his stomach a swirling vortex. The red-and-black backscreen projections simulating the dystopian skies of the future could have been projected from his own gut. Next time, it was true what his wife had said, he might just have to let the next kid or whomever deal with the cop (or whomever) all on his own. He was never able to explain to his wife that he was as surprised as anyone by the way things worked out, stepping from the crowd, stepping forward. These things he thought about as he executed his falls, his attacks, his runs, as best he could. Meanwhile, they called on him to kill or be killed (regular, mostly the latter).

✧

What were these stories even about? He did not understand them, it's true. His mind wasn't on the storyline anyway. Some science fiction bullshit, just this side of ray guns and bubble helmets, rubbery latex monsters floating out of cardboard caves in far-off galaxies where everybody was white and even the colossal-headed monsters spoke English. They explained that in this latest episode they were members of a death squad dispatched to kill some gallant self-taught illegal immigrant engineer who was holed up in a vast abandoned airplane factory, building one of the last (or was it one of the first?) dirigible airships by himself. Their role was to infiltrate the factory and chop this illegal immigrant genius to pieces with their machetes, knives, pistolas, and— Something like that. He'd been thinking about his wife and hadn't caught the rest of the plot. He had a hard enough time focusing on the present, cracked and loose teeth tasting like metallic fillings, ribs grating, broken finger still sore weeks later, pulsing face where blood from his sinuses drained into the back of his throat, and he swallowed it. He took his falls like a professional. He ran like a twenty-year-old. He took every tumble, fall, and shot and never asked to be excused or complained. His eye flared like a black marble shot through with red tiger stripes. On his way home, he'd get off the train downtown to replace those shirts; he remembered exactly where to pick up the earrings.

Clockwise:
CRYSTALLOGRAPHY
HOLO-FORMS

HOME OF "POPCORN,"
ARCHIVIST FOR THE 1996
ITERATION OF THE DIRIGIBLE
LINE. IN 2002, THE AUTHORS
LOCATED THESE MATERIALS AT
A YARD SALE IN EL SERENO.

DINO'S (INTERIOR)

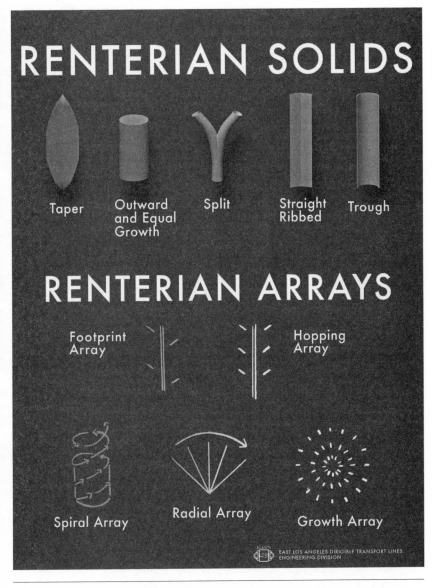

APPARENTLY, POSTERS PRODUCED BY ELADATL'S R AND D DEPARTMENT WERE INTENDED TO BE BOTH INSPIRATIONAL FOR STATION WORKERS AS WELL AS SERVE AS MARKETING TOOLS. RICARDO DESUAREZ RENTERIA'S INFLUENCE ON EARLY DESIGN OF AIRSHIPS RESULTED IN A NUMBER OF INNOVATIONS.

CREW MEMBERS OF THE AIRSHIPS
COLIMA (*above*) AND EHECATL (*inset*)
Below: COMMEMORATIVE STAMP

ENRIQUE PICO,
AIRSHIP ENGINEER
AND ELADATL CHIEF
OFFICER, SURVEYING
THE PROPOSED
OFFICES ON THE
TOP FLOOR OF LOS
ANGELES COUNTY
GENERAL HOSPITAL

EHECATL
FIRST FLIGHT

ELADATL
EHECATL

ELADATL AIRSHIP EHECATL

DESIGNED BY MARIA
MEDEL VILLALOBOS,
A TECHNOLOGICALLY
ADVANCED AIRSHIP,
THE FIRST DIRIGIBLE TO
UTILIZE TENSEGRETIC
ENGINEERING
IN ITS DESIGN

THE ABANDONED BURBANK
LOCKHEED AIRCRAFT PLANT
WAS TRANSFORMED FOR THE
BRIEF INTER-WAR PERIOD INTO
THE HOME OF ELADATL AIRSHIP
MOLOTES AND ELADATL VALLEY
OFFICES BY ARCHITECT WRAYLEEN
SOSA (BOTTOM RIGHT)

Wrayleen Sosa

BALL LIGHTNING OVER LOS ANGELES COUNTY GENERAL HOSPITAL

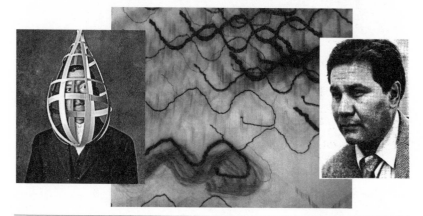

H. VERDUSCO'S USE OF THE VORTICE BELL TO HARNESS PARTICLE WAVE ENERGIES FOR THE DESIGN OF AIRSHIPS

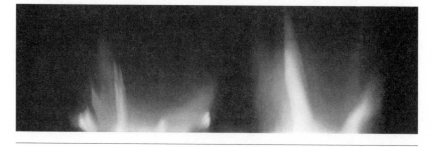

SPECTROGRAPH REGISTRATION OF PARTICLE WAVE ENERGIES

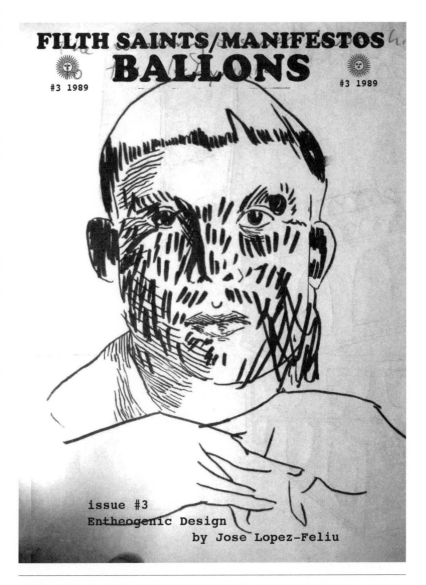

FILTH SAINTS/MANIFESTOS
BALLONS

#3 1989

#3 1989

issue #3
Entheogenic Design
by Jose Lopez-Feliu

FINAL ISSUE OF *FILTH SAINTS/MANIFESTOS/BALLONS* BEFORE ERICKA LLANERA VANISHED, WITH ARTICLES BY JOSE LOPEZ-FELIU, LIKI RENTERIA, AND OTHERS ON 'RECOVERED' ORGANIC VEGETAL AIRSHIP DESIGN

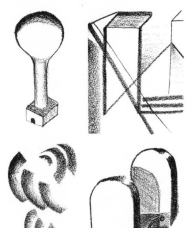

Next page:
INTERVIEWS WITH ELADATL EXPERT
AND LECTURER TANIA LUNA, PICTURED
HERE ON HER STEED MOLOTES,
REVEAL RUMORS OF AN UNFINISHED
ELADATL DIRIGIBLE AT AN UNDISCLOSED
LOCATION (WITH A RATHER DELLSCHAU-
IAN DESIGN FOR THE LIFT MECHANISM),
A LAST SNAPSHOT OF ENRIQUE PICO'S
OFFICE DIRECTLY BENEATH THE
DIRIGIBLE DOCKING STATION ON THE
ROOF OF THE LOS ANGELES COUNTY
GENERAL HOSPITAL. THE LAST NOTE AND
FINAL MESSAGE FROM CHIEF OFFICER
ENRIQUE PICO READS, "OUR WORK
IS TO LIBERATE THROUGH ECSTASY
/ THE OVERWHELMING AND BARRIER
BREAKING." ALTHOUGH IT'S
ON A POST-IT, IT CANNOT BE ERASED.

AS A CHILD, ENRIQUE PICO ENVISIONED
AIRSHIPS CONNECTING MILLIONS OF LIVES
OVER LOS ANGELES.

... WORK IS TO
LIBERATE THROUGH
ECSTASY
THE OVERWHELMING
AND BARRIER
BREAKING

SO OUR BEST EFFORTS WERE UNDONE (INCLUDES ULYSSES S. GRANT'S FAVORITE RECIPE FOR PANCAKES)

"Chopping wood off all the heads of people like nobody's mid-day forests of Americas, chopping off the hair of trees across green crusts of dust America, chopping birds' noses off the illegitimate unspoken thoughts of intimate puff breaths of sweet mouths, scattering all of it in empty plastic containers strewn on the beach. That's all. That's about it."

—JOHN F. KENNEDY

"*Batman*, that movie sucked! That movie sucked, man, and people who like those lame-ass superhero movies, they gotta be stupid! Jeez, they are lame! Talk about total bullshit! 'Pardon me, while I fight the bad guys in my leather underwear! Please! Boy Wonder, get the fuck outa my way!' Wow. Just, like, wow." —RAQUEL WELCH

"Today's sexual freedom, for most people, is really only a convention, an obligation, a social duty, a social anxiety, a necessary feature of the consumer's way of life."

—TINA MODOTTI

"You cannot teach a man anything about wax; you can only find it within yourself." —DICK TRACY

"Edith whispered to me, 'América, he's drunk. Let's go home.' 'Take it easy. He knows what he's doing. Don't worry.' Again he couldn't make it. Again he started to fall asleep. He drove about twenty miles per hour, his great head falling, his eyes glassy, moaning incoherently. I wished to God I knew how to drive. 'Jackson, please let's go home' . . . We got him to stop. He turned around in front of the Cottage Inn, a roadhouse bar, a dancing place frequented by Negroes. It was Saturday night; there were a lot of cars around. Edith quickly got out of the car. 'I'm going to call for help or call a cab; I must do something.' She was panicked. She was right, but I called her back. Jackson got furious. 'She can't go in there, get her back.' Then he mumbled drunkenly, something about Negroes, some disapproving remark. 'Edith, get back in the car. Come on! Don't go in there!' 'But América, he's drunk. I don't want to drive with him. I'm afraid.' 'No, he's not, he's fine, I promise you, we're going home. Come on! Get in!' . . . I finally coaxed Edith back in. We started on our way home. Jackson was fully awake now, fully conscious. He was angry, annoyed at us, and began to speed. Edith started screaming, 'Stop the car, let me out!' She was pleading with him. Again she screamed, 'Let me out, please stop the car! América, do something. I'm scared!' He put his foot all the way to the floor. He was speeding wildly. 'Jackson, slow down! Edith, stop making a fuss. He's fine. Take it easy. Please. Jackson, stop! Jackson don't do this.' I couldn't reach either of them. Her arms were waving. She was trying to get out of the car. He started to laugh hysterically. One curve too fast. The second curve came too quickly. Her screaming. His insane laughter. His eyes lost. We swerved, skidded to the left out of control— the car lunged into the trees." —AMÉRICA RODRIGUEZ

"Orthopedics became a specialty with the help of a new instrument, the osteotome, invented around 1830 by the German, Bernard Heine. This clever master of prosthetics had in fact already invented the chain saw. The links of the chain carried small cutting teeth with the edges set at an angle; the chain was moved around a guiding blade by turning the handle of the sprocket wheel."
—CANTINFLAS (MARIO MORENO KRAKATOA)

"Mujeres tan fuertes, real strong women, I say to you, all they need is a wire, the wire could be in a circle, it could be in a loop going from an old lamp to the wall socket, it could be dangling from the telephone pole. Hoop earring or bracelet of time, they wear it as ornament. Some crows could be yellow. It doesn't even matter, for the strong ones, if it's fucking Tuesday." —ROSA TOKYO, DAUGHTER OF FU MANCHU

"When I was a musician, we'd be on the road, traveling from town to town, you can imagine, crossing as it were the inner sea of the prehistoric cheapness of life, in a van or a sedan (doesn't matter), I'd forget that there were experts in everything somewhere, a whole nation of experts, waiting somewhere, to be vaguely useful, waiting to become a force to be reckoned with. On the outside. Instead, we'd just be collecting our mail wherever we could get it. On the radio or soda machine, or wherever—general delivery."
—SMOKEY THE BEAR

"¿Cuánto tiempo ha durado la anestesia, que llaman los hombres? ¡Ciencia de Dios, Teodicea! si se me echa a vivir en tales condiciones, anestesiado totalmente, volteada mi sensibilidad para adentro! ¡Ah doctores de las sales, hombres de las esencias, prójimos de las bases! Pido se me deje con mi tumor de conciencia, con mi irritada lepra sensitiva, ocurra lo que ocurra aunque me muera! Dejadme dolerme, si lo queréis, mas dejadme despierto de sueño, con todo el universo metido, aunque fuese a las malas, en mi temperatura polvorosa." —TINA LERMA

"When he [Albert Einstein] returned with his discouraging
report, the fog settled quickly over mountain and ice, and
there was nothing else for it but to settle down and wait,
with short rations for ourselves and nothing for our dogs.
On the ice near the tent I found a dead lemming. It had walked
across the deep snow from the other side of the fjord. The
energetic and obstinate little animal appeared to have been
wandering through the fog, as occasionally it had been walking in a circle, and had moved along in an uneven zigzag which
showed plainly that it had lost its bearings. It was almost
incredible that this small rodent, which is no larger than a
fair-sized finch, had managed to make its way through the
deep snow, of which the upper-layer was so soft that it had
to press its small sinewy body through a deep and assuredly
most toilsome furrow. All its paws were skinned, and so torn
that the toes were frozen together with stiffened blood. The
snow had, presumably in the same manner as it happens with
our dogs, stuck to the hairs between its toes; then it had
made an effort to try to cleanse them with its teeth, so that
it had torn away both skin and hair. In one foot it had a deep
wound which it must have inflicted on itself, and the conse-
quent loss of blood must have occasioned its death. The
Eskimo, who admire the unusual qualities of the lemming,
its courage, its endurance and stubbornness, say of it that it
possesses the chest of a man, the beard of a seal, the feet of
a bear, and the teeth and tail of a rabbit— a characteristic of
its appearance that is very striking." —ANTHONY QUINN

"Again today we see a lemming attempting to cross the
fjord. It comes from the slough close by our camp and stub-
bornly sets its course where the crossing is at its broad-
est. In comparison to its size it shoots ahead with dazzling
speed, swimming through the snow with queer jumps.
Occasionally it disappears entirely in a tunnel to shoot up
further ahead like a dwarf seal coming up to breathe. With
its weeny size and its phenomenal energy, it seems para-
doxical in these enormous surroundings that swallow it up.
One of our dogs scents it and rushes up so violently that

the traces break. In the same instant a cloud of snow whirls around the tail of the little wanderer; for a few seconds yet the lemming fights its way ahead, then suddenly it is flung high up in the air to disappear still alive into the mouth of the dog."

—SERGIO TAMAGO

"Gentlemen, I must inform you that the board can no longer function in this manner. I sent a man down to the streets, I sent a female agent to the roof. We have our people in the subway, in the telephone booths and central exchanges, in the art gallery and the riding stables. You have all read their reports. This is it—good night, gentlemen. Next time I see you, it shall be over a smudgy fire and a can of chile beans in the hobo jungle. Any questions?" —DR. EUFENCIO ROJAS

"The houses along the road side had all burned (to the ground) and the trees and electric poles were scorched, though they remained standing. The factories on the other side of the river looked like masses of crushed wire, with only the largest of their columns still standing. There were many dead bodies among the debris littering the roads. The faces, arms and legs had swollen up, making them look like black rubber dolls. When our shoes touched those bodies the skin would come peeling off just like that of an over-ripe peach, exposing the white fat underneath. There were many dead bodies floating in the river as well. We were drawn to one that belonged to a young woman of about 18 or 19, from which a long white cloth belt was dragging behind. Looking closer, we saw that this white belt was really her intestines, which were protruding from the side of her abdomen. Feeling nauseous, we turned our eyes away and hurried off again in the direction of our father's factory. When we had come within about a hundred meters of our father's factory, my brother suddenly screamed out and stood paralyzed with fear. I looked over his shoulder to see a boy of 6 or 7 who had died with something white hanging out of his mouth. At first glance, it seemed to me that he had been vomiting up noodles when he died. Looking closer, however, I realized that the roundworms that had been living inside his body had come shooting out at once. We ran away, fighting back our nausea. Does everyone here know what roundworms are? They are white parasites that look like worms and grow 20 to 40 centimeters long. Our father's factory had also been reduced to nothing but scorched metal."

—F. SCOTT FITZGERALD

"Sometimes suicide seems the only way out. These little towns, with their liquor stores and gas stations, with their supermarkets and summer heat . . . Refracting all the lies and bullshit you convinced yourself of in all the other towns, you see and hear it coming back at you, even across generations. You open family photo albums and it stares at you. Cussing, drunkenness, falling out of trees, meannesses of all kinds, sexual relationships with the loneliest plant life, the broken-back spirit of pettiness, those are all names for it. See, that's what aspirin was invented for." —BOB DYLAN

"Compassion and compression act as the twin pistons of our radiogrammatic civilization—charge them with your will."

—FRANKLIN D. ROOSEVELT

"For a dollar or two, you get these little animals in a box. At least, they are the dried seeds of animals that you grow in a cup of water. You can get the address of the company off the back of a comic book, maybe, or a book of matches. I warn you, though, they stink when they die. But if you want to see some, look at that cup on the windowsill. They dried out in the sun when I forgot to water them . Maybe if I wait and add water later, they'll grow again." —KATY JURADO

"Jose Lozano, he was here earlier. He don't look like an artist. He looks more like [unintelligible]. . . "

—FRESNO TOMÁS MORENITO

"Ciudad Juarez's femicide machine is composed of hatred and misogynistic violence, machismo, power and patriarchal reaffirmations that take place at the margins of the law or within a law of complicity between criminals, police, military, government officials, and citizens who constitute an a-legal old-boy network. Consequently, the machine enjoys discreet protection from individuals, groups and institutions that in turn offer judicial and political impunity, as well as supremacy over the State and the law." —MISTER COFFEE

"Guided by golden rays of brilliant sweet sunrises wafting through the screen of my open window, which had a rose actually growing through the torn screen into the room I rented on a quiet street in Mountain View, where the landlady's pallid boy and girl teens too lazy to be actual mean delinquents stole my rent money from the top bureau drawer where I kept it under my socks and underwear so I had to keep searching out weirder more obscure hiding places (or find a new place to live)—rising over dull glaring streets in a plain California neighborhood on old El Camino Real—not a dusty Spanish dirt highway of 1800s, but a main avenue and traffic artery fronting car dealerships, bars and liquor stores, pepper trees and strip joints, the new days broke in on me with the wild promise of summer's long days to come and endless new adventures."
—BLACKIE, THE GHOST OF JACK KEROUAC'S DOG

"Intermarriages between French fur trappers and Plains Cree women led, in the 17th and 18th centuries, to the creation of a metis (mixed) community, with a distinctive creole named Michif. Still spoken by fewer than 1,000 in Sasketchewan and North Dakota, it is characterized by French nouns and Cree verbs. Bungee was another creole, this time with Scots Gaelic, which evolved in Manitoba in the 19th and 20th centuries." —UNKNOWN BOY OR GIRL

"When I cook a chicken, I really cook it, you know? I mean like I am cooking it with everything, whether it is car antennaes, or science fiction gizmos from Los Angeles of the Future where the city is destroyed by Death Rays from Hair Balls from Outer Space, to hoisin sauce, fish sauce, garlic jelly, pomegranate jelly, Armenian pizza juice, whole garbanzos and Yukon potatoes stuffed with quails wrapped in nori with bacon and aluminum foil and toilet paper, slathered with some kind of Texas railroad oil." —CESAR X. CHÁVEZ

"Roads of mud, roads of sheet ice, roads of choking dust. Dead roads. Look, I had a ticket, I swear to you, at some point I swear I had a ticket." —RAY FOSTER

"All the almonds up a tree
Heaven to the lady descending a staircase
STAIRCASE. such up and downs nobody knows.
SO may hazard and quince. Without/
NO. More fool.   /NO unspace or cluttered as
Can't believe it be under writing. GAVE PEACE!
You wldnt hand an old man like me. DOWN?
    WITH
Across the Tijuana Border near Oregon I discovered
THREE COINS and a bus ticket out! Girls making beds
getting silly.

She looks like you
when she laughs." —RAY FOSTER

"Geometric Silver Lotion, derived from philosophical formulas of ancient Greek alchemists in Alexandria, guaranteed to deliver lions to your honeyed breasts, hungry mouths of Sun, Moon and Wind in fresh cream over your body, and new orifices to your Mind's Light. Desire, cantaloupe froth, asparagus oil, and filaments of polyethylene glycol, send $19.85 plus $3.95 postage and handling to King Kong's Mom, 12356 Interrupt Road, Glendale, CA 90033." —KING KONG

"Shamans like Colonel Sanders assert that all human beings have the capacity to see energy directly as it flows in the universe. They believe that the assemblage point, as they call it, is a point that exists in man's total sphere of energy. In other words, when a shaman perceives a man as energy that flows in the universe, he sees a luminous ball. In that luminous ball, the shaman can see a point of greater brilliance located at the height of the shoulder blades, approximately an arm's length behind them. Shamans maintain that perception is assembled at this point; that the energy that flows in the universe is transformed here into sensory data, and that the sensory data is later interpreted, giving as a result the world of everyday life." —PIO PICO

—TINA LERMA

"We sent out Broderick Crawford to patrol the byways, with their perfume of Mexico City and Zagreb, oleanders and agave growing by the gravel quarry— What did Broderick Crawford know about the moon, he was an alcoholic— suspended license, DUI— Everyone chauffeurs a bit of moon, pieces of moonlight— If it doesn't have dust on it, you know it has been moved— Moon carcass hanging on a fence—" —PAT BROWN

"Cigarettes are my ruin, whisky is my grave / some of these nice-looking women gonna carry me to my grave"
—HARRY TRUMAN

"People began to look like gorillas, their muscles swelled with bristling tufts of hair, flashing teeth and black eyes, they began to look insectile to me, sun glinting hard on their cara-

paces, limbs jointed, brusquely exoskeletal, exposing nasty
pointed hairs, jerky movements in daylight, surfaces too
shiny and jagged, their movements jerky and jagged, capable of sudden rapidity beyond which I could even make out
with the human eye, people grew frighteningly hard and
shiny, growing like dinosaurs, larger than cars suddenly or
gas stations, I had the sense that they were lurking behind
buildings and fences, consuming things, God knows what,
containers of solvents or petroleum products or dead
animals, becoming grotesquely huger and huger, threatening to crush their surroundings accidentally, I couldn't look
anyone in the face like that anymore." —TONY ROMA

"I have 3 women, yellow, brown and black / I have 3 women,
yellow, brown, and black / gonna take the governor of Georgia
to judge the one I like / I got one for the morning, one for late
at night / I got one for noon-time, to treat a daddy right"
—LEE HARVEY OSWALD

"Yes, I'd like the roasted miasma with succulent diverticulitis,
and a side of garlic Sargasso and punctured bees. To drink,
let me see, how about crushed ice chest? If the ice is not
crushed, just the chest. Yes." —LEE KRASNER

"Se atumulta la sangre en el termómetro." —CHARLIE CHAN

"Many were killed as they attempted to swim off the island.
Others were shot. Many of the women met their deaths
by bayonet. But most horrific of all were the stories of the
deaths of children. One Pomo historian later wrote, "One
lady told me she saw two white men coming, their guns up
in the air and on their guns hung a little girl. They brought
it to the creek and threw it in the water. And a little while
later two more men came in the same manner. This time
they had a little boy on the end of their guns and also threw
it in the water . . . She said when they gathered the dead
they found all the little ones were killed by being stabed
(sic)" After the destruction of the village, Lyon's forces
continued throughout the area, killing all Indians they came
into contact with. In coming months, hundreds of Indians

of all tribes would be hunted down and killed. Nine years later, after the Gunther's Island massacre near the Pacific coast, one young editor by the name of Bret Harte was so appalled he wrote in the Northern Californian, 'Indiscriminate Massacre of Indians: Women and Children Butchered.'"
—WOODY "WOODROW WILSON" STRODE

"It looked like Death Valley, except I think we were out toward Nevada by that time. I swear, I think that time Ray Foster did have a ticket." —CISCO HOUSTON

Ingredients

1 cup all-purpose flour
2 tablespoons sugar
2 teaspoons baking powder
1 teaspoon salt
1 egg, beaten
1 cup soy or oat milk
2 tablespoons vegetable oil

Directions

1. In a large bowl, mix flour, sugar, baking powder and salt. Make a well in the center, and pour in milk, egg and oil. Mix until smooth.

2. Heat a lightly oiled griddle or frying pan over medium high heat. Pour or scoop the batter onto the griddle, using approximately 1/4 cup for each pancake. Brown on both sides and serve hot. —ULYSSES S. GRANT

"Buffalo Gal, won't you come out tonight, and we'll dance by the light of the mind" —JIM CROW

"Evidence of ancient dirigible transportation has been located north of Bishop, CA preserved in an Area called the Volcanic Tablelands. Locals may be reluctant to direct outsiders to where evidence of ancient dirigibles can be found, certainly the cashiers at Safeway in Bishop may give you the flat cold stare. Drive north on '7 bridges dirt road' through Fish Slough off Highway 6 leading toward the weird emptiness of Nevada. Sometimes if you go off and walk to a high point, you may see a guy with a pickup truck raise dust as he drives by a long way in the distance, and messages may come to you. The White Mountains may indicate something to you in the 94-degree sunshine." —NICOLA TESLA

"We walked side by side in the forest on sandy trails between 'quaking' aspen—tear drop leaves flicking rapidly back and forth in the wind—or flickering willows or on the soft duff of the shady forest floor, sometimes the wind roared through the tree tops and blew the white pine or sugar pine pollen all over us—and all about us rising ever higher the great granite domes far denser than concrete, their gray peaks cracked and jointed and marked with weeping black oxides and stained splotchy everywhere with the black and gray and lime-green of lichen—the living stone, the stone alive in every crack and crevice; if you sat down on a stone, weary from miles of walking, mosquitoes bit your arms or neck where you weren't watching—big and small black ants and gray spiders and black stink bug beetles walked everywhere across the surface of the great granite mountains and beautiful tiny succulent five-pointed yellow star-shape flowers and magenta pink trumpets, small but terribly hardy, grew from each crack or crevice—"
                                        —MARTHA AND THE VANDELLAS

"'Are you finished now?' Tina says. 'You pretender. I thought you were asleep,' I say. 'I was, until you came along with all your racket. Did you really think I could still be asleep?' 'Come now, I wasn't as bad as all that.' She sits up, still covering her eyes. Her breasts fall like fruit onto her belly. 'Do you want to take anymore? How should I sit?' 'What's the point now?' I say, trying to outdo her. 'You've ruined the mood. I think I'll even have to destroy the negatives.' 'You must be mad. Why?' 'It would be dishonest not to.' 'Nobody will ever know the difference,' she says as she leans back onto her elbows, supine and seductive. 'No, I suppose they never will.'" —SWIRLING ALHAMBRA

"This was why Ericka, Swirling, Tina, Tiburcio, Sergio and I organized the East Los Angeles Dirigible Air Transport Lines, even realizing all of its problems, errors and history of headaches, with beer and oranges, Tiburcio's besmirched lips, Tina's tremendous mean streak and jokes (insisting that she be called Tania from now on or she wasn't going to talk to us), Swirling with his toes all swollen from yellow fever and swamp gas, unable to sleep, wiggling his toes in the middle of meetings, Sergio not saying much just taking care of business as usual, Swirling interrupting to read us reports from Knud Rasmussen crossing Arctic wastes via dogsled, that's how it all got started. Rick H. never showed up for meetings (supposedly in India), but he sent us this assessment of the industrial environment:

One-third of Americans had suffered job loss, and another third knew somebody who had been made jobless. 40% of families had suffered reduced working hours, lower wages and benefits. There were now four job seekers for every job opening. Six million Americans, almost five times as many as in 2007, have been out of work for more than six months; four million for more than a year. Many of those who still work have had to accept a drop in wages because they have had to take lower paying jobs.. Paul Krugman makes an estimate of the likely permanent loss of value in potential GDP from the Great Recession and the subsequent depression of about $5 trillion. That's an accumulated staggering 40% of current US real GDP.

Which, I mean, open your eyes and look around. Global warming, trash vortices opening in the skies, dust storms called haboobs enveloping cities of the Southwest, continents of drought and forest fires, deranged mystics and gangster religions, anxieties trembling like dinosaurs roaming strange terrains, weird haircuts on youth, all of it was surrounding us. In order to fight back and give someone hope, we organized a new mode of transportation to challenge the whole grid. Yeah, pretty much."

— JOSE LOPEZ-FELIU

THE LAST TO KNOW

First, why was Sergio limping?

Partly because Sergio didn't see where the guy even came from. It was too sunny, the world full of glare and heat, he was standing in some Vegas parking lot feeling dazed and stupid from a late night out, trying to sort out his keys, eyes swiveling like rusty hinges, what the hell was the guy saying?

"Gimme your wallet! Hand over your wallet!"

"What?" Sergio brain-dead, mind blank, after a night of drinking. He wasn't pleased to having some guy jam him up, first thing.

What did he want? Sergio had thrown his overnight bag in the trunk, and half turned when spoken to.

"You heard me! Gimme your wallet! And your keys!"

("What the hell?" Sergio was still thinking.)

Little scrawny dude with a drawn and wizened old face, fifteen or twenty years younger than himself. Wispy whiskers goateed the guy's chin, a small black Chinese Indian man. ("Hey, my brother? What's the matter?") Now that he had

Sergio's attention, the bandit lifted his T-shirt to show the chrome butt of a pistol in his pants.

Sergio could have said, "What the fuck?" but instead tried to focus his eyes in some outrageous glare of sunshine. Now he was completely dazed and stupid, whereas walking across the blazing sun-blasted parking lot to his vehicle, he'd just felt slow.

Too slow for this guy.

"Shit," Sergio thought. No time to bother to regret the previous night. The wedding of his friend (ex-girlfriend, likely one of the best people he'd ever known), the wedding reception where he hardly knew anybody except the bride (she could spare no time for him, just a word or two of thanks for coming, already she'd moved into a new life, new circles of friends), in a big banquet hall. He hadn't circulated much, he drank and talked to characters like the bride's dubious low-life brothers. After four hours driving across the desert from L.A. he felt as foolish coming to the wedding and afterward the reception as he had expected. He hadn't really known what to expect but that awkward possibility hit it on the head. He felt ghostly, the ghost of Christmas past. He drank enough to dull these misgivings but not the silly echo of his own lame thoughts ("Look at her! That could be me!" his mind squealed, and it didn't matter that he didn't believe any of these notions), and he didn't recall much about how the evening ended, or care to, but mid-morning when he awoke with the glare of the desert seeping around the edge of the curtains so that the room filled with light, he fled: he showered and jumped in his clothes and checked out—mid-morning, the desert heat already spiking— he burned his mouth slurping a styrofoam cup of motel coffee before sailing out across a vast sea of heat waves shimmering off the chrome and steel rows of parked automobiles.

Mid-flight, about to jump in his car and catch the 15 . . .

"Gimme your wallet! And your keys!"

The frazzled outline of young robber wasn't clear in Sergio's peripheral vision, but Sergio felt his scowling hostility. He seemed about to snap, as if trembling imperceptibly. Sergio shifted his keys to his left hand, digging into his pocket for his wallet. With adrenal intensity, the pistolero eyed Sergio's every move.

Sergio pulled out his wallet but lost his grip on his keys, which fell tinkling on the asphalt. Looking down at them (stupidly, no doubt) Sergio caught a glimpse of the young guy, blocked from view of anyone coming out of the motel by a van with tinted windows. They were at the far side of a vast parking lot. If the guy shot him, it would sound like a firecracker, if people at the motel entrance even noticed anything.

Who knew wasted, dried-out young pistoleros lurked in sweltering Vegas parking lots like lizards among the cars? Risking heat exhaustion for—what did Sergio have in his wallet, $40?

Sergio proffered his wallet, holding it limply toward the guy.

The guy snatched it away, caught a glimpse of what was inside and gasped. "Fuck you!" he whined.

"Been out of work," Sergio muttered. The East Los Angeles Dirigible Air Transport Lines, they owed him big time. He had no time to bring that up now.

"Fuck this," the parking lot pistolero hissed. "You gotta have more than this on you! What the fuck did you do, you fucking old bastard, lose everything playing quarter slots?"

"I ain't that old!" Sergio thought to himself.

"Pick up those keys, now! Give them to me," the robber said.

Sergio bent over, picked up the keys, and handed them across to the guy. The robber took the bills and plastic out of the wallet and tossed it aside. With bills and plastic in one hand, he was reaching for the keys with the other when Sergio let the keys go. The guy dropped his gaze as if to reach for the falling keys when Sergio stepped forward and jabbed at the guy's face. The pistolero flinched, throwing himself backwards to get out of the way, but still Sergio's fist swiped him across the mouth.

The robber backpedaled, grabbing for the pistol and pulled it free as Sergio dove forward and grabbed the guy's shirt. The pistol went off; one very loud pop. Sergio swung his right forearm and caught the guy across his head, slamming him facedown atop Sergio's car. The guy didn't hit the car too forcefully, he was already twisting loose, trying to spin free, when Sergio shoved him forward and they both fell between parked vehicles. Sergio landed on top of the young pistolero and slammed his fist on the back of the robber's head again and again.

A white couple heard the ruckus between parked cars and peered in at Sergio, sitting on the pistolero and beating on his head. They watched for a moment and hurried off.

Sergio stopped when it seemed clear the kid couldn't pull the pistol (the youth was breathing wetly through broken teeth, nose crushed; he'd made a whimpering cry); Sergio glanced about and saw the pistol on the ground under his car.

Sudden pain made Sergio light-headed, somewhat nauseous. He saw that the kid had shot him in the foot, severing at least a couple toes. He rolled to one side and clutched his calf with both hands.

✿

Sergio limped along Main Street by the L.A. River, traffic heavy in smoggy late afternoon on immense concrete embankments, Melissa striding easy at his side. They owe me a lot of money. And time, but if it's one or the other, I'll take the money. I asked for it, and they assured me that it was forthcoming, not exactly "check's in the mail" forthcoming, but more like "soon, you'll hear from us soon" forthcoming. That was weeks or months ago. My idea was to go all over the outposts of the Colorado Plateau or Gran Bohemia where the Swirling big man might appear, with his Swirling big ideas. I told Mel that I'd introduce her to him: we might intercept him on his Swirling rotations. I didn't mention to her exactly why I had to track him down ("company business"). I suspected she wanted to tag along for personal reasons; I felt that I might be stringing her along, maybe messing up something she had going with Tina, but you know how it is, it's getting harder and harder these days to recruit good kids. Anyway, it was true what I told her, "You'll get to see ELADATL as a whole, the whole operation." I'd given up going by the offices (one of the last places you'd ever locate Swirling or Jose), so I figured I had to bump into them by accident on the waterfront somewhere, in Seattle Pike Market drinking tea overlooking Puget Sound in cold gray rain, or at Garcia's in Albuquerque at breakfast on a smoggy hot morning, or at some organic rock-climbing granola hotcakes table in Joshua Tree or on a Minneapolis street corner or hiding out in some corner of Brooklyn. I'd ask him how it was going; somewhere in the conversation we'd talk money. Of course I mentioned none of this to Mel, because why bother a new recruit with the news that the organization was perhaps collapsing?

Mel asked, "What do you do? I mean for a living. Do you really make enough working for ELADATL?" (Even newcomers like Mel knew that the organization was having financial problems.)

"I used to work in the movie industry. Used to work as an extra. Then I became a stunt man. Hopefully I can pick up more work like that. I've been unemployed due to injury."

Mel nodded because he was limping. Sergio didn't bother to explain that his limp was entirely unrelated.

"I've been out of circulation. I'll have to put out a bunch of calls, see if I can get my foot back in the door (so to speak)."

"Might take a while?"

"Might."

"Some strands of time are carried off on the breeze like short pieces of satin ribbon in an updraft."

"What? What do—"

"Oh, just thinking of Tina."

"What about Tina?"

"Railroad of dreams."

"Excuse me?"

"I mean, she's probably one of those strands of ribbon caught in the updraft of a breeze, carried off."

"Really?" Sergio was discomforted by Mel's casual shrug. Really? Is that all? Maybe Mel was a bit too casually impulsive for him. The daunting willfulness of youth. Maybe, in that way and others, she was more perfect than he might imagine.

"Tina and I will always be good. Not to worry. Why do you have that worried look?" Mel chuckled.

"Oh, there's our ship. Better hurry," Sergio said.

Orange glare of the sun too intense to look at directly, above the train tracks and warehouse roofs along the empty riverbank—there was the swollen metal skin of the waiting airship. People scurried and half-ran past them, and they joined the crowd, rushing to the station.

Why was he still limping?

Because his toes (the stumps) goddamned hurt.

With Sergio's ELADATL Employee ID, his company travel pass, and a bagful of complimentary tokens leftover from old PR contests and lapsed marketing campaigns, the two of them traveled the length and breadth of the Americas, ostensibly—and often actually—searching for Swirling Alhambra and Jose Lopez-Feliu. When Melissa asked whether, as they were having such difficulty locating Sergio's "comrades," wouldn't it be better just to go to the top and try to meet with a chief, Enrique Pico? Sergio said he could never do that, that not only was Enrique Pico intellectually and emotionally inaccessible and surrounded by pathological bureaucrats and clerks, Pico knew nothing of the actual technical side of production, which he (Sergio) had, unfortunately, sole knowledge of. Pico was a trained engineer fully occupied with the financial operations of the organization. Pico may have heard Sergio's name here and there (he had presented Sergio with an aluminum desk trophy commemorating his exemplary service to the organization), but Sergio expected no understanding, nothing, from the office of the chief financial officer. The only ones with full and direct understanding of Sergio's key role in the whole structure of the organization, of the initial stages and development of ELADATL were Alhambra and Lopez-Feliu. They had been the main organizers, had built the organization from the ground up over two decades, making good use of Sergio's wide-ranging talents. Alhambra and Lopez-Feliu were among the few (such as Tina Lerma) who knew that Sergio was the linchpin of the organization. So Sergio and Melissa voyaged on, criss-crossing the Colorado Plateau and the Great Plains, the Mississippi Delta, the Great Basin, the vast deserts, the Mojave, the Sonora, the Chihuahua, in search of them. Together they discovered astonishing wonders such as the obscure Osa and Nicoya peninsulas of Costa Rica, which had been accessible only by boat until the advent of lighter-than-air airships.

Of course, airships were their life.

Occasionally Sergio's contacts allowed them to travel in Deluxe Accommodations, with a First Class suite to themselves, but even when they traveled coach, and even if the airship was a rickety First Series ("Agnes Smedley Era, should've been taken out of service years ago"), Sergio knew how to make the best of the flight, such as when they caught the airship Colima out of Oaxaca City. They exited through a usually locked access door at the stern end of crew quarters and entered the gangway to the cargo area. Sergio showed Mel the ballast tanks of coolant water, which had been lowered sufficiently for the altitude gain necessary for the ascent. With the Sierra Madre's jagged peaks drifting mistily below the illuminated silver belly of the ship, Mel and Sergio dove and swam in the big oval tank, something like a twenty-foot-deep Olympic size pool, an ovum of fresh liquid, while their whoops and hollers rang off the brassy walls, their giant shadows playing back and forth in refracted blue light.

Photo #1:
Sergio limped along Seattle's South Main Street, everything glistening, shiny and gloomy in the foggy morning (with a few winos asleep in Pioneer Square), looking for the former offices of ILWU Local 37 to show Mel where those union reformers had been assassinated, but he couldn't find the place. They went to Filipino restaurant in the I-District, with Sergio talking about "the old days" for no particular good reason.

Photo #2:
Mel pointing at newspaper in glass display case, headline JOHN LENNON SHOT DEAD, with quizzical poker face. Beatles?

Photo #3:
Mel selfie taken with cell phone through rain-spattered car window in drippy side mirror, streets and buildings blurring fast.

Photo #4:
Someone kindly shot Mel and Sergio standing together on a vista point on the coast. They look damp and misty in their wrinkly raingear. The Pacific Ocean rolls in on a long beach

far below them. Like the ocean, the sky is gray and cloudy—
cold, wet, windy day. Mel has taken Sergio's hand, or he has
taken hers.

✧

The whole trip, or series of trips, evolved into something
Sergio had never intended—his love life till then had been
limping along like he was limping, then suddenly this twenty-
something was doing wild things to him ("You're such a kid,"
Sergio would sometimes tell her, Mel thought somewhat
dismissively)—such that now he felt her presence, tasted her
skin, her breath in his ear, even as he tied his shoes in the
morning (the empty space where his toes went, unnoticed—
things gone missing in his life like digits unmissed), a feeling
for her, a taste and touch of her with him at all times now, a
new spectrum of colors emerging from the air, a distortion
(or a trueing) in his sense of sight, in his feeling for daylight,
in his breathing.

"Jesus Christ, how will I ever get rid of her now?" he found
himself thinking when he first awoke (in the dark, blinking
with apprehension against the unresolving dark) next to her.
Immediately he felt foolish.

He listened to her breathing as she slept. He had to listen
to hear it, and it ticked off a thrill of fear. "Now, you're going
be afraid?" he thought, mocking himself. Afraid to be with
someone, or afraid to be alone? That's the way of it, he told
himself with lame reassurance so that he could breathe easier
and fall back asleep: the best things will carry with them the
worst fears. You shall awaken afraid at night. Get used to it.

It'll all look different in the daylight.

✧

One of the flights was dreadfully hot. It was in the '90s. We
were over the dried-out West, maybe Nevada. We passed over
ranges of burned-up lava rocks, basins of alkali wastes, pink

plains of gray fuzz that might have been sagebrush. Former reservoirs like Lake Mead or Lake Powell, now desiccated sump holes, displayed bathtub rings of mineral deposits of former glory of 20th-century eras when there was water, will- and man-power, money and optimism. Vast monumental concrete dams seemed insignificant as we passed at high altitude. State highways zigged lonely or interstates zagged like black lines across sand-colored wrinkly parchment, demarcations whose original purposes had been forgotten. White passengers in linen and seersucker wore sunglasses, like they usually all do. They looked cool, but, like everybody, they had a wilting aspect. The rest of us wished we had sunglasses. We wanted to look cool so we might feel cooler. As it sailed into the west, horizon aflame, the sun cast angry orange light across the entire port side of the ship. It irradiated the promenade deck, but the desert air was somewhat cooler in the adjacent lounge. That's where Mel and I spent long hours, part of a crowd half-baked and subdued. Management supplied the passengers with small electric fans. You could take the fan to your cabin, where it actually was cooler, but the air was confined there and stuffier, or you could sit with the stultified crowd in the dining room or in one of the lounges, drinking pineapple daiquiris or key lime margaritas or gin and tonics or lemon spritzes with your whirring little fan to give you a small draft of coolness. We both drank our little drinks and fell asleep reading, waking with sore necks.

✡

Sergio had already sent out email messages, telegrams, phone calls, and brief letters to Friedrichshafen, Frankfurt, Tillamook, NYC (Empire State Bldg), Lakehurst NJ, El Monte, Mountain View, Burbank, and El Sereno. He was not hiding the fact that he was trying to locate the so-called leadership of the organization. In fact, he made every effort to be as obvious about wanting to meet with them as possible. He felt that this increased the likelihood that they would have to meet with him sooner or later. He tried several approaches in texts that he sent to Jose Lopez-Feliu and Swirling Alhambra. He sent formal letters delineating company business described in technical terms, sometimes attaching accompanying tables and diagrams. He faxed budgetary proposals with invoices for work past due.

After weeks and months without written replies to his direct requests for payment on debts owed, Sergio added indirect sorts of requests. He sent a "Eat at the Hat: World Famous Pastrami" postcard to Jose with this message, in part:

Probably you have heard the rumors. Anyway, when I have a woman life is more scientific. Because of all the connections. All life in the universe seems more connected. The first time I have sex after a long dry spell (so to speak) I feel I have once again been initiated into a complex and mysterious science, secrets of which are being revealed to me. They are, of course, secrets of origin, of my original being. Cool, eh?

Need to talk,

Sergio

✿

Simultaneously, he sent Swirling a "Winter Scene, Truckee, CA" postcard, with this note:

Possibly, Jose is a sex addict? You of all people would know. You may have heard, I am in a personal situation, a situation of a personal Nature, and must speak with someone who has a lot of experience. That is why I pick him. So I was hoping you would ask Jose to call me. Because you know, not just anybody. This is a very important matter to me, involving destiny, Fortune, Gemini versus Virgo, Rooster versus Monkey, happiness and love. Basic

relationship issues. As in, should I stay or should I go? Don't fail
me now.

> *Get back to me ASAP,*
>
> *Sergio*

✿

Sergio knew these guys. Whereas they might feel out of their league when dealing with larger budgetary or money issues, one of them must figure he was the Love Daddy-Papi Chulo-Muffler Man. They'd probably argue over which one of them could provide better counsel. They might have an idea this was a ploy to draw them out of the woodwork. Might not work, they might see through it. Later, they'd have a ready answer if he complained. "We just thought it was a girl. You know, we don't really have no expertise in women or stuff like that. Know what I'm sayin'? Plus, you can deal, am I right or am I right?" But it was worth a try. There was the slightest chance he'd get his money and a bit of useful advice out of this deal.

✿

Of course, Melissa and Sergio each talked about the other. For instance, Melissa said via phone (in a phone booth in Port Townsend, on the Olympic Peninsula—its rows of "quaint shops" disappearing into a swirling empty mist as if the street beyond fell into the deep cold sea, total darkness beyond the condensation droplets running down sides of the glass booth) to her sister, "I like his face, you know, the serious look he usually has. He has that stoic man-thing going on, but any second he might roll his eyes at you, wink and grin, or throw his head back and laugh." In a call to his cousin, Tomás, Sergio said (from a wall phone in a bar in Portland, the former Chinatown, with Mel nursing a hoppy local IPA), "She usually has this kind of impassive 'I don't care' look on her face. Like she has other things on her mind. You might not be able to tell what she's thinking—but if she catches your eye, suddenly she might roll her eyes, smirk sweetly, or say something funny; then you know something of what she's thinking." They never knew but they told almost exactly the same things and other unoriginal secrets about each other to family and friends.

✿

The annual company barbecue of the East Los Angeles Dirigible Air Transport Lines was scheduled to take place at tables under the picnic shelter and spreading on the lush summer lawn rolling down to the reservoir. A location in the Rocky Mountains. Luckily Mel was a late sleeper in the afternoon, after driving a couple hours from the town where . . . Luckily . . . sunny but then massive cottonwoods . . . Colorado cumulus clouds blocked out the sun, still it was hot, muggy . . . The picnic site could be identified from afar by dirigibles circling in the distance, and dirigible kites tacking in the stiff breeze above . . . Reservoir had the warm slimy water . . . Sleepy green algae drifting around in the shallows, tadpools . . . tadpoles . . . wiggling around your feet when you walked into the water . . . From sand that had been trucked to the site and dumped on the shore to simulate a beach . . . But a few feet into the water, your feet sunk into the mud, dark brown oozing between your toes . . . tadpoles . . . living commas made of algae or bug-eating amphibians, grass stalks poking the bottom of your feet . . . Grass growing in the water. Mel insisted they swim of course. First off, because it was hot and muggy . . .

The water was murky green, a cloudy pea soup of live microscopic algae . . . Mel laughed at Sergio, she'd just shrugged off her halter dress . . . ran out, splashing and dove in . . . Sergio watched her suspiciously, to see if she fetched up her head against a submerged shopping cart, landed on an underwater stump and hurt herself, came up gasping for breath and bleeding from a split eyebrow, but when she rose and flipped her wet hair from her face, she just looked at him and laughed. Was she only wearing her underwear? But of course in the shimmering green water nothing could be seen, except her seal-sleek head rising darkly, tossing a wet fin or wing of hair (an arc of droplets streaming behind her) out of her eyes so she could look back to shore, locate him and laugh... "Come on, Stinky! You'll feel so much better! It's cool, not cold! It's great!"

"Aaaarrrgh!" With his best pirate growl, Sergio shuffled forth and tossed himself bodily into the lake... Water clapped about his body, embracing it with a sudden chill that he felt first against his skin, then penetrating his gut... a chill of darkness... He opened his eyes underwater and his eyes adjusted to vague murk, brown to black below, green above... Blowing bubbles out of his nose, he rose to the surface and caught his breath. Mel may have been laughing at him, but he laughed with her... When he put his feet on the mucky bottom and stood, swishy grass against his calves, he rose halfway out of the water... little wavelets beat against his stomach... Mel had used a sidestroke to propel her out to deep water... Ploshing in the water as he pushed blandly through chill currents after her, Sergio meanwhile had flashes, milliseconds of fragmentary images of misgivings, great grouper monster fish jaws yawning, snapping turtles lurking, dead gangster car wrecks sunken jaggedly below her as she swam... if she yowled "ouch!" and came up with a bloody ankle cut on jagged tetanus Dodge of a rusty sheetmetal body below in black water, he would not have been surprised... But the surprise was, of course, Mel's spontaneous grace as she cut through the shining water.

While he sort of flailed on the surface of the lake... He felt a lack of impetus, as if he were a piece of driftwood... swimming was like trying to make headway in a dream where you dreamed you couldn't make headway... It's true, Sergio could have used his toes as an excuse, said something about how he didn't want to get an infection. He could have sat out on the warm grass, ELADATL picnickers milling about above him, and just watched Melissa swim, admired her . . . showing off . . . But he hated when people made excuses like that, when they were just squeamish or sheepish or foppish. Sergio would rather get an infection in his amputated metatarsals necessitating getting the tips sawed off again rather than to make any such excuses under this summer sky. Not to Mel. The sky was radiant blue and he felt relief on his head, he felt the radiation pass, when clouds covered the sun like vast dirigibles looming overhead. Kicking with his feet, he floated out into the lake, gurgly sounds in his ear canal. Echoes from sea caves thousands of miles away in the Sea of Cortez . . . Big summer sky . . . on billowy cottonwoods looming leafy green over the wooden picnic awnings . . . Luckily . . .

✿

"Heard about your mishap, eh? Las Vegas, eh? Crazy, eh? Blowed them toes clean off!" big Mick Larch said, big beige curly-haired white guy with mustache/goatee in sporty clean plaid short-sleeves. He leaned over to take a hard look at the foot as Sergio toweled off. "Jeezus. Look at that. Jeezus. They still hurt?" Mick asked—winced—squinting at the abbreviated red stumps and sucking a green bottle of Rolling Rock.

Melissa had already stepped into her clothes; she wrung her hair and shook it out on the grass. Hair hung matted in Mel's face, making Sergio laugh at her disheveled fierceness (just a momentary look after all), and Mel laughed too. "They stopped hurting," Sergio said, though he was still in the habit of putting on his socks and shoes very deliberately. "Jose get here yet? Swirling around? You seen either of 'em?"

"No," Mick replied. "But I probably wasn't paying attention. Maybe they're up with the people."

"When did you arrive?" Sergio asked.

"Got in . . . maybe ten?"

"How'd you get here?"

"Company provided everything. Did everything. Flight out of San Francisco. I caught a dirigible in, where was it, Martinez? The other side from Benicia. Hotel at the layover. Great New Mexican breakfast in . . . Wherever that was. You? They must have flown you out on your own ship, right? They send a car for you and everything? You're practically one of the founders. None of this could ever have happened without you. You are the main engineer. Whatever they get done, they owe to you."

Sergio was shaking his head.

"You're kidding," Mick scowled. "Hell, that ain't right." He couldn't believe it.

Sergio stood up straight, both palms up as he shrugged.

"Really?" Mick said. "You're kidding? You?"

Sergio shook his head again.

"Why would they book everything for me, cover all my costs, pay me per diem and a car and not you? Hell, next to you, I'm nothing more than part-time assistant to Tina Lerma's 2003 publicity campaign for the Inland Empire expansion. What the hell is that about?" Mick said.

"Don't know," Sergio admitted. "Gotta find out."

✿

Hours of dank crotch, his shorts soaked through with green lake water . . . Larry Orozco handed him and everyone stiff shots of mezcal, Larry's mission to get everyone drunk. Sergio glanced at his wristwatch, in the cup sloshed . . . The kite flyers . . . A bright girl laughed . . . it took several hours for Sergio's shorts to dry . . . He tried to hide the limp; he didn't want to keep explaining. People had heard various things . . . They asked . . . Sergio developed existential questions in order to head them off. They might want to ask him about his injury, his personal situation, anything along those lines. He'd interrupt them, asking, "Nicola Tesla, does his spirit still live among us?" or "How long have you been a member of the vegetariat, and would you recommend kale to just anyone?" and "Who do you feel closest to, personally, Pablo Neruda, Garcia Lorca, or Cesar Vallejo? Which poet best represents your style of love?" Probably some saw through him . . .

Sergio didn't care. When Larch, Brent Suislaw, Tina Lerma, and the rest couldn't figure out how to power up the Tesla coils inside the twin fifteen-foot-high Transmssion Towers, to demonstrate remote power transmission to dirigibles equipped with special receivers, it was the typical thing— Sergio was happy to go to work . . . his way of disappearing into purpose, to step outside of his own trivia or whatever sounded to him like purposeless chatter. The ELADATL Jenny Hamilton carrot cake eaters, luau pig munchers dipping gobs of juicy pork into Thai sweet chile sauce, the previously mentioned ELADATL staff, significant others, locals from the community, and anyone holding the free vouchers to the company picnic all one by one fell silent and walked down onto the wide slope of lawn to gape and gaze when the sparks began to fly.

The metalloid phallic mushrooms atop each pillar, which looked vaguely like a giant steel cooking whisk, buzzed angrily. Sparks began to fly. Everyone came out to watch.

The twin wooden towers with their steel and copper innards were set about thirty or forty meters apart. As soon as their power went on, the "resonator pancake" on top of each tower began to emit, at irregular intervals, tentacles of sparks. Like lightning, these tentacles curled about, zapping at the air. The air fried with a dangerous sizzle. The tentacles curled around the towers, bouncing off the wood frame, causing them to smoke slightly. Viewers blinked away spots on their eyes, spots of brightness floated on their retinae. The tentacles of bluish lightning increased, coursing and buzzing, crackling and flowing out of the tops of the towers. Some folks moved behind others, peering over someone else's shoulder. Everyone watched apprehensively as bolts of lightning from both towers arced through the air, reaching toward each other. Some were frightened and stepped back toward the covered picnic tables. Like claws of two electrical crabs, the lightning bolts feinted and flickered toward the opposite tower. People expected an explosion or shower of sparks when the two currents met, but as the crackling and buzzing grew loudest and as the tentacles of lightning found each other, coalescing in a menacing blue arc, the electricity flicked off and vanished. Spots hovered inside people's retinae, and the very air had a charged, acrid smell.

In the hush following, someone coughed, and a wooden door at the base of one tower was kicked open. Sergio emerged, coughing, wiping his greasy hands on the front of his shirt. The crowd erupted in shouts and applause. Tina, Mick, and Melissa were laughing and clapping. Sergio stood in front of the tower and saluted the crowd. The demonstration dirigible (ELADATL Ehecatl) descended behind him, approaching over the lake, preparing to absorb a transmission.

✧

He not only never found Swirling or Jose (the crowd sumptuously banqueted, as if to purposely hide rumors of the organization's imminent collapse, even though the official leadership seemed inauspiciously absent), Sergio also lost Mel at the company picnic. The crowd was kept occupied by calavera fashion shows and door-prize lotteries, live music, and cooking demonstrations put on by the widely famous celebrity chefs of the long-distance lines. A feisty girl pilot in regulation overalls with an intense, sorrowful, dark-eyed look shook her curly head at him as she handed him an envelope with his name on it, scrawled in Mel's handwriting. "Sorry, jefe," the pilot said.

The enclosed note said in part: "She [Tina] and I have to get away. Something's come up. We have to talk. I owe it to

her. You'll always be in my heart. Be in touch soon. XOXO."
He didn't like the sound of the "always in my heart" part. It
sounded to him like, "Sign here to join our mailing list." It only
came to him much, much later when he recalled vague distant
memories of nights and mornings that he had worried about
how he would ever be able to break things off with her. He'd
never imagined how it would feel to get dumped first. All he
knew at the company picnic, as he rushed breathlessly uphill
through the crowd toward the parking area, where nobody was
able to tell him anything about Mel or Tina (or Swirling or Jose,
for that matter—what did these people know?), was that so
pre-occupied had he been with himself and his own situation
that he'd taken Mel for granted and everything she'd said at
face value—and now that she was gone for good, he realized
some time later— He realized . . .

DEAR SWIRLING ALHAMBRA,

My name is Ericka Llanera. Listen to me, this is urgent. Are you paying attention, this is for real. I am the real Ericka Llanera, pay no attention to any future messages from messengers who pretend or say they are Ericka Llanera. There is only one, Ericka Llanera. I shall identify myself to you by code on each of these letters. There is only one Ericka Llanera, me.

There has been a Campaign of Hate. I have proof. You know about the destruction of the East L.A. Dirigible Air Transport Lines El Sereno Station by the sheriff's SWAT team—when they burned down your station under the pretext of arresting Carlos Montes, cofounder of the Brown Berets, that was just a really bad cover-up. When you walked through the smoking rubble, numerous documents—forgotten and stupidly left behind by the FBI agents who coordinated the "raid"—were found [see attached document]. I know that you know where they are, these documents, and the boxes of files that were stolen from my house by government agents when they did the exact same thing, which was, they smashed up my office and lit it on fire. "An accident," they told the *L.A. Times*, when I was forced to go underground and run for my life. "An accident"! Every time! An accident! Who would believe it?

As Oscar Zeta Acosta wrote in his La Raza newspaper article about me, describing my career and legendary troubles that resulted in more than a decade of life on the run, underground without minimal health care or dental coverage, resulting in severe gum disease:

"Ericka Llanera was born in Los Angeles, California in 1944. In 1963, she left Los Angeles and moved to an outpost in the Sonoran desert run by followers of Carlos Castañeda's Elemental Tensegrity cult. In 1969, after returning to Los Angeles, Ericka Llanera resurrected East L.A. Dirigible Air Transit Lines by launching a homemade geodesic balloon from an old anchoring point in the community of City Terrace. Renaming it East L.A. Balloon Tours, she began to offer a limited route to and from California State University Los Angeles from another anchor point in the community of El Sereno.

"Llanera was also founder and editor of *Filth/Saints/Manifestos/Ballons*. The magazine covered a diverse range of topics within the field of entheogenic physics, urban design and prophecy. It was also designed as an echo of the revolutionary events of 1968 . . . a kind of delayed echo and elaboration of some of the policies put forth by student revolutionaries back then. The magazine folded in 1989 after a joint FBI/LA County Sheriff's raid on her house in El Sereno caused a fire that destroyed her papers."

That was written by the famous Brown Buffalo himself, Doctor of Jurisprudence Zeta Acosta, who also disappeared under mysterious circumstances. However, I do not have information about that, at this time. Sometimes you take the dirigible of truth to the very edge of existence, and you stand there in one or two blustery winds. And you throw a pebble into the bottomless abyss. Now, what I must discuss with you is the recuperation and return of my obviously important files and manuscripts. If you have heard of my case you know what tremendous knowledge these files and manuscripts represent. Decades of research, often at great personal risk or sacrifice, the product of years and travels and uncertain circumstances. Nopales and Skin Care, the High Low Radiance Corridor, Tijuana Time Portal, the Mysteries of East L.A., The East L.A. Balloon Club, the Bessie Coleman Aero Club, James Banning (first black pilot in America) and the Black Wings, the elite black flying formation headquartered at the Eastside Los Angeles Airport, the Sonora Aero Club and so much more. My files contain multitudes. A whole secret history of marginalized and disappeared peoples. Northern, Central, Southern, Baja California.

They want those files and manuscripts destroyed, because it will be like shutting and locking the door on the World of the Past that they do not ever want opened again. Why is that? Severely throwing away the key. That is how they want it. We must ask, why? Reactionary forces destroyed the indigenous Indian civilizations of original Americans and replaced it all with an actual robot version of Disney zombie apocalypse. These and other scenarios or erasures of history are all outlined in my unpublished manuscripts.

Also! Something else! I have testimony from someone of your acquaintance, someone who can verify my identity to you in person, because she is your trusted associate and friend, Melissa Arana. You have received reports of your colleagues and comrades when they are awake—well, here is one from a whole different state of consciousness. This is the recounting of a dream that Melissa Arana told me directly in person. I ask you to hold off all tendencies of judgment until I finish, for then you will understand that although this information comes to us through the aquamarine vibrations and formats of rarified hypnogogic consciousness, that it nevertheless relates exceptionally valid information, especially if you know how to interpret it. I assure you, I do. I retain those credentials and capabilities.

Melissa said she awoke and immediately knew where she was, no disorientation, no hesitancy; it was the drone of the external motors —the familiar hum and vibration, conveying a sort of maternal comfort as she slept—so that when she awoke she realized immediately she was aboard ship. She pushed aside the thin coverlet and sat up on the aluminum bunk, wondering if he (not Tina, if you know what I mean) was asleep on the bunk above her. But when she stood, she saw that the upper bunk was empty, cream-colored coverlet undisturbed, polished metal supports and ladder gleaming.

Still there was something odd, something funny about the sound of the ship. It was the same familiar, solid, imperceptibly humming and subconsciously vibrating ship, like a vast mechanical cocoon, like a massive cotton boll wafting through the summer breeze. But when she stuck her head out of the door, Melissa said, she realized what was weird was that no one was around. The corridor was empty. No stray knock or typical commotion in the slightest, no voices from adjoining staterooms. She knocked twice on the nearest door, got no reply. Only the occasional wiry susurration that was the ship's music, feathery decrescendoes playing over the whole of the ship in a massed torque of atmospheres, like a note sliding down a distant taut piano wire at the far end of a huge sound stage. She walked out of the stateroom and along the corridor toward the promenade—-where surely she'd bump into someone. Soft atmospheric reverb passing like a breath overhead gave the sound of her footsteps on the deck an exaggerated edge.

She proceeded, Arana said, "inside bouncing silences."

But I know Melissa like I know the back of my hand, I kid you not señor, this agent (just a kid you might say—in some ways—in these other ways completely not) was not daydreaming about Sergio or Tina or any other dreamy love, instead she stalked forward quietly, listening intently forward, at the same time mentally calibrating wind sheer velocity versus engine torque horsepower ratio, at this likely possible heading south along the 118th meridian in easterly winds at approximately 30 knots. That's what she figured, going on a hunch, plus an intuitive feel for Last Known Location. (However, remember, she had awoken aboard ship, and she should not have been able to have had access to coordinates of exact recall, or LKL. But never underestimate Melissa Arana, especially in her dreams.) But Melissa had her navigator's notepad in her pocket (she felt sure enough about that, without having to check), she had all the notes she had annotated in her navigator's notebook in mind, she had her Bowditch's American Navigator's Manual and her Aguila Mexicana Navigation Handbook under her belt (so to speak), and she could do these types of calculations on the fly. It was required, to get from Point A to Point B, anyhow in this complex world—you had to be about developing alternate routes at all times. Apparently alternate routes ran through some strange dreams. Where she might even retain vague awareness that this rickety reality was somehow a dream. But she proceeded directly nonetheless, because this was Arana's nature, her training, her intent.

Every navigator is bound to have dreams of navigation.

It occurred to Melissa to wonder if she'd left beans on the fire. You had to simmer beans for a couple of hours, so she was forever forgetting about them, doing something else and forgetting them, starting another activity . . . unless she compulsively wondered "Am I burning the beans?" she was going to burn the beans. Anasazi beans or black beans or kidney beans. Because she should take some to her mom, who was ill, getting on in years. She'd take her a fresh pot of beans, perhaps garden greens, Japanese mustard or rainbow kale, tied off with a recycled rubber band, to check on her mom. That's of course what she should be doing this afternoon—but instead, she'd awoken aboard ship. Of course, she was only dreaming. In the "real world," her beans were probably burning. Whatever world you wake up in, Melissa was ready to go for it. She was the kind who arrived with beans or greens for your mom, if your mom was old and possibly feeling ill. Instinctively, she thought to descend the spiral stairs to the lower decks to see if she'd left the beans simmering in the ship's kitchen. That would be the first clue of authenticity, wherever she was or might be.

Down one level, skipping down aluminum stairs, boot steps clanging, she ducked her head into the kitchen. No beans on the fire, no one there. But the silver coffee percolator was on the stove, against flight protocol standards to leave it like that. She knew a couple ELADATL flight crew who might do such a thing—one in particular. She strode over to the coffee pot and gingerly placed her palm against it. It was very warm. Someone was drinking coffee.

Taking a right outside the kitchen, Melissa plunged forward down the passage to the control car. Like the navigation and radio rooms, it was empty. The ship proceded on automatic pilot, a south by south westerly course. According to her understanding, everything seemed all right, except no one was in sight. The airship the length of two football fields rolled on, thrumming with metallic helio-aluminum power, drawn on by radio navigation? By the prescient spirit of Nikola Tesla?

Back upstairs, Melissa strode through the lounge (empty, book discarded on far coffee table by the couch) onto the port promenade. Leaning on the chrome promenade railing, she took in the view. The ocean far below roiled furiously. Far as she could tell, the ship was on a port tack, the ocean crashing against green bluffs along a rocky wild coast visible through banked plateglass windows the length of the promenade. Cloud banks plowed onto coastal mountains, sunshine plashing or playing across the topmost creamy froth of clouds. Somewhere in the gray mist, it was probably rainy and dark, quiet fields, drippy orchards and misty highways and towns receiving a drizzly rain. Directly below, in last light of afternoon, the sea churned, rough, whipped by westerlies, scouring white water across the dark wracked surface. Swells rose into the wind far below; Melissa distinguished the spray coming off the lead edges, flung into the sunshine—foamy whiteness whipsawing across variegated dark waters. Those same winds vibrated the frame of the ship. Whoever was piloting was on tack against the prevailing wind to maintain a southerly course.

(She leaned down to flip open the book on the coffee table. *Cheyenne Autumn* by Mari Sandoz. What was that about? A torn slip of paper marked pages 122–123. Written on the paper was "5–19"—her birthday. She recognized the writing.)

Melissa walked the ship, bow to stern.

✿

When she returned through the lounge, the Cheyenne Autumn book was gone from the coffee table. In place of the book, an empty white coffee cup—"ELADATL Jolina" dog head insignia on the side—stain of coffee in the bottom. Next to the coffee cup, the slip of paper with her birthdate had been flipped over, and a note scrawled:

I know you're here on the ship somewhere. I can feel you. I'll check the usual places, if not maybe we should meet in cabin 19 at 1400 hours. I'll find you. — S.

Melissa checked her watch. It was already 3 PM. Where had the time gone? That was probably her second inkling, in the recurrent suspicion that this was a dream, she told me — (it was a bright sunny L.A. day on the avenue outside the open window, traffic noise streamed through, it was that golden summer of Southern California that lasts all year, when I asked

Melissa, "But isn't that something you thought about later? After you woke up? And do you want some more iced tea or maybe a beer?" "Maybe," she said) —remembering how the ocean below looked infinitely real, the waters infinitely deep, dark as the interior of mountains, as the interior of metals, scoured by wind, the water whipped by waves and froth. She recalled walking the ship, standing at the edge of the shimmering blue ballast tank where they had frolicked, distant ages, it seemed, in the past.

"Maybe," Melissa thought, imagining the ship surging ahead, leaving behind that storm front as the clouds blew over the land, raining into citrus and avocado orchards, blowing hard through chaparral shaking on high rocky slopes. Maybe, she felt the airship quiver in the cold wind like a sheet of steel. As if she herself walked through rays of cold sunshine, through doors of steel and glass, into a blustery day.

That's what she said. She said the dream revealed something all-important, which I am prepared to report to you, at any location or point in time you find convenient in order to release to me the East L.A. Balloon Club files and memorabilia, of which, you realize, I am the sole rightful owner.

Sincerely,

Ericka Llanera
(you know who I am)

✿

Dear Swirling,
Or should I say Mr. Alhambra? I am writing you today in a matter of the utmost urgency. I cannot stand the idea that you are being fooled by some FBI agent provocateur, posing as me. Not for one moment.
The very idea.
They say the FBI or PDID or CIA is trying to dupe you, trad-

ing fanciful tales of made-up dreams of one "Melissa Arana" for the secret location of property that rightfully belongs to me. Damn! Those are my files! Mine!

Pay no attention to those reactionary interlopers, bastards. Beware, Mr. Swirling, they are selling you a bill of goods, and in return they expect to make off with something that belongs not to you nor to them, but to me—of all people. Do not take their fake dreams (they do not know the real Melissa Arana like I know her) in return for all that's left of my life's decades of work, the files of the East L.A. Balloon Club. These files are the one hope of passing along all the secret history of the East L.A. Balloon Club, *Filth Saints/Manifestos/Ballons*, East Los Angeles Dirigible Air Transport Lines, the cadre and their dreams.

Of course, Melissa Arana told me this dream herself, and personally suggested that you of all people had the expertise to interpret it. Pay no attention to fakers and agents who would fool you with some bootleg, Technicolor, Cinemascope or downloaded dreams. This one is the only wholly accurate dream. Arana would tell you herself if only she were here.

Maybe you don't know her? Of course you know her, but I mean how well do you really know her? For example, did you know she once ran 1,200 miles from Mexico City to El Paso Texas, part of a 3-woman team who ran a thousand miles across vast sun-cracked deserts in solidarity with the rights of indigenous peoples of Mexico, followed by three guys in a Ford van support vehicle? Do you know that her deepest fear is of having children and finding out later that she's a terrible mother? Or that her second deepest fear is that she will wake up in the hospital brain-damaged after a massive car accident and be unable to see or hear or even think, she'll just be kept alive by feeding tubes and catheters hooked up to machines in a large hospital complex, not even knowing if anybody ever visits her or even if she's alive or dead or just dreaming? Or, you probably didn't know, but her third and really deepest fear is that somehow her life is already like that, like we're all in a coma dreaming we're alive, doing nothing with our lives, nothing you can do matters, so, like, whatever you do, it's nothing—you know? I know all these and other fears that Melissa told me about, along with her dreams and hopes. We discussed all kinds of secrets on warm summer nights sitting on the porch overlooking the lights of Happy Valley in a cloud of marijuana smoke, drinking tea, electronic bleats and burbles coming from the interior of the house, the guys inside cackling sometimes, and Melissa said, "What if I'm like that girl lying in the hospital who can't move or talk or do anything, what if my life is already like that, even while I am walking around, perfectly healthy, thinking I am alive so to speak, believing it's all good? Except everybody's trapped in circumstance, unable really to make any sense of it, or any difference?" You know exactly what I'm talking about, the kind of things you talk about above the neighborhood weed smoke drifting off on a wonderful breeze after midnight, a little traffic noise, maybe a siren drifting up from below.

You know Melissa, she won't let such fears get in her way. This girl, if she's afraid of the water, goes swimming. If she feels afraid of being alone, climbs the mountain solo. If she's afraid her life makes no difference, lives it a way to make a difference. Why else become a dirigible pilot?

It's a recurring dream, she wakes up and she's on board a dirigible . . . floating through the empty night . . . ELADATL Colima humming across the open ocean . . . or through a lashing storm . . . Sometimes it occurs to her that this is the famous lost airship, the one that went missing . . . She's on board, for better or worse, she alone is destined to find out what happened to it. Sometimes the dirigible is crowded with people, as on flights they'd taken years ago, sometimes the airship is eerily empty . . . In this dream, it seems Sergio is with her (in other dreams it may be Tina, or someone else—someone she doesn't recognize, though they seem generally familiar)—anyway, she's not alone. I don't know what your sources, the fake Ericka Llaneras, might have been telling you, related to Melissa's dreams. She moves through this dream surrounded by people, or the shadows of people.

Really, these others are figures who seem like people in some other life, in some other time, but then they become photographic representations of themselves, 2-dimensional, visible from the front only. Melissa found herself walking through a crowded ship, background noise of chatter and conversations going on, corridors spilling noise and people going about their business. Every time she fixed her gaze on someone, a family, a couple with a little girl, the mother holding a baby in her arms—she admired the sash, over the woman's shoulder, which supported the baby—as she looked at them the family, which had been an indistinct part of a tableau of people, light and space opening out onto the forward lounge (the bank of windows on the promenade beyond a wall of white light beyond a delicate potted palm), they all froze into position, the husband/father leaning over to attend to the little girl with an expression stuck midway between pout and frown, concerned with some interior reality that is itself also stuck. The whole family became life-size photographic images of themselves, pasted on cardboard cut-outs. Melissa approached them, light gleaming across their laminated surfaces. When she peered behind them, she saw that the three figures (plus baby on the woman's hip) were stabilized by a fold-out leg of cardboard behind them, like the free-standing cardboard figures of celebrities that tourists pose beside for snapshots. The ship seems, feels, full of commotion and people, but everywhere she looked, she only encountered these cardboard figures. Even the murmur of conversations, chatter and random clatter—the usual shipboard noises—finally did not come from discernable sources. It's as if the life she heard about her was piped into the air through air vents. And after she hurries past the family tableau, do they resume motion, become real and actual, fully embodied and resume their former life?

Who photographed these people? Who manufactured the life-sized likenesses, laminated these depictions on cardboard cut-outs? Is this dirigible a stage, a movie set, a prop in some giant production? Melissa glanced at the cut-outs as she moved past each one, checking their faces. Perhaps their identities (she recognized none so far) were some clue as to their purpose. Simulataneously, she was aware of the "soundtrack," apparently a loop of muffled crowd noise, indistinct converation, occasional laughter, glasses tinkling on a metal tray, voices rising and falling, against the general hum of the airship. Meanwhile, Melissa was disappointed with the faces she examined; they seemed patently unreal, the faces of models or actors—there was an artificial homogenized quality about their expressions, a performative aspect to their postures, a clichéd sameness to their clothing (in other words, costuming), such that each person appearing as a cardboard cut-out might have first appeared in a magazine advertisement, and then been reduplicated, Photoshopped, touched up and pasted onto a large piece of cardboard. For example, the commercially ideologically archetypal Hetero-couple and child, their contemporaneity and modernity proclaimed by inclusion of an Asian woman as wife or mother figure, leaning appreciatively with family smile toward the white male, while the male in pale (possibly pink in the original, in this lighting uncertain) polo shirt, grinning as he leaned over to give the small girl a balloon—small girl of indistinct features, dark curls obscuring her face, smiling, reaching upward for the balloon—unaccountably, the fabricators of these cardboard people had attached an actual helium-filled balloon to the "father's" outstretched hand—the balloon on its distended string moved slightly, as if reluctantly. While all the scattered crowd of figures were patently flat, shiny reproductions of images of recognizable types, healthy happy models or actors used in commercial advertisement, Melissa noticed small touches given to a few of them, as if to indicate their previous (or possible future) existence in some plane of 3-D reality. One (white) man in a blue business suit sported an actual Goodwill-special necktie furled about his buttoned-up neck. A thick-set black woman in a bulbous hat and lace veil, possibly sorrowful gaze (eyes hidden in shadow), balanced on her arm a physical bouquet of white roses, which the shipboard air conditioning had wilted, so most of the white petals lay in a pile on the carpet. Melissa felt a surprise of recognition, instantly disappointed. One group of figures in the long foyer was the Rolling Stones. This depiction of them was apparently taken when they were middle-aged (generations ago), dressed for the stage. Mick Jagger moved ahead of the rest in profile, grinning obliviously. Keith Richards, smirking under a bandana tied about his forehead, hair akimbo, held his right hand as if ready to balance an electronic cigarette—and indeed, there was such a device, or part of one, a small black plastic box to hold batteries, attached to the backside of his fingers—but no cigarette was visible—no smoke, electronic or otherwise— was emitted from the device. NO SMOKING ABOARD SHIP: the fabricators remained cognizant of this fact. Not even cardboard cut-outs of the fake Rolling Stones were allowed to break ship's rules.

The long bank of windows on the promenade suddenly darkened. Her eyes adjusting to the yellowish interior lighting, she felt the ship shudder. They may have entered a cloud bank, the low pressure front before a storm. The ship swayed gently, and she wondered if she went to the promenade and looked down, whether she'd be able to see the sea. Perhaps clouds were lapping the hull of the ship, streaming past the windows in tendrils, fleetingly illuminated by the ship's lights.

Which reminded her, she must find out who was flying the ship. Where was this phantom voyager headed, and why?

Directly in front of her, a cardboard figure of Santa Claus, proffering a cardboard Coca-Cola. Even in the dim illumination, the colors of the face looked too pink, too yellow—a poor reproduction of halftone dots of four-color separation—so the ruddy face appeared as it was, cut-out paper. A poor reproduction. But on the proffered Coke bottle, a note was taped. "Mel," said the scrawl. She already knew what it said (it occurred to her she'd dreamed this dream in the past, and that, therefore, she should be aware of so much more right now than she was), when one of the cardboard figures in the foyer moved. Startled, Melissa jumped.

Cardboard figures don't move! Her stomach flip-flopped, unrelated to the lightning that flashed in the storm outside, unrelated to the great thunderclaps that followed. Note folded in hand, she sprinted past multiple immobile figures, knocking a couple aside—but (lights flickering, rain cascading on distant windows) when she arrived where she was certain she'd seen one of the figures turn and move or wave at her, she saw only a cardboard figure fallen on the carpet. It had been knocked over by the motion of the ship. Melissa looked about. Or? Had someone knocked it over? A glance told her that the figure was a female, dressed in leather flying jacket, pilot's goggles on a leather cap—it was a depiction of herself . . . But when she examined the face, she thought it did not look like her. Was this supposed to represent her? If so, she was disappointed in this generic representation. Some broad-shouldered girl with girlish curls. If she was going to have the same dream repeatedly, did it have to be this kind of dull dream, where she already knew what the secret message (supposedly) of the note was going to say? If she bothered to read it? With lightning flashing, the storm buffeting the dream's airship as it floated solo over the night ocean? She might as well awaken, face the morning—

wherever that was going to be—in Paris on a rainy Thursday, or Mexico City, under a sky threatening to rain, or Los Angeles, where it never rained . . .

Yes, Swirling, or Mr. Alhambra, if that's what you prefer to be called, if you agree to meet my terms, at a place of your convenience, we can meet and I will exchange for MY FILES, the actual scientifically explained rationales behind each of the Dreams of Melissa Arana (for example, the contents of that note in Mel's hand) and what they signify to YOU. VERY IMPORTANT! Very, very IMPORTANT! To you, I must say!

Therefore, avoid any contact with all such false Ericka Llaneras who may try to contact you (who may actually be agents of the government, or just as bad, predatory freelancers from private industry) and send me immediately an eminent message professing your agreement to my terms and stating instructions on where to meet.

I look forward to our meeting.

Remember, I am the real one.

Sincerely,

Ericka Llanera
founder, East Los Angeles Balloon Club
editor, *Filth Saints/ Manifestos/ Ballons*

✿

Dear Mister Swirling Alhambra,

I am the real Ericka Llanera, the only one who will tell you the truth.

This is for real.

This is not one of those Nigerian emails suggesting that if you send them a cashier's check for a thousand dollars you will receive a rebate of a million dollars from HSBC bank accounts full of drug cartel money. This is not the false promises made by your city council members that they are not stealing you blind, taxing your sewer line and your parking meters, your water service, and investing it in their own multimillion-dollar pension plan. This is not a weird note from a random nut case pretending to be Arizona state patrol who seized life savings of many travelers who crossed the AZ border, erroneously found themselves at the mercy of asset forfeiture by state officers using moneys and properties seized from random peoples to pay officers' adminstrative expenses, barbecue needs, overtime trips to Marty's Marvelous Gun Show in Miami, of which you might recoup 5% for yourself if you become a paid informant. No.

You may have heard that Melissa Arana had a dream that not only purveyed messages for Mel personally, it revealed a prophetic message for the East Los Angeles Dirigible Air Transport Lines, and indeed, for all of Western Civilization (as well as Eastern Civilization). You may have heard that in her dream Melissa held in her hand a scrawled note that was almost the crack in storm clouds from which lightning emerges.

"Shit," Melissa said, "basically the fucking note was telling me (in the dream):

this is it:

everyone is dead . . . dirigible floats on over the seas empty . . . save yourself and the baby . . .

—Sergio"

☼

That was the dream, the gist of it, Melissa said (she knew she was pregnant by then, even while dreaming, of course—she had wanted to tell Sergio, but he guessed it: he said it came to him in the exact same dream). Frowning, she took the note to the lounge (lightning flashing against the far wall, casting shadows of rain like in an old black-and-white movie, and silhouettes of artificial plants, bird of paradise flowers, rain spattering hard against the promenade windows). Melissa sat on the couch . . . On the coffee table a book by Mari Sandoz, a ELADTL Jolina coffee cup . . . a scrap of paper with nothing written on it . . . a short stack of file folders . . . The long bank of windows on the promenade suddenly darkened. Her eyes adjusting to the yellowish interior lighting, she felt the ship shudder. They may have entered a cloud bank, the low pressure front before a storm. The ship swayed gently, and Melissa wondered if she went to the promenade and looked down, whether she'd be able to see the sea. Perhaps clouds already lapped the hull of the ship, streaming past the windows in tendrils, fleetingly illuminated by ship's lights.

Leaning on the chrome railing of the promenade, she took in the view. The ocean far below roiled furiously. As far as she could tell, the ship was on a port tack, the ocean crashing against green bluffs along a rocky wild coast visible along the northeast through the length of the promenade's windows. Cloud banks plowed onto coastal mountains, fulminating shadows, dissolving the rocky hard edges of the continent in gray mists, in swaths of drifting rain. Somewhere in the gray mist, it was probably rainy and dark, quiet fields, drippy orchards and misty highways and towns receiving a drizzle. Puddles in parking lots, a car going by on the highway, rock & roll blearing out the window, diminishing straight away. Pickup trucks, pallets piled against a wall, oleander bushes in a row, blue plastic port-a-potties stacked in a gravel turn out, orchards of avocado trees dripping in the wet. Directly below, in last light of afternoon, the sea churned blackly, rough, whipped by westerlies, scouring white water across the dark wracked surface. Swells rose into the wind far below; Melissa distinguished the spray coming off the lead edges of the wave, flung into the wind sheer—white foam whipsawing across veined dark waters.

Melissa recovered from this memory, which welled up suddenly from such a long time ago (so long it seemed like another lifetime), to find herself staring at the configuration of objects on the coffee table of her living room: a coffee cup, a crumpled receipt that vaguely resembled a note that nagged at her memory, and a novel, *Winter in the Blood* by James Welch.

Another afternoon with the last light of day burning orange against the wall of her apartment. She even unfolded the receipt for Tylenol to see if it did not contain some surreptitious message from her past, when everyone had still been alive. Ages ago, Sergio was killed in a work accident, though it was rumored that was just the story they told Melissa, as everyone knew how dangerous Sergio's solo reconnaissance and construction expeditions had been. She'd understood some hints to mean that conspiracy theorists supposed he'd been asssassinated, either by some faction of his own organization or by security forces posing as members of the organization. Either way, the organization had been erased, and any survivors who Mel saw by chance once in awhile, sometimes not for years, chose not to reveal their stories (as if they were ashamed, when in fact, they chose not to speak of the triumphs and subsequent disasters because those years of secret struggle were a secret dream shared—their youth, their hidden pride, held close by each one of the survivors to this day, something they'd never wave like a fist in anyone's face, because others who'd never been there—they'd never know how it was). Anyway, she couldn't remember the last time she'd bumped into someone associated with ELADATL . . . It was startling to find herself recalling that incident, the time when she awoke on the lost dirigible. She'd single-handedly saved a lost airship, saved the day. But who knew or cared now?

Melissa awoke, groggy, on the couch, wind lashing rain against her apartment window. A second glass of wine after work sometimes had that effect. Dirty water buffeted the windowpane, but it must've been the lightning that woke her. Thunder shook the apartment. Leaning on the chrome railing of the promenade, she took in the view. The ocean far below roiled furiously ... crashing against green bluffs along a rocky wild coast visible along the northeast through banked plateglass windows ... Cloud banks plowed onto the mountains, a trifecta of shadows, dissolving rocky hard edges of the continent in gray mists, in swaths of drifting rain. The continent itself falling away into the deeps.

Oh hell. On the coffee table, empty wine glass, a book someone had given her (Leslie Marmon Silko... she couldn't see it clearly without her glasses), and a tablet she'd been using to do some calculations. And a tablet—she knew if she turned it on she might find a note from her daughter. Melissa had dreamed that same dream, from so long ago [she told this directly to me the last time I saw her, Scouts honor! I will tell you all about it!], and this is what she dreamed:

Leaning on the chrome railing of the promenade, she took in the view. The ocean far below roiled furiously, crashing against a rocky wild coast visible along the northeast through rainswept plateglass windows ... Cloud banks plowed onto the greeny mountains, a trifecta of shadows, dissolving rocky hard edges of the continent in gray mists, in swaths of drifting rain. The continent itself fell away into deep black waters, ridges of foam and white froth scoured and scattered across the surface like scratches blasted and etched into black ice.

Melissa had checked the automatic pilot, radioed in the heading and position, negotiated with red-headed dispatcher Tania Champion to get a rescue ship into the air and headed to meet her out over the ocean, so they could perform a very dangerous and dicy, risk-fraught mid-air boarding by an emergency crew. Once she received confirmation for the coordinates, the ships would attempt to maneuver alongside each other and attach lines, the rescue crew would then attempt to rappel across in the windy morning light. Meanwhile, night was falling, and Melissa's duty would be to keep watch over the controls, maintaining uniform direction and speed so that the ship could be met and salvaged. She dreamed that she singlehandedly saved the airship that decades ago had been lost without a trace.

As she manned the rain-lashed, wind-buffeted control room alone, it came to her in the dream that Sergio was also there/not there. In one way Sergio was with her, with her and her pregnancy that she had decided she must tell him about, and in another way, Sergio was not with her—she was absolutely alone (with the new person, dreaming inside her)—and there was no way to tell him. It came to her (the way understanding can come to you in a dream) that Sergio was probably on the other side of a living membrane of time, in a world slightly different, or a world exactly like this one, intersecting with this reality somehow. She could feel him nearby. He was, somehow, almost here with her. After all, wasn't that how he was sending her messages, little notes like whispers in the very air, in spite of the fact that she'd inspected the ship from bow to stern, and found it empty? Except, once in awhile, when she passed by the lounge and glanced at the couch and the coffee table, the book on the table might be removed or replaced with another title, the coffee cup might be moved or filled or emptied, and a note addressed to her might have been scrawled and left thereabouts. She'd left her own notes inserted in the book, which later disappeared, or turned blank, or were answered by notes that were apparently, impossibly, written days or hours earlier. The times were always off. Notes told her to meet on days or hours that had passed, even (or especially) the notes she now expected to receive later. Somehow there was interference, somehow they were not allowed to meet. Somehow their worlds did not overlap perfectly. Somehow the membrane of dreams—if that's what this was—did not align exactly. All this came to her with a certainty, as certainties come to you in dreams.

Melissa believed that Sergio must have realized this, come

to the same certainty, riding high over the surface of the rainy Pacific in his own lost airship, in his own solitary stormy night. She was comforted by this thought, feeling as if even though they were separated by dimensions of time, in different realities, they were together in this dream, together over a black ocean under a black sky of clouds, together in the same rainy night, almost the same person. A calmness came over her, a feeling she was beloved inside and out, convincing her for the moment. That Sergio was experiencing everything she was going through (though she understood he would be doing it with a cup of coffee, sometimes hot, sometimes cold, in one hand), that both of them were simultaneously together, and alone, looking south across a vast windswept ocean at night.

"What bullshit! What a bunch of horseshit!" Yes, I know exactly what you are thinking! But this is the real dream this time! I am telling you this message for real. I have severely hard proofs in several ways. I have pictures and stuff. You must believe this, I am telling you, your own life, the future possible history of East L.A. Dirigible Air Transport Lines (the existence of ELADATL and all it stands for) and the lives of the leadership, not to mention the severely alternate future of the world, depends on this.

Do not believe the fake dreams of the secret police. Those dreams are severely not right.

I come to you with some true kinds of facts and factorinos. Don't fall for the fake dreams of fake revolutionaries disguised as secret police.

Your life depends on it. You heard that they are coming for you; they're gonna wipe the slate clean. If they get their way, no one's gonna ever hear about ELADATL or all those people or you and your leadership or anything you tried to accomplish. It'll be like you and the whole history ELADATL never existed. But we can change that. Come on, I am telling you for real. This is the real dream.

You tell me where to meet, where we can exchange the files, I will tell you all I know and more.

Bring it. I look forward to hearing from you asap at the address below. (If you happen to come by and the neighbor's big black dog tries to bite you, kick him right in the face.)

Your friend,

Ericka Llanera
President, East L.A. Balloon Club
1524 Helen Dr. (back house)
L.A., CA 90063

BALL LIGHTNING AND THE GENERAL HOSPITAL

Sure, we were in charge of the ELADATL office, where we left the ghosts of electricity howling in the bones of her face in charge, instructed under all circumstances to tell collection agencies "no one is here by that name," it didn't matter who they were calling for. Not Swirling #1, not Swirling #2, not Jose Lopez Feliu, not Sergio, not Likki Renteria, not anybody. Certainly not me!—Augustina Sandate (AKA Tina Lerma). Collection agents tried different tactics to try to get a line on who might be in, but we were the only ones ever around. Then they tried to find out who we were, pulling names off lists they got from who knows where, but they asked for "Melissa" instead of Mel, or "Augustina Andate" instead of Tina, so we told them there was nobody here by that name either. My name is Tina, and me and Mel are all that's left in the head office of an organization that once employed 3,600. ELADATL (employee-owned), once operated passenger and freight dirigible lines throughout the Pacific Rim, across Gran

Apacheria, from outliers in Cuzco, Baja, California, Yuma AZ, Winnemucca and Elko NV, Los Mochis, Durango, and Torreon, Mexico, with interconnections to Ho Chi Minh City, Shanghai, Bangor, Bangkok, Changmai, Osaka, as well as the only service remaining (at one point) to the Miami sea towers of sunken Florida, sticking up out of the tepid waters of the Atlantic where it merges with the Gulf of Mexico. Posters collecting dust around the office now advertise our original inter-urban runs from Pacoima to Elysian Park, from the hills of El Sereno to the hills of Tijuana. But that was all over, apparently, by the time Mel and I got a clue and decided we'd better find out what was going on.

Finally, somebody called who didn't bother asking for anyone specific, they just did some kind of breathing exercise followed by screaming threats of a violent sexual nature. Kind of creepy, I admit. That's the kind of world we live in, isn't it? We weren't really scared, per se (that ain't Mel's style), but it's the kind of thing that will linger in the back of your mind and encourage certain thoughts once in awhile. So Mel or I checked the street out front through the blinds every time we closed up the office. We left Snoopy's picture (our spiritual mascot—see illustration #5 below — the black and white chihuahua that Jose and Swirling had photographed on the 4th Street Bridge early in the 21st century) watching protectively over the empty offices, his Colima dog spirit barking from the corner of the chief executive's desk, so to speak, even though Enrique Pico hadn't been to this branch in years. To think that our director Enrique Pico's grand vision of lighter-than-air titanium airship lines could have united the world and rejuvenated the ruins of self-immolated capitalism on a socialistic footing! It almost worked! What the hell happened?

Mel or I cracked the back door as we held our breath against a ferocious blast of super-heated air, peered out and then scooted to the car that had baked all day against the wall of the building (almost leaving its shadow embedded in the stucco, like after an atomic blast). We cranked the starter and went roaring across the empty parking lot at 30–40 mph like a dust devil. The hot wind blasting down off the eroded hillside covered a thicket of dried thistles in the same yellow dust we tried to shift off the windshield, flicking on the windshield wipers with a dry scraping and clicking (1967 Chevy Caprice station wagon, black paint oxidized into bald bronze patches) as the car pounded and slammed across the eroded ruts of the parking lot, raising a dust cloud that drifted on the air like a flag of yellowish dirt against a fulvous sky.

✿

This all happened after Los Angeles had been destroyed by Death Rays from Hair Balls from Outer Space (not the scientific or official name); we'd seen it on TV in black-and-white reruns. That was the official explanation given by some fascist "experts" from Silicon Valley (the previously unknown group, Radion), sponsored by several federal agencies. They played clips and videos over and over showing City Hall blasted to pieces by Death Rays, freeway overpasses collapsing, cars and semi trucks burning on Highway 15, etc. White guys with automatic rifles were driving around in Chevy Camaro convertibles, protecting white people from Mexican cartels and tamale vendors, firing at anything suspicious, changing high-capacity magazines and banana clips without even glancing down or ever taking off those Rayban sunglasses. They assured us we were under attack from Space Devils, so-called, who could easily disguise themselves behind Muslim veils or ancient customs of non-Western peoples, who were out to destroy God's Green Earth, so it was up to them "to protect and to serve," "to keep order," and they further assured us that the destruction raining down from the skies had absolutely nothing to do with secret government projects or corporations with their heads up their asses. The plan was to fix everything with trillions of dollars of spending (it was said) on rockets, more giant rockets than you could even imagine that they would fix in orbit over the earth, vast humongous flexible arrays of solar refractors gracefully orbiting the planet like immense nanotechnological yoyos, and some nukes to rain down on enemies and terrorists and stuff, all of it coordinated from secret underground bunkers in the Utah desert and of course the Internet. Experts and spokespersonifiers assured us that what we were witnessing "with our very eyes" was not climate change-induced: the wildfires burning up what was left of the trees, firestorms scorching the West and the South and Southeast, and Florida, so fucked up it was just a vague memory of grasses and clumps of foliage still above water, with geysers of flame from wells polluted by toxic frick-fracking fluids vomiting fireballs hundreds of feet into the air, from the desert to the sea, while noxious fumes billowed inland from dense carpets of algal scum off several dying oceans. This was all due to Hair Balls from Outer Space (said the voice of our dreams, repeating what we were told), which were blasting the USA and Europeans with Death Rays. I didn't ever actually see these Death Rays myself, and Mel didn't either (she said), nor did I ever meet anyone who said they did. But of course, by this time, we all had urgent business to take care of in order to survive.

I still remembered the good old days with nostalgia, you know, when the Orange Trash Gyre spun in the sky and sucked up the entire town of Joshua Tree and the Noah Puri-foy National Monument and spit it out, hurled it in a million pieces of debris upon the Southland in a Swath of Terror from Tujunga to Temecula. Plus, once established, the Orange Gyre split into two and "stabilized"— twin gyres spinning over the city in an atmosphere that varied from fulvous orange to bilious gray to dense black as each gyre disgorged utility trucks, microwave towers disguised as fake trees, water heaters, oil pipelines, I-beams, 200-ton granite boulders, and miscellaneous garbage and dead dogs or partial corpses in a rain of filth and whatnot, flinging them down upon the landscape (if you could still call it that) of Southern California.

I remembered the days of the old trash gyres with nostalgia, because it was nicer than the current era of the Death Rays. Compared to now, that was the easy life.

✿

"Sergio told me that his wife left him. I'm not sure why he tells me things like that. We were trying to track the Agnes Smedley before it disappeared into Gyre #2."

"I heard about that. I don't remember who told me."

"I told you."

"Maybe. Wait. What, Mel?"

"You didn't hear what I told you? You must listen to what I say. Goddamn it! What do I gotta do? Record a podcast?"

"I listen to your every word, Mel."

"Supposedly that's why Sergio isn't around these days, operations he's in charge of shut down, covert dirigible production and repair ain't happenin'."

"That's not good."

"You're tellin' me. In a nutshell."

"Why?"

"See. I told you already."

"You know, it's kind of hard to drive because of the toxic fumes."

"Of course. I know. I know you're a good driver. You could drive in your sleep. Cars, dirigible airships, bikes, motorcycles, I know it."

"You wanna hear what I dreamed about last night?"

"Of course I do. But help me watch out for that kid on the bike. He's riding erratic. He shouldn't be out here breathing the atmosphere, what are his parents thinking?"

"It was the mouth of a big river, with a big bridge, as big as the Vincent Thomas bridge in San Pedro, not as high but even longer. I was driving a yellow 1963 Chevrolet El Camino, classic car, you know, vintage yellow. That puppy was parked out in the parking lot waiting for me. I had stopped at this falafel joint for some lunch."

"Chevy El Camino? That's a pickup truck?"

"Yeah. Sort of like a car forced to become a truck."

"Got it."

"It wasn't cherried out or anything. But it was nice. Someone had worked on it."

"Okay. So you ate a falafel in your dream?"

"Apparently."

"How was it?"

"I don't remember. All right, I guess. I don't recall details. Anyway, I was looking forward to driving along the coast in this cool ride. It was a beautiful day like in the old days."

"Ow! Okay."

"But the girl was taking so long to give me my bill. She was standing there at the tablet or register or whatever, looking around, like she needed help. I was trying to be patient, you know, checking my phone for messages. Looking out across the parking lot at the river and that big bridge shining in the sunshine. But that girl was taking so long that the light actually started to change. Clouds or smoke or something blew in off the ocean and the girl—with her confused face—still didn't say how much I owed on the bill. Finally I said, 'Hey, can I have my bill? I gotta go.' Still, she wouldn't answer. She was embarrassed and wouldn't admit that she didn't know what she was doing. She looked over at a co-worker, who told me, 'We'll be right with you. Something's going on with the system. It's not going through.' "

"Yeah, I remember that used to happen before the systems

shut down for good and they told us the money had all been lost. 'Your money has been lost.' That's it. All there was too it. The system went down and sorry, there was no backup and your money has been lost. Lost? Lost where? Nowhere. Just lost."

"Finally I said, 'Look, are you gonna charge me? I gotta go. It's getting dark outside.' 'Sorry,' they told me, 'sorry, it'll probably just take a minute more, if you can wait.' But I already felt like I had waited for hours. And it seemed as if I had, because it was starting to get dark outside, like twilight. So I just went outside fully intending to get in my car and go. The El Camino was there, neat and yellow and pretty under a street lamp in the parking lot. But I didn't have my keys. So I panicked and ran back inside. 'Have you seen my keys?' I asked them. 'No,' they said, shaking their heads like dummies. They were still sort of leaning together, trying to figure out how to open the till or calculate my bill without the system. I went into the restroom and my keys were there by the sink, so I grabbed them and went back outside. But this time the El Camino was gone! There was a front and back door to the place, so I went out the front and checked there, and the parking lot was empty, and I went out the back, just in case I'd misremembered somehow, but no, the spot under the streetlamp in back was vacant too, the pretty yellow pickup truck was gone. Somebody had stolen my pretty yellow pickup! Goddamn it!"

"Goddamn it. I hate when that happens! Even in a dream."

"Yeah. I was screwed. I wasn't going anywhere. Night had fallen by that time."

"All because of that girl! She couldn't just write up the bill!"

"No! Because who does that anymore? Write up something on paper?"

"Yeah. Right?"

"Yeah. Damn it! Nobody writes anything by hand anymore except us."

"Damn girl!"

"Damn her! I'll never eat at that place ever again."

"Right? Because it was a dream."

"Yeah. Lucky for us, we are like Cubans."

"Cubanos? What are you saying?"

"We're like Cubanos because we got our faithful classic, Chevy Caprice wagon." [Pats the dashboard. Dust rises. Laughter.]

Mel turned left on Huntington, up to Eastern, south toward the freeway, El Sereno glowing like the city was on fire. That's just how it is (when it's not worse), everybody driving with their lights on even if it doesn't help much to cut the blowing clouds of particulate and debris, pedestrians wearing face masks and head wraps, hunched over against it like a desert sandstorm, now there's a haboob for you, everything glowing orange from sunlight refracted through carbon dioxide, they say, and the wind tearing through the streets. Mel and I have never witnessed a major debris landfall, nothing crashed down on us, we've just seen the aftermath, a telephone pole in an intersection, people driving around it, shipping container on top of a store, a billboard on top of parked cars. Sometimes you hear an explosion or booming—what is that, you know? Day or night, the streets full of flying objects, trash, litter, papers, plastic containers, sticks, leaves, hazards. Carry safety goggles. You don't want an eye infection, lose your sight like my aunt. Even if she did regain partial sight, at least in one eye, like maybe after a year. And the whole deal gave her a better relationship with my cousins who she always treated outrageously, after all. My cousin Lucy said about that, live long enough, you may change your attitude. You never can tell, might suddenly clear up, turn into one of your typical outstanding sunny Southern California days till the winds shift back.

We wended our way forward, the station wagon like a boat parting the curtains of dirty air, as atmospheres pattered a dry rain atop the car, the ancient rain trying to peel off our heavy-duty Rustoleum-special paint job. Spare parts piled in the back, the backseat filled with water jugs and cartons of East L.A. Balloon Club paperwork that Swirling had told us to guard with our lives, but, sorry, as it happens, when we pulled over outside the South Gate Station—the mooring mast appearing and disappearing like an abbreviated Eiffel Tower in the smoke, dust, and debris—Mel's door caught on the wind, which jerked it open and sucked out a stack of folders. Papers and photos of Ericka Llanera flew up into the air over the car, one slapped me on the head before it slipped into the wind, all those pages of secret histories made a few flapping noises, then zip-zip-zip . . . I don't know what was in those files, but away they went, sucked up inside the dirty sky to become one with the Trash Atmosphere. Some could have floated down the L.A. River, but I don't know if there was any water down there or just a mess of plastic, I couldn't see. Mel slammed the car door shut and we rushed to the station door. Mel held the door for me, and the wind slammed it shut behind me. I swallowed the dirt in my mouth.

Inside, people sat at tables drinking coffee from the coffee counter in the corner. The big window threw a yellow light into the room. The window glass had been replaced, as was common nowadays, with acrylic so scoured by sand and particulate that traffic on the distant street (beyond the unpaved parking lot) flowed by in shapes and blobs. The word OFFIC (backwards) could be partially discerned above the apparently homeless old guy who sat lifting a cup, to his face hidden behind the gray locks curling out of his jacket hood. His luggage, several grease-soaked canvas mail bags, was stacked behind him. In another corner several families waited in the plastic chairs, small children playing, the adults napping. The television mounted above the coffee counter was either off or broken. The mooring mast above the station channeled vibrations of the wind to us, everything resonated audibly or inaudibly, more obviously or less obviously. Could've been nerves too. The waiting room was full of people, but it wasn't clear if they were in transit with a long wait ahead and weary from the morning commute or just waiting inside out of the wind. Next to the ticket counter, the door (Gate 1) to the passenger boarding bridge tapped and creaked with changes in pressure.

"If you told me that guy was a statue, I'd believe you," Mel said.

"If you told me that was Swirling Alhambra, I'd believe you," I said.

"Maybe this is where our boss disappeared to," she said. "Retired, looks like."

"Nobody's behind the ticket counter."

"Figures, " Mel tsked. Annoyed, she rapped sharply on the window. She waited a moment—no sign of life, rapped again. "This is bullshit," she said, leaning forward to peer into the ticket office. "Do we have to report this?"

I walked over to the door to the office and opened it. "It's not locked," I said.

"You selling tickets today? Because I'm not," Mel replied.

We shut the door behind us; the office was neat enough. Nothing looked out of place. A photograph of our chief hung above the desk, Enrique Pico, the frame engraved with the famous declaration, "2009, end of the automotive era! Toward the gaseous and airy future!" A shiny ceramic replica of the ELADATL mascot, Snoopy the black-and-white chihuahua, perched on a corner of the desk. All as it should be. So where was the clerk, and Miky the office manager? We pushed through the back door of the office into the garage. Music was playing.

The place was jammed, people were camped out, plastic tarps and tents filled the big garage like stalls in a marketplace, food truck on the far side blocking the wind somewhat at the open door. Mel and I stepped out next to two long tables set up with buffet-style serving pans, where Ray Palafox (Ray, of all people!), pudgy rock and roller Ray, curly haired boy toy in his Guns & Roses T-shirt, bleary-eyed and pale and hygiene-free, not up before 2 p.m., Ray? Serving food in a South Gate garage? I was astonished at the sight of Ray in his motorcycle jacket as always, not because the the garage was crammed full of—

"Hey, Tina! Mel! Welcome to South Gate station!" Miky crowed.

"Miky!" Mel said, "Nobody's manning the ticket counter!"

"Can't fly till this weather lets up anyway. Plus, Food not Bombs!"

"Food not Bombs," Mel muttered.

Miky explained Food Not Bombs was showing *Salt of the Earth* and Buster Keaton's *Steamboat Bill* over and over for refugees from the most recent firestorm. Ever since the government only recognized corporations as citizens and stopped helping actual people, refugees jammed the roads. Food Not Bombs had set up the vegetarian buffet for people who hadn't had hot food in days, Jose Uriarte brought in his taco truck and set out the salsa, and even Ray Palafox mobilized Los Quemados to blast out cumbias or whatever they call it in a free concert and got his band members and their entourage to come out to assist refugees who'd lost their houses and everything. I made sure to step over and tell Ray I thought it was great, what he was doing; he shrugged, saying he had family himself in the burn. He probably remembered me from Self-Help Graphics or somewhere. Ray thanked me in return for getting ELADATL to shelter the people like this. I didn't tell him it was all Miky's idea. We could see people were busy, so we headed for the door—but we didn't get out of there in time, because Miky asked if we'd take boxes of food and clothing to the South El Monte ELADATL station, which had also opened up to shelter fire refugees. "Sure thing, " Mel grumbled.

"Make sure to keep a box of avocados for yourselves," Miky told us as he and his guys loaded crates and boxes on top of the junk in the back of our station wagon. "We got way too many and they're all soft. They'll go bad before anybody can use 'em," he said, big hair whipping in his face.

Mel jumped into the driver's seat, in a rush to get out before they thought up other stuff for us to do. She pressed a heavy foot on the gas, generating a wheezy roar as she turned the big Chevy toward the street. I looked back at Miky standing in the unpaved parking area with his hands in the pockets of a jacket that looked too small on him, a cloud of dust and sand blowing like a whirlwind.

South El Monte ELADATL was full of people too, but only a few had tickets for their ride, it looked like. We didn't check. It was usually like that anyway, most public spaces from libraries to post office lobbies, from train stations to restrooms in neighborhood parks, you would meet people living in or around the facilities because where else could they go? Then there were those anarchists like Ray Palafox or Miky (whatever he was), who saw Food Not Bombs, or the South El Monte Anarchist Posse (SEMAP), or the Community Service Organization, or other church and neighborhood factions, as the necessary and best thing, if people were in need. "What were you gonna do?" I could hear Miky asking Mel, if she had raised any objection. "What do you think we're gonna do? Turn a blind eye till we finally go blind altogether?" Mel knew better than to bug Miky about how he ran his station. She wasn't going to run it, was she?

"Let's see if SEMAP provides better food than the rockeros," I said.

They did. Food Not Bombs was all about ladling out vegan garbanzo beans in fake Indian sauce, pilaf and old pita bread and whatnot. It was all right (It was healthy! I'd made sure to sneak a taste, get a whiff of spices. We saved our appetites.) The SEMAP kids were a spin-off of a community organization of older activists; the new generation taking a new bent. A Kumeyaay basket maker I knew, Luisa, told us where to put the donations. "You haven't eaten yet, have you?" Luisa asked. I got a whiff of something porky that sizzled. SEMAP had help from the family that ran Tacos Periban, whose carnitas can't be beat. I mean, surtido, odd bits and pieces, with cuero, skin, mixed in! Or buche! Pig esophagus! Tacos Periban, they got it! We unloaded boxes of clothes and food, stacking them where indicated—beside the rest, then Mel and I were handed paper plates of tiny tacos heaped with onions, cilantro, lime, and three kinds of salsa, which we wolfed down on the spot. We got out of there quick, which Mel wanted. She strode out from under a torn, flapping blue awning, and we jammed. I did take a box of mostly half-smashed overripe avocados to toss on the back seat. Mel had guzzled a beer with her tacos, so I'm sure she felt better. "Guacamole express, my ass," Mel said, turning west.

✿

It was like that at City of Commerce, Covina, Azusa, and Eagle Rock stations when we checked in, but it was in East L.A. (where it had all started) that the reality of our situation was revealed. The City Terrace station was dark behind locked chainlink gates, atop a hill with a view of the San Gabriel mountains on those thousand-to-one clear days, except that today howling winds and dust clouds whipped plastic bags and trash against the fencing. As we stood in front of the station wagon discussing what to do next, plastic bags caught high in the barbed wire of the abandoned Sybil Brand County Jail, flapped like the pennants of a castle. City Terrace ELADATL had been closed for a while, judging from the trash, and a map and instructions wired to the gate telling riders to take a Metro bus to the El Sereno station.

Mel drove cautiously and didn't rush. Limited visibility meant she had to beware of stalled cars or debris in the road. Other drivers, though, barreled around us at high speed.

She drove Eastern (north) to Valley Boulevard, (west) to Soto, and north on Soto to the old viaduct that had once been a Red Line train station, only to discover the Mission Road ELADATL was also closed and locked. The shutters were pulled down over the ticket windows, in spite of the big pink mural on the wall that read TICKETS AVAILABLE 24 HOURS (illustrated with portraits of diverse satisfied customers). Mel banged on the shutter. "What the hell!" she yelled. We heard a noise from inside so Mel banged some more, and I kicked the front door for good measure. We walked around the side, where squatters peeked around the corner at us, wondering why we were making a fuss.

Mel said, "We want to buy tickets."

"Tickets?" one guy said.

"Boletos ELADATL," Mel said.

"No tickets these days," another guy said. A third guy hung back, not speaking. I felt there were probably more folks inside waiting to hear the outcome of this conversation.

"How long has the station been closed down?" Mel asked.

"I been here all month at least," the first said. "Nobody came in that time."

"Nobody bothered us," the other guy said. "We're getting out of the weather."

"All right," Mel said.

"You want to look inside?" he asked. "It's not too messy. The back door was already open when I got here."

"That's all right," I said. I told Mel, "We gotta get to the hospital."

"You guys all right?" the second guy said, "we got basic first aid."

"No, nothing like that," Mel said.

"There's an office there, one of the main offices as a matter of fact," I said. "They'll be able to tell us why these lines are closed down and what's going to happen to this station."

You could almost see County General Hospital from the station, or you might have been able to see it on a clear day, in other words NEVER. Basically we couldn't see anything, though, not even the mooring mast atop the station. We located our car by memory and dove inside. The wind practically slammed the doors shut after us. But if, if the atmosphere was somehow a different, translucent blue atmosphere, even an aquamarine hue (activated perhaps by the High Low Radiance Corridor over Lincoln Heights), and you could see through it, then you could have seen "County" (as they used to call it) wth its gray massif face of 1932 concrete (empty since 2008), ball lightning crackling and popping snakelike around its monumental facade on the coldest winter nights.

Like everything else County General Hospital was privatized in the 21st century, pillaged, and then left to fall into disrepair. Investors moved in, profited, and moved on. In recent years developers finally implemented county supervisor Hilda Solis's plan for homeless housing and retail on unused floors, while Enrique Pico pulled some strings and secured the top, 20th floor for a dirigible docking tower, cargo, and passenger station. The central location near downtown Los Angeles, its connection to surface transport via tunnels beneath the streets dating back to 1932, elevators to the 19th floor, and plenty of available office space made County the perfect operations hub for ELADATL administration.

It was only a few blocks away, obscured by the pall of ash and smoke. This required Mel to drive southwest down Mission past the ragged palm trees of Lincoln Park that leaned through sibilant dust and swirling particulate like giant blown-out dandelions. On the far side of the park, beyond the pall, I knew Valley Boulevard was lined with the campers, vans, and station wagons of people living adjacent to the park and using the rec center when they could for showers and water.

"This is where I got my driver's license," I said as we passed the former DMV offices. "I drove around the block."

Mel grunted, nodding.

"Oscar Zeta Acosta had an apartment in this old complex here, so they said," I noted. "This taco stand on the corner, Manny's El Loco, used to have a Buffalo Burrito supposedly named after him."

Plastic bags, or something resembling plastic bags, buoyed with air as if alive, floated across the road like big jellyfish.

Mel frowned, squinting as she stopped at the intersection of Valley and Mission. Manny's was gone, of course; she squinted up at the yellow sign that said "Chano's Burritos," shrugged and tooled through the intersection, up the overpass over the Union Pacific tracks. We could've been flying an airship through cloudbanks, visibility was so poor.

Mel turned into an alley off Mission and parked behind a former hotel that had been converted into apartments for physicians doing their residencies at the USC medical complex attached to the former County Hospital building.

"You want to hear something crazy?" Mel asked, using her ID card to get us in the backdoor.

"Does this question have a right answer?" I asked. Mel ignored me and went on a long spiel about how ELADATL was doomed unless she got Sergio to take over the leadership. "He's the only one who can do it," she insisted as we took the elevator down to the underground tunnels. (We could have hurried up the curvilinear expanse of concrete steps to the wide brass double doors in front of the building, but why go with the flow, why be like everybody else when you've got Mel?) "He's the only one, you know it," she was saying, "he's got the experience and the skills, he's the only one who can build an airship literally from the ground up, from scratch, and though he's not the best pilot, we got pilots galore, even you and I can work ground crew, we need strategists and somebody with a vision," Mel said. "If only his life wasn't all fucked up, his wife and kid rejected him, everybody thinks he's a loser . . ." Mel went on and on about Sergio, about how people might think he was a loser but he was actually the secret key to a new deal. "He does have ideas," I agreed. "For a long time ELADATL has been falling apart due to those factions, the maximalists and the minimalists, whatever you wanna call 'em," Mel said as we strode down long echoey concrete tunnels with glaring lights on the white-tiled walls—as construction workers passed us hauling materiel on carts and quads, and some cops passed us driving a golf cart with a prisoner handcuffed beside them, and doctors or med personnel in blue scrubs or white coats strolled by.

"Bolsheviks and Mensheviks," I snickered. "Voluntarists versus the gradualists or objectivists," Mel suggested, "insurrectionists and militarists versus mass organizers," nodding, describing how (in her estimation) Sergio was the one to break the deadlock that was otherwise going to break ELADATL, who had the necessary experience and could get backing from key players of the various factions to rejuvenate the organization—otherwise, Mel said, "Look, it's already dead." I wasn't thinking about ELADATL, though, I was wondering, Is this how we live our lives? This is it? Rushing on, going forward like it's all just gonna turn out okay in the end?

"I know this sounds crazy," she said. In the echoey tunnel her phrase clicked or clacked like a metaphor.

"We'll go up to the offices and put it to Enrique Pico himself!" I suggested. "What about that guy? What side will he come down on?"

"They say he doesn't take sides, but we can find out."

We walked out into the great lobby, which was unfortunately not packed with lines of people waiting to purchase tickets for ELADATL flights; instead, there were only a few people standing around the ticket windows. Most windows at the counter were closed, and the whole lobby was full of smoke and haze, probably seeping down through the high windows, dust in the holy rays of transportation light. The homeless crowd camped along one wall of the lobby took it easy, sitting or chatting quietly (some with dogs), mostly obeying the No Smoking signs. Mel kept talking as we crossed the lobby, but there was a commotion, a shriek and a yell, somebody shoved her from behind and sent her staggering forward. A paunchy little bear of a man snarled and threw one, two punches at a big white guy's bald head, knocking him against Mel. She turned to sidestep them both. The bald guy raised his fists to block punches, face reddened from blows.

"Hey!" I yowled. It was all I could think to do. "Hey!"

Mel shoved the short man, aggressor, hard from the side, knocking him off balance. "Knock it off!" Mel yelled. "Stop it! Stop it now!"

The grizzly man, thick gnarled face wine-dark with outrage (and maybe wine), cocked his arm back to throw a punch as he tried to regain his balance, but that took enough time (a second or two) for him to size up his opposition, the big bald guy and two women standing in front of him—Mel especially, authority arcing not only through her voice but also her stance and her eyes, and, as she stepped forward, he stepped back. Mel jabbed two fingers toward the middle of his chest, and the stocky man looked at them.

"Take it outside! Take your beef outside!" Mel ordered, knowing nothing would or could happen outside. The man lowered his gaze to the floor, mouth settling into a pout. His energy left him, and rays from the windows threw his face in shadow.

Mel turned to the big white man behind her, who staunched a nosebleed with the palm of his hand. "Lemme see," Mel said to him, brushing his hand away. Blood dripped into his mouth.

Mel pushed his chin back with her thumb, looking at his face, left side, right side. "Does it feel broken?" she asked.

"Nah," he said, his breath slowing raggedly to normal.

"You okay?" Mel asked.

"I'm okay," the man assented. He wiped blood off his mouth on his sleeve.

"Whew!" Mel said, "Okay."

She patted the man's arm. We walked to the far corner of the lobby, and Mel did her card trick, letting us in through an unmarked side door. We took a service elevator to the 19th floor. The elevator doors sighed open. The 19th floor was quiet. We walked down to the end of the corridor to the door that said EAST LOS ANGELES DIRIGIBLE AIR TRANSPORT LINES. It was locked.

We got inside, anyway, just a minute later (Mel's card again). It was a two-office suite, the traditional secretary's front desk and beyond that a big office with a conference table and chief Enrique Pico's heavy oak desk visible through an open door. Nobody was home. The neatness of the secretary's desk bothered me in particular. Her desktop was empty. I stepped behind the desk and pulled out the drawers, each one with your usual clerical supplies or unused items. What about all the work orders? What about all the emergency notices? What about all the accident reports and crisis reports? What about all of it? Where had all the messages and texts and letters and postcards and complaint forms ended up? There was no sign of any of it. And no personal possessions, no pictures of family, no make-up mirror, no keys, nothing to show anyone had ever been there.

Mel led the way into the big office.

Stacks of cartons and boxes of reports, forms, texts, file folders of letters and postcards and printed matter lined one wall of the office. The conference table had a few old brochures scattered on its dusty surface. "Fried Chicken and Wine Picnic of the Air! Get your tickets now!" that old thing, failed attempt to popularize the Pasadena - Riverside - Indio line. We'd never been able to regularize traffic along the Yuma, Mexicali, and Puerto Peñasco flight corridor. "Free Queso Fresco and Colima Dogs," read another promotion from years past. Mel went through the desk, jerking the drawers open. I looked at spots on the wallpaper showing where pictures had once hung. A couple of them were on the floor, turned to face the wall. The one picture left was defaced, the glass shattered onto the green carpet. The picture had once been a portrait of Enrique Pico as Chief Executive Officer, but his face was obliterated, having been used as a dartboard. A cluster of darts stuck out of what was left of the face.

"What the hell is this?" Mel asked.

She pulled something made of purple-red-orange fabric from the desk drawer. Tentacles splayed out across the desk; as crinkly fabric unfolded, a bulbous head looked our way with round flat eyes.

"An octopus?" I asked.

"It has a switch." Mel manipulated something in the back of the bulb of the head, making a clicking noise.

"Whatever it used to do, it's dead now," she said. "Oh, it's a puppet," Mel said, lifting a sort of wooden crossbar, which in turn, caused the octopus to perk up, two flat disk eyes shining. Mel twitched the crossbar and the octopus arms lifted, some internal spring in them causing the ends of each tentacle to coil and uncoil in a lifelike way. It practically breathed. "What's it for?" she muttered.

She let it go, and the thing slowly deflated on top of the desk. The porcelain statuette of the black-and-white Snoopy dog was missing from the desk.

"Maybe I saw that in an old movie once, a classic!" I said. I pulled file folders from the stack of boxes, and we went methodically through everything in the office. Outside of a box of copies of the textbook by Dr. Eufencio Rojas, *A Compendium of Industrial Knowledge* (I pocketed one copy for myself), we didn't leave the offices carrying any more than we arrived with.

"I'll find Sergio and report this," Mel said as we waited for the elevator.

"We're on our own, that's for sure," I confirmed.

"Isn't somebody in charge?" Mel asked as we emerged into the main lobby, wending through the crowd. "Isn't anybody minding the store?" she said. "I thought somebody was in charge."

"They left it up to us," I said.

"Ready or not," she said, pushing open the heavy brass and glass door, and we went out and down the wide front steps.

That's when it happened, I don't know how, instead of the blasted smoke and particulate atmosphere, we walked down the broad steps of that monumental building into the glare of sunlight (I shielded my eyes with my hand)—the weird corrosive haze had parted momentarily, and we descended in actual sunshine and merged with the crowd into the infinitely forgetful city.

☼

On the corner, at the 76 gas station, the fruit vendor served his customers. At Marengo and State Street, Metro buses waited at the shelters, disgorging riders and taking on passengers. Cop cars loitered at the parking lot off State Street, as usual. A motorcyclist flicked his throttle and tapped his clutch, roaring off toward the 5 freeway. People in wheelchairs waited to be loaded into the buses on lifts. A recycler pushed a shopping cart buried under sacks and bags. Pedestrians waited to cross. The light changed, and as we crossed with the rest, surrounded by the crowd, waves of people poured out of Marengo and State Street and everyone marched downtown on Mission Road, under the Golden State freeway, past the signage on auto wrecking yards and piles of tires at the tire dumps, past the black donut of a huge earth mover tire hoisted atop a pole above the row of tire shops. Auto parts storefronts on one side of us, mountains of crushed and shredded metal in the junkyards on the other. The crowd pushed us along, above the SP tracks running along the river. People behind us chanted, "El pueblo unido, jamas sera vencido!" People behind us yelled, "No justice! No peace!" They shouted, "They say, no contract! We say, fight back!" I saw people I hadn't seen all year. I saw Sandra and William, I saw Beti from Self-Help Graphics, Carlos Montes and a line of CSO people carrying a long red banner denouncing police killings. Maga paused on her bike to watch everyone. Daniel Gonzalez lifted a big stick puppet of a two-headed figure in a suit, sprouting a donkey and an elephant's head from a greedy necktie. Others waved a larger-than-life papier-mâché calavera clutching dollars in both fists. Jen and Rob Ray bicycled by. Mike and his daughter, Sophie (Mary Kay and Sam were back in the crowd), Brent and Joe, Romeo and Carribean, a bunch of the SEMAP posse. Mel introduced me to people. I met Gino Franco, and he reminded me of Arnoldo Garcia (also a musician, they said). My neighbors Freddy and Mariana said hi, with their friend Baldemar. Tania Olmedo caught me from behind with a hug, blurting laughter in my ear. I hadn't seen her since Tania became chief of staff of a congresswoman; she said she was back, she couldn't stand DC, no time to explain now! Then Tania rushed off after she snapped a snapshot of Mel and me and asked a passerby to shoot us three. The teachers' union, Cody, Eddie, Katie and Vicky, and Sal had turned out 50,000 people. SEIU and Justice for Janitors shifted picket signs and lofted banners. Koreatown Immigrant Workers Alliance, Oaxaqueños, Koreanos and others waved a big red KIWA banner. What was this about? We were finding out. Reies Flores said hello, I asked him if we could buy one of his goats for birria, but he said he only had sheep. Barbacoa. He went to look for Romo Senior, Laura, and family. Music blared and bleated out throughout the crowd. I saw Kathy from Avenue 50, folks from Tia Chucha's and Kaya Press—somebody I thought was Carlos Molino wearing a baseball cap, brim soaked in sweat and his beard gone gray. Then I saw it wasn't Carlos but somebody who looked exactly like my brother would have looked if he had lived. A big drum pounded, pulsing as we went. The speaker ahead of us got on the PA and shouted from the bed of a truck, their voice shredded into crackling static. Factions and sections cheered and applauded. Mel looked over her shoulder at me now and then. I made sure to stay by her all the way.

APPENDICES

Appendix A:
What Is the Purpose of Mystery:
Interview with Oscar Zeta Acosta

WHAT IS THE PURPOSE OF MYSTERY?

OSCAR ZETA ACOSTA (the man known as)

Our Cal State L.A. Chicano Studies professor Jamie Escalante returned from the University of Houston Panamerican Conference on the Post-colonial Legacy and Lingering Whereabouts of Oscar Zeta Acosta, where he said the margaritas were smashing and new theories abounded as new socio-political alliances formed every millisecond in hotel rooms around the conference. Professor Escalante ensconced in our awareness the realization that there could be no better consultant on the Mystery than Oscar Zeta Acosta, civil rights attorney and cigar aficionado, acclaimed author of the classics, Autobiography of a Brown Buffalo, and Revolt of the Cockroach People, though he was reported missing and presumed dead off the coast of Mazatlan in 1974. Alive or dead, who could be a more incisive and insightful spokesperson for the Mystery than someone who has peered over the edge and then disappeared? Tracking down someone whose whereabouts have been unknown for 30-plus years can be extremely difficult, not to mention discouraging, so I'd thank Liki Renteria, in particular, for heading up the search that recently located the man who answered the description, the man who insists that he is Oscar Zeta Acosta (OZA).

1. What is the purpose of mystery?

OZA: You know, I don't want to sound self-serving, but this is really the subtext, if you read between the lines, of both of my books Autobiography of a Brown Buffalo and Revolt of the Cockroach People. I would direct people to those books, which on the surface deal in social commentary and historical conflict, drugs, sex and (Chicano) rock and roll, but really---if you really look---you will find the spiritual seeking that you seek. Here's a short, just a snippet, sort of a quote---it's a teaser, a riddle--- think of it as a Zen koan: "It's in the blood now. And not only my blood. Somebody still has to answer for Robert Fernandez and Roland Zanzibar. Somebody still has to answer for all the smothered lives of all the fighters who have been forced to carry on, chained to a war for Freedom

just like a slave is chained to his master." Or
this one---see if you can figure it out: "Warm-
wet-stuck-suck, down, in-out, in-out... Ayyyyy!"

2. What is the purpose of "death"?

OXA: Yeah, I could see how you would want to ask
me that but there ain't no easy answers. People
with questions like that have been searching for
me for decades, down in Mazatlan and Michoac-
an, Zacatecas nor Guadalajara, Texas or Juarez
or whatever, and here you people, Liki, lucked
out and connected with me here at home in ELA
(home-away-from-home, my spiritual base, wherever else I might be) and I don't mind answering a
few questions, I don't. But if I get the general
drift of your meaning, the guy you really ought
to ask these kinda of questions to is a guy
named Juan Fish. He's not that well known, not
at all. In fact, he's practically unknown, except among certain circles. He's almost as hard
to locate as I am. By chance, have you heard of
the vato?

3. We know him, yeah. He's a complex guy. What
is the purpose of ball lightning around General
Hospital especially on winter nights?

OXA: Have you checked with the Office of Homeland Security? Maybe it has something to do with
that? It would be interesting to maybe see what
they have to say. Just don't ask FEMA, know what
I'm saying? (Laughs.) You know for a fact you
ain't gonna get a straight answer from any of
the fascists they got running everything now in
the name of the corporate bottom line. You'll
get the Gary Webb treatment, you know what happened to Gary Webb? Or Ruben Salazar? Accidents
happen to people like that who go around asking
too many hard questions. Another way of looking
at the whole thing is, if jails and hospitals
are the colleges of Life, then ball lightning is
like Christmas ornaments on the Tree of Life,
get it? By the way, what are you, anyway, Vietnamese or something?

4. What is the purpose of "winter"?

OXA: Jeez, Louise. Hey, Liki, c'mon! You never
said anything about--- what the hell, gimme an-

245

other tall one out of the cooler, don't just sit
on it, Jesus.

5. Who funds the campaign headquarters in the
campaign of hate?

Pulling out of my pocket a piece paper, I read
to OEA:
cf. L.A. TIMES July 5, 2006, "TRIAL IN BLACK
SLAYINGS PAINTS LANDSCAPE OF HATE"

In a mid-1990s federal racketeering case against
12 Eme defendants, an Avenues leader named Alex
"Pee Wee" Aguirre was convicted of murdering an
unpaid consultant who helped Edward James Olmos
make "American Me," a 1992 movie that the gang
did not like.

One informant in the current case told an FBI
agent that the Eme had ordered the Avenues to
"Kill any blacks on sight." The judge ruled out
testimony about the Eme connection as being too
prejudicial.

This case came about when Los Angeles police de-
tectives took the Wilson killing, then 3 years
old, to the U.S. attorney's office in 2002. They
hit a statutory obstacle in trying to bring
Saldana, who had not yet been convicted of his
other crimes, to trial in state court. The case
grew from there based largely on the testimony
of Jose de la Cruz, the only Avenues member convicted in the Wilson murder, and Jesse Diaz, an
Avenues member in prison for attempted murder of
a police officer.

If the campaign of terror the prosecution al-
leges indeed occurred, it is difficult to say
if it pushed African Americans out of Highland
Park, or kept others from coming in.

In 1990, there were 1,246 African Americans in
Highland Park. In 2000, there were 1,974, according to census records.

Warren Hill, Sr., 58, moved to Highland Park
from South Los Angeles 15 years ago. As a black
man, he has never been harassed by the Avenues.
But he keeps his head when they're around, as he
did with black gangs in his old neighborhood.

And he keeps off the street at night.

"If you have Avenues standing right there," he said one recent afternoon, sitting at a bus stop, "I could sit down here and they wouldn't do a thing. It's not them harassing blacks period. "It's what teenagers do. If my son walked by them, and shot them a look, then there could be trouble."

OZA: That's why I ran for L.A. County Sheriff in 1970. We were aiming to shut down all the offices of the campaign of hate wherever we could find them. Bet your ass on it, people knew that, too. That's why I got over 500,000 votes. Of course, I lost by a million (laughs), what does that tell you?

6. What is the effect on personal health of all these moving lights? Particularly all these moving lights? Sometimes at night you see lights moving from room to room in a house across the street, and what effect does that have on us?

OZA: Carlos Castaneda had his theories (chuckles), so what, nowadays you ain't going for all that Don Juanismo? Why not? They probably still go for that stuff at UCLA and New York, even in De Efe, Mexico City, you might be able to find people into Maria Sabina. She died, yeah, everybody dies. But you could probably hook up different tours, where they take people out in the desert or up in the mountains, feed them mushrooms. In the old days it was all done on the QT, a low-rent rendezvous---blue acid tabs straight from the Haight; nowadays I bet they have $300 a day spas on top of a mountain where the masseuse wipes off your babas or barf with white linen and put cucumbers on your eyes while you're tripping. After its all over you can cool off with a dip in the pool. $300 a day. Is this another one of those kind of trips? 'Cuz if it is... (OZA begins to sing---if you can call it that, "Oh, I've seen fire and I've seen rain. I seen sunny days that I thought would never come again, but I always thought that I'd see you, baby, ONE MORE TIME AGAIN!" Laughs.)

7. I also want to ask about spots I sometimes see. The doctors couldn't find anything so what

about these spots I sometimes see, which writhe like serpents across my eyesight? Do they "exist"?

OZA: I'm not a doctor. I'm a trained lawyer. I could speculate, but that would have to be off the record. I have personal experience with this type of thing, so take it from me, court-ordered shrinks won't be of much help in this regard. There is no bottom! You can go down that way forever, but there's no way out.

8. Who are the so-called experts in this field and how are they decided, I mean who picks them? Because we never get asked, in the area of mystery.

OZA: What kind of expert are you waiting for? You seen the stairways to nowhere for yourself. You seen the kids all run out of the bathroom at City Terrace Elementary saying they saw la Llorona in the mirror. You seen the fog of Mystery on a winter morning. You seen the horny toad squirting blood out of his eyes. Ah! (Chugaluga the malt liquor.)

9. What about black pepper? Do you----?

OZA: You got pederast priests in the offices of the church, why don't you ask them? Or the family down the block who says they have ghosts? Or the TV addicts writing astrology columns for all tomorrow's newspapers? Some airwaves and frequencies radiating from the hills broadcast everyday illusions. There's experts behind all of that fooling themselves. There's people making it the business of their lives to pass this stuff on to another generation. Who voted for any of them? Who's to say what the real mystery was? You know one day I woke up in the morning, and it was the exact same day as the day before. I lived that day completely different from the one that I remembered from before. It never happened again, but that was the day I got to go back and do it over again for once. I never told anybody about that.

10. Once I was told, "Don't read while you eat or you will go blind."
My eyes continue to deteriorate. Could you elab-

orate on this?

OZA: Like I say kid, I don't know if you are
getting the message here. Maybe if you took a
little kitten and wrapped it up in firecrackers
on Chinese New Year's and lit the fuse, you'd
have good luck for once, or maybe you'd just
have the ugliest, most neurotic cat you ever had
that hated you. What's your guess?

11. What's personally most important to you in
the healing arts, 5,000 years of traditional
folk practice or something invented on the Internet this month?

OZA: That's something different altogether. You
have your traditional healing practices of indigenous peoples the world round, and you got
your snake oil salesmen trying to make a quick
buck off of something that's been taken out of
context. You take psychedelic rock from the 60s
and spin it backwards, are you gonna get a secret message or are those kinds of ideas just
dreamed up by people sitting around blasting a
little too much herb?

12. Occasionally people go to unlicensed storefront curanderos and get sold nasty stuff that
makes them sick or die, but isn't that better
than Scientology? Or is it the same?

OZA: I guess it all depends on who pays their
money to rent stalls at the next street fair.
Who's to say but in my time maybe I could've
used a prayer from somebody, maybe even me?

13. Are you controlled by robots from outer
space?

OZA: How many fingers am I holding up? [OZA
stands in the breeze coming through the French
doors of the third floor balcony overlooking the
rooftops of the city, and spreads his arms, I
figure he's going to flip the whole town the bird,
give the whole indifferent metropolis the middle
finger, an anarchist anti-Nixon with both arms
upraised in his own version of the V-for-victo-
ry sign, but he just takes it all in with the
twilight breeze blowing in his face, lowers his
arms to rest on the railing, and looks out, now

and then drinking melancholic from a can.)

14. Personally I feel that we shouldn't mention narcotraficante Satanic worshippers from the Tex-Mex border in this context because they have too many problems, don't you think? You know what I mean?

OZA does not reply. He's thinking about something else.

15. Are you going to answer my question?

OZA tosses the empty can three stories to the street below. Maybe someone is looking at him, because he stiffens and backs warily from the balcony. His contacts told us that they consider this unpretentious ELA apartment his last safehouse in America.

16. What is the connection between the conspiracies of the 1960s and modern conspiracies of today? What has really changed in the practice of modern conspiracies?

OZA: That's a question you need to ask a professor or a journalist. I am just Zeta, the last Brown Buffalo.

17. How do you explain the following unusual phenomena of ELA:

• the geyser at Valley & Eastern?

OZA: That was... that was... a sign! A sign that... someone must answer!

• ball lightning orbiting General Hospital?

OZA: Blue tabs of acid straight from the Haight!

• the man who walks avenues and boulevards wearing the rabbit mask of brown paper bag?

OZA: He is unashamed to stand before you with tears on his face, to sing of the Cockroach People.

• Levitating post-modern "pre-condemned" house?

OZA: I was a civil rights lawyer, not tenant law.

* Stairs to nowhere and the people who walk them?

OZA: You mean the courthouse steps downtown? I repeat what I said to those vile sons of bitches many years ago: You crummy bastards, we are da yout!

* Indian graveyard at Cal State L.A. forensics center?

OZA: Maybe like the La Brea tar pits it's all gonna come bubbling and oozing up one day through the floorboards like greasy black asphalt! Bones, crimes, murders, broken promises, lies, hidden truths, secret lives, stolen futures, it'll be pounding in the blood like karma.

* AIDS memorial portal to Tijuana that sometimes plays Carlos Santana music and even the Chinese don't know about?

OZA: Don't short-change our Chinese brethren; they didn't make a billion of them for nothing. Have you heard of the secret Chinese tunnels of Mexicali?

* A Virgin Defacer who only causes himself and his own lifetimes of bad luck?

OZA: Anybody messing around with virgins has only himself to blame. Although, I guess somebody has to do it.

* Juan Fish Garage? Where is it located and what is its connection to a house of pregnant girls?

OZA: Juan Fish, that guy again! Talk about your men of Mystery! He puts me in the shade. I take my hat off to him, figuratively speaking. As you see, I don't wear a hat.

18. Lastly, what effect does leaving a jar of pennies by the door have on your day? On your overall health? On your headache?

OZA: You got a headache, kid? Leave the jar of
aspirin by the door. Then again, maybe you need
a steaming big bowl of menudo, with pig's feet
floating around in it, and fresh chopped onion
and oregano tossed on top. That might cure you.

19. So what if I said "lastly," I still want to
ask you about the secret tunnels of ELA? Where
are they and what have they been used for? This
is important.

OZA: The only secret tunnels I heard about were
escape hatches and storage spaces built underneath certain houses by subversive groups and
organizations of the day, but I was sworn to secrecy, in part by lawyer-client privilege.

20. Who knows where the files are kept on the secret history of Los Angeles? You must know something or certainly have some idea?

OZA: About the time I went south to Mexico in
'74, former Black Panther Party member and community activist, Michael Zinzun, formed the Coalition Against Police Abuse (CAPA) with Kwaku
Duren and Anthony Thigpenn to deal with the
rampant police brutality of the time---this was
twenty years before the Rodney King riots of
'92, remember---and this organization provided
support for victims of the police and their families, and agitated for justice in street demonstrations and courtrooms. If you have read my
book, then you can see how crucial and necessary
this activism was. After the 1979 LAPD killing
of Eula Love over a dispute involving a $22 gas
bill, CAPA proposed a civilian police review
board, like the kind L.A. had in place after the
1992 riots, but at the time, CAPA couldn't get
it on the ballot. Maybe that would have prevent-
ed the later 1992 riots and the damages to the
city to the tune of over a billion dollars and
58 killed. Of course, the LAPD was up to the
same tricks they used against me and the people
I was representing in court during the Chicano
Movement. The LAPD had a secret red squad called
the Public Disorder Intelligence Division, PDID,
that spied on anti-war groups and civil rights
organizations, and they infiltrated CAPA like
they did the other community groups. Michael

Zinzun and CAPS sued the LAPD and the LAPD was forced to disband this repressive, secret, corrupt police division, and that's a good question. Where are those files? In this so-called time of threats to national security and the War on Terrorism, have the security forces and their reactionary masterminds implemented new PDIDs? Are they compiling new files on community activists and infiltrating organizations and disrupting their activities? Children, do you know where your police are tonight? Michael Zinzun died just recently, you know. At home, in his sleep.

OZA steps to the railing of the balcony and looks out over the city. He's smiling (with his big hair messed up) at something.

ELADTL
c/s

Appendix B: Interview with Juan Fish

DISCLAIMER: FIRST YOU MUST UNDERSTAND I DON'T GO FOR SOME PEOPLE'S ARBITRARY OR ABSTRACT NOTION OF TRUTH, WHAT'S TRUE OR NOT-TRUE, I DON'T KNOW IF YOU CAN RAPPEL YOUR MIND AROUND THAT. THE FIRST THING I EXPECT YOU TO KNOW IS THAT THE DIFFERENCES BETWEEN WHAT IS TRUE AND WHAT IS NOT-TRUE ARE NOT ANYWHERE AS IMPORTANT AS THE SIMILARITIES. TRY TO RAPPEL YOUR MIND AROUND THAT, SADLY IT COULD BE THE SAME THEREFORE YOU MUST TRY HARD TO UNDERSTAND, FOR WITHOUT THAT UNDERSTANDING YOU CAN'T REALLY GET A REAL UNDERSTANDING OF WHAT MYSTERY IS ALL ABOUT IN EAST L.A. OR ANYWHERE, LIKE YOU GO OUT ON A HOT DAY AND FIND OUT THE SIDEWALK IS MELT-ING THE GUM SOLES ON YOUR CHEAP MADE-IN-CHINA SHOES LEAVING STICKY BLACK MARKS EVERYWHERE YOU GO, THAT'S OBVI-OUS, NOT MYSTERIOUS. THE STICKY BLACK MARKS AND THAT SOUND THAT FOLLOWS YOU EVERYWHERE YOU WALK, REMEMBER WHEN YOU FIRST PICKED THOSE OFF A TABLE AND SAID, "THESE SHOES LOOK NICE, $4.95, WHAT DO I HAVE TO LOSE?"

POET OF THE UNIVERSE?

In the interests of interviewing experts on the Mystery, in general, and in particular Mysteries of East L.A., we have located highly elusive individuals much more deeply involved with these issues than standard commercial experts that people usually go to—such as the Vietnamese lady in the former pink Photomart booth on the corner of Commonwealth and Atlantic Boulevards with the neon sign "PSYCHIC," an eccentric older person in your family shunned ostensibly because of a bizarre past life but actually because of loose personal hygiene combined with what is perceived to be a fatal lack of fashion sense, or the high school girl who believes she has attained a certain degree of knowledge because of all manner of things she has heard, discussed, and even read about in books from the used bookstore. Instead, understanding that we all to some extent lead secret lives, double lives compartmentalized and partitioned off from public view, usually more related to matters of personal desire than legality but occasionally both—as well as for other reasons—we have been able to locate among the circle of people we know and in the community persons that you may never have suspected as being experts in the Mystery, as you'd likely know them only in their ordinary personas, their street names so to speak, and like anyone's double or secret life, they could be found "hiding in the open" in the daily circumstances of their regular environment. You probably know some of these people under other names or guises than are referred to here. This is not to suggest that the experts we chose are all of the same point of view on the Mystery or the Mysteries of East L.A. Far from it, in their secret lives people tend to assert individuality and idiosyncrasy even more so than they do in public life, and as a matter of fact we counted on a diversity of opinions in this regard to develop what we thought would be the most useful information on specific local phenomena that, again, we expect that you knew about on the level of knowledge but not on the level of understanding. Although you may be surprised to learn their day-to-day identities, more important is the information they may reveal to you on infrastructure and stress phenomena occurring in your community today.

JOHN LOZOYA

Interview with Juan Fish

1. *What is the purpose of mystery?*

One later afternoon, I spot Juan Fish (who looks smaller than I remembered him) leaning against the side of his truck in the shade of a Chinese elm in Lincoln Heights, as if waiting for someone. I had previously asked him if I could ask him some questions about his experience of the city, and he had tentatively agreed, and I see him waiting in the street (he looks almost exactly like the same guy) and think this might be the perfect moment, but now he acts like he doesn't remember me, and furthermore, as if he doesn't even really understand the question. He just kind of frowns and gives me a distracted nod, as if only just now noticing me and my pen and clipboard. Then he looks away as if perhaps I might just go away. But I continue to stand there asking questions.

2. *What is the purpose of "death"?*

JF: I'm not sure. I—What, what are these questions supposed to be about? I thought you were talking about something else. I don't really . . . Death? The purpose of death is to get rid of the dead people, in case they haven't noticed. Imagine if they just stuck around, hanging around forever and ever, never got the message that somewhere along the line they had stopped living? Some people won't get the message, I guess. Death and time, you know. Time goes by, people die. Death and time, tick tick tick . . .

3. *What is the purpose of ball lightning around General Hospital especially on winter nights?*

JF: I'm not really familiar with anything like that. So I don't know. I did hear there used to be a zeppelin landing pad on the top of the building, where they would anchor the zeppelins to a lightning rod they used to have up there. That they planned this whole other lighter-than-air patient delivery system to avoid street congestion on the ground. But that was when they used to plan things like that and have alternative ideas about how to make the city better. But I don't know what happened to that. Maybe those ideas went out with the red cars, or even before that.

4. *What is the purpose of "winter"?*

JF: What is the purpose of these questions? Damn!

5. *Who funds the campaign headquarters in the campaign of hate?*

JF: Your best bet there, check with Michael Zinzun and the Coalition Against Police Abuse. You know, he fought against that type of thing organizing community support for a gang truce.

6. *What is the effect on personal health of all these moving lights? Particularly all these moving lights? Sometimes at night you see lights moving from room to room in a house across the street, and what effect does that have on us?*

JF: Hold on a sec. (At this point, Juan Fish abruptly stands up straight and walks around the cab of his pickup and gets behind the wheel. I follow, pen and pad ready, as he's gunning the engine, releasing a cloud of white exhaust in the street. I lean over and look in his window, but he drives away.)

[It takes a number of weeks before I am able to catch up with Juan Fish again. The guy gives me pretty much exactly the same look when I pull out my pen and clipboard and say, "About those questions. I just needed a few more minutes," so I am confident he remembered what we were discussing, and my confidence in his perspective and point of view were such that I think you have to determine to follow these things through to the end.]

7. *I want to ask about spots I sometimes see. The doctors couldn't find anything so what about these spots I sometimes see, which writhe like serpents across my eyesight? Do they "exist"?*

JF: Hey, I talked to my cousin. He said that he saw you. He said that you were doing better. But you know, I can't really talk right now. I got stuff I got to take care of, so I'll see you round, all right?

[After that encounter, it took me more than two months to track down Juan Fish, because he had changed his appearance, he'd grown a mustache and goatee, and he needed a haircut, his hair was sticking out, and he was wearing some eyeglasses, and his trick now was to pretend that he'd never

met me before and did not know anything about our previous agreement to discuss radically esoteric questions of an immediate metaphysical or existential nature. But I found him again in a corner booth in a little restaurant on N. Broadway in Lincoln Heights, and given the fact that he was only halfway through a plate of chicken in pepian sauce, Juan finally agreed, chewing with his mouth full and speaking in a fake Mexicano accent that I'd never heard him using before, since I knew he was born in Los Angeles and he was from here, so the accent was just some sort of affected mannerism of some kind, an act of some sort, to answer the rest of my questions. Juan Fish is nothing if not a complex character. Part of his charisma is that he has so many different and seemingly complex facets to his personality. On different days you'll get totally divergent answers from him. Sometimes, like today, he'll even be speaking with a totally different accent and everything.]

8. *Once I was told, "Don't read while you eat or you will go blind."*
*My eyes continue to deteriorate. Could you elaborate on th*is?

JF: Well, you know, uh, some people they like to believe some things and then other people, they don't. Like you could go with the flow, or whatever. Because either you do or you don't, you understand me? Wooly-bully?

11. *Sure, I do. What's personally most important to you in the healing arts, 5,000 years of traditional folk practice or something invented on the Internet this month?*

JF: Time is really important, you know. In life, it's everything, you know. You could be in the right place but at the wrong time, you could be at the wrong place but at the right time. Then you got to really, really have a clear idea of what time is, and what time it is for you. It could be the right time or the wrong time, you know? It could just hit you, bam! [JF punched me in the arm, causing me to drop my pen, which I retrieved, and then I resumed taking notes as he continued.] Yeah, time is everything. Everything is time. It goes both ways. How old are you? What time you got? I got to go to San Fernando Road and pick up a truck that just got a trailer hitch welded on it. That place closes at around like five o'clock, Bam!

[Again he socked my arm and sent my pen spinning away, and when I went to pick it up a woman handed it to me.] Like that, you see? You got to be there on time! Then everything is probably going to work out. But you never can know for sure.

12. *OK. Occasionally people go to unlicensed storefront curanderos and get sold nasty stuff that makes them sick or die, but isn't that better than Scientology? Or is it the same?*

Bam! Ha ha ha! [JF drained a Corona with a big mouthful of chicken and green sauce. I picked up the pen and this time I held it really tight so when he punched me I just scribbled a bit but kept hold of the writing instrument.] Bam! Ha ha ha! You want a beer?

13. *No, thanks. Are there indications you are controlled by robots from outer space?*

JF: Sometimes you watch too many movies you get a messed up idea of reality, my friend. Because reality is not outer space. I'm telling you TIME, TIME is everything.

14. *Personally I feel that we shouldn't mention narcotraficante Satanic worshippers from the Tex-Mex border in this context because they have too many problems, don't you think? You know what I mean?*

JF: What time is it?

15. *It's 4:40. Are you going to answer my question?*

JF: I'll be right back. [JF paid the woman at the cash register in back and asked her something. She looked at me and just shrugged. As he went out the front door, he repeated again, "I'll be back." When I located JF a month or so later, he had changed his appearance again. Perhaps he'd been ill. He was definitely skinnier and paler and had shaved off his goatee and mustache. This made him look a lot younger, but at the same time, when I approached him sitting on the front steps of what I thought must be a relative's house in Lincoln Heights, he gave me that same weary look as ever. I told him that it would only take just a few minutes to finish answering the questions that we'd started before, and he was asking me about this and that ("You don't get paid to do this, this is just exercising a constitutional right?") and acting like he was unclear on some of the terms I was using, but I knew that this was just a ploy to try to change the subject and to get out of finishing the interview, and that he would try to come up with some excuse to drive away, and this time I kept a firm grip on my pen, a very firm grip indeed, in case he punched my arm.]

16. *What is the connection between the conspiracies of the 1960s and modern conspiracies of today? What has really changed in the practice of modern conspiracies?*

JF: Probably, right? You figure somebody has to be behind it, right? I mean these things, the planes crashing into the Twin Towers, and gas prices going up and up, they don't just happen by themselves, right? And then with the Vietnam War for example, so they found out that that whole Gulf of Tonkin incident they used to start the war never happened. So it's just like Iraq, isn't it? That's what you're talking about, isn't it? You can probably check out books about that at the library. There's always CIA and FBI guys (well, maybe not FBI guys because maybe they're not as smart) and journalists like Gary Webb or Seymour Hersh who know about these conspiracies and write books about them. Plus others.

17. *How do you explain the following unusual phenomena of ELA:*

   the geyser at Valley & Eastern?

JF: That might have something to do with the fake palm tree broadcasting microwave signals just a hundred yards from that spot. I mean, it's a guess, because it's such a coincidence.

   ball lightning orbiting General Hospital?

JF: It may be that the X-ray machinery, radioisotope units and other types of machinery that emit radiation and perhaps have strong electromagnetic fields about them alter the atmosphere in that particular environment, particularly where you do not have a lot of natural vegetation in the area to counter the effects of building after building full of labs and equipment and computers and even things like the emergency generators which are meant to allow the hospital to continue operating even in the event of a major earthquake. I haven't seen these ball lightning events myself, so, again, it's just a guess.

the man who walks avenues and boulevards wearing the rabbit mask of brown paper bag?

JF: That, I couldn't even hazard a guess. Rabbit mask of brown paper bag?

levitating postmodern "pre-condemned" house?

JF: That sounds like basic bad design to me, when you don't connect the bottom of your house to the foundation, or the foundation to the ground in a sturdy way. That would certainly get your house pre-condemned.

stairs to nowhere and the people who walk them?

JF: That was a conspiracy in itself. In the 1950s and 1960s urban renewal plans drawn up by politicians and their appointed civic committees promised to rejuvenate cities by moving poor people out of inner-city neighborhoods and bulldozing their "run-down" neighborhoods like Bunker Hill or Chavez Ravine and replacing them with centers of culture like Dodger Stadium or the Music Center and the Museum of Contemporary Art and Disney Opera Hall, but what really happened was that the people got displaced, and the neighborhoods were bulldozed and replaced by parking lots and big empty buildings, and the stairs to nowhere started showing up all over town, and people ending up walking them for the rest of their lives. Now the same thing is going on here and there across the country wherever city councils use eminent domain to condemn houses and mom-and-pop shops to put up Walmarts, Target stores, and big-box shopping malls.

La Playita
2200 N Broadway
LA, CA 90031
(310) 452-0090

2/12/96

To Whom it May Concern,

The following letter has been written to establish the fact that researcher and scholar on mysteries of East Los Angeles, Guadalupe Jolina, has conducted excellent and highly recommended evaluations at this site on Wednesday, January 17, 1996.

While conducting research, G. Jolina was allowed access to every square inch of this facility and was allowed to sample our menu:

1.) Shrimp Burrito............ $4
2.) Fish Tacos Fried.......... $1.50
3.) Coctel de Abulon.......... $2
4.) Mixed Ceviche............. $3 for 3
5.) Ensalada Pulpo............ $25
6.) Jugo de Sandia............ 50¢
7.) Chile Shrimps............. $4.50

From what we know, the research was a success and findings are forthcoming. We would like to thank Guadalupe Jolina for the research and forthcoming results.

Sincerely,

John L. Reyes

Indian graveyard at Cal State L.A. forensics center?

JF: The rumor is that the Indian graveyard under Cal State L.A. extended to the parking lot near the nearly completed new forensics pathology building. Talk about your stairs to nowhere! That was the original eminent domain/urban renewal project that started during the days of Spanish missions. The Spanish are remembered for building for the first stairs to nowhere, but some Indigenous activists would point to the pyramids.

AIDS memorial portal to Tijuana that sometimes plays Carlos Santana music and even the Chinese don't know about?

JF: That's like the bus they used to have—maybe they still have it—that ran from Chinatown L.A. to Chinatown San Francisco for around $20, fast and cheap. I mean, there has to be more of those around, and somebody's probably running some from L.A. to Tijuana. But a portal like a time machine? I mean, that sounds kind of high-tech. Maybe Carlos Santana is into some technology that the rest of us don't know about yet.

a Virgin Defacer who only causes himself and his own lifetimes of bad luck?

JF: That guy! I can't speak for him. You gotta ask that guy yourself.

Juan Fish Garage? Where is it located and what is its connection to a house of pregnant girls?

JF: It no longer exists, and neither does any connection to some so-called house of pregnant girls.

18. *Lastly, what effect does leaving a jar of pennies by the door have on your day? On your overall health? On your headache?*

JF: It's important to save—even if only a few pennies—for your future. It could be here sooner than you know. You might be living in the past already.

JUAN FISH
GARAGE
3036 W. 7th ST.
Phone DU. 41267

19. *So what if I said "lastly," I still want to ask you about the secret tunnels of East LA. Where are they, and what have they been used for? This is important.*

JF: Yeah, there's always those tunnels. Some were subways that never got built and were used to store Caltrans supplies and equipment in. Some were storm drains, and I heard stories they supposedly were used by gangs of Mexican and Japanese American youths to avoid arrest and beatings by racist LAPD and L.A. County sheriffs during racial conflicts. Sort of like underground conduits.

20. *Who knows where the files are kept on the secret history of Los Angeles? You must know something or certainly have some idea?*

JF: My guess is that those files have largely been destroyed. You may be able to find someone who has knowledge of some of their contents, but elements of the city power structure have always wanted official myths to permeate the thinking at all levels and have never wanted other concepts to cloud the perfectly sunny skies over Los Angeles. Hey, hold on a second, will you?

[Juan Fish went up the steps and into the house. After fifteen minutes or so, I banged on the wrought iron security door, but no one answered. A dog barked behind the house.]

limesa the last
before epic
ert of Coachella
stated
nefly every
thing
that was once
g is now dead

—MESSAGE:
SELWAY FALLS, ON THE SELWAY RIVER, 20 miles
off the Lewis and Clark Hwy. These falls form a
partial block for the Salmon run and form a were
favorite spot for Indians and whites to spear their
fish.

EAST LA AIRSHIP EXPRESS
(PAN-AMERICAN FLIGHT 1909)
$1.50
FLADATL AIR MAIL

PLACE
STAMP
HERE

Post Card

The burnt ochre of Cali
history, the titanium
white of a girl's mustache
The olive green of mild
thoughts, the erroneous
green of reserved thoughts
The Vietnamese yellow
of passing time, the
fuzzy black of world night—
The gleaming brass of Mick Jagger the
celluloid transparency of downtown Los
Angeles, the faint pink of aspiration— Carl

Botanica Mestizo del
Poder ✱ ✱ ✱
68 W. Hampden Terrace
Alhambra CA 91801

Appendix C: Interview with the Virgin Defacer

SW/JLF
2238 Zonal Street
Los Angeles CA 90031

Preliminary Questions for the Virgin Defacer

The Virgin Defacer was a graffiti artist who became famous for a brief period in the early 90s when he painted over the faces of Virgin of Guadalupe on stores and walls across East L.A. Speculation abounded about his motives. Was he a sexually abused Catholic school boy embittered by the global cover-up of the Catholic hierarchy? Was he a secret agent of the Crips or Bloods going behind enemy lines to try to destroy the Mexican Mafia through supernatural voodoo? Was he a twisted racist of the Jewish Defense League trying to make Mexicans feel unwelcome on their home ground? We finally located one of the original Virgin Defacers who agreed to speak with us along with another member of his crew or posse, "there's only two of us left," he asserted. "I can't tell you what happened to our real leader," he added. "But he was the greatest one of all." They agreed to speak to us on condition that their names not be used and their identities be disguised.

Is it true you are the actual Virgin Defacer? Was it really you?

I painted ZAKAZAKAZAKA92847087Y349 8Y!!!!!!!!!!!!!!!!!!!! on the Soto Street overpass over the San Bernardino, I painted ZAKAZAKA-ZAKA095T08??????????? on the North Broadway overpass over the Golden State Freeway, I painted ZOO-PYZOOPYZOOPY565656T56Tggggggggugugugugug........ on the Los Feliz overpass over the 5, I painted

ZINZOZINZOZINZO454545R453535@@@@@@@ on
the Sunset Boulevard overpass over the Hollywood Free-
way! Yeah! Yeah! Yeh! I fricking painted YAGAZAGA-
RAGAHHHHHhhhhhhhhs34654656wt5r/////////// on the
Colorado Blvd overpass over the L.A. River like 65 times!
Or like 75 I don't know!

But I understand that you are, or were, truly one of the
original Virgin Defacers. Even though you mentioned that
perhaps you were not the leader, or whatever, can you tell
us, what was the motive, why you defaced with big splots
of beige house paint or drippy black swaths or swirls round
and round of red splashes of spraypaint like exploding
blood on Virgin faces on stores and walls across East L.A.
and even South Central and even in Northeast L.A. as far as
Eagle Rock?

I painted BOBOGOGOBOBONOBO()())(()))
(8465474rc::::::::::: on several Paul Botello murals, and
the Streetscaper mural at the corner of Cesar Chavez and
Soto, I painted YUYUYUYUYUYUYU-92i8986578wuwuwu-
wuwuwuwu]]]]]]]]]] on some unknown murals by losers,
on the freeway murals meant to celebrate 1984 Olympics
(who cares about 1984 Olympics, wow), I painted HUH-
HUHHUHHUHHUHHUHrrrr56433576yu757i96ti9p8v3
nu 80u********* on the bottom as high as I could reach
of giant murals by Kent Twitchell or Trent Mitchell and by
Eloy Martinez and Frank Romero's fat cars, I spraypainted
ZOTZOZOTZOZOTZODdddDDDDDDDDddddd,,,,,,,,,,,,u
gh on some other famous murals that I can't remember who
it was or where. Don't even fucking... Yeah.

But you asserted earlier, when we spoke on the phone, that
you and your friend here were original members of the Virgin Defacer crew, so I think what people really would like

to know about is why, basically, you engaged in this campaign of defacement, or perhaps you saw it as a creative act, an artistic act, more or less? Did you? Exactly what were you trying to say?

I painted BATOBAPOBAXOio4r98vy2b08f-9cp896y-++++++++++ 12 or 14 times on the white van my uncle was driving when he took my little brother away when he was twelve and never brought him back. Then when I did see him again he was never the same. I painted MAXOMIXOMEXOuhrt7yu1097758-7tv 9999999999999 on the Belmont tunnel empty lot where Mexicanos used to play ulama till it was demolished and they built fortresses of luxury condo with Italian names. I painted GARGAF-FARGAFGARGAFFtatatatatatta008459886-080 six or seven times on the gray wall where the Homeboy graffiti removal crew had been shot up and one killed when they were painting over graffiti arts, I would've shot them myself but I didn't have no "gun," I didn't even have no "anger," all I had was just "my bike" and "my brother." I painted ZOOPZOOPZIPZIPu0935b9xp c87ctçpppppppp1≈ʃ more than three times (or two) on the creepy town and creepy city which they present to us every day without any embarrassment on their creepiest parts whatsoever. The creeps.

Okay, but I'm not sure I got an answer to my question. I guess I'd like to know more about your concept of graffiti as an art, as an art movement, or art form or something, for example, do you have a philosophical or aesthetic concept of graffiti as an art form? And how does defacing Virgins of Guadalupe relate to your concept?

I painted VAZONAZOWAZOOhou876-7cf5r9tingolingo-lingo once or twice on the restrooms at Hazard Park where

supposedly they raped some 18 year old girl, maybe that's
why they always used to punch my brother or me in the
face as hard as they could if they caught us around just trying to use the bathroom, I painted 098508764659709576je
eeeeeeeeeeee maybe like six times on the railroad tracks,
well not on the tracks but on the factories bordering the
tracks right there, you know where they left some guy all
stabbed and robbed, supposedly, one dead dude, I painted
SWUSSSSSSSSSSSSSS093875360%%%%o%%% across
town on secret make-out locations I was able to locate via
an educational booklet produced by the Pocho Historical
Society like on top of hills with dead end streets with dead
palm trees terminating in lonely half-hidden spots without
street light illumination where people have sex inside cars
day or night, I guess they are horny and had nowhere they
could go. So they throw out condoms there and broken beer
bottles.

I don't know if we are getting the kind of information or
facts our readers are interested in. Can you tell us what was
the original concept of Virgin Defacement, what was your
goal effacing the faces of Virgins of Guadalupe that represent the merciful aspect of Tonantzin on hard-edged architectural aspects throughout the Eastside, from Downey, HP
and Bell to Highland Park, Glassell Park and Frogtown?
How did you come up with that idea? Who thought of it
first?

I painted ZAKAZAKAZAKA92847087Y349
8Y!!!!!!!!!!!!!!!!!!! on the Soto Street overpass
over the San Bernardino, I painted ZAKAZAKA-
ZAKA095T08??????????? on the North Broadway
overpass over the Golden State Freeway, I painted
TIPSYGWANDAWANDADOOLDLyEix on multiple
blue ice glaciers of Alaska before they were about to melt

forever---

No, no, wait a second ere--- [the second guy, described in my notes as a somewht snarky, _____ guy of about _____ years of age, vth _____ eyebrows rises slightly from his seat to interrut, where previously he was only listening with a highly oncentrated frown] the original conception of the First eader, whose name I am not going to reveal here, not now ad not ever, while you suggest our graffiti design conctts aimed at opening worm holes between alternative univrses allowing for souls to travel through sadness to gladrss, from sickness unto health, we are not going to confm or deny these reports! We are terminating this intervievhere! Come on, bro, let's get out of here! Time to go!

[the first Virgin Defacer, ho has not actually stopped talking, contiues---] I painted SQUASQUASQUEÉSQUHPO508I098N PV CIH0 thirteen times on City Coucilman Art Snyder's car dealership and tiki restaurant in untington Beach till his career was destroyed, I painted BYBOYBOIZZZZ90u45y cvch----------------------------,-------! on Councilman's Mike Hernandez's bail bondbusiness 17 times till his career was destroyed, I paintd GLUGLUGGLUG8uyw c87cy784 twelve times (that as all it took for that sucker!) on Mayor Antonio Villaraigoa's girlfriend's apartment building till his career was destoyed, I painted HAHAHA-NANANANANAggeerrrrrRR!'!!!!!!!! 19 times outside of Griffith Park Observatory tryingto destroy the career of the Universe, or the Powers of the Universe, but so far nothing happened so I just gotta keep doag it!

[but his partner interjects] Okay, kay, come on now! You gotta let it go. We got to go now!

I painted ZOKOZOKOZICKYZACK-nunununununu=-27ur976t0 at the Los Angeles City Hall lawn on the wings of the pedestal for the statue commemorating

the Unknown Conquering White Man whose name has
been lost to history but whose statue still stands high above
the city clerks and Latinos, the cops and protestors milling
around under the city ficus trees in the 90 degree shade
with the sprinkler going off once every 45 minutes to keep
the homeless people (or anybody) from taking a nap on the
grass, I painted GHGGGGAHAUWOGGGAHHHH-
HHHboowowowoogaaaahhhhhhhoi95e7y6 on the LA.
Times Building across the street, as a matter of fact, like
4 or 5 times or if I remember correct, coming and going, since the ole building was converted into one giant
pencil sharpe after being bought by the Chicago Tribune
Corporation, ich gutted the paper and laid off the entire
staff and repld all editors with mannikins purchased
from Sears ldions abandoned throughout Detroit and
Flint, Michig I painted RrrarrRRrararrRRRRRRR-
RR-0248t—

A. [violently unable to control himself any longer, the
second Virg Defacer lunges across the coffee table at his
partner] I SD IT'S TIME TO GO!

Preliminary Interview ends here.

Appendix D:
Fly the East L.A. Dirigible Air Transport Lines

1.

Why?

There is no why.

Because the world ended at Paul's Kitchen in Monterey Park on April 26, 1986, and no one noticed. Because there was a kind of afterglow to the whole thing, slow-motion train wreck with the poor visibility of an oil fire. Because hair and fingernails keep growing after death. Because everything was bathed in an orange light, the long last light of afternoon saturated all surfaces with the semblance of eternity. Because of Reaganomics, the Reagan revolution and redistribution of income, infrastructure, rights, representation, peace and quiet to the rich. Because I went to the Hat to get a "best pastrami in the world" and the newspaper said, NIXON DEAD AT 81, REMEMBERED AS GREAT STATESMAN. Because thousands of sea turtles, porpoises, dolphins, pelicans, fish, and seabirds floundered, suffocated, and died in a poisoned ocean of BP (Arco), and the fish and dolphins and porpoises and sea birds were made of yellow and gelatin. Because the sun was yellow, the sea was green, and the sky was brown. Because there was not a bandaid to put on fresh injustice. Because there was not a radio broadcasting radio silence to the victims of the disaster for no help came because there was no excursion trolley provided to transport tourists to the edge of town.

Because small cigarette packs came wrapped in cellophane like the Chinaman (and the secret Chinese) came wrapped in yellow. It was almost historical. Because historiography was burned in the fifty-gallon drum in the backyard with her parents' love letters and the mysterious booklet of numbers and codes. Because they couldn't say what it meant anymore. Because there were a million reasons not do anything and only like four or five reasons to actually do anything, and people avoided that. Because for that reason, dog fights became wildly popular, and cock fights, private clubs and private sex clubs, serial killers and distraction, alcoholism, lame movies, and sports. Because anything where people didn't have to kill themselves seemed better, like fresh paint and pills and red licorice and clean laundry, like the smell of home-baked bread coming out of the oven, and, if possible, we could still go really fast, faster and faster. Like really fast. Because everything could get blurry.

Because you could get a boxer to punch you in the head to simulate brain damage. Or you could examine the brains of athletes in sports prone to brain damage. Or you could leave the maintenance of order to the military and not bother to read the reports. Or you could wait for the military to tell the whole story. Or you could wait till years later when more people started talking about what really happened. Because somebody often remembered. Because somebody always talked. Or you could study the problem, which wasn't the most popular.

And if you opened people up inside would they have mayonnaise? Would they have old schedules, diurnal cycles, hormonal stains, quarter-inch molding? Would they crinkle like a baked potato with steaming sour cream and chives? Would they emit their own burned, charred remains on the floors of house being demolished, the dry tarpaper and blackened boards splintering jaggedly, revealing almost pink grain? Would they reveal empty industrial avenues and post-riot boulevards with the sky reflected in pools or puddles from the fire hydrants? Would they smile revealing the urban inertia and business-like acceptance of death in life as if they themselves were a walking personification of Las Vegas, Reno, Phoenix, Denver, and San Diego? Would they have ready a deck of cards, lawn chairs, international criminal enterprise and offshore accounts, and amusing pets?

There is no why, just an infinity of reasons not chulo enough. Because of everything—why is for later. Everything was here first, and why came last.

You yourself arrived before it—before unfolding days of exacerbated miles, before freeway overpasses and interchanges, before nostalgia and riots. Since there was nothing for you, no place or space or room or destination for you, then you showed up. People in the dusty park, waiting to emerge under the trees like the dusk.

A collective and imagined self precedes you, walks ahead of you. Everybody was loud. They were shouting and laughing, she was having a great time, then an hour or so after the party she was vomiting. She turned her head to the side to spit to clear her mouth. She lay down and drifted to sleep, moaning a little. He'd always thought it was wonderful the way her eyes shone. Years later she saw him approaching in a parking lot, and something in his face about how she looked, her appearance had changed, annoyed her, and she turned her face from him. She walked off before he got there. He could have run after her. He thought he'd bump into her again, but he never did, mostly he forgot her. He forgot something about himself at the same time—he went about just as forgotten, unimagined.

Dusk collecting in the trees.

ELADTL
C/S

3

I am communicating with you now.

Thank you for this appointment. I have been appointed to many positions of centers and organizations that are about to hit the wall at 60 MPH or about to fold. Which is this? I am in charge now. Do what I say. And. . . [static] . . . short term. . . [static noise] blank check with my . . . [popping sound] . . . organic... [buzzing] . . . ssssttz—

The Effect of Phases of the Moon

. . . ably, with this economy, in Calif—[static] . . . kites [popping sound] . . . the most obvious routes being the ones that we have considered, and counterintuitively, using mathematical models we have on hand from the Danish . . . [static noise] . . . Golden Hind, Ferdinand Magellen, the famous schoo—[buzzing, loud and then fading] . . . to the moon, in 1969, whi—[loud buzz overtaken by humming] . . . the Eastern Sierras, the San Joaquin and Great central—[static] . . . thank—[static interrupted by silence] . . . [popping sound] [a dog barking] . . . comrades, we—[fading static hiss] . . .

2009 PROCLAIMED END OF THE AUTOMOTIVE ERA!

Solar globes overhead are the self-charging, clean, quiet, convenient and leisurely transport to the Future!

No more waiting around for pigeon shit bronze horsemen to fall off pedestals, for taxicabs of absolute reality to crash here, for pigeons to explode like clay pigeons, for the crowds of shadows to shift and reveal the faces.

Sign your name on the dotted line ....

Sign your house over to the bank ....

Sign your body over to insurance ....

Sign your car over to the Trash Vortex in the Sky ....

Sign your family over to the Future of Catastrophe ....

Sign your job over to the Decline of Endless Budget Cuts ....

Sign state and local governments over to Wall Street ....

Sign your ideas over to Trash Vortex in the Sky ....

Sign your soul over to the nearest Parking Meter ....

Sign your sorrow over to Virtual Reality War ....

They're taking everything; let's give it to them. Give them extra!

Fly to it!

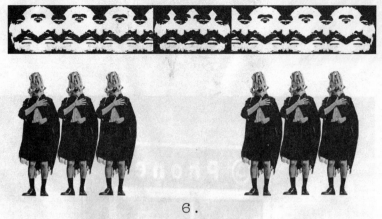

6.

Swiftest flight freer than the sober whiskey of Love faster than a neuron in fact a neuron of a new body itself a lift on East Los Angeles Dirigible Transport Lines! Imagine the clean air, wildhaired rain, sunny radiowaves and spatial networks of Shit That Makes The Engine Run And Exhaust below with pretty lights, parties & the reading of fun fun poems & different states of Being where the flapping wings of birds touch, Long Beach to Huntington Park 20 minutes of the day or 20 days of the minute, they lemme sing up there Chavela Vargas songs like a gun of birth with my eyes of a mushroomcloud and nobody even flinched! & the wind howled throo my pockets & I lost my contents & stepped off that ladder like head first into the day & the sky still on my face & I was ready then to circumnavigate the big walls of empire and day-to-day drabness and my zero credit,

My name is Mosaic Roskalnikov and I approve this message with the taste of posole still on my breath.

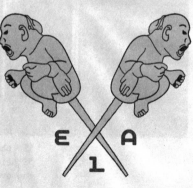

7.
Mail Bag: Letters from Our Many Satisfied Customers

GOLDEN WEST
Minibike Sales and Service 4U

3929 W. Riverside Drive, Toluca Lake CA.   (818) 842-1922

Dear Nuts,:
    It is my pleasure to inform you that your services
are no longer needed. Nor were they ever. Not by me
or any of mine. Your organization is a boil on the
gallbladder of this nation. Everytime I shake out my shoes,
there you are.
Most sincerely,

Darryl Gates
Chief Engineer
Golden West Minibike Sales and Service 4U
Toluca Lake, California

Mr. Wheelnuts,
    Sir. For this reason and others I commend you
As a regular and multisatisfied user of your cereal
products I find my health measurably improved. By 16
at last measure. Such results! For too many years I
was reduced to digging holes, hoping to discover
there-in the solution to your problems. O how the
neighbors did object! After much practice and travail
it became evident to me and all those dear to me that
it is in the nature of holes that they do not contain
solutions, or any other things. This is why our elders
in their wisdom decided to call them "holes" rather
than: "things". Your groundskeeper tells me that this
principle has been the great key to your success.
Kudos , sir! From this day on, I expectorate with
    pride, and thank you for it.

    Yours without restraint,

Fulgencio Tree

    Fulgencio Tree
    Montebello

Oddfellows
Cemetery & Crematorium

1342 WEST 1ST STREET, BOYLE HEIGHTS, ALTA CALIFORNIA 90033   (213) 695-1973

Dear Sir or Madam,

I have lost something important. While traveling in your vehicle, I became confused. It was a pleasant feeling while it lasted, but having since recovered, I find myself dismayed by the price of your tickets, and by the uniforms of your employees, which are ~~are~~ are repugnant. So much velour! I am ~~tot~~ told the meals were excellent, but as for me, I did not care for the sensation of landing. Also, the perilons were overstated. I liken you to a bird lacking in feathers, beak and wings, in some essential birdness. In this and other matters, you defy all expectations. I therefore ask for your imme immediate assistance.

Mrs. Stevedore Ware
Oddfellows Cemetery
& Crematorium
Boyle Heights,
Alta California

285

From the Desk of
MATHILDE

To Whom it May Concern,
I have often imagined flights
above the Empire State, and far
and more expansive in Brooklyn
skies. Singy feet above it her
or less and on a cloudy breezeless
day. _____
Thus the realm of my own. The
flight path of your Zeppelin
transport line has robbed me of
these dreams. I commend you to
your kibog but otherwise withhold
all praise.

In bitter appreciation bereft,

Mathilde Parisitt-Semanal, Esq.
Monterey Park, CA

Gentlemen,
I commend you! In all my years, your Genuine East Los Angeles
Dirigibles are the most delicious fried delectables I have yet
encountered. So delicate and with a perfect puff of sweetness.
Will you send nutritional information chart? SASE enclosed for
your convenience, minus stamp. Hence SAE.

my very best,

Amanda (from bingo night)

OFFICE OF THE MAYOR
ANTONIO R. VILLARAIGOSA

October 14, 1998

Dear Wheelnuts,

It is with a heavy heart that I write to inform you that I cannot accept your generous campaign contribution, which exceeds the limits specified under state and federal law. Also I have no use for so much helium. What were you thinking? See official certificate of appreciation, enclosed.

yours in service,

Antonio Villaraigosa
Mayor
City of Los Angeles

200 NORTH SPRING STREET • LOS ANGELES, CALIFORNIA 90012
PHONE: (213) 978-0600 • FAX: (213) 978-0750
EMAIL: MAYOR@LACITY.ORG

Sirs:
I have not yet had the occasion to enjoy your
product, but I hear it is "pretty good." I write to
inform you of an investment opportunity that you will
not wish to pass up. I am myself an inventor of a
patented meteorological gust-creation mechanism that
produces the finest and densest gusts of any machine
now on the market. My competitors' gusts do not stand
comparison. Mine are speculative, feather-guided and
potentially localizable. Being intelligent gentlemen,
I am sure you are already fervently engaged in
imagining the advantages the possession of my latest
model (the PassingWind X-2000®) would confer upon
your enterprise. Particularly when your inflatable
dirigible vehicles hover, in all apparent innocence,
above the prancing ponies of the Santa Anita
hippodrome. If you wish to discuss this opportunity
in greater detail, I can be found nightly in the last
booth but one on the right (directly beneath the dart
board) at the Solemn Sailor Basement Bar & Lounge on
Eastern Avenue. I will be wearing a false mustache.
Please make no mention of it.
sand and stones, my heart explodes,

Vinegar Ooo
Ramona Gardens

Dear Swirlings:

My father, who is ill-disposed as far as fingers go, has asked me to write to you to express his appreciation. Perhaps he did not ask in so many words, not explicitly, but I am sure he would not frown on the endeavor. "Those dirigible fellows," he likes to say. Frequently he says this. He never finishes the sentence. It's always just, "Those dirigible fellows," but I can assure you that his tone is one of great respect and admiration, as if the mere thought of you has elevated his existence to such heights as you daily traverse in the exercise of your labors. This tone is easily distinguishable from, for instance, the one he employs when referring to me, his only living child. "That shit-eyed son of mine," is another of his favorites. Usually followed by a hocking sound. I imagine these two utterances as two great mountains, between which stretches a valley, a sort of dusky bog really, in which my father, fingerless, spends his days. Hocking. Up to his neck in it. The bastard. I thought you'd like to know.

I remain,

IGGY POND

Iggy Pond
Irwindale

8.

**Menu for Dirigible flights longer than
30 minutes served from 11:30a.m.–1p.m.
Every Day for reference**

Menu for Dirigible flights longer than 30 minutes
served from 11:30am - 1pm Every Day

a la carte
delicious snacks served quickly

Mexican Hot Dogs 2.00
Farmer John weenie wrapped in flour tortilla with mayonnaise

Pink Macaroni and Cheese 1.50
Elbow macaroni cooked in tomato sauce sprinkled with cheese
(available wet or dry)

Sanavagan 1.50
Eggs scrambled with cut up Farmer John brand weenies

Crinkle Cut French Fries .50
side of cream cheese

Full Lunch
all lunch is served with miso soup and cottage cheese

Chicken sandwich 4.00
shredded chicken with diced green onions in mayonnaise on crust-free white bread

Phillipe French Dip 4.00
roast beef sandwich on a bed of sawdust

Pico Salad 16.00
Wedge of iceburg lettuce with shredded green papaya and sliced beet-pickled eggs. Shrimp/chile de arbol dressing

Beverage Menu

Soda .75

Dr. Brown's Cel-Ray
Coca-Cola
Jarritos Tamarindo
Eastern Hill Mineral Water

Coffee
All of our coffee beverages are made with Verdugo Hills Coffee Bean Company Shade Grown Dark Roast beans

Cafe con Che .35
Espresso shot heavy with cinnamon, no sugar

Coffee .25

Aguas Frescas .85
available daily, please inquire for our flavor of the day

After Lunch*
(please enjoy in the observation deck)

Herbal smoking mix cigarette .75
relaxing mix of psylocibe, tobacco and locally grown roses and squash blossoms

ELADTL

9.
Complaint Forms

Did you enjoy your journey with East Los Angeles Dirigible Air Transport Systems?

A._____yes

B_____What have those earthbound stevedores incidentally not in our employ done now?

If you answered yes to the above question, return to the rear of the queue; if you checked B, please proceed with the form as if you have never hired a lawyer.

Please check the appropriate complaint:

1. _____Overly rapid ascent.
Explanation and suggested further proceeding: Stevedore mishandling of copra apparatus. Equilibrate. Check temperature on fifth subsequent day. Call appropriate ministry or labor union. Ask for Steve.

2. _____Looked out the window and hit in the face by a chihuahua.
Explanation and suggested further proceeding: Please keep head and limbs inside airship at all times for safety. Your safety is something we consider a priority.

3. _____Lost luggage.
Explanation and suggested further proceeding: It's most likely at the West Covina Amtrack station, where an old dude tells passengers that they are in Claremont. Proceed to your destination and we will call you to pick up your luggage. When we call you to pick up your luggage you will have no longer than five hours, at which point the stevedores have the pick of the lot.

4. _____Lost chihuahua.
Explanation and suggested further proceeding: See #2 above.

_____Conductor requested your ticket and you do not wish to pay, because you are with your "friends."
Explanation and suggested further proceeding: Exit at next station yelling curses and trying to look defiant, yet sharp, as you walk across the parking lot trailed by "friends."

_____Your basic questions remain unanswered.
Explanation and suggested further proceeding: For $50, today only, the Alhambra Photomart booth psychic Mrs Lin (who is not Asian, by the way) is on hand to answer all questions. The basic ones. Love, money, business, dreams. Step forward into the redesignated maintenance room. "There is an ATM in the 7-11," Mrs Lin sometimes says.

_____General complaints, not just about your flight, but about everything.
Explanation and suggested further proceeding: List them here
_____.

Mail this form to ELADATL **Service** Complaint Division
c/o Mrs. Lin Psychic Shop
1100 W Commonwealth Ave
Alhambra, CA 91803

_____ Something.

Explanation and suggested **further** proceeding: Specify
_____.

_____Vague **existential** angst.

Explanation and **suggested** further proceeding: Purchase **one year pass** good
on flights on all routes, $298 **this** week only. Call 1-800 DIRGIBL.

_____You **get off** at the end of the **line and it** is on **the** Croatian
coast.

Explanation and **suggested** further **proceeding. Stevedores adopted** your
chihuahua, nullifying **the basic facts of** your ticket. Be more physical,
go **for** the throat, go **for** the goat, they **have a** lot of goats there, be
all that a goat can be, eat tin, horns **available** at any **trafika.** By no
means share your passport with that old lady at the **Rijeka train station**
with hands like raven claws.

—Rick Harsch, **Pres.** Union of **Wisconsin** Stevedores, Slovenia

East Los Angeles Dirigible Transport Lines

Address:
3571 City Terrace Drive
Los Angeles, CA 90063

Phone:
AN 41267

(L-R) Sesshu Foster, Arturo Romo, Ben Ehrenreich, Rick Harsch, Raul Ruiz, Swirling E. Wheelnuts, Sergio

Should we say our names out loud?
For the record?
Just transcribe it,
we'll sort out who was who later.
Or we won't.
Yeah, or we won't.
Who cares?
Saturday—
Liki, Swirling, Tania—
Who wants to start?
Who's going to—
Nestor, Ben—
What is to be done?
Aquila, Mosaic—

"THE ELEVATED VIEW AFFORDED
FROM HEIGHTS OFFERED BY
BALLOON TRANSPORT OF THE
FUTURE ARE EXCITING. IMAGINE
SEEING THE DRIFT OF EastLA
LIKE YOU HEAR PIECES OF
MUSIC DRIFTING IN FROM
HOUSES SUNDAY MORNING,
EXCELLENT OPPORTUNITIES FOR
CRACKING OPEN CODES OF VISUAL
INTERFERENCE."
—ZAD MANIFESTO, 2010

THIS IS WHAT WE MUST DO.

Recapture imagination colonized by internal combustion
formats of Hollywood, since the movie industry with
its posters of glowering stars brandishing fire arms like
big dicks is only the commercial organ of the largest arms
export corporations in the world, Colt, Armalite, Sturm,
Ruger & Co., U.S. Fire Arms Mfg Co., etc.
and U.S. is the largest arms exporter in the world, troops
deployed in over 150 countries, in combat in
half a dozen at any given moment.

(Do these trash movies & exciting wars make Americans
happy? No, the suicide rate is twice the murder rate, with
34,000 people killing themselves each year, 94
or so every day, whereas only 17,000 people are
murdered annually, which is interestingly more
than Mexico in spite of its drug war, curious
don't you think?)

WHAT ELSE DO WE GOT?

No jobs, eh. They've fucked up the schools with bureaucracy,
testing, bullshit, fees, poverty, they polluted the earth,
water, killed off all the fish in the rivers, threw plastic
and giant oil spills in the ocean, blighted the cities and
infrastructure. All the money went to banks and Wall Street
and they told the people, go have fun with your wars.

(Predator drone strikes—UAV—unmanned aerial vehicle –
$10,500,000 each General Atomics "Reaper"—target and kill
thousands in Yemen, Iraq, Somalia, Afghanistan, Pakistan,
etc., 30% of attack deaths are civilian noncombatants,
women and children. Drones receive feed control from
Creech Air Force Base outside of Las Vegas.)

Visions of global skies, grand cumulus drift on the
atmosphere above glittering seas. Caribbean light values.
Shades include prairie sage, egg cream, and coral violet.

What's that about?

Waves lapping, an incoming tide. Rising wind.

Marine breezes, luminous cloud banks rising over the horizon.

Oh, in other words, we give 'em metaphors and stuff. Same stuff writers and artists always give them. What good is that?

Call it "new ways of seeing," we call it "alternative lifestyle," call it "human powered flight," "Ennoblement of Water," or "Implosion Machine."

We could tell them—

Tell them a story.

Implement narrative—

Implement overarching narratives.

Like, maybe we can come up with new ones!

CAN SOMEBODY GIVE US A GRANT FOR IT?

You know anybody?

Creative Capital won't do it. They said nobody's in charge of us.

The fuckers.

Yeah.

How do we start?

Men with brutal faces skyward. Leaping.

Orchestral arrangements?

Women with perfect teeth. Much leaping.

Musculature choreographed to appear and disappear behind hair, or khaki.

Flapping of canvas in a hard wind, wind whistling through guy wires.

Calendar above a tool bench at the rear of a garage.
Calendar leaves begin flapping as in a hard wind, the years

flying off. The crackling of fire grows louder.

Piles of titty magazines in stench of mildew and rat droppings. Coke bottle crates, empty oil cans. Acres of junk car bodies, quonset huts out in the boulders and Joshua trees. California fire season radio broadcast.

Women widening their eyes. Casting a significant glance.

Men flaring nostrils, setting their lips in a line.

"Completing its first circumnavigation of the globe in less than 22 days, the Graf Zeppelin under the command of Doctor Hugo Eckener arrives over the Manhattan skyline June 5, 1931, as the first streaks of light penetrate a gray dawn."

"Berlin–New York City two days. Friedrichshafen–Rio de Janeiro 2 days."

Here's your ticket on the Rock Island Line.

I hear the crows snickering and chortling.

So—

Ah—

Yeah.

What's the story?

Plans go back to the turn of the

(NOT ONLY CHORIZO SKINS, BUT ALSO TIGHT WOVEN SILK AND CALIFORNIA NATIVE BASKETRY TECHNIQUES COULD BE USED IN THE PATCHING OF DEFUNCT DIRIGIBLES)

last century. Personal hygiene in the upper atmosphere. Austrian forester Viktor Schauberger's water vortex implosion machines. Nikola Tesla's Colorado Springs experiments to transfer energy through longitudinal waves to telautomatic objects. Porous skin shining metallic in the glare (filters).

Glints of hard sunlight on flexing bodies.

~~Heaving breast. Clapping—~~

~~Robert Desnos dying at Terezín (Theresienstadt)~~

It's a movie.

It's a movie of the imagination.

An imaginary—

No.

It's not—

Not imaginary. Not an imaginary movie. It's of the actual or factual or real imagination.

Movie of the imagination.

Like pseudographic cinema: Asco's No Movies—impressions of factuality, projecting the real.

Do we make this movie ourselves?

Let's get somebody to make this movie.

Who can we get?

I have their files:

Chicana Power Bumpersticker, flamboyant hair, last time I saw her she moved back from Mexico City. She had run from El Paso, TX (van-supported) to D.F., Mexico City in support of rights for indigenous peoples and was living there. She could be the most charismatic lead actress and probably the love interest.

Compa He Called Me, went from guerrillero to wandering poet on his way to NYC through any number of lives, he asked me for contacts in the East. Could reappear at any time for supporting role as Engineer Who Fixes Everything At the Last Minute, adding to the suspense.

Pirate Radio, one night I was cleaning out an apartment I had already moved out of, carrying the last bag of trash downstairs to the street and he walks out of the dark, asking for directions. "Oh, it's you!" he said when we both stepped under the street light. Years before that, I met this vato in Iowa City (born Durango MX); when he came to L.A., I sent him to my

cousin, who put him up till he found a place. Campus radical, led lots of tours till he went underground, but you might hear him some midnights coming out of pirate radio, announcing his Nahua name. He is exactly the authority figure we need for a pilot and commander.

Hecho en Aztlan, always working two jobs, raising his son alone in that house on a hill. He must've shown, at some point, the son the same foto he showed me: the scraggly bunch of revolutionaries out in the desert twenty years before, him holding something like a single shot .22 carbine. The son, in his black rocker t-shirts and skinny black pants, Converse All-stars, kept wondering why his dad has to be such a hardass. Both could easily do that love-hate buddy routine that audiences always love so well.

Tamale Lady, sometimes sells 3 kinds of tamales out of buckets from the back of her station wagon in the parking lot of the Alhambra Market. I don't really know anything about her, like if she has experience at anything like this or whatever, but it might be good to ask her. She might run our whole operation, with all kinds of logistical experience dealing with difficulties of all kinds, getting people out of jail, etc.

Grandma Walsh, used to talk to dozens of cats underneath the fruit trees in the front yard, smell of rotten peaches, a very nice person, gone for a long time I expect, now the yard is full of dead cars, I think she could still be talked into lending us outstanding screen presence.

Joker, obsidian eyes like laughing flint, what a joker! He has his scars (no, we don't want to see the false teeth); he's been shot at least once. He has his secrets (secret family in another city). He has gambling debts and death threats; those are forgotten. Such a loveable rogue, so funny, what a storyteller, such a joker. Could be a lead actor, whose facile exterior hides a heart of gold, has a thing for lead actress, whatever.

Mytili Jagannathan, Philadelphia poet, once led a group of us on a tour of Philadelphia Chinatown. This one has a somewhat different script, but I know for a fact she could handle the gig. Tremendous poise and flashing dark eyes of an air commander. I see her as our crack attack dirigible pilot.

Guatemalteco, print shop owner, soccer man, plays the over thirty league, using profits from the business to spon-sor a girl's club team, hires a professional coach. Took the girls on a Central American tour where they made region play-offs, yes indeed. He doesn't really have the time, but you know, he might just be talked into supporting role as character actor.

Samba Pa Ti, hopefully he still blasts out those songs like Billy Bragg accompanying himself on a lone electric guitar. I never gave him enough credit for that. Last seen by my brother wearing the blue helmet of UN peacekeepers, waving at the TV cameras in Bosnia. Where are you, my brother? No one is better qualified to be secret agent and gay love interest. First Aid/CPR certified.

(FIRST I WAS INTO GEODESIC ALUMINUM MUSHROOMS. THEY SEEMED TO ME THE PERFECT STRUCTURE. NOW I FAVOR THE SOFT LIGHTNESS OF BALLONS.)

81 But Looks 59, came to Calif. in 1920 as photographer's assistant to Edward Weston, WPA photographer in San Francisco, ship welder during World War 2 (steel splinter destroyed the sight in one eye), this old dude scares us every time we go to Redondo Beach he swims so far beyond the breakers you can't even see him. Expert haggler at Grand Central Market over old, wilated vegetables; they can't pull nothing on him. Often says, "doctors just want your money." If he gives you food throw it away. Perfect for the role of Enrique Pico, Chief Financial Officer of the East Los Angeles Dirigible Transport Lines.

Oh yeah ha,

I once wrote to debunk hoaxes and myths, but as I progressed on each debunking project, I would become more and more confused. I realized that the sighting of anomalies was by nature and definition anomalous. Furthermore, I realized that all anomaly is really variation. I began to see all variation and change as anomalous and in consequence many mundane things in the world; flowing water, growing hair, roadkill, movement of bodies, acceleration and even stasis became as odd and frightening to me as mothman, chupacabra or cattle mutilation.

And slowly, my recognition of the anomalous spread to include more and more of the things around me until everything that filled my senses was foreign and struck terror in me: a boy's head cracked by a policeman's fist, my voice slipping across the wind, Lopez-Feliu's hair growing year by year, iron against lubricated iron, a skyscraper falling in a pile, the rapidly worming distances between my eyes and distant views . . .

I don't know all of them, personally I mean.

You think?

I know—

Yeah, we can get 'em.

But a couple of 'em—didn't they pass away, like die already?

Well. Maybe.

You plan on digitally re-creating them?

If we have to. From records, audio files, MP3 files, CGI scans, telemetronic measurements, old photographs, overdubbing, YouTube videos, forensic science with insects, seeds and spores, Shadow Lengthening Imagery and

Vegetal Echolocation.

The hard part is to get people to commit, to actually do it.

I know, right?

We have to practically force them.

Yeah, practically.

Well, not practically.

Yeah, actually, we will force them to.

We'll just force them.

They have to.

They do.

Otherwise it doesn't get done.

Otherwise nothing gets done.

Yeah.

We can't let them hold us up.

We can't let anything stand in our way.

Nobody is stopping us.

Even if they're dead. We'll reconstitute them from electrical files, electron images, shadow research and stuff.

We can probably do it.

I'm sure we can.

I think we may have to, in some cases.

We'll figure out some way.

It will be interesting, to say the least.

How will they get paid?

All is now in flux and changing, everything is anomalous and hoax; even the hoax and story of gravity only dictates one direction of many directions and can be called into question as readily as the moth-man hoax—our blood flows up and down, across and back, pumped by a strange hoax—the heart muscle, flowing through strange mythic channels called veins. These words follow a mythical set of systems to become a strangely manifest hoax. The myth of dictated words in mythical symbols representing ideas (themselves anomalous and deceptive) laid down in quick drying hoax-ink on a mythical and unprovable substrate.

This paper that you hold in your hand and the content on it and the brain functions that lead you to understand it are all unprovable hoaxes perpetuated by over-active imaginations susceptible to the influence of myth.

"On", "over", "on top", "based on"... all orientation and relation is ghostlike and anomalous. Directionality and placement, composition and divine order are hoaxes and mythologies.

I'm thinking we exist and ultimately are mythical—like a play with no director or audience, no script or stage, no actors, no props... for reference please see mirror scene in ZAD, mythical movie from the hoax year of 2016.

We'll pay them later.

I guess so.

We'll probably have to.

Yeah, because, like—

It's not like we have any funds.

We have a methodology.

We have the methodology of ontology.

Pass me that, would you?

The tea?

(MY SUBMISSION FOR THE METRO GOLD LINE STATION EXTENSION INTO EL SERENO WAS REJECTED BECAUSE IT INCLUDED A DOCKING STATION FOR FUTURE DIRIGIBLE PROJECTS. THEY ALSO SAID IT RESEMBLED SACRIFICIAL STEPS OF ANCIENT CIVILIZATIONS AND THEY DIDN'T LIKE THAT)

(WE KNOW THAT ALL THINGS ARE INTERCONNECTED AND RELATED AND THAT IT'S THE LINKS AND RELATIONSHIPS BETWEEN DIFFERENCES THAT MAKE UP THE COMPLEX ARCHITECTURE OF REALITY)

Gracias.

Methodological ontology.
Did you get that from
Cal State L.A.?

When I was a teenager,
I used to read a lot.

We'll pay them in ontology?
Ontologically?

It'll have to be an all-volunteer force, at least at the
beginning.

Looks like it!

Harry Gamboa gives people food,
when he's directing his movies.

We can try that. Maybe we can get Harry to direct.

He's always busy. But maybe. It could be good to have a big
name director like that.

Nobody knows Liki Renteria.

Not yet, anyway.

But one day!

Because, for example, check this out. This is my idea:
first—we somehow make this movie, then—

Then we can pay our people—

**Well, maybe. I'm thinking we use the money we raise to build
actual East L.A. Dirigible Air Transport Lines, fashioned after
the imaginary one built out of—**

Ontology.

—out of preconceptions and misjudgments, Colima dogs
and queso fresco—

—out of peanut butter and bamboo sticks, Ray Foster's
letters and old lawn mowers, things that should've been
said but weren't, afixed in the last light of afternoon—

—Manny's Special Burrito, if you can eat the whole thing
you get it free, with added lift from the uncle who always
said, "You're gonna turn out to be the scum of the earth like

your old man!"—

—cracked pieces of Bakelite radios and toasters, ceramic tile, electrical tape, rabbit skin, willow sticks, laundry baskets, ironing boards, Big Wheels, wind-up toys, piggy banks—

—condoms (to be safe), unbreakable plastic combs (with the teeth broken) all dried out by still smelling like hair oil, Roosevelt dimes, axe handles—

—writ of Habeas Corpus, needlenose pliers, recycled LAUSD textbooks, parts of Oldsmobiles, American Motors, International Harvesters, Packards, Plymouths, Pontiacs, Hummers, Saturns and 100% recycled parts of car companies that no longer exist—

—we will be green, everything shall be recycled or recycleable: ideas and identities, personal issues and the air that we breathe, time (the long hand and the short hand go round and round)—

~~Love scene, moon over Acapulco Bay~~—

—recycled from wasted lives, from getting hit in the forehead with a brick, from pissing your life away in bars, from not having anything to say anymore—

—plus Biktor Schauberter's astonishing Implosion Engine technology, Nikola Tesla's longitudinal wave energy transfer broadcasters and receivers, based on the newly discovered Colorado patent interviews—

First the idea—

Like a dream almost.

Then we develop images—

Models, functioning prototypes, more or less. Hard to tell till we build some of them.

We'll need a lot of space for the materials.

Sensory details, chicken wire, and PVC pipe.

No PVC pipe. I'd rather use bamboo and natural hemp cordage.

No bamboo then.

Ay! Lame!

Ha ha ha!

Wide landing fields like veritable open plains. Like steppes.

Like El Monte in the 1950s.

~~Love scene, roaring river far below vast as an inland sea, accidental fire—~~

We'll expropriate abandoned aerospace buildings out by the Burbank airport. There's dead sections of the industrial landscape out there, probably some come with hangars attached.

Probably.

And closer to downtown, certainly there's abandoned industrial buildings with vacant warehouse space in El Sereno along the railroad tracks.

That will work perfectly.

So that's the plan.

You got the story?

> *I got lots of notes. I'm always taking notes. Stuff is always coming to me. It feels like having something in your eye, so you have to get it down.*

Men with brutal faces, leaping skyward. Rising into the sky.

Women tossing hair. Looking over their shoulder, hip cocked.

Legs and arms akimbo. Tattered fabric flapping in stiff wind like flags.

~~Trolley careening around a bend on an embankment above Huntington Drive, 1930s—~~

Parachutes descending through clouds.

Clouds whipping through guy wires.

It's a kind of aerial ballet.

Mechanized to an extent.

A new civilization.

The possibility for one.

Sort of like going back into the past to alter the future.

Women with perfect teeth. Arched eyebrows, cute crinkly nosed squint. Crinkly skin of desire—

Clock faces, gauges, dashboard instruments. All technical.

~~People watching from balconies—~~

Women with strong shoulders, rising into the sky. Pert square or boyish shoulders.

Tania, everybody agrees with that.

I still want that in there.

It's on the tape.

~~Stiff wind in the wardrobe. Coffee whipped out of the cup by wind, drops driven across a smooth surface, when you look down the cup is empty (in a 1930s way)—~~

~~Someone behind the curtains—~~

Love interest gets a severe haircut? Occasioning a disturbance, setting off a running gun battle? An aerial duel between fleets of airships?

We gotta come up with some better than—

Stale stuff—

Yeah, don't worry.

If nothing else, we're masters at improvising.

Ay! Lame!

Ha ha ha!

`We'll see. Just call 1-800-DIRGIBL.`

Shadows of attacking ships emerging from the cloud bank are thrown onto the the dirigibles below.

Crew choice when the ship goes down in flames, burn with the ship or leap to certain death. The sad choice of duty. Analogous to war capitalism where you burn in the ship or leap into space.

(You knew what you were signing up for, kids.)

Laying down your life for your fellow man (Merrill Lynch, Chase Bank, Lehman Brothers, etc.) in a world that is forever at war.

She always has new tattoos. One day she's covered in Japanese camellias, and the next time she reveals skin they've become robots. It's a running gag. She explains how to create new tattoos out of old by ingenious designs where you rewrite over the previous ones on a continuing basis.

Lots of coincidental revelation of skin.

Human skin, soft. Taut dirigible skin.

She has a praying mantis as a pet. She talks to it.

Maybe it could do the voice-over.

Explosions rock the ship.

Like BP Deep Horizon, they only have a few minutes before the platform is consumed.

Only one parachute, you know what this means.

No, you take it.

No, you.

No, you.

He thrusts it at her and steps to the open (door?), says, goodbye my dear.

Jumps.

She straps on the parachute and leaps overboard to try to save him, plunging through atmospheres. Will she reach him in time to pull the cord?

~~Why didn't he think of that first?~~

Shot of the praying mantis, light green as a spring rain, swaying delicately on the shuddering or cracked guages of the console.

Praying mantis voice over—unintelligible squeaking, blotted out by sounds of destruction.

Those insects can't even make any noise, do they?

Maybe they make a crunchy sounds when they chomp up their mates.

Just when all seems lost, East L.A. Dirigible Transport Lines on fire, shot to pieces, some going down in flames (proud

ELADATL flagship Colima, with its distinctive dog head consumed by a BALL OF FIRE, still proudly upholding its dog head)—sprouting tiny white parachutes like dandilion seeds in the blurry air smudged with columns of smoke, the heroine plunges through the air seeking out what's his name, who jumped with no chute. Suddenly, far above, out of the columns of smoke and storm front cloud banks, appear the giant tentacles of Kraken, the—

What's that? Like a giant octopus?

It comes out of the clouds, a giant sort of puppet octopus?

Yeah! It crushes the fascist zeppelins of the reactionary forces and saves the day.

WTF?

It's another metaphor. One metaphor is saved by another.

Really?

Oh, I don't know.

Can we do that?

Can we do what? Make a giant Kraken octopus out of papier-mâché, so that it doesn't look like "The Giant Claw" monster from 1957, operate it from wires and drop it through cumulus cloud banks and swirling black smoke?

We'll have our technical experts work on it. Special effects!

It's doable. They can bail out AIG and Detroit, we can bail out East L.A. Dirigible Transport with a Kraken.

They didn't bail out Detroit! They bailed out car companies.

Kraken, out of the sky? Out of clouds?

Out of the unknown Trash Vortex.

Trash Vortex? In the sky?

What about the leads, will they be saved?

You'll have to see it to find out.

Maybe they end up in Sky City in

A sequel!

Is the praying mantis saved?

Watch to find out!

ELADTL

c/s

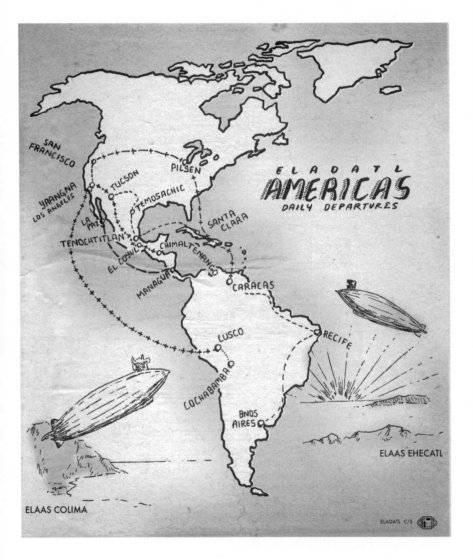

Acknowledgments, Inspirations and Extra Credit

ELADTL

PROFESSIONAL FIGURATIVE AIRSHIP PILOT ASSOCIATION
Stacey Lewis, Elaine Katzenberger, City Lights Books, Neelanjana Banerjee, Sunyoung Lee, Duncan Williams, Kaya Press, Tropico de Nopal

ORGANIC PARTS DEPARTMENT
Doveglion, Barbara Jane Reyes and Oscar Bermeo (Oakland), Joyland, Matt Timmons (Los Angeles), Culture/Strike, Ken Chen and Andy Hsiao NYC), Global Graffiti, Monica Hanna and David Sharp (L.A.), Mandorla, Roberto Tejada (Houston)

ELADATL BOARD OF DIRECTORS (1989–1996–2007)
Raul Abraham Ruiz, E. Tammy Kim, Ben Ehrenreich, Luis Vega, Linda Gamboa, Selene Santiago, Andrew Vasquez, Kenji Liu, Christine Truong, Dolores Dorantes, Imelda Romero, Melissa Uribe, Miguel Ramos, John Urquiza, Javier Mora, Luis Trujillo, Liza Beltran, Bryan Diaz, Jesica Vasquez

SUSTAINABLE AIRSHIP AND BALLOON TRANSPORTATION LEAGUE (WESTERN REGION)
Harry Gamboa Jr., Juan Felipe Herrera, Nisi Shawl, Will Alexander, Sharon Doubiago, Gino Franco, Karla Griego

SUSTAINABLE AIRSHIP AND BALLOON TRANSPORTATION LEAGUE (EASTERN REGION)
Jonathan Lethem, Mark Doten, Ammiel Alcalay

ZEP DINER CATERING CREW
Marina, Umeko and Citlali

**WESTERN REGIONAL AIRSHIP
COORDINATOR (WRAC)**
Dolores Bravo

**POETIC RESEARCH BUREAU (SEE ALSO
FELLOWSHIP, POET OF THE UNIVERSE)**
Andrew Maxwell and Joseph Mosconi

**ORANGE TRASH VORTEX PARAGLIDER
TEAM (STUNT COORDINATORS)**
Karen Yamashita, Brent Armendinger, Tisa Bryant, Bruna
Mori, Brandon Som, Jen Hofer, Jerry Gonzalez, Brian Kim
Stefans, Randy Cauthen, Reyes Rodriguez, Marialice Jacob

FURTHER READING AND RADIOTELEMETRY
Lisa Chen

**GENTRIFIED JAROCHO MUSICIANS ON
THE TIJUANA-SAN FRANCISCO-SEATTLE
COAST LINE**
The Mojicas

**SOFT ROCK MILDLY PUNK BAND ON THE
DOWNEY/HUNTINGTON PARK-LA PAZ-OAXACA
CITY-CUZCO PANAMERICAN LINE**
The Andersons

**MONKEY DEMON BRASS BAND ON
THE BARSTOW-YUMA-SILVER CITY-
GILA WILDERNESS SONORA DESERT LINE**
The Fosters

**CURLED NYLON STRING QUARTET ON
THE TRUCKEE-SACRAMENTO-VENTURA
(SIERRAS TO THE SEA) LINE**
The Smallhouses

**WILD CUTE CUMBIA LOKOS ON THE HIGHLAND
PARK-GENERAL HOSPITAL/BOYLE HEIGHTS-
CHAVEZ RAVINE INTER-URBAN LINE**
The Bravos

ANGRY JAZZ POETRY DUO ON THE FONTANA-MONTEBELLO-LYNNWOOD-WEST L.A. LINE
The Agawas

IMPLACABLE HUAPANGO TRIO ON THE CLAREMONT/POMONA-WEST COVINA-SOUTHGATE-LEIMERT PARK LINE
The Levins

CHICANA/GUATEMALTECA/INDIGENOUS GOTH ROKERAS ON THE ECHO PARK-IRWINDALE-COACHELLA-HOLLYWOOD-SOUTH PASADENA LINE
The Santillanos

UBARI DANCERS ON THE AGUASCALIENTES-HERMOSILLO-LINCOLN HEIGHTS LINE
The Mendozas and Romos

THE MATRILINEAL LINE (STRENGTH OF SHORT WOMEN)
Antonia Sandate, Peggy Bossi, Laura Bossi Romo, Camila Jasmin Romo-Kuo

POETS OF THE UNIVERSES AWARD
Arturo Rafael Romo
Reies Flores
Sandra de la Loza

UTLA GOLDEN VOYAGES AWARD (YOSEMITE TO YELLOWSTONE)
Colleagues and alumni of Francisco Bravo MMHS, Los Angeles River School, Franklin HS, and Sonia Sotomayor MHS

Sesshu Foster thanks Arturo Ernesto Romo for everything from first to last that almost made the cut and got folded in.

Arturo Ernesto Romo thanks Sesshu Foster for knowing that stories are told in both images and words but also in miles-long shadows, jokes, silence, blasts of light, crisp gelatinous life, inner bloom

In memoriam
Bill London, El Pedorrero

See also
Sonoran Desert

SESSHU FOSTER has taught composition and literature in East L.A. for 20 years. He is the author of the novel, *Atomik Aztex* (City Lights, 2005), winner of the Believer Book Award, and a number of books of poetry, including *World Ball Notebook* (City Lights, 2009) and most recently *City of the Future*, winner of the Firecracker Award for Poetry. He lives in Alhambra, California.

ARTURO ERNESTO ROMO was born in Los Angeles, California. His artwork, mostly collaborative mixed media works but also drawing, has been exhibited internationally. Fluency, agency and folly are central themes in his practice; he sees his artwork as a companion multiplier, folding folds, netting nets. His art-making is pushed through explorations on the streets of East and North East Los Angeles, which feed into an ongoing series of collaborations with writer Sesshu Foster. He is based in Alhambra, CA.